VOYAGERS

VOYAGERS

Twelve Journeys through Space and Time

ROBERT SILVERBERG

THREE ROOMS PRESS
New York, NY

VOYAGERS
Twelve Journeys through Space and Time
BY Robert Silverberg

ISBN 978-1-953103-04-8 (trade paperback)
ISBN 978-1-953103-05-5 (ebook)
Library of Congress Control Number: 2020949595

TRP-088

Pub Date: April 20, 2021
First Edition

BISAC Coding:
FIC028090 Science Fiction: Action and Advanture
FIC029000 Science Fiction Short Stories (single author)
FIC028000 Science Fiction Space Exploration
FIC038040 Science Fction / Collections & Anthologies

BOOK COVER AND INTERIOR DESIGN:
KG Design International | www.katgeorges.com

DISTRIBUTED BY:
Publishers Group West / Ingram Content Group | www.pgw.com

Visit our website at www.threeroomspress.com or
write us at info@threeroomspress.com

Once more, for Karen

Companion on the voyage

"Make voyages. Attempt them. There's nothing else."

—Tennessee Williams—

TABLE OF CONTENTS

INTRODUCTION
BY ROBERT SILVERBERG

EVERY SCIENCE FICTION STORY IS a voyage of some kind—to a world of a far-off galaxy, to our own world of the distant future or the remote past, to some interior corner of the human soul. That's the point of science fiction: to envision the unknown, the previously unexplored, what Gulliver's Houyhnhnms would call *the thing which is not.*

They are, by definition, imaginary voyages. Gulliver was no mean voyager himself, and Jonathan Swift's novel about him can be considered an example of early science fiction, but Lilliput and Brobdignag and all the other remarkable places Gulliver visited did not exist until Swift invented them, and in fact do not exist anywhere but in Swift's imagination—and, thanks to him, in ours. There are novels of voyages that aren't science fiction, or even really imaginary—Nordhoff and Hall's *Mutiny on the Bounty,* though a work of fiction, tells of events that actually happened, involving people who actually lived. Then there are complete fictions, like Katherine Anne Porter's *Ship of Fools,* for example, or that other one about the white whale, which are imaginary in so far as both situation and characters were invented by their author, but are set in real-world contexts. These are imaginary voyages too, but not quite the same kind that science fiction writers create.

Science fiction carries things to the next level of imagination, into a new universe of the mind. What's imaginary about *Moby-Dick* is Moby himself, and Ahab and Ishmael and the rest of the crew, but apart from them the book is solidly realistic, virtually a documentary account of the nineteenth-century American whaling industry. E. E. Smith's classic science fiction novel, *The Skylark of Space*, though, takes place aboard a vessel that never existed or could have existed, traveling to worlds no human being will ever visit. Robert A. Heinlein's generation-ship saga *Orphans of the Sky*, better known in its novella form as "Universe," is an imaginary-voyage tale. Imaginary too are the travels of Gully Foyle in Alfred Bester's *The Stars My Destination*, and the exploits of Paul Atreides in Frank Herbert's *Dune*. The starship *Enterprise*—the adventures of Luke Skywalker—the journey of the spaceship *Discovery* in Arthur Clarke's *2001*—all imaginary. The voyage of Captain Nemo's *Nautilus*, and Professor Cavor in H.G. Wells' *The First Men in the Moon*—imaginary. What science fiction writers do, what they have always done since the days of Verne and Wells, is just make the stuff up. It goes without saying, really.

The imaginary voyage is an ancient tradition among us, far older than the concepts of "science" and "fiction." We have *The Odyssey*, of course, but there is an Egyptian story, the twelfth dynasty "The Shipwrecked Sailor," a thousand years older than Homer, in which we hear of an enchanted island inhabited by a wise old cobra fifty feet long who rules over seventy-five of his kin. From Roman times comes the *True History* of Lucian of Samosata, a satirical account of a voyage to the Moon. The medieval authors of the stories we call *The Arabian Nights* gave us the varied exploits of Sindbad the Sailor. Cyrano de Bergerac—the real one, not the character in Edmond Rostand's nineteenth-century play—provided several methods of reaching the moon in his playful *Voyage dans la Lune* of 1650, of which the best, I think, involved traveling in a chariot made of iron and throwing magnets upward that would pull the chariot after them.

Some time ago I came upon an interesting reference book that deals comprehensively with the early literature of the imaginary voyage. It's *The Imaginary Voyage in Prose Fiction*, by Philip Babcock Gove, first published in 1941 and reprinted by Octagon Books in

1975. Its subject is the novel of the imaginary voyage in the eighteenth century, a golden age for such fantasies, a period when works of that genre occupied more or less the niche in publishing that science fiction does today, and it brings to our attention a host of glorious speculative works, some as well known to us as *Gulliver's Travels*, and others totally obscure today and covering a range from the seriously thoughtful to the wildly goofy.

Dipping in to Gove's book here and there, I find references to all sorts of wondrous stories, books that I suppose few of us will ever read, which provide the foundation for the science fiction of modern times.

He proposes five types of imaginary voyages. "The term *Extraordinary Voyage* is . . . a fictitious narrative, purporting to be the veritable account of a real voyage . . . to an existent but little known country—or to several such countries—together with a description of the happy condition of society there found. . . . Another type is the *Fantastic* or *Marvelous*, in which dreams, witchcraft, or other supernatural agencies preclude any serious attempt at realistic authentication." Cyrano's adventures fall into the class of *The Extra-Terrestrial Voyage.* Then there is the *Satirical or Allegorical* type, which includes various utopias and dystopias, and, finally, *The Subterranean Voyage*, in which a world beneath the surface of the Earth is explored.

In the multitude of works Gove describes, I was particularly taken by Robert Paltock's *The Life and Adventures of Peter Wilkins* (1750), which a contemporary reviewer called "the illegitimate off-spring of no very natural conjunction between *Gulliver's Travels* and *Robinson Crusoe*." Wilkins, a mariner from Cornwall, is ship-wrecked near the South Pole, and, says the title page, the book relates how he entered into a "wonderful Passage thro' a subterraneous Cavern into a kind of new World; his there meeting with a Gawry or Flying Woman, whose Life he preserv'd, and afterwards married her; his extraordinary Conveyance to the Country of Glums and Gawrys, or Men and Women that fly. Likewise a Description of this strange Country, with the Laws, Customs, and Manners of its Inhabitants, and the Author's remarkable Transactions among them."

Peter Wilkins was a great success in its own day, going through dozens of editions by 1848, and reprinted from time to time even in the twentieth century. Another best-seller of this genre was *Nicholas Klim* by Ludvig Holberg, a book published (in Latin) in Copenhagen in 1741, and subsequently translated into many languages, going through 34 editions in the eighteenth century alone. It is a story that has for Scandinavian readers much the same appeal that *Alice in Wonderland* has for us. Nicholas Klim, a mountaineer, descends by rope into a mysterious cavern; the rope breaks and he finds himself plummeting into the interior of the Earth, where he floats suspended in space until a flying monster appears and carries him off to Nazar, a planet within our world. There he encounters trees with human heads, headless people whose mouths are in the middle of their chests, and many another wonder, all described in the greatest detail. He travels from country to country, each one with customs quite opposite to anything found in our surface world, telling of them with much the same satiric effect that Swift achieves in *Gulliver's Travels.*

Gove goes on to list scores of other tales of imaginary voyages, most of them long forgotten and all but unobtainable today, such as *John Daniel* (1751), attributed to one "Ralph Morris," in which we learn of John Daniel's shipwreck on a desert island, "His accidental discovery of a Woman for his companion. Their peopling the island. Also, a description of a most surprising Engine, invented by his Son Jacob, on which he flew to the Moon, with some Account of its inhabitants. His return, and accidental Fall into the Habitation of a Sea Monster, with whom he lived two Years. . . . " And there is a multitude of other works of the same sort. *The Travels and Adventures of William Bingfield*, from 1753, gives us "that amazing Animal called The Dog Bird," and tells of Bingfield's "dispersing an amazing multitude of African Cannibals, Who were feasting on the miserable wretches they had taken Captives. . . . " 1774 brought *The Travels of Hildebrand Bowman, Esquire, Into Carnoviria, Taupiniera, Olfactaria, and Auditante in New Zealand; in the Island of Bonhommica, and in the powerful Kingdom of Luxo-Volupto, on the Great Southern Continent. . . .* And so forth—much, much else.

I think my favorite, though, is the sequel to *The Adventures of Baron Munchausen* that some unknown hand turned out in 1792. Munchausen himself was a real person, an eighteenth-century German baron who told many a lively story of his adventures far and wide. In 1785 a writer named Rudolf Erich Raspe put together a collection of Munchausen's tales, somewhat enhanced by his own rich imagination—the baron rides a cannonball, is swallowed by an immense fish in the Mediterranean, fights a forty-foot crocodile, travels to the Moon, et cetera, et cetera. Raspe's book has held readers entranced to this day, and has been the source for several delightful movies. But it is the lesser-known anonymous sequel of seven years later that provides even greater fun. A look at the title page hints at the pleasures within:

"Containing his expedition into Africa. How he out-does Alexander.—Splits a rock at the Cape of Good Hope.—Wrecked on an island of ice.—Becomes acquainted with the Sphinx, Gog and Magog. —Overcomes above a thousand lions.—Buried in a whirlwind of sand.—Feasts on live bulls and Kava.—Is declared Sovereign of Africa, and builds a bridge from thence to Great Britain, supported by a single arch.—Battle of his retinue with the famous Don Quixote.—Becomes acquainted with the Colossus of Rhodes.—Chase of Wauwau through America.—Meets with a floating island.—Visits the islands in the South Sea.—Becomes acquainted with Omai.—Cuts a canal across the Isthmus of Darien.—Discovers the Alexandrian Library.—Besieges Seringapatam.—Overcomes Tippoo Saib.—Raises the hull of the Royal George; together with a variety of other very Surprising Adventures."

Now, *there's* an adventurer for you. The doings of Baron Munchausen in the sequel make his earlier exploits seem like very weak tea indeed. Builds the Panama Canal! Puts a single-arch bridge across the Mediterranean to London! Duels with Don Quixote and chats with the Colossus of Rhodes! What a movie it would make! (Special effects budget, $200 million.) And, best of all, the Munchausen sequel has recently been reissued and is currently in print, so you can thrill and chill along with the valiant baron as he dines on those live bulls and wrangles the thousand-plus lions. (All at once, I wonder?) I don't think there's anything to match it in the rest of Philip Gove's huge compendium of fantastic voyages.

Today there are no unexplored corners of the Earth in which imaginative writers can discover places like Olfactria and Luxo—Volupto, and we are quite certain that no planets like Nazar lurk beneath the surface of the world. We are forced to go farther out for our imaginary destinations—Dune, Ringworld, my own planet Majipoor. But the impulse is the same: to invent, to divert, to extend the realm of the imagination. It is an aspect of ourselves that must have been there in Cro-Magnon days and, I think, will never leave us.

For most of my life I have been a voyager myself. I remember my first major trip on my own—all the way from New York City to Philadelphia, when I was fifteen. It was a 90-mile journey by bus, and in those days, more than seventy years ago, a trip like that was a big venture for a boy like me. I had never gone far from my native turf of Brooklyn. And now here I was in exotic Philadelphia, where one of the first things that struck me was that the lampposts were of a different design than those of Brooklyn. It had never occurred to me that different cities would have different styles of lamppost. That was the beginning of my education as a traveler, an education that took me to England and France by the time I was 21—oh, were the lampposts different there!—and eventually on to a multitude of distant places, Italy, Greece, Turkey, Egypt, Spain, Morocco, Tunisia, Croatia, the Scandinavian countries, the Baltic countries, Ireland, Finland, Russia, Mexico, Kenya, Zanzibar, Australia, Japan, Guyana, Surinam, various islands of the Caribbean, et cetera, et cetera, a vast catalog of trips. I have seen plenty of strange lampposts, eaten plenty of strange things, stared in wonder at a host of exotic splendors: the Pyramids and the Sphinx, the Parthenon, the Great Barrier Reef, the Grand Canyon, the Roman Colosseum, the streets of Pompeii, the Sacred Well of Chichen Itza, the Labyrinth of Crete, the giant tortoises of the Galapagos, the Alhambra, and ever so much more. My travels have been the making of me as a writer; for how can one invent alien worlds and write of far-off times if one is not reasonably familiar with the enormous collection of marvels that our own small planet provides?

And so, in my fiction, I have taken my characters from one end of the universe to the other, from the dawn of time to its final hours. I have made a fair sampling of my tales of imaginary voyagers here: time-travelers from the future coming back to witness a catastrophe of our own time, Spanish *conquistadores* looking for—and finding—the Fountain of Youth, a tourist in Mexico stepping into an alternative universe, spacefarers going among the stars to make a surprising discovery, and a good many more. The range of these stories, the kinds of voyages they describe, just begins to demonstrate the scope of science fiction; for, as writers from Verne and Wells on up through Robert Heinlein and Isaac Asimov and Ray Bradbury to last month's newest novelist, nothing can limit its infinite variety.

—Robert Silverberg
June, 2020

VOYAGERS

IN ANOTHER COUNTRY

Writing "In Another Country" was one of the strangest and most challenging things I've ever done in a writing career that now is more than sixty years old.

The impetus to do it came from the anthologist Martin H. Greenberg, who told me one wintry day in 1988 that he was editing a series of books for which contemporary science fiction writers would be asked to produce companions to classic s-f novellas of the past. The new story and the old one would then be published in the same volume. He invited me to participate; and after hardly a moment's thought I chose C. L. Moore's *Vintage Season*, her classic tale of jaded, sophisticated time-travelers coming back from some unspecified time in the future to witness as sightseeing tourists a terrible catastrophe in the America of the twentieth century, as the story I most wanted to work with.

Now and then I have deliberately chosen to reconstruct some celebrated work of literature in a science fictional mode, as a kind of technical exercise. My novel *The Man in the Maze* of the 1960s is based on the Philoctetes of Sophocles, though you'd have to look hard to find the parallel. *Downward to the Earth*, from the same era, was written with a nod to Joseph Conrad's *Heart of Darkness.* My story "To See the Invisible Man" develops an idea that Jorge Luis Borges threw away in a single sentence. In 1989, I reworked Conrad's famous story "The Secret Sharer," translating it completely into an s-f context.

But in all those cases, though I was using the themes and patterns of earlier and greater writers, the stories themselves, and the worlds in which they were set, were entirely invented by me. Essentially I was running my own variations on classic themes, as Beethoven did with the themes of Mozart, or Brahms with Haydn. The task this time was to enter a world already created by a master artist—the world of Moore's highly regarded 1946 story, *Vintage Season*—and work with her material, finding something new to say about a narrative situation that had already been triumphantly, and, one would think, completely, explored in great depth.

The solution was not to write a sequel to *Vintage Season*—that would have been pointless, a mere time-travelogue to some era other than the one visited in the original story—but to produce a work interwoven with Moore's actual story the way the lining of a cape is interwoven with the cape itself. My story is set during the same few weeks as hers, and builds toward the same climax. I used many of her characters, but not as major figures; they move through the background, and the people in the foreground are mine. She told her story from the point of view of a man of the twentieth century who finds himself in the midst of perplexing strangers from the future; I went around to the far side and worked from the point of view of one of the visitors. Where I could, I filled in details of the time-traveling society that Moore had not provided, and clarified aspects of her story that she had chosen to leave undeveloped, thus providing a kind of Silverbergian commentary on her concepts. And though I made no real attempt to write in Moore's style, I adapted my own as well as I could to match the grace and elegance of her tone.

There is perhaps an aspect of real lèse-majesté in all of this, or maybe the word I want is hubris. Readers of my autobiographical anthology, *Science Fiction: 101*, will know that C.L. Moore is one of the writers I most revere in our field, that I have studied her work with respect verging on awe. To find myself now going back over the substance of her most accomplished story in the hope of adding something to it of my own was an odd and almost frightening experience. I suspect I would not have dared to do any such thing fifteen or twenty years ago, confident though I was then of my own technical abilities. But now, when my own science fiction-writing career had extended through a period longer than that of

Moore's own, I found myself willing to risk the attempt, if only to see whether I could bring it off.

It was an extraordinary thing for me to enter Moore's world and feel, for the weeks I was at work at it, that I was actually writing, if not *Vintage Season* itself, then something as close to it as could be imagined. I was there, in that city, at that time, and it all became far more vivid for me than even my many readings of the original story over a 40-year period had been able to achieve. I hope that the result justifies the effort and that I will be forgiven for having dared tinker with a masterpiece this way. And most profoundly do I wish that C.L. Moore could have seen my story and perhaps found a good word or two to say for it.

Gardner Dozois published it in the March, 1989 issue of *Asimov's Science Fiction* and Tor Books brought it out the following year bound with Moore's original story in a double volume.

THE SUMMER HAD BEEN CAPRI, at the villa of Augustus, the high summer of the emperor at the peak of his reign, and the autumn had been the pilgrimage to golden Canterbury. Later they would all go to Rome for Christmas, to see the coronation of Charlemagne. But now it was the springtime of their wondrous journey, that glorious May late in the twentieth century that was destined to end in sudden roaring death and a red smoking sky. In wonder and something almost like ecstasy Thimiroi watched the stone walls of Canterbury fade into mist and this newest strange city take on solidity around him. The sight of it woke half-formed poems in his mind. He felt amazingly young, alive, open . . . vulnerable.

"Thimiroi's in a trance," Denvin said in his light, mocking way, and winked and grinned. He stood leaning casually against the rail of the embankment, a compact, elegant little man, looking back at his two companions.

"Let him alone," said Laliene sharply. In anger she ran her hands over the crimson nimbus of her hair and down the sides of her sleek tanned cheeks. Her gray-violet eyes flashed with annoyance. "Can't you see he's overwhelmed by what he sees out there?"

"By the monstrous ugliness of it?"

"By its beauty," Laliene said, with some ferocity. She touched Thimiroi's elbow. "Are you all right?" she whispered.

Thimiroi nodded.

She gestured toward the city. "How wonderfully discordant it is! How beautifully strident! No two buildings alike. And the surfaces of everything so flat. But colors, shapes, sizes, textures, all different. Not even the trees showing any sort of harmony."

"And the noise," said Denvin. "Don't forget the noise, if you're delighted by discordance. Machinery screeching and clanging and booming, and giving off smelly fumes besides—oh, it's marvelous, Laliene! Those painted things are vehicles, aren't they? Those boxy-looking machines. Honking and bellowing like crazed oxen with wheels. That thing flying around up there, too, the shining thing with wings—listen to it! Just listen!"

"Stop it," Laliene said. "You're going to upset him."

"No," Thimiroi said. "He's not bothering me. But I do think it's very beautiful. Beautiful in its ugliness. Beautiful in its discordance. There's energy here. Whatever else this place may be, it's a place of tremendous energy. And energy is always beautiful." His heart was pounding. It had not pounded like this when they had arrived at any of the other places of their tour through antiquity. But the twentieth century was special: an apocalyptic time, a time of such potent darkness that it cast an eerie black radiance across half a dozen centuries to come. And this was its most poignant moment, when the century was at its highest point, all its earlier turmoil far behind—the moment when splendor and magnificence would be transformed in an instant, by nature's malevolent prank, into stunning catastrophe. "Besides," he said, "not everything here is ugly or discordant anyway. Look at the sky."

"Yes," Laliene said. "That's a sky to remember. It's a sky that absolutely demands a great artist to capture, wouldn't you say? Someone on the order of Nivander, or even Sathimon. Those blues, and the white of the clouds. And then those streaks of gold and purple and red."

"You mean the pollution?" Denvin asked.

She glowered at him. "Don't. Please. If you don't want to be here, tell Kadro when he shows up, and he'll send you home. But don't spoil it for the rest of us."

"Sorry," said Denvin, in a chastened tone. "I do have to admit that that sky is fantastic."

"So intense," Laliene said. "It comes right down and wraps itself around the tops of the buildings like a shimmering blue cloak. And everything so sharp, so vivid, so clear. The sun was brighter back in these days, someone said. That must be why. And the air more transparent, a different mix of elements. Of course, this was an unusual season even for here. That's well known. They say there had never been a month like this one, a magical springtime, everything perfect, almost as if it had been arranged that way for maximum contrast with—with—"

Her voice trailed away.

Thimiroi shook his head. "You both talk too much. Can't you simply stand here and let it all come flooding into your souls? We came here to *experience* this place, not to talk about it. We'll have the rest of our lives to talk about it."

They looked abashed. He grasped their hands in his and laughed—his rich, exuberant, pealing laugh, which some people thought was too much for their delicate sensibilities—to take the sting out of the rebuke. Denvin, after a moment, managed a smile. Laliene gave Thimiroi a curiously impenetrable stare; but then she too smiled, a warmer and more sincere one than Denvin's. Thimiroi nodded and released them, and stepped forward to peer over the edge of the embankment.

They had materialized just a few moments earlier, in what seemed to be a park on the highest slopes of a lush green hillside overlooking a broad, swiftly flowing river. The city was on the far side, stretching out before them in dizzying vastness. Where they stood was in a sort of overlook point, jutting out of the hill, protected by a dark metal railing. Their luggage was beside them. The hour appeared to be midday; the sun was high; the air was mild, and very still and clear. The park was almost empty, though Thimiroi could see a few people strolling on the paths below. Natives of this time and place, he thought. His heart went out to them. He would have run down to them and embraced them, if he could. He longed to know what they were really like, these ancients, these rough earthy primitives, these people of lost antiquity.

Primitives, he thought? Well, yes, what else could they be called? They lived so long ago. But this city is no trifling thing. This is no squalid village of mud-and-wattle huts that lies before us.

In silence Thimiroi stared across the river at the massive blocky gray towers and wide, busy streets of the great metropolis, and at the shimmering silvery bridges to his right and to his left, and at the endless rows of small white and pink houses that rose up and up and up through the green hills on the other side. The weight and size and power of the place were extraordinary. His soul quivered with—what? Joy? Amazement? Fear?—at such immensity. How many people lived here? A million? Five million? He could scarcely conceive of such a number, all packed into a single place. The other ancient cities they had visited on this tour, imperial capitals though they were, were mere citylets—towns, even; piddling little medieval settlements—however grand they might have imagined themselves to be. But the great cities of the twentieth century, he had always been told, marked the high point in human urban concentration: cities of ten million, fifteen million, twenty million people. Unimaginable. This one before him was not even the biggest one, not even close to the biggest. Never before in history had cities grown to this size—and never again, either. Never again. What an extraordinary sight! What an astounding thing to contemplate, this great humming throbbing hive of intense human activity, especially when one knew—when one knew—when one knew the fate that was soon to befall it—

"Thimiroi?" Laliene called. "Kadro's here!"

He turned. The tour leader, a small, fragile-looking man with thick flame-red hair and eerie blue-violet eyes, held out his arms to them. He could only just have arrived himself—they had all been together mere minutes before, in Canterbury—but he was dressed already in twentieth-century costume, curious and quaint and awkward-looking, but oddly elegant on him. Thimiroi had no idea how that trick had been accomplished, but he accepted it untroubledly: The Travel was full of mysteries of all sorts, detours and overlaps and side-jaunts through time. It was Kadro's business to understand such things, not his.

"You'd better change," Kadro said. "There's a transport vehicle on the way up here to take you into town."

He touched something at his hip and a cloud of dark mist sprang up around them. Under its protective cover they opened their suitcases—their twentieth-century clothes were waiting neatly inside, and some of the strange local currency—and set about the task of making themselves look like natives.

"Oh, how wonderful!" Laliene cried, holding a gleaming, iridescent green robe in front of herself and dancing around with it. "How did they think of such things? Look at how it's cut! Look at the way it's fitted together!"

"I've seen you wearing a thousand things more lovely than those," said Denvin sourly.

She made a face at him. Denvin himself had almost finished changing: he was clad now in gray trousers, scarlet shirt open at the throat, charcoal-colored jacket cut with flaring lapels. Like Kadro, he looked splendid in his costume. But Kadro and Denvin looked splendid in anything they wore. The two of them were men of the same sort, Thimiroi thought, both of them dandyish, almost dainty. Perfect men of fashion. He himself, much taller than they and very muscular, almost rawboned, had never quite mastered their knack of seeming at utter ease in all situations. He often felt out of place among such smooth types as they, almost as though he were some sort of throwback, full of hot, primordial passions and drives rarely seen in the refined era into which he had happened to be born. It was, perhaps, his creative intensity, he often thought. His artistic nature. He was too earthy for them, too robust of spirit, too much the primitive. As he slipped into his twentieth-century clothes, the tight yellow pants, the white shirt boldly striped in blue, the jet-black jacket, the tapering black boots, he felt a curious sense of having returned home at last, after a long journey.

"Here comes the car," Kadro said. "Hold out your hands, quickly! I have your implants."

Thimiroi extended his arm. Something silvery-bright, like a tiny gleaming beetle, sparkled between two of Kadro's fingers. He pressed it gently against Thimiroi's skin, just above the long rosy scar of the inoculation, and it made the tiniest of whirring sounds.

"This is their language," said Kadro. He touched it to Denvin's arm also, and to Laliene's. "And this one, the technology and social customs. And this is your medical booster, just in case." Buzz, buzz, buzz. Kadro smiled. He was very efficient. "You're all ready for the twentieth century now. And just in time, too."

A vehicle had pulled up in the roadway behind them, yellow with black markings, and odd projections on its roof. Thimiroi felt a quick faint stab of nausea as a breeze, suddenly stirring out of the quiescent air, swept a whiff of the vehicle's greasy fumes past his face.

The driver hopped out. He was very big, bigger even than Thimiroi, with immense heavy shoulders and a massive column of a neck. His face was unusual, the lips strongly pronounced, the cheekbones broad and jutting like blades. His hair was black and woolly and grew very close to his skull. But the most surprising thing about him was the color of his skin. It was dark brown, almost black: his eyes were bright as beacons against that astonishing chocolate-hued backdrop. Thimiroi had never imagined that anyone might have skin of such a color. Was that what they all were like in the twentieth century? Skin the color of night? No one on Capri had looked like that, or in Canterbury.

"You the people called for a taxi?" the driver asked. "Here—let me put those suitcases in the trunk—"

Perhaps it is a form of ornamentation, Thimiroi thought. They have it artificially done. They think it makes them look more beautiful when they change their skins, when they change their faces, so that they are like this.

And it *was* beautiful. There was a brooding somber power about this black man's face. He was like something carved from a block of some precious and recalcitrant stone.

"I'll ride up front," Kadro said. "You three get in back." He turned to the driver. "The Montgomery House is where we are going. You know where that is?"

The driver laughed. "Ain't no one in town who don't know the Montgomery House. But you sure you don't want a hotel that's a little cheaper?"

"The Montgomery House will do," said Kadro.

* * *

THEY HAD RIDDEN IN MULE-DRAWN carts on the narrow winding paths of hilly Capri, and in wagons drawn by oxen on the rutted road to Canterbury. That had been charming and pretty, to ride in such things, to feel the jouncing of the wheels and see the sweat glistening on the backs of the panting animals. There was nothing charming or pretty about traveling in this squat glass-walled wheeled vehicle, this *taxi.* It rumbled and quivered as if it were about to explode. It careered alarmingly around the sharp curves of the road, threatening at any moment to break free of the driver's tenuous control and go spurting over the edge of the embankment in a cataclysmic dive through space. It poured forth all manner of dark noxious gases. It was an altogether terrifying thing.

And yet fascinating and wonderful. Crude and scary though the taxi was, it was not really very different in fundamental concept or design from the silent, flawless vehicles of Thimiroi's world. Contemplating that, Thimiroi had a keen sense of the kinship of this world to his own. We are not that far beyond them in time, he thought. They exist at the edge of the modern era, really. The Capri of the Romans, the Canterbury of the pilgrimage—those are truly alien places, set deep back in the pre-technological past. But there is not the same qualitative difference between our epoch and this twentieth century. The gulf is not so great. The seeds of our world can be found in theirs. Or so it seems to me, Thimiroi told himself, after five minutes' acquaintance with this place.

Kadro said, "Omerie and Kleph and Klia are here already. They've rented a house just down the street from the hotel where you'll be staying."

Laliene smiled. "The Sanciscos! Oh, how I look forward to seeing them again! Omerie is such a clever man. And Kleph and Klia—how beautiful they are, how refreshing to spend time with them!"

"The place they've taken is absolutely perfect for the end of the month," said Kadro. "The view will be supreme. Hollia and Hara wanted to buy it, you know. But Omerie got to it ahead of them."

"Hollia and Hara are going to be here?" Denvin said, sounding surprised.

"*Everyone* will be here. Who would miss it?" Kadro's hands moved in a quick playful gesture of malicious pleasure. "Hollia was beside herself, of course. She couldn't believe that Omerie had beaten her to that house. But, as you say, Laliene, Omerie is such a clever man."

"Hollia is ruthless," said Denvin. "If the place is that good, she'll try to get it away from the Sanciscos. Mark my words, Kadro. She'll try some slippery little trick."

"She may very well. Not that there's any real reason to. I understand that the Sanciscos are planning to invite all of us to watch the show from their front window. Including Hollia and Hara, naturally. So they won't be the worse for it. Except that Hollia would have preferred to be the hostess herself. Cenbe will be coming, you know."

"Cenbe!" Laliene cried.

"Exactly. To finish his symphony. Hollia would have wanted to preside over that. And instead it will be Omerie's party, and Kleph's and Klia's, and she'll just be one of the crowd." Kadro giggled. "Dear Hollia. My heart goes out to her."

"Dear Hollia," Denvin echoed.

"Look there," said Thimiroi, pointing out the side window of the taxi. He spoke brusquely, his voice deliberately rough. All this gossipy chatter bored and maddened him. Who cared whether it was Hollia who gave the party, or the Sanciscos, or the Emperor Augustus himself? What mattered was the event that was coming. The experience.

The awesome, wondrous, shattering calamity. "Isn't that Lutheena across the street?" he asked.

They had emerged from the park, had descended to the bank of the river, were passing through a district of venerable-looking three-story wooden houses. One of the bridges was just ahead of them, and the towers of the downtown section rose like huge stone palisades on the other side of the river. Now they were halted at an intersection, waiting for the colored lights that governed the flow of traffic to change; and in the group of pedestrians waiting also to cross was an unmistakably regal figure—yes, it was Lutheena, who else could it be but Lutheena?—who stood among the twentieth-century folk like a goddess among mortals. The difference was not so much in her clothes, which were scarcely distinguishable from the street clothes of the people around her, nor in her features or her hair, perfect and flawless though they were, as in the way she bore herself: for though she was slender and of a porcelain frailty, and no more than ordinary in height, she held herself with such self-contained majesty, such imperious grace, that she seemed to tower above the others, coarse and clumsy with a thick-ankled peasant cloddishness about them, who waited alongside her.

"I thought she was coming here *after* Charlemagne," Denvin said. "And then going on to Canterbury."

Thimiroi frowned. What was he talking about? Whether she came here first and then went to Canterbury, or journeyed from Canterbury to here as they had done, would they not all be here at the same time? He would never understand these things. This was another of the baffling complexities of The Travel. Surely there was only one May like this one, and one 1347 November, and one 800 December? Though everyone seemed to make the tour in some private order of his own, some going through the four seasons in the natural succession, others hopping about as they pleased, certainly they must all converge on the same point in time at once—was that not so?

"Perhaps it's someone else," he suggested uneasily.

"But of *course* that's Lutheena," said Laliene. "I wonder what she's doing all the way out here by herself."

"Lutheena is like that," Denvin pointed out.

"Yes," Laliene said. "She is, yes." She rapped on the window. Lutheena turned, and stared gravely, and after a moment burst into that incandescent smile of hers, though her luminous eyes remained mysteriously solemn. Then the traffic light changed, the taxi moved forward, Lutheena was lost in the distance. In a few minutes they were on the bridge, and then passing through the heart of the city, alive in all its awesome afternoon clangor, and then upward, up into the hills, up to the lofty street, green with the tender new growth of this heartbreakingly perfect springtime, where they would all wait out that glorious skein of May days that lay between this moment and the terrible hour of doom's arrival.

* * *

After the straw-filled mattresses and rank smells of the lodges along the way to Canterbury, and the sweltering musty splendors of their whitewashed villas on the crest of Capri, the Montgomery House was almost palatial.

The rooms had a curious stiffness and angularity about them that Thimiroi was already beginning to associate with twentieth-century architecture in general, and of course there was no sweepdamping, no mood insulation, no gravity gradients, none of the little things that one took for granted when one was in one's own era. All the same, everything seemed comfortable in its way, and with the proper modifications he knew he would have no trouble feeling at home here. The rooms were spacious, the ceilings were high, the windows were clean, no odors invaded from neighboring chambers. There was indoor plumbing: a blessing, after Canterbury. He had a suite of three rooms, furnished in the strange but pleasant late-twentieth-century way that he had seen in museums. There was a box in the main sitting-room that broadcast images in color, flat ones, with no sensory augmentation other than sonics. There were paintings on the wall, maddeningly motionless. The walls themselves were painted—how remarkable!—with some thick substance so porous that he could almost make out its molecular structure if he looked closely.

Laliene's suite was down the hall from his; Denvin was on a different floor. That struck him as odd. He had assumed they were lovers and would be sharing accommodations. But, he reflected, it was always risky to assume things like that.

Thimiroi spent an hour transforming his rooms into a more familiar and congenial environment. From his suitcase he drew carpeting and draperies and coverlets of his own time, all of them supple with life and magic, to replace the harsh, flat, dead ones that they seemed to prefer here. He pulled out the three little tripod tables of fine, intricately worked Sipulva marquetry that went with him everywhere: he would read at the golden one, sip his euphoriac at the copper-hued one, write his poetry at the one that was woven in scarlet and amber. He hung an esthetikon on the wall opposite the window and set it going, filling the room with warm, throbbing color. He sat a music sphere on the dresser. To provide some variation in psychological tonality he activated a little subsonic that he had carried with him, adjusting it to travel through the entire spectrum of positive moods over a twenty-four hour span, from *anticipation* through *excitation* to *culmination* in imperceptible gradations. Then he stood back, surveying the results, and nodded. That would do for now. The room had been made amiable; the room was *civilized* now. He could bring out other things later. The suitcase was infinitely capacious. All it was, after all, was a pipeline to his own era. At the far end they would put anything in it that he might requisition.

Now at last he could begin to explore the city.

That evening they were supposed to go to a concert. Denvin had arranged it; Denvin was going to take care of all the cultural events. The legendary young violinist Sandra di Santis was playing, in what would turn out to be her final performance, though of course no one of this era could know that yet. But that was hours away. It was still only early afternoon. He would go out—he would savor the sights, the sounds, the smells of this place—

He felt just a moment of hesitation.

But why? Why? He had wandered by himself, unafraid, through the trash-strewn alleys of medieval Canterbury, though he knew that cut-throats and roisterers lurked everywhere. He had scrambled alone across the steep gullied cliffs of Capri, looking down without fear at the blue rock-rimmed Mediterranean, far below, into which a single misstep could plunge him. What was there to be cautious about here? The noisy cars racing so swiftly through the streets, perhaps. But surely a little caution and common sense would keep him from harm. If Lutheena had been out by herself, why not he? But still—still, that nagging uneasiness—

Thimiroi shrugged and left his room, and made his way down the hall to the elevator, and descended to the lobby.

At every stage of his departure wave upon wave of unsettling strangeness assailed him. The simplest act was a challenge. He had to call upon the resources of his technology implant in order to operate the lock of his room door, to summon the elevator, to tell it to take him to the lobby. But he met each of these minor mysteries in turn with a growing sense of accomplishment. By the time he reached the lobby he was moving boldly and confidently, feeling almost at home in this strange land, this unfamiliar country, that was the past.

The lobby, which Thimiroi had seen only briefly when he had arrived, was a somber, cavernous place, intricately divided into any number of smaller open chambers. He studied, as he walked calmly through it toward the brightness at the far end, the paintings, the furnishings, the things on display. Everything had that odd stiffness of form and flatness of texture that seemed to be the rule in this era: nothing appeared to have any inner life or movement. Was that how they had really liked it to be? Or was this curious deadness merely a function of the limitations of their materials? Probably some of each, Thimiroi decided. These were an artful, sophisticated folk. Of course, he thought, they had not had the advantage of many of our modern materials and devices. All the same, they would not have made everything so drab unless their esthetic saw beauty in the drabness. He would have to examine that possibility more deeply as this month went along, studying everything with an artist's shrewd and sympathetic eye, not interested in finding fault, only in understanding.

People were standing about here and there in the lobby, mainly in twos and threes, talking quietly. They paid no attention to him. Most of them, he noticed, had fair skin much like his own. A few, Thimiroi noticed, were black-skinned like the taxi driver, but others had skin of still another unusual tone, a kind of pale olive or light yellow, and their features too were unusual, very delicate, with an odd tilt to the eyes.

Once again he wondered if this skin-toning might be some sort of cosmetic alteration: but no, no, this time he queried his implant and it told him that in fact in this era there had been several different races of humanity, varying widely in physical appearance.

How lovely, Thimiroi thought. How sad for us that we are all so much alike. Another point for further research: had these black and yellow people, and the other unusual races, been swept away by the great calamity, or was it rather that all mankind had tended toward a uniformity of traits as the centuries went by? Again, perhaps, some of each. Whatever the reason, it was a cause for regret.

He reached the grand doorway that led to the street. A woman said, entering the hotel just as he was leaving it, "How I hate going indoors in weather like this!"

Her companion laughed. "Who doesn't? Can it last much longer, I wonder?"

Thimiroi stepped past them, into the splendor of the soft golden sunlight.

The air was miraculous: amazingly transparent, clear with a limpidity almost beyond belief, despite all the astonishing impurities that Thimiroi knew were routinely poured into it by the unthinking people of this era. It was as though for the long blessed moment of this one last magnificent May all the ordinary rules of nature had been suspended, and the atmosphere had become invulnerable to harm. Beyond that sublime zone of clarity rose the blue shield of the sky, pulsingly brilliant; and from its throne high in the distance the sun sent forth a tranquil, steady radiance that was like no sunlight Thimiroi had ever seen. Small wonder that those who had planned the tour had chosen this time and this place to be the epitome of springtime, he thought. There might never have been such beauty before. There might never be again.

He turned to his left and began to walk, hardly knowing or caring where he might be going.

From all sides came powerful sensory signals: the honking of horns, the sharp spicy scent of something cooking nearby, the subtler fragrance of the light breeze. Great gray buildings soared far into the dazzling sky. Billboards and posters blared their messages in twenty colors. The impact was immediate and profound. Thimiroi beheld everything in wonder and joy.

What richness! What complexity!

And yet there was a paradox here. What he took to be complexity in this street scene was really only a studied lack of harmony. As it had in the hotel lobby, a second glance revealed the true essence of this world's vocabulary of design: a curious rough-hewn plainness, even a severity, that made clear to him how far in the past he actually was. The extraordinary May light seemed to dance along the rooftops, giving the buildings an intricacy of texture they did not in fact possess. These ancient styles were fundamentally simple and harsh, and could all too easily be taken to be primitive and crude. In Thimiroi's own era every surface vibrated in at least half a dozen different ways, throbbing and rippling and pulsating and shimmering and gleaming and quivering. Here everything was flat, stolid, static. The strangeness of that seemed oppressive at first encounter; but now, as he ventured deeper and deeper into this unfamiliar world, Thimiroi came to see the underlying majesty of it. What he had mistaken for deadness was in fact strength. The people of this era were survivors: they had come through monstrous wars, tremendous technological change, immense social upheaval. Those who had outlasted the brutal tests of this taxing century were rugged, hearty, deeply optimistic. Their style of building and decoration showed that plainly. Nothing quivering and shimmery for them—oh, no! Great solid slabs of buildings, constructed out of simple, hard, unadorned materials that looked you straight in the eye—that was the way of things, here in the late twentieth century, in this time of assurance and robust faith in even better things to come.

Of course, Thimiroi thought, there was savage irony in that, considering what actually *was* to come. For a moment he was swept by deep and shattering compassion that brought him almost to tears. But he forced himself to fight the emotion back. Would Denvin weep for these people? Would Omerie, would Cenbe, would Kadro? The past is a sealed book, Thimiroi told himself forcefully. What has happened has happened. The losses are totaled, the debits are irretrievable. We have come here to experience the joys of jarring contrasts, as Denvin might say, not to cry over spilled milk.

He crossed the street. The next block was one of older-looking single-family houses, each set apart in a little garden plot where bright flowers bloomed and the leaves of the trees were just beginning to unfold under springtime's first warmth.

There was music coming from an upstairs window three houses from the corner. He paused to listen.

It was simple straightforward stuff, monochromatic in tone. The instrument, he supposed, was the piano, the one that made its sound by the action of little mallets striking strings stretched across a resonating board. The melodic line was both sinuous and stark, carried in the treble with a little commentary in the bass: music a child could play. Perhaps a child was indeed playing. The simplicity of it made him smile. It was quaint stuff, charming but naive. He began to move onward.

And yet—yet—

Suddenly he felt himself caught and transfixed by a simple, magical turn of phrase that came creeping almost surreptitiously out of the bass line. It held him. Unexpectedly, it touched him.

He remained still, unable to go on, listening while the lovely phrase fled, waiting in hope for its return. Yes, there it was again! And as it came and went, it cast startling illumination over the entire musical pattern. He saw its beauty and its artfully hidden depth now, and he grew angry at himself for having responded at first in that patronizing way, that snide, condescending Denvin-like way. Quaint? Naive? Hardly. Simple, yes: this music achieved its effects with a minimum of means. But what was naive about that? Was a quartet for strings naive, because it did not make use of the resources of a full symphony orchestra? There was something about this music—its directness, its freedom—that the composers of his own time might well want to study, might even look upon with a certain degree of envy. For all their colossal technical resources, could the best of them—yes, even Cenbe—manage to equal the quiet force, Thimiroi wondered, of that easy, graceful little tune?

He stood listening until the music rolled to a gentle climax and a pleasant resolution and came to a halt. Its sudden absence brought him up short. He looked up imploringly at the open window. Play it again, he begged silently. Play it again! But there was no more music.

Impulsively he burst into applause, thinking that that might encourage an encore.

A woman's face appeared at the window. Thimiroi was aware of pale skin, long straight golden hair, warm blue-green eyes. "Very lovely," he called. "Thank you. Thank you very much."

She looked at him in apparent surprise, perhaps frowning a little. Then the frown was replaced for a moment by a quick amiable smile of pleasure; and then, just as quickly, she was gone. Thimiroi remained before her house a while longer, still hoping the music would begin again. But there was no more of it.

* * *

He returned to the hotel an hour later, dazzled, awed, weary, his mind full of wonders great and small. Just as he entered his suite, a small machine on the table beside the bed set up a curious insistent tinkling sound: the telephone, it was, so his technology implant informed him. He picked up the receiver.

"This is Thimiroi."

"Back at last." The voice was Laliene's. "Was it an interesting walk?"

"One revelation after another. Certainly this year is going to be the high point of our trip."

Laliene laughed lazily. "Oh, darling Thimiroi, didn't you say the same thing when we came to Canterbury? And when we had the audience with the emperor on Capri?"

He did not reply.

"Anyway," she continued. "We're all going to gather in my suite before we go to the concert. Would you like to come? I've brewed a little tea, of course."

"Of course," he said. "I'll be right there."

She, too, had redone her rooms in the style of their own period. Instead of the ponderous hotel bed she had installed a floater, and in the sitting room now was a set of elegant turquoise slopes mounted around a depth baffle, so that one had the illusion of looking down into a long curving valley of ravishing beauty. Her choice of simso screens was, as usual, superb: wondrous dizzying vistas opened to infinity on every wall. Laliene herself looked sumptuous in a brilliant robe of woven silver mesh and a pair of scarlet gliders.

What surprised him was that no one else was there.

"Oh," she said lightly, "they'll all be coming along soon. We can get a head start."

She selected one of the lovely little cups on the table beside her, and offered it to him. And as he took it from her he felt a sudden transformation of the space between them, an intensification, an amplification. Without warning, Laliene was turning up the psychic voltage.

Her face was flushed, her eyes were glistening. The rich gray of them had deepened almost to purple. There was no mistaking the look. He had seen it many times before: Laliene in her best flirtatious mode, verging on the frankly seductive. Here they were, a man, a woman, well known to one another, together in a hotel room in a strange and distant city, about to enjoy a friendly sip or two of euphoriac tea—well, of course, Laliene could be expected to put on her most inviting manner, if only for the sport of it. But something else was going on here besides mere playful flirtation, Thimiroi realized. There was an odd eagerness to the set of her jaw, a peculiar quirk in the corners of her mouth. As though she *cared*, he thought. As though she were *serious*.

What was this? Was she trying to change the rules of the game?

Deftly she turned a music sphere on without looking away from him. Some barely audible melodikia came stealing like faint azure vapor into the air, and very gradually began to rise and throb. One of Cenbe's songs, he wondered? No. No, too voluptuous for Cenbe: more like Palivandrin's work, or Athaea's. He sipped his euphoriac. The sweet coiling fumes crept sinuously about him. Laliene stood close beside him, making it seem almost as if the music were coming from her and not the sphere. Thimiroi met her languid invitation with a practiced courteous smile, one which acknowledged her beauty, her grace, the intimacy of the moment, the prospect of delights to come, while neither accepting nor rejecting anything that was being proposed.

Of course they could do nothing now. At any moment the others would come trooping in.

But he wondered where this unexpected offer was meant to lead. He could, of course, put down the cup, draw her close: a kiss, a quick caress, an understanding swiftly arrived at, yes. But that did not seem to be quite what she was after, or at least that was not all she was after. And was the offer, he asked himself, all that unexpected? Thimiroi realized abruptly that there was no reason why he should be as surprised by this as he was. As he cast his mind back over the earlier weeks of their journey across time, he came to see that in fact Laliene had been moving steadily toward him since the beginning—in Canterbury, in Capri, a touch of the hand here, a quick private smile there, a quip, a glance. Her defending him so earnestly against Denvin's snobbery and Denvin's sarcasm, just after they had arrived here: what was that, if not the groundwork for some subtle treaty that was to be established subsequently between them? But why? Why? Such romance as could ever have existed for Laliene and him had come and gone long, long ago. Now they were merely friends. Perhaps he was mistaking the nature of this transaction. But no . . . no. There was no mistake.

Sparring for time, he said, keeping his tone and style carefully neutral, "You should come walking with me tomorrow. I saw marvelous things just a few blocks from here."

"I'd love to, Thimiroi. I want you to show me everything you've discovered."

"Yes. Yes, of course, Laliene."

But as he said it, he felt a deep stab of confusion. Everything? There was the house where that music had been playing. The open window, the simple, haunting melody. And the woman's face, then: the golden hair, the pale skin, the blue-green eyes. Thinking of her, thinking of the music she had played, Thimiroi found himself stirred by powerful and inexplicable forces that made him want to seize Laliene's music sphere and hurl it, and with it the subtle melodikia that it was playing, into the street. How smug that music sounded to him now, how over-civilized, how empty! And Laliene herself, so perfect in her beauty, the crimson hair, the flawless features, the sleek slender body—she was like some finely crafted statue, some life-sized doll: there was no reality to her, no essence of humanity. That woman in the window had shown more vital force in just her quick little half-frown and half-smile than Laliene displayed in all her repertoire of artful movements and expressions.

He stared at her, astounded, shaken.

She seemed shaken too. "Are you all right, Thimiroi?" she whispered.

"A little—tired, perhaps," he said huskily. "Stretched myself farther today than I really knew."

Laliene nodded toward the cup. "The tea will heal you."

"Yes. Yes."

He sipped. There was a knocking at the door. Laliene smiled, excused herself, opened it.

Denvin was there, and others behind him.

"Lutheena—Hollia—Hara—come in, come in, come in all of you! Omerie, how good to see you—Kleph, Klia—dear Klia—come in, everyone! How wonderful, how wonderful! I have the tea all ready and waiting for you!"

* * *

THE CONCERT THAT NIGHT WAS an extraordinary experience. Every moment, every note, seemed freighted with unforgettable meaning. Perhaps it was the poignancy of knowing that the beautiful young violinist who played so brilliantly had only a few weeks left to live, and that this grand and sumptuous concert hall itself was soon to be a smoking ruin. Perhaps it was the tiny magical phrase he had heard while listening in the street, which had somehow sensitized him to the fine secret graces of this seemingly simple twentieth-century music. Perhaps it was only the euphoriac they had had in Laliene's room before setting out. Whatever it was, it evoked a mood of unusual, even unique, attentiveness in Thimiroi, and as the minutes went by he knew that this evening at the concert hall would surely resonate joyously in his soul forever after.

That mood was jarred and shaken and irrevocably shattered at intermission, when he was compelled to stand with his stunningly dressed companions in the vestibule and listen to their brittle chirping chatter. How empty they all seemed, how foolish! Omerie stalking around in his most virile and commanding mode, like some sort of peacock, and imperious Lutheena matching him swagger for swagger, and Klia looking on complacently, and Kleph even more complacent, mysteriously lost in mists like some child who has found a packet of narcotic candies. And then of course there was the awesome Miss Hollia, who seemed older than the Pyramids, glowering at Omerie in unconcealed malevolence even while she complimented him on his mastery of twentieth-century costuming, and Hollia's pretty little playmate Hara as usual saying scarcely anything, but lending his support to his owner by glaring at Omerie also—and Denvin, chiming in with his sardonic, too-too-special insights from time to time—

What a wearying crew, Thimiroi thought. These precious connoisseurs of history, these tireless voyagers of the eons. His head began to ache. He stepped away from them and began to walk back toward the auditorium. For the first time he noticed how the other members of the audience were staring at the little group. Wondering what country they came from, no doubt, and how rich they might be. Such perfection of dress, such precision of movement, such elegance of speech—foreign, obviously foreign, but mystifyingly so, for they seemed to belong to no recognizable nationality, and spoke with no recognizable accent. Thimiroi smiled wearily. "Do you want to know the truth about us?" he imagined himself crying. "We are visitors, yes. Tourists from a far country. But where we live is not only beyond your reach, it is beyond even your imaginations. What would you say, if I revealed to you that we are natives of the year—"

"Bored with the concert?" Laliene asked. She had come up quietly beside him, without his noticing it.

"Quite the contrary."

"Bored with us, then." It was not a question.

Thimiroi shrugged. "The intermission's an unfortunate interruption. I wish the music hadn't stopped."

"The music always stops," she said, and laughed her throatiest, smokiest laugh.

He studied her. She was still offering herself to him, with her eyes, her smile, her slightly sidewise stance. Thimiroi felt almost guilty for his wilful failure to accept the gambit. Was he infuriating her? Was he wounding her?

But I do not want her, he told himself.

Once again, as in her room that afternoon while they were sipping euphoriac together, he was struck by the puzzling distaste and even anger that the perfection of her beauty aroused in him. Why this violent reaction? He had always lived in a world of perfect people. He had been accustomed all his life to Laliene's sort of flawlessness. There was no need for anyone to have blemishes of face or form any more. One took that sort of thing for granted; everyone did. Why should it trouble him now? What strange restlessness was this century kindling in his soul?

Thimiroi saw the strain, the tension, the barely suppressed impatience in Laliene's expression, and for a moment he was so abashed by the distress he knew he must be causing her that he came close to inviting her to join him in his suite after the concert. But he could not bring himself to do it. The moment passed; the tension slackened; Laliene made an elegant recovery, smiling and slipping her arm through his to lead him back to their seats, and he moved gratefully into a round of banter with her, and with Kleph, who drifted back up the aisle with them. But the magic and wonder of the concert were forever lost. In the second half he sat in a leaden slump, barely listening, unable to find the patterns that made the music comprehensible.

That night Thimiroi slept alone, and slept badly. After some hours of wakefulness he had to have recourse to one of his drugs. And even that brought him only partial solace, for with sleep came dark dreams of a singularly ominous and disruptive kind, full of hot furious blasts of anguish and panic, and he felt too drained of energy to get up again and rummage through his kit for the drug that banishes dreams. Morning was a long time in coming.

* * *

Over the next few days Thimiroi kept mostly to himself. He suspected that his fellow voyagers were talking about him—that they were worried about him—but he shied away from any sort of contact with them. The mere sight of them was something that caused him a perceptible pain, almost like the closing of a clamp about his heart. He longed to recapture that delicious openness to experience, that wonderful vulnerability, that he had felt when he had first arrived here, and he knew that so long as he was with any of them he would never be able to attain it.

By withdrawing from them in this morose way, he realized, he was missing some of the pleasures of the visit. The others were quite serious, as serious as such frivolous people ever could be, about the late twentieth century, and they spent each day moving busily about the city, taking advantage of its wealth of cultural opportunities—many of them obscure even to the natives of the era themselves. Kleph, whose specialty was Golconda studies, put together a small festival of the films of that great actor, and for two days they all, even Hollia, scurried around town seeing him at work in actual original prints. Omerie discovered, and proudly displayed, a first edition of Martin Drexel's *Lyrical Journeys.*

"It cost me next to nothing," Omerie declared in vast satisfaction. "These people don't have the slightest idea of what Drexel achieved." A day or two later, Klia organized a river trip to the birthplace of

David Courtney, a short way north of the city. Courtney would not be born, of course, for another seventy years, but his birthplace already existed, and who could resist making the pilgrimage? Thimiroi resisted. "Come with us," Laliene pleaded, with a curious urgency in her voice that he had never heard in it before. "This is one trip you really must not miss." He told her, calmly at first and then more forcefully, as she continued to press the point, that he had no desire to go. She looked at him in a stricken way, as though he had slapped her; but at that point she yielded. The others went on the river journey and he stayed behind, drifting through the streets of the downtown section without purpose, without goal.

Troubled as he was, he found excitement nevertheless in the things he saw on his solitary walks. The vigor and intensity of this era struck resonances in his own unfashionably robust spirit. The noise here, the smells, the colors, the expansive, confident air of the people, who obviously knew that they were living at one of history's great peak periods—everything startled and stimulated him in a way that Roman Capri and Chaucerian Canterbury had not been able to do.

Those older places and times had been too remote in spirit and essence from his native epoch to be truly comprehensible: they were interesting the way a visit to an alien planet can be interesting, but they had not moved him as this era moved him. Possibly the knowledge of impending doom that he had here had something to do with that. But there was something else. Thimiroi sensed, as he had not in any way sensed during the earlier stops, that he might actually be able to *live* in this era, and feel at home in it, and be happy here. For much of his life he had felt somehow out of place in his own world, unable all too often to come to terms with the seamlessness of everything, the impeccability of that immaculate era. Now he thought he understood why. As he wandered the streets of this booming, brawling, far-from-perfect city—taking joy in its curious mixture of earthy marvelous accomplishment and mysterious indifference to its own shortcomings, and finding himself curiously at ease in it—he began to perceive himself as a man of the late twentieth century who by some bewildering prank of the gods had been born long after his own proper time. And with that perception came a kind of calmness in the face of the storm that was to come.

* * *

TOWARD THE END OF THE first week—it was the day when the others made their pilgrimage up the river to David Courtney's birthplace—Thimiroi encountered the golden-haired woman who had been playing the piano in the house down the block from the hotel. He caught sight of her downtown while he was crossing a plaza paved with pink cobblestones, which linked twin black towers of almost unthinkable height and mass near the river embankment.

Though he had only seen her for a moment, that one other time, and that time only her face and throat at the window, he had no doubt that it was she. Her blue-green eyes and long straight shining hair were unmistakable. She was fairly tall and very slender, with a tall woman's quick way of walking, ankles close together, shoulders slightly hunched forward. Thimiroi supposed that she was about thirty, or perhaps forty at most. She was young, at any rate, but not *very* young. He had no clear idea of how quickly people aged in this era. The first mild signs of aging seemed visible on her. In his own time that would mean nothing—there, a woman who looked like this might be anywhere between fifty and a hundred and fifty—but he knew that here they had no significant way of reversing the effects of time, and what she showed was almost certainly an indication that she had left her girlhood behind by some years but had not yet gone very far into the middle of the journey.

"Pardon me," he said, a little to his own surprise, as she came toward him.

She peered blankly at him. "Yes?"

Thimiroi offered her a disarming smile. "I'm a visitor here. Staying at the Montgomery House."

The mention of the famous hotel—and, perhaps, his gentle manner and the quality of his clothing—seemed to ease whatever apprehensions she might be feeling. She paused, looking at him questioningly.

He said, "You live near there, don't you? A few days ago, when I was out for a walk—it was my first day here—I heard you playing the piano. I'm sure it was you. I applauded when you stopped, and you looked out the window at me. I think you must have seen me. You frowned, and then you smiled."

She frowned now, just a quick flicker of confusion; and then again she smiled.

"Just like that, yes," Thimiroi said. "Do you mind if we talk? Are you in a hurry?"

"Not really," she said, and he sensed something troubled behind the words.

"Is there some place near here where we could have a drink? Or lunch, perhaps?" That was what they called the meal they ate at this time of day, he was certain. Lunch. People of this era met often for lunch, as a social thing. He did not think it was too late in the day to be offering her lunch.

"Well, there's the River Cafe," she said. "That's just two or three blocks. I suppose we—" She broke off. "You know, I never ever do anything like this. Let myself get picked up in the street, I mean."

"Picked up? I do not understand."

"What don't you understand?"

"The phrase," Thimiroi said. "Pick up? To lift? Am I lifting you?"

She laughed and said, "Are you foreign?"

"Oh, yes. Very foreign."

"I thought your way of speaking was a little strange. So precise—every syllable perfectly shaped. No one really speaks English that way. Except computers, of course. You aren't a computer, are you?"

"Hardly."

"Good. I would never allow myself to be picked up by a computer in First National Plaza. Or anyplace else, as a matter of fact. Are you still interested in going to the River Cafe?"

"Of course."

She was playful now. "We can't do this anonymously, though. It's too sordid. My name's Christine Rawlins."

"And I am called Thimiroi."

"Timmery?"

"Thimiroi," he said.

"Thim-i-roi," she repeated, imitating his precision. "A very unusual name, I'd say. I've never met anyone named Thimiroi before. What country are you from, may I ask?"

"You would not know it. A very small one, very far away."

"Iran?"

"Farther away than that."

"A lot of people who came here from Iran prefer not to admit that that's where they're from."

"I am not from Iran, I assure you."

"But you won't tell me where?"

"You would not know it," he said again.

Her eyes twinkled. "Oh, you *are* from Iran! You're a spy, aren't you? I see the whole thing: they're getting ready to have a new revolution, there's another Ayatollah on his way from his hiding place in Beirut, and you're here to transfer Iranian assets out of this country before—" She broke off, looking sheepish. "I'm sorry. I'm just being weird. Have I offended you?"

"Not at all."

"You don't have to tell me where you're from if you don't want to."

"I am from Stiinowain," he said, astounded at his own daring in actually uttering the forbidden name.

She tried to repeat the name, but was unable to manage the soft glide of the first syllable.

"You're right," she said. "I don't know anything about it at all. But you'll tell me all about it, won't you?"

"Perhaps," he said.

* * *

THE RIVER CAFE WAS A glossy bubble of pink marble and black glass cantilevered out over the embankment, with a semicircular open-air dining area, paved with shining flagstones, that jutted even farther, so that it seemed suspended almost in mid-river. They were lucky enough to find one vacant table that was right at the cafe's outermost edge, looking down on the swift blue riverflow. "Ordinarily the outdoor section doesn't open until the middle of June," Christine told him. "But this year it's been so warm and dry that they opened it a month early. We've been breaking records every day. There's never been a May like this, that's what they're all saying. Just one long run of fabulous weather day after day after day."

"It's been extraordinary, yes."

"What is May like in Stiin—in your country?" she asked.

"Very much like this. As a matter of fact, it is rather like this all the year round."

"Really? How wonderful that must be!"

It must have seemed like boasting to her. He regretted that. "No," he said. "We take our mild climate for granted and the succession of beautiful days means nothing to us. It is better this way, sudden glory rising out of contrast, the darkness of winter giving way to the splendor of spring. The warm sunny days coming upon you like—like the coming of grace, shall I say?—like—" He smiled. "Like that heavenly little theme that came suddenly out of the music you were playing, transforming something simple and ordinary into something unforgettable. Do you know what I mean?"

"Yes," she said. "I think I do."

He began to hum the melody. Her eyes sparkled, and she nodded and grinned warmly, and after a moment or two she started humming along with him. He felt a tightness at his throat, warmth along his back and shoulders, a throbbing in his chest. All the symptoms of a rush of strong emotion. Very strange to him, very primitive, very exciting, very pleasing.

People at other tables turned. They seemed to notice something also. Thimiroi saw them smiling at the two of them with that unmistakable proprietorial smile that strangers will offer to young lovers in the springtime. Christine must have seen those smiles too, for color came to her face, and for a moment she looked away from him as though embarrassed.

"Tell me about yourself," he said.

"We should order first. Are you familiar with our foods? A salad might be nice on a beautiful warm day like this—and then perhaps the cold salmon plate, or—" She stopped abruptly. "Is something wrong?"

Thimiroi struggled to fight back nausea. "Not a salad, no, please. It is—not good for me. And in my country we do not eat fish of any sort, not ever."

"Forgive me."

"But how could you have known?"

"Even so—you looked so distressed—"

"Not really. It was only a moment's uneasiness." He scanned the menu desperately. Nothing on it made sense to him. At home, he would only have to touch the screen beside anything that seemed to be of interest, and he would get a quick flavor-analog appercept to guide his choice. But that was at home. Here he had been taking most of his meals in his room, meals prepared many centuries away by his own autochef and sent to him down the time conduit. On those few occasions when he ate in the hotel dining room with his fellow travelers, he relied on Kadro to choose his food for him. Now, plunging ahead blindly, he selected something called carpaccio for his starter, and vichyssoise to follow.

"Are you sure you don't want anything warm?" Christine asked gently.

"Oh, I think not, not on such a mild day," Thimiroi said casually. He had no idea what he had ordered; but he was determined not to seem utterly ignorant of her era.

The carpaccio, though, turned out to be not merely cold but raw: red raw meat, very thinly sliced, in a light sauce. He stared at it in amazement. His whole body recoiled at the thought of eating raw meat. His bones themselves protested. He saw Christine staring at him, and wondered how much of his horror his expression was revealing to her. But there was no helping it: he slipped his fork under one of the paper-thin slices and conveyed it to his mouth. To his amazement it was delicious. Forgetting all breeding, he ate the rest without pausing once, while she watched in what seemed like a mixture of surprise and amusement.

"You liked that, didn't you?" she said.

"Carpaccio has always been one of my favorites," he told her shamelessly.

Vichyssoise turned out to be a cold dish too, a thick white soup, presumably made from some vegetable. It seemed harmless and proved to be quite tasty. Christine had ordered the salmon, and he tried not to peer at her plate, or to imagine what it must be like to put chunks of sea-creatures in one's mouth, while she ate.

"You promised to tell me something about yourself," he reminded her.

She looked uneasy. "It's not a very interesting story, I'm afraid."

"But you must tell me a little of it. Are you a musician by profession? Surely you are. Do you perform in the concert hall?"

Her look of discomfort deepened. "I know you don't mean to be cruel, but—"

"Cruel? Of course not. But when I was listening there outside the window I could feel the great gift that you have."

"Please."

"I don't understand."

"No, you don't, do you?" she said gently. "You weren't trying to be funny, or to hurt me. But I'm not any sort of gifted pianist, Thimiroi. Believe me. I'm just a reasonably good amateur. Maybe when I was ten years old I dreamed of having a concert career some day, but I came to my senses a long time ago."

"You are too modest."

"No. No. I know what I am. And what the real thing is like. Even *they* don't have an easy time of it. You can't believe how many concert-quality pianists my age there are in this country. With so many genuine geniuses out there, there's no hope at all for a decent third-rater like me."

He shook his head in amazement, remembering the magical sounds that had come from her window. "Third-rater!"

"I don't have any illusions about that," she said. "I'm the sort of pianist who winds up giving piano lessons, not playing in Carnegie Hall. I have a couple of pupils. They come and go. It's not possible to earn a living that way. And the job that I did have, with an export-import firm—well, they say that this is the most prosperous time this country has seen in the past forty years, but somehow I managed to get laid off last week anyway. That's why I'm downtown today—another job interview. You see? Just an ordinary woman, an ordinary life, ordinary problems—"

"There is nothing ordinary about you," said Thimiroi fervently. "Not to me! To me you are altogether extraordinary, Christine!" She seemed almost about to weep as he said that. Compassion and tenderness overwhelmed him, and he reached out to take her hand in his, to comfort her, to reassure her. Her eyes widened and she pulled back instantly, catching her breath sharply, as though he had tried to stab her with his fork.

Thimiroi looked at her sadly. The quickness and vehemence of her reaction mystified him.

"That was wrong?" he said. "To want to touch your hand?"

Awkwardly Christine said, "You surprised me, that's all. I'm sorry. I didn't mean—it was rude of me, actually—oh, Thimiroi, I can't explain—it was just automatic, a kind of dumb reflex—"

Puzzled, he turned his hand over several times, examining it, searching for something about it that might have frightened or repelled her. He saw nothing. It was simply a hand. After a moment she took it lightly with her own, and held it.

He said, "You have a husband? Is that why I should not have done that?"

"I'm not married, no." She glanced away from him, but did not release his hand. "I'm not even—involved. Not currently." Her fingers were lightly stroking his wrist. "I have to confess something," she said, after a moment. "I saw you at Symphony Hall last week. The De Santis concert."

"You did?"

"In the lobby. With your—friends. I watched you all, wondering who you were. There was a kind of glow about the whole group of you. The women were all so beautiful, every one of them. Immaculate. Perfect. Like movie stars, they were."

"They are nothing compared with you."

"Please. Don't say any more things like that. I don't like to be flattered, Thimiroi. Not only does it make me uncomfortable but it simply isn't effective with me. Whatever else I am, I'm a realistic woman. Especially about myself."

"And I am a truthful man. What I tell you is what I feel, Christine." Her hand tightened on his wrist at that. He said, "So you knew who I was, when I approached you in the plaza up above just now."

"Yes," she murmured.

"But pretended you did not."

"I was frightened."

"I am not frightening, Christine."

"Not frightened of you. Of me. When I saw you that first day, standing outside my house—I felt—I don't know, I felt something strange, just looking at you. Felt that I had seen you before somewhere, that I had known you very well in some other life, perhaps, that—oh, Thimiroi, I'm not making any sense, am I? But I knew you had been *important* to me at some other time. Or *would* be important. It's crazy, isn't it? And I don't have any room in my life for craziness. I'm just trying to hold my own, don't you see? Trying to maintain, trying to hang on and not get swept under. In these wonderful prosperous times, I'm all alone, Thimiroi, I'm not sure where I'm heading, what's going to come next for me. Everything seems so uncertain. And so I don't want any extra uncertainties in my life."

"I will not bring you uncertainty," he said.

She stared and said nothing. Her hand still touched his.

"If you are finished with your food," he said, "perhaps you would like to come back to the hotel with me."

There was a long tense silence. After a time she drew her hand away from him and knotted her fingers together, and sat very still, her expression indecipherable.

"You think it was inappropriate of me to have extended such an invitation," he said finally.

"No. Not really."

"I want only to be your friend."

"Yes. I know that."

"And I thought, since you live so close to the hotel, I could offer you some refreshment, and show you some treasures of my own country that I have brought with me. I meant nothing more than that, Christine. Please. Believe me."

She seemed to shed some of her tension. "I'd love to stop off at your hotel with you for a little while," she said.

* * *

He had no doubt at all that it was much too soon for them to become lovers. Not only was he completely unskilled in this era's sociosexual rituals and procedures, so that it was probably almost impossible for him to avoid offending or displeasing her by this or that unintentional violation of the accepted courtship customs of her society, but also at this point he was still much too uncertain of the accuracy of his insight into her own nature. Once he knew her better, perhaps he would be less likely to go about things incorrectly, particularly since she already gave him the benefit of many doubts because she knew he came from some distant land.

There was also the not inconsiderable point to consider that it was a profound violation of the rules of The Travel to enter into any kind of emotional or physical involvement with a native of a past era.

That, somehow, seemed secondary to Thimiroi just now. He knew all about the importance of avoiding distortion or contamination of the time-line; they drilled it into you endlessly before you ever started to Travel. But suddenly such issues seemed unreal and abstract to him. What mattered was what he felt: the surge of delight, eagerness, passion, that ran through him when he turned to look at this woman of a far-off time. All his life he had been a stranger among his own people, a prisoner within his own skin; now, here, at last, it seemed to him that he had a chance of breaking through the net of brittle conventions that for so long had bound his spirit, and touching, at last, the soul of another human being. He had read about love, of course—who had not?—but here, he thought, he might actually experience it. Was that a reckless ambition? Well, then, he would be reckless. The alternative was to condemn himself to a lifetime of bitter regret.

Therefore he schooled himself to patience. He dared not be too hasty, for fear of ruining everything.

Christine appeared astounded by what she saw in his rooms. She wandered through them like a child in a wonderland, hardly breathing, pausing here and there to look, to reach out hesitantly, to hold her hand above this or that miraculous object as though afraid actually to touch it but eager to experience its texture.

"You brought all this from your own country?" she asked. "You must have had fifty suitcases!"

"We get homesick very easily. We wish to have our familiar things about us."

"The way a sultan would travel. A pasha." Her eyes were shining with awe. "These little tables—I've never seen anything like them. I try to follow the weave, but the pattern won't stand still. It keeps sliding around its own corners."

"The woodworkers of Sipulva are extremely ingenious," Thimiroi said.

"Sipulva? Is that a city in your country?"

"A place nearby," he said. "You may touch them if you wish."

She caressed the intricately carved surfaces, fingers tracing the weave as it went through its incomprehensible convolutions. Thimiroi, smiling, turned the music sphere on—one of Mirtin's melodikias began to come from it, a shimmering crystalline piece—and set about brewing some tea. Christine drifted onward, examining the draperies, the glistening carpets, the pulsating esthetikon that was sending waves of color through the room, the simso screens with their shifting views of unknown worlds. She was altogether enthralled. It would certainly be easy enough to seduce her now, Thimiroi realized. A little sensuous music, a few sips of euphoriac, perhaps some surreptitious adjustments of the little subsonic so that it sent forth heightened tonalities of *anticipation* and *excitation*—yes, that was all that it would take, he knew. But easy conquest was not what he wanted. He did not intend to pass through her soul like a frivolous tourist drifting through a museum in search of an hour's superficial diversion.

One cup of tea for each of them, then, and no more. Some music, some quick demonstrations of a few of the little wonders that filled his rooms. A light kiss, finally, and then one that was more intense; but a quick restoration, afterward, of the barriers between them. Christine seemed no more willing to breach those barriers today than he was. Thimiroi was relieved at that, and pleased. They seemed to understand each other already.

"I'll walk you home," he said, when they plainly had reached the time when she must either leave or stay much longer.

"You needn't. It's just down the street." Her hand lingered in his. Her touch was warm, her skin faintly moist, pleasantly so. "You'll call me? Here's my number." She gave him a smooth little yellow card. "We could have dinner, perhaps. Or a concert—whatever you'd like to see—"

"Yes. Yes, I'll call you."

"You'll be here at least a few more days, won't you?"

"Until the end of the month."

She nodded. He saw the momentary darkening of her expression, and guessed at the inward calculations: reckoning the number of days remaining to his visit, the possibilities that those days might hold, the rashness of embarking on anything that would surely not extend beyond the last day of May. Thimiroi had already made the same calculations himself, though tempered by information that she could not conceivably have, information which made everything inconceivably more precarious. After the smallest of pauses she said, "That's plenty of time, isn't it? But call me soon, Thimiroi. Will you? Will you?"

* * *

A LITTLE WHILE LATER THERE was a light knocking at the door, and Thimiroi, hoping with a startling rush of eagerness that Christine had found some pretext for returning, opened it to find Laliene. She looked weary. The perfection of her beauty was unmarred, of course, every shining strand of hair in its place, her tanned skin fresh and glistening. But beneath the radiant outer glow there was once again something drawn and tense and ragged about her, a subliminal atmosphere of strain, of fatigue, of devitalization, that was not at all typical of the Laliene he had known. This visit to the late twentieth century did not seem to be agreeing with her.

"May I come in?" she asked. He nodded and beckoned to her. "We've all just returned from the Courtney birthplace," she said. "You really should have gone with us, Thimiroi. You can feel the aura of the man everywhere in the place, even this early, so many years before he even existed." Taking a few steps into the room, Laliene paused, sniffed the air lightly, smiled. "Having a little tea by yourself just now, were you, Thimiroi?"

"Just a cup. It was a long quiet afternoon."

"Poor Thimiroi. Couldn't find anything at all interesting to do? Then you certainly should have come with us." He saw her glance flicking quickly about, and felt pleased and relieved that he had taken the trouble to put the teacups away. It was in fact no business of Laliene's that he had had a guest in here this afternoon, but he did not want her, all the same, to know that he had.

"Can I brew a cup for you?" he asked.

"I think not. I'm so tired after our outing—it'll put me right to sleep, I would say." She turned toward him, giving him a direct inquisitorial stare that he found acutely discomforting. In a straightforward way that verged on bluntness she said, "I'm worried about you, you know, Thimiroi. Keeping off by yourself so much. The others are talking. You really should make an effort to join the group more often."

"Maybe I'm bored with the group, Laliene. With Denvin's snide little remarks, with Hollia's queenly airs, with Hara's mincing inanity, with Omerie's arrogance, with Klia's vacuity—"

"And with my presumptuousness?"

"You said that. Not I."

But it was true, he realized. She was crowding him constantly, forever edging into his psychic space, pressing herself upon him in a strange, almost incomprehensible way. It had been that way since the beginning of the trip: she never seemed to leave him alone. Her approach toward him was an odd mix of seductiveness, protectiveness, and—what?—inquisitiveness? She was like that strangest of antique phenomena, a jealous lover, almost. But jealous of what? Of whom? Surely not Christine. Christine had not so much as existed for him, except as a mysterious briefly-glimpsed face in a window, until this afternoon, and Laliene had been behaving like this for many weeks. It made no sense. Even now, covertly snooping around his suite, all too obviously searching for some trace of the guest who had only a short while before been present here—what was she after?

He took two fresh cups from his cabinet. "If you don't mind, Laliene, I'll put up a little more tea for myself. And it would be no trouble to make some for you."

"I said I didn't want any, Thimiroi. I don't enjoy gulping the stuff down, you know, the way Kleph does."

"Kleph?"

"Certainly you know how heavily she indulges. She's euphoric more often than not these days."

Thimiroi shrugged. "I didn't realize that. I suppose Omerie can get on anyone's nerves. Even Kleph's."

Laliene studied him for a long moment. "You don't know about Kleph, then?" she asked finally. "No, I suppose you don't. Keeping to yourself this way, how would you?"

This was maddening. "What about Kleph?" he said, his voice growing tight.

"Perhaps you should fix some tea for me after all," Laliene said. "It's quite a nasty story. It'll be easier for me with a little euphoriac."

"Very well."

He busied himself over the tiny covered cups. In a short while the fragrant coiling steam began to rise through the fine crescent opening. His hands trembled, and he nearly swept the cups from the tray as he reached for them; but he recovered quickly and brought them to the table. They sipped the drug in silence. Watching her, Thimiroi was struck once more by the inhuman superfluity of Laliene's elegance. Laliene was much too perfect. How different from Christine, whose skin had minute unimportant blemishes here and there, whose teeth were charmingly irregular, whose hair looked like real hair and not like something spun by machines. Christine probably perspired, he thought. She endured the messiness of menstruation. She might even snore. She was wonderfully real, wonderfully human in every regard. Whereas Laliene—Laliene seemed—scarcely real at all—

"What's this about Kleph, now?" Thimiroi said, after a time.

"She's become involved with the man that the Sanciscos are renting their house from."

"Involved?"

"An affair," said Laliene acidly. Her glistening eyes were trained remorselessly on his. "He goes to her room. She gives him too much tea, and has too much herself. She plays music for him, or they watch the simsos. And then—then—"

"How do you know any of this?" Thimiroi asked.

Laliene took a deep draught of the intoxicating tea, and her brow grew less furrowed, her dark rich-hued eyes less troubled. "She told Klia. Klia told me."

"And Omerie? Does he know?"

"Of course. He's furious. Kleph can sleep with anyone she cares to, naturally—but such a violation of the Travel rules, to get involved with one of these ancient people! And so stupid, too—spending so much of the precious time of her visit here letting herself get wrapped up in a useless diversion with some commonplace and extremely uninteresting man. A man who isn't even alive, who's been dead for all these centuries!"

"He doesn't happen to be dead right now," Thimiroi said.

Laliene gave him a look of amazement. "Are you defending her, Thimiroi?"

"I'm trying to comprehend her."

"Yes. Yes, of course. But certainly Kleph must see that although he may be alive at the present moment, technically speaking, the present moment itself isn't really the present moment. Not if you see it from our point of view, and what other point of view is appropriate for us to take? What's past is past, sealed and finished. In absolute reality this person of Kleph's died long ago, at least so far as we're concerned." Laliene shook her head. "No, no, Thimiroi, completely apart from the issue of transgression against the rules of The Travel, it's an unthinkably foolish adventure that Kleph's let herself get into. Unthinkably foolish! It's purely a waste of time. What kind of pleasure can she possibly get from it? She might as well be coupling with—with a donkey!"

"Who is this man?" Thimiroi asked.

"What does that matter? His name is Oliver Wilson. He owns that house where they are, the one that Hollia is trying to buy, and he lives there, too. Omerie neglected to arrange for him to vacate the premises for the month. You may have seen him: a very ordinary-looking pleasant young man with light-colored hair. But he isn't important. What's important is the insane, absurd, destructive thing Kleph is doing. Which particular person of this long-gone era she happens to be doing it with is completely beside the point."

Thimiroi studied her for a time.

"Why are you telling me this, Laliene?"

"Aren't you interested in what your friends are getting themselves mixed up in?"

"Is Kleph my friend?"

"Isn't she?"

"We have come to the same place at the same time, Kleph and I," Thimiroi said. "Does that make us friends? We *know* each other, Kleph and I. Possibly we were even lovers once, possibly not. My relationship with the Sanciscos in general and with Kleph in particular isn't a close one nowadays. So far as this matters to me, Kleph can do what she likes with anyone she pleases."

"She runs the risk of punishment."

"She was aware of that. Presumably she chooses not to be troubled by it."

"She should think of Omerie, then. And Klia. If Kleph is forbidden to Travel again, they will be deprived of her company. They have always Traveled together. They are accustomed to Traveling together. How selfish of her, Thimiroi."

"Presumably she chooses not to be troubled by that, either," said Thimiroi. "In any case, it's no concern of yours or mine." He hesitated. "Do you know what I think *should* trouble her, Laliene? The fact that she's going to pay a very steep emotional price for what she's doing, if indeed she's actually doing it. That part of it ought to be on her mind, at least a little."

"What do you mean?" Laliene asked.

"I mean the effect it will have on her when the meteor comes, and this man is killed by it. Or by what comes after the meteor, and you know what that is. If the meteor doesn't kill him, the Blue Death will take him a week or two later. How will Kleph feel then, Thimiroi? Knowing that the man she loves is dead? And that she has done nothing, nothing at all, to spare him from the fate that she knew was rushing toward him? Poor Kleph! Poor foolish Kleph! What torment it will be for her!"

"The man she loves?"

"Doesn't she?"

Laliene looked astounded. "What ever gave you that idea? It's a game, Thimiroi, only a silly game! She's simply playing with him. And then she'll move along. He won't be killed by the meteor—obviously. He'll be in the same house as all the rest of us when it strikes. And she'll be at Charlemagne's coronation by the time the Blue Death breaks out. She won't even remember his *name*, Thimiroi. How could you possibly have thought that she—she—" Laliene shook her head. "You don't understand a thing, do you?"

"Perhaps I don't." Thimiroi put his cup down and stared at his fingers. They were trembling. "Would you like some more tea, Laliene?"

"No, I—yes. Yes, another, if you will, Thimiroi."

He set about the task of brewing the euphoriac. His head was throbbing. Things were occurring to him that he had not bothered to consider before. While he worked, Laliene rose, roamed the room, toyed with this artifact and that, and drifted out into the hall that led to the bedroom. Did she suspect anything? Was she searching for something, perhaps? He wondered whether Christine had left any trace of her presence behind that Laliene might be able to detect, and decided that probably she had not. Certainly he hoped not. Considering how agitated Laliene seemed to be over Kleph's little fling with her landlord, how would she react if she knew that he, too, was involved with someone of this era?

Involved?

How involved are you, really? he asked himself.

He thought of all that they had said just now about Kleph and her odd little affair with Oliver Wilson. A cold, inescapable anguish began to rise in him. How sorry he had felt for Kleph, a moment ago! The punishment for transgression against the rules, yes—but also the high emotional price that he imagined Kleph would pay for entangling herself with someone who lay under sentence of immediate death—the guilt—the sense of irretrievable loss—

The meteor—the Blue Death—

"The tea is ready," Thimiroi announced, and as he reached for the delicate cups he knocked one into the other, and both of the pretty things went tumbling from the tray, landing at the carpet's edge and cracking like eggshells against the wooden floor. A little rivulet of euphoriac came swirling from them. He gasped, shocked and appalled. Laliene, emerging from one of the far rooms, looked down at the wreckage for a moment, then swiftly knelt and began to sweep the fragments together.

"Oh, Thimiroi," she said, glancing upward at him. "Oh, how sad, Thimiroi, how terribly sad—"

* * *

After lunch the next day, he telephoned Christine, certain that she would be out and a little uneasy about that; but she answered on the second ring, and there was an eagerness in her voice that made him think she had been poised beside the phone for some time now, waiting for him to call. Did she happen to be free this afternoon? Yes, yes, she said, she was free. Did she care to—his mind went blank a moment—to go for a walk with him somewhere? Yes, yes, what a lovely idea! She sounded almost jubilant. A perfect day for a walk, yes!

She was waiting outside her house when Thimiroi came down the street. It was a day much like all the other days so far, sharp cloudless sky, brilliant sun, gold blazing against blue. But there was a deeper tinge of warmth in the air, for May was near its end now and spring was relinquishing its hold to the coming summer. Trees which had seemed barely into leaf the week before now unfurled canopies of rich deep green.

"Where shall we go?" she asked him.

"This is your city. I don't know the good places."

"We could walk in Baxter Park, I suppose."

Thimiroi frowned. "Isn't that all the way on the other side of the river?"

"Baxter Park? Oh, no, you must be thinking of Butterfield Gardens. Up on the high ridge, you mean, over there opposite us? The very big park, with the botanical gardens and the zoo and everything? Baxter Park's right near here, just a few blocks up the hill. We could be there in ten minutes."

Actually it was more like fifteen, and no easy walk, but none of that mattered to Thimiroi. Simply being close to Christine awoke unfamiliar sensations of contentment in him. They climbed the steep streets side by side, saying very little as they made the difficult ascent, pausing now and again to catch their breaths. The city was like a giant bowl, cleft by the great river that ran through its middle, and they were nearing its rim.

Baxter Park, like its counterpart across the river that Thimiroi had seen when he first arrived in the twentieth century, occupied a commanding position looking out and down toward the heart of the urban area. But apart from that the two parks were very different, for the other was intricately laid out, with roads and amusement sectors scattered through it, and this one seemed nothing more than a strip of rough, wild semi-forest that had been left undeveloped at the top of the city. Simple paths crudely paved led through its dense groves and tangles of underbrush.

"It isn't much, I know—" Christine said.

"It's beautiful here. So wild, so untamed. And so close to the city. We can look down and see houses and office buildings and bridges, and yet back here it's just as it must have been ten thousand years ago. There is nothing like this where I come from."

"Do you mean that?"

"We took our wilderness away a long time ago. We should have kept a little—just a little, a reminder, the way you have here. But it's too late now. It has been gone so long, so very long." Thimiroi peered into the hazy distance. Shimmering in the midafternoon heat, the city seemed a fairytale place, enchanted, wondrous. Shading his eyes, he peered out and downward, past the residential district to the metropolitan center by the river, and beyond it to the bridges, the suburbs on the far side, the zone of parks and recreational areas barely visible on the opposite slope. How beautiful it all was, how majestic, how grand! The thought that it all must perish in just a matter of days brought the taste of bile to his mouth, and he turned away, coughing, sputtering.

"Is something the matter?" Christine asked.

"Nothing—no—I'll be all right—"

He wondered how far they were right now from the path along which the meteor would travel.

As he understood it, it was going to come in from this side of the city, traveling low across the great urban bowl like a stone that a boy has sent skimming across a stream and striking somewhere midway down the slope, between the zone of older houses just below the Montgomery House hotel and the business district farther on. At the point of impact, of course, everything would be annihilated for blocks around. But the real devastation would come a moment later, so Kadro had explained: when the shock wave struck and radiated outward, flattening whole neighborhoods in a steadily widening circle, as if they had been swatted by a giant's contemptuous hand.

And then the fires, springing up everywhere—

And then, a few days later, when the invading microbes had had a chance to spread through the contaminated water supply of the shattered city, the plague—

"You look so troubled, Thimiroi," Christine said, nestling up beside him, sliding her arm through his.

"Do I?"

"You must miss your homeland very much."

"No. No, that isn't it."

"Why so sad, then?"

"I find it extremely moving," he said, "to look out over your whole city this way. Taking it all in in a single sweep. Seeing it in all its magnificence, all its power."

"But it's not even the most important city in the—"

"I know. But that doesn't matter. The fact that there may be bigger cities takes nothing away from the grandeur of this one. Especially for me. Where I come from, there are no cities of any size at all. Our population is extremely small . . . *extremely* small."

"But it must be a very wealthy country, all the same."

Thimiroi shrugged. "I suppose it is. But what does that mean? I look at your city here and I think of the transience of all that is splendid and grand. I think of all the great empires of the past, and how they rose, and fell, and were swept away and forgotten. All the empires that ever were, and all those that will ever be."

To his surprise, she laughed. "Oh, how strange you are!"

"Strange?"

"So terribly solemn. So philosophical. Brooding about the rise and fall of empires on a glorious spring day like this. Standing here with the most amazing sunlight pouring down on us and telling me in those elocution-school tones of yours that empires that don't even exist yet are already swept away and forgotten. How can something be forgotten that hasn't yet even happened? And how can you even bother to think about anything morbid in a season like this one?" She moved closer to him, nuzzling against his side almost like a cat. "Do you know what I think, standing here right this minute looking out at the city? I think that the warmth of the sun feels wonderful and that the air is as fresh as new young wine and that the city has never seemed more sparkling or prosperous and that this is the most beautiful spring day in at least half a million years. And the last thing that's going to cross my mind is that the weather may not hold or that the time of prosperity may not last or that great empires always crumble and are forgotten. But perhaps you and I are just different, Thimiroi. Some people are naturally gloomy, and always see the darkest side of everything, and then there are the people who couldn't manage to be moody and broody even if their lives depended on—" She broke off suddenly. "Oh, Thimiroi, I don't mean to offend you. You know that."

"You haven't offended me." He turned to her. "What's an elocution-school voice?"

"A trained one," she said, smiling. "Like the voice of a radio or TV announcer. You have a marvelous voice, you know. You speak right from the center of your diaphragm, and you always pause for breath in the right places, and the tone is so rich, so perfect—a singer's voice, really. You can sing very well, can't you? I know you can. Later, perhaps, I could play for you, and you could sing for me, back at my place, some song of Stiino—of your own country—"

"Yes," he said. "We could try that, yes."

* * *

He kissed her, then, and it was a different sort of kiss from either of the two kisses of the day before, very different indeed; and as he held her his hands ran across her back, and over the nape of her neck, and down the sides of her arms, and she pressed herself close against him. Then after a long moment they moved apart again, both of them flushed and excited, and smiled, and looked at each other as though they were seeing each other for the first time.

They walked hand in hand through the park, neither of them saying anything. Small animals were everywhere, birds and odd shiny bright-colored little insects and comical four-legged grayish beasts with big shaggy tails lalloping behind them. Thimiroi was amazed by the richness of all this wildlife, and the shrubs and wildflowers dazzling with early bloom, and the huge thick-boled trees that rose so awesomely above them. What an extraordinary place this century was, he told himself: what a fantastic mixture of the still unspoiled natural world and the world of technology and industry. They had these great cities, these colossal buildings, these immense bridges—and yet, also, they still had saved room for flowers, for beetles and birds, for little furry animals with enormous tails. When the thought of the meteor, and the destruction that it would cause, crept back into his mind, he forced it furiously away. He asked Christine to tell him the names of things: this is a squirrel, she said, and this is a maple tree, and this a grasshopper. She was surprised that he knew so little about them, and asked him what kinds of insects and trees and animals they had in his own country.

"Very few," he told her. "All our wild things went from us long ago."

"Not even squirrels left? Grasshoppers?"

"Nothing like that," he said. "Nothing at all. That is why we travel—to experience life in places such as this. To experience squirrels. To experience grasshoppers."

"Of course. Everyone travels to see things different from what they have at home. But it's hard to believe that there's any country that's done such ecological damage to itself that it doesn't even have—"

"Oh, the problem is not ecological damage," said Thimiroi. "Not as you understand the term. Our country is very beautiful, in its way, and we care for it extremely well. The problem is that it is an extremely civilized place. Too civilized, I think. We have everything under control. And one thing that we controlled, a very long time ago, is the very thing that this park is designed to provide: the world of nature, as it existed before the cities ever were."

She stared. "Not even a squirrel."

"Not even a squirrel, no."

"Where is this country of yours? Did you say it was in Arabia? One of the oil kingdoms?"

"No," he said. "Not in Arabia."

They went onward. The afternoon's heat was at its peak, now, and Thimiroi felt the moisture of the air clinging close against his skin, a strange and unusual sensation for him. Again they paused, after a while, to kiss, even more passionately than before.

"Come," Christine said. "Let's go home."

They hurried down the hillside, taking it practically at a jog. But they slowed as the Montgomery House came into view. Thimiroi thought of inviting her to his room once again, but the thought of Laliene hovering nearby—spying on him, scowling her disapproval as he entered into the same transgression for which she had so sternly censured Kleph—displeased him. Christine reminded him, though, that she had offered to play the piano for him, and wanted him to sing for her. Gladly, eagerly, Thimiroi accepted the invitation to go with her to her house.

But as they approached it he was dismayed to see Kleph standing on the steps of a big, rambling old house just opposite Christine's, on the uphill side of the street. She was talking to a sturdy square-shouldered man with a good-natured, open face, and she did not appear to notice Thimiroi.

Christine said, "Do you want to say hello to her?"

"Not really."

"She's one of your friends, isn't she? Someone from your country?"

"She's from my country, yes. But not exactly a friend. Just someone who's taking the same tour I am. Is that the house where she's staying?"

"Yes," Christine said. "She and another woman, and a tall somber-looking man. I saw them all with you, that night at the concert hall. They've rented the house for the whole month. That man's the owner, Oliver Wilson."

"Ah." Thimiroi drew his breath in sharply.

So that was the one. Oliver. Kleph's twentieth-century lover. Thimiroi felt a stab of despair. Looking across the way now at Kleph, deep in conversation with this Oliver, it seemed to him suddenly that Laliene's scorn for Kleph had not been misplaced, that it was foolish and pathetic and even a little sordid for any Traveler to indulge in such doomed and absurd romances as this. And yet he was on the verge of embarking on the same thing Kleph was doing. Was that what he really wanted? Or should he not leave such adventures to shallow, trivial people like Kleph?

Christine said, "You're looking troubled again."

"It's nothing. Nothing." Thimiroi gazed closely at her, and her warmth, her directness, her radiant joyous eyes, swept away all the sudden doubts that had come to engulf him. He had no right to condemn Kleph. And in any case what he might choose to do, or Kleph, was no concern of Laliene's. "Come," he said. He caught Christine lightly by the arm. "Let's go inside."

Just as he turned, Kleph did also, and for an instant their eyes met as they stood facing each other on opposite sides of the street. She gave him a startled look. Thimiroi smiled to her; but Kleph merely stared back intently in a curiously cold way. Then she was gone. Thimiroi shrugged.

He followed Christine into her house.

It was an old, comfortable-looking place with a great many small, dark, high-ceilinged rooms on the ground floor and a massive wooden staircase leading upstairs. The furnishings looked heavy and unstylish, as though they were already long out of date, but everything had an appealing, well-worn feel.

"My family's lived in this house for almost a hundred years," Christine said, as though reading his mind. "I was born here. I grew up here. I don't know what it's like to live anywhere else." She gestured toward the staircase. "The music room is upstairs."

"I know. Do you live here by yourself?"

"Basically. My sister and I inherited the house when my mother died, but she's hardly ever here. The last I heard from her, she was in Oaxaca."

"Wah-ha-ka?" Thimiroi said carefully.

"Oaxaca, yes. In Mexico, you know? She's studying Mexican handicrafts, she says. I think she's actually studying Mexican men, but that's her business, isn't it? She likes to travel. Before Mexico she was in Thailand, and before that it was Portugal, I think."

Mexico, Thimiroi thought. Thailand. Portugal. So many names, so many places. Such a complex society, this world of the twentieth century. His own world had fewer places, and they had different names. So much had changed, after the time of the Blue Death. So much had been swept away, never to return.

Christine said, "It's a musty old house, I know. But I love it. And I could never have afforded to buy one of my own. Everything's so fantastically expensive these days. If I hadn't happened to have lived here all along, I suppose I'd be living in one of those poky little studio apartments down by the river, paying umpty thousand dollars a month for one bedroom and a terrace the size of a postage stamp."

Desperately he tried to follow what she was saying. His implant helped, but not enough. Umpty thousand dollars? Studio apartment? Postage stamp? He got the sense of her words, but the literal meanings eluded him. How much was umpty? How big was a postage stamp?

The music room on the second floor was bright and spacious, with three large windows looking out into the garden and the street beyond. The piano itself, against the front wall between two of the windows, was larger than he expected, a splendid, imposing thing, with ponderous, ornately carved legs and a black, gleaming wooden case. Obviously it was old and very valuable and well cared for; and as he studied it he realized suddenly that this must not be any ordinary home musical instrument, but more likely one that a concert performer would use; and therefore Christine's lighthearted dismissal of his question about her having a musical career must almost certainly conceal bitter defeat, frustration, the deflection of a cherished dream. She had wanted and expected more from her music than life had been able to bring her.

"Play for me," he said. "The same piece you were playing the first time, when I happened to walk by."

"The Debussy, you mean?"

"I don't know its name."

Thimiroi hummed the melody that had so captured him. She nodded and sat down to play.

It was not quite as magical, the second time. But nothing ever was, he knew. And it was beautiful all the same, haunting, mysterious in its powerful simplicity.

"Will you sing for me now?" Christine asked.

"What should I sing?"

"A song of your own country?"

He thought a moment. How could he explain to her what music was like in his own time—not sound alone, but a cluster of all the arts, visual, olfactory, the melodic line rising out of a dozen different sensory concepts? But he could improvise, he supposed. He began to sing one of his own poems, putting a tune to it as he went. Christine, listening, closed her eyes, nodded, turned to the keyboard, played a few notes and a few more, gradually shaping them into an accompaniment for him. Thimiroi was amazed at the swiftness with which she caught the melody of his tune—stumbling only once or twice, over chordal structures that were obviously alien to her—and traveled along easily with it. By the time he reached the fifth cycle of the song, he and she were joined in an elegant harmony, as though they had played this song together many times instead of both improvising it as they went. And when he made the sudden startling key-shift that in his culture signaled the close of a song, she adapted to it almost instantaneously and stayed with him to the final note.

They applauded each other resoundingly.

Her eyes were shining with delight. "Oh, Thimiroi—Thimiroi—what a marvelous singer you are! And what a marvelous song!"

"And how cunningly you wove your accompaniment into it."

"That wasn't really hard."

"For you, perhaps. You have a great musical gift, Christine."

She reddened and looked away.

"What language were you singing in?" she asked, after a time.

"The language of my country."

"It was so strange. It isn't like any language I've ever heard. Why won't you tell me anything about where you come from, Thimiroi?"

"I will. Later."

"And what did the words mean?"

"It's a poem about—about journeying to far lands, and seeing great wonders. A very romantic poem, perhaps a little silly. But the poet himself is also very romantic and perhaps a little silly."

"What's his name?" she asked.

"Thimiroi."

"You?" she said, grinning broadly. "Is that what you are? A poet?"

"I sometimes write poetry, yes," he said, beginning to feel as uneasy as she had seemed when he was trying to praise her playing. They looked at each other awkwardly. Then he said, "May I try the piano?"

"Of course."

He sat down, peered at the keys, touched one of the white ones experimentally, then another, another. What were the black ones? Modulators of some sort? No, no, their function was very much like that of the white ones, it seemed. And these pedals here—

He began to play.

He was dreadful at first, but quickly he came to understand the relationship of the notes and the range of the keyboard and the proper way of touching the keys. He played the piece that she had played for him before, exactly at first, then launching into a set of subtle variations that carried him farther and farther from the original, into the musical modes of his own time. The longer he played, the more keenly he appreciated the delicacy and versatility of this ancient instrument; and he knew that if he were to study it with some care, not merely guess his way along as he was doing now, he would be able to draw such wonders from it as even great composers like Cenbe or Palivandrin would find worthwhile. Once again he felt humbled by the achievements of this great lost civilization of the past. Which to brittle, heartless people like Hollia or Omerie must seem a mere simple primitive age. But they understood nothing. Nothing.

He stopped playing, and looked back at Christine.

She was staring at him in horror, her face pale, her eyes wide and stricken, tears streaking her cheeks.

"What's wrong?" he asked.

"The way you play—" she whispered. "I've never heard anyone play like that."

"It is all very bad, I know. But you must realize, I have had no formal training in this instrument, I am simply inventing a technique as I go—"

"No. Please. Don't tell me that. You mustn't tell me that!"

"Christine?"

And then he realized what the matter was. It was not that he had played badly; it was that he had played so well. She had devoted all her life to this instrument, and played it with great skill, and even so had never been able to attain a level of proficiency that gave her any real satisfaction. And he, never so much as having seen a piano in his life, could sit down at it and draw from it splendors beyond her fondest hope of achieving. His playing was unorthodox, of course, it was odd and even bizarre, but yet she had seen the surpassing mastery in it, and had been stunned and chagrined and crushed by it, and stood here now bewildered and confounded by this stranger she had brought into her own home—

I should have known better, Thimiroi thought. I should have realized that this is *her* art, and that I, with all the advantages that are mine purely by virtue of my having been born when I was, ought never to have presumed to invade her special territory with such a display of skills that are beyond her comprehension. Without even suspecting what I was doing, I have humiliated her.

"Christine," he murmured. "No. No, Christine."

Thimiroi went to her and pulled her close against him, and kissed the tears away, and spoke softly to her, calming her, reassuring her. He could never tell her the truth; but he could make her understand, at least, that he had not meant to hurt her. And after a time he felt the tension leave her, and felt her press herself tight to him, and then their lips met, and she looked up, smiling. And took him lightly by the hand, and drew him from the room and down the hall.

Afterward, as he was dressing, she touched the long, fading red scar on his arm and said, "Were you in some kind of accident?"

"An inoculation," he told her. "Against disease."

"I've never seen one like that before."

"No," he said. "I suppose you haven't."

"A disease of your country?"

"No," he said, after a time. "Of yours."

"But what kind of disease requires a vaccination like—"

"Do we have to talk of diseases just now, Christine."

"Of course not," she said, smiling ruefully. "How foolish of me. How absurd." She ran her fingers lightly, almost fondly, over the inoculation scar a second time. "Of all things for me to be curious about!" Softly she said, "You don't have to leave now, you know."

"But I must. I really must."

"Yes," she said. "I suppose you must." She accompanied him to the front door. "You'll call me, won't you? Very soon?"

"Of course," Thimiroi said.

Night had fallen. The air was mild and humid, but the sky was clear and the stars glittered brilliantly. He looked for the moon but could not find it.

How many days remain, he wondered?

Somewhere out there in the airless dark a lump of dead rock was falling steadily toward earth, falling, falling, inexorably coming this way. How far away was it now? How soon before it would come roaring over the horizon to bring unimaginable death to this place?

I must find a way of saving her, he told himself.

The thought was numbing, dizzying, intolerably disturbing.

Save her? How? Impossible. Impossible. It was something that he must not even allow himself to consider.

And yet—

Again it came. *I must find a way of saving her.*

* * *

THERE WAS A MESSAGE FOR him at his hotel, just a few quick scrawled sentences:

Party at Lutheena's. We're all going. See you there?

Laliene's handwriting, which even in her haste was as beautiful as the finest calligraphy. Thimiroi crumpled the note and tossed it aside. Going to a party tonight was very close to the last thing he would want to do. Everyone in glittering clothes, making glittering conversation, trading sparkling anecdotes, no doubt, of their latest adventures among the simple sweaty blotchy-skinned folk of this interestingly raucous and crude century—no. No. No. Let them trade their anecdotes without him. Let them sip their euphoriac and exchange their chatter and play their little games. He was going to bed. Very likely, without him there, they would all be talking about him. How oddly he had been behaving, how strange and uncouth he seemed to be becoming since their arrival in this era. Let them talk. What did it matter?

He wished Kleph had not seen him going into Christine's house, though.

But how would Kleph know whose house it was? And why would Kleph—Kleph, with her own Oliver Wilson entanglement preoccupying her—want to say anything to anyone about having seen some other member of the tour slipping away for an intimate hour with a twentieth-century person? Better for her to be silent. The subject was a delicate one. She would not want to raise it. She of all people would be unlikely to disapprove, or to want to bring down on him the disapproval of the others. No, Thimiroi thought. Kleph will say nothing. We are allies in this business, Kleph and I.

He slept, and dark dreams came that he could not abide: the remorseless meteor crossing the sky, the city aflame and shrieking, Christine's wonderful old house swept away by a searing blast of destruction, the piano lying tumbled in the street, split in half, golden strings spilling out.

Wearily Thimiroi dosed himself with the drug that banishes dreams, and lay down to sleep again. But now sleep evaded him. Very well: there was the other drug, the one that brings sleep. He hesitated to take it. The two drugs taken in the wrong order exacted a price; he would be jittery and off balance emotionally for the next two or three days. He was far enough off balance as it was already. So he lay still, hoping that he would drift eventually into sleep without recourse to more medication; and gradually his mind grew easier, gradually he began the familiar descent toward unconsciousness.

Suddenly the image of Laliene blazed in his mind.

It was so vivid that it seemed she was standing beside him in the darkness and light was streaming from her body. She was nude, and her breasts, her hips, her thighs, all had a throbbing incandescent glow. Thimiroi sat up, astonished, swept with waves of startling feverish excitement.

"Laliene?"

How radiant she looked! How splendid! Her eyes were glowing like beacons. Her crimson hair stood out about her head like a bright corona. The scent of her filled his nostrils. He trembled. His throat was dry, his lips seemed gummed together.

Wave after wave of intense, overpowering desire swept through him.

Helplessly Thimiroi rose, lurched across the room, reached gropingly toward her. This was madness, he knew, but there was no holding himself back.

The shimmering image retreated as he came near it. He stumbled, nearly tripped, regained his balance.

"Wait, Laliene," he cried hoarsely. His heart was pounding thunderously. It was almost impossible for him to catch his breath. He was choking with his need. "Come here, will you? Stop edging away like that."

"I'm not here, Thimiroi. I'm in my own room. Put your robe on and come visit me."

"What? You're not here?"

"Down the hall. Come, now. Hurry!"

"You are here. You have to be."

As though in a daze, brain swathed in thick layers of white cotton, he reached for her again. Like a lovestruck boy he yearned to draw her close, to cup her breasts in his hands, to run his fingers over those silken thighs, those satiny flanks—

"To my room," she whispered.

"Yes. Yes."

His flesh was aflame. Sweat rolled down his body. She danced before him like a shining will-o'-the-wisp. Frantically he struggled to comprehend what was happening. A vision? A dream? But he had drugged himself against dreams. And he was awake now. Surely he was awake. And yet he saw her—he wanted her—he wanted her beyond all measure—he was going to slip his robe on, and go to her suite, and she would be waiting for him there, and he would slip into her bed—into her arms—

No. No. No.

He fought it. He caught the side of some piece of furniture, and held it, anchoring himself, struggling to keep himself from going forward. His teeth chattered. Chills ran along his back and shoulders. The muscles in his arms and chest writhed and spasmed as he battled to stay where he was.

He was fully awake now, and he was beginning to understand. He remembered how Laliene had gone wandering around here the other day while he was brewing the tea—examining the works of art, so he had thought. But she could just as easily have been planting something. Which now was broadcasting monstrous compulsions into his mind.

He switched on the light, wincing as it flooded the room. Now Thimiroi could no longer see that mocking, beckoning image of Laliene, but he still felt her presence all around him, the heat of her body, the pungency of her fragrance, the strength of her urgent summons.

Somehow he managed to find the card with Christine's telephone number on it, and dialed it with tense, quivering fingers. The phone rang endlessly until, finally, he heard her sleepy voice, barely focused, saying, "Yes? Hello?"

"Christine? Christine, it's me, Thimiroi."

"What? Who? Don't you know it's four in the morn—" Then her tone changed. The sleepiness left it, and the irritation. "What's wrong, Thimiroi? What's happening?"

"I'll be all right. I need you to talk to me, that's all. I'm having a kind of an attack."

"No, Thimiroi!" He could feel the intensity of her concern. "What can I do? Shall I come over?"

"No. That's not necessary. Just talk to me. I need to stir up—cerebral activity. Do you understand? It's just an—an electrochemical imbalance. But if I talk—even if I listen to something—speak to me, say anything, recite poetry—"

"Poetry," she said. "All right. Let me think. '*Four score and seven years ago—*'" she began.

"Good," he said. "Even if I don't understand it, that's all right. Say anything. Just keep talking."

Already Laliene's aura was ebbing from the room. Christine continued to speak; and he broke in from time to time, simply to keep his mental level up. In a few minutes Thimiroi knew that he had defeated

Laliene's plan. He slumped forward, breathing hard, letting his stiff, anguished muscles uncoil.

He still could feel the waves of mental force sweeping through the room. But they were pallid now, they were almost comical, they no longer were capable of arousing in him the obsessive obedience that they had been able to conjure into his sleeping mind.

Christine, troubled, still wanted to come to him; but Thimiroi told her that everything was fine, now, that she should go back to sleep, that he was sorry to have disturbed her. He would explain, he promised. Later. Later.

Fury overtook him the moment he put the receiver down.

Damn Laliene. Damn her! What did she think she was doing?

He searched through the sitting room, and then the bedroom, and the third room of the suite. But it was almost dawn before he found what he was looking for: the tiny silvery pellet, the minute erotic broadcaster, that she had hidden beneath one of his Sipulva tables. He pulled it loose and crushed it against the wall, and the last faint vestige of Laliene's presence went from the room like water swirling down a drain. Slowly Thimiroi's anger receded. He put on some music, one of Cenbe's early pieces, and listened quietly to it until he saw the first pale light of morning streaking the sky.

* * *

CASUALLY, EASILY, WITH A WONDERFUL recklessness he had not known he had in him, he said to Christine, "We go anywhere we want. Anywhen. They run tours for us, you see. We were in Canterbury in Chaucer's time, to make the pilgrimage. We went to Rome and then to Emperor Augustus' summer palace on the island of Capri, and he invited us to a grand banquet, thinking we were visitors from a great kingdom near India."

Christine was staring at him in a wide-eyed gaze, as though she were a child and he were telling her some fabulous tale of dragons and princes.

He had gone to her at midday, when the late May sun was immense overhead and the sky seemed like a great curving plate of burnished blue steel. She had let him in without a word, and for a long while they looked at each other in silence, their hands barely touching. She was very pale and her eyes were reddened from sleeplessness, with dark crescents beneath them. Thimiroi embraced her, and assured her that he was in no danger, that with her help he had been able to fight off the demon that had assailed him in the night. Then she took him upstairs, to the room on the second floor where they had made love the day before, and drew him down with her on the bed, almost shyly at first, and then, casting all reserve aside, seizing him eagerly, hungrily.

When finally they lay back, side by side, all passion slaked for the moment, Christine turned toward him and said, "Tell me now where your country is, Thimiroi."

And at last he began—calmly, unhesitatingly—to tell her about The Travel.

"We went to Canterbury in the autumn of 1347," he said. "Actually Chaucer was still only a boy, then. The poem was many years away. Of course we read him before we set out. We even looked at the original Old English text. I suppose the language would be strange even to you. '*When that Aprill with his shoures soote The droghte of March hath perced to the roote.*' I suppose we really should have gone in April ourselves, to be more authentic; but April was wet that year, as it usually is at that time in England, and the autumn was warm and brilliant, a season much like the one you are having here, a true vintage season. We are very fond of warm, dry weather, and rain depresses us."

"You could have gone in another year, then, and found a warmer, drier April," Christine said.

"No. The year had to be 1347. It isn't important why. And so we went in autumn, in beautiful October."

"Ah."

"We began in London, gathering in an inn on the south side of the river, just as Chaucer's pilgrims did, and we set out with a band of pilgrims that must have been much like his, even one who played a bagpipe the way his Miller did, and a woman who might almost have been the Wife of Bath—" Thimiroi closed his eyes a moment, letting the journey come rushing back from memory, sights and sounds, laughter, barking dogs, cool bitter ale, embroidered gowns, the mounds of straw in the stable, falling leaves, warm dry breezes. "And then, before that, first-century Capri. In the time of Augustus. In high summer, a perfect Mediterranean summer, still another vintage season. How splendid Capri is. Do you know it? No? An island off Italy, very steep, a mountaintop in the water, with strange grottos at its base and huge rocks all about. There comes a time every evening when the sky and the sea are the same color, a pale blue-gray, so that it is impossible to tell where one ends and the other begins, and you stand by the edge of the high cliff, looking outward into that gray haze, and it seems to you that all the world is completely still, that time is not moving at all."

"The—first century—?" Christine murmured.

"The reign of the Emperor Augustus, yes. A surprisingly short man, and very gentle and witty, extremely likable, although you can feel the ruthlessness of him just behind the gentleness. He has amazing eyes, utterly penetrating, with a kind of light coming from them. You look at him and you see Rome: the Empire embodied in one man, its beginning and its end, its greatness and its power."

"You speak of him as though he is still alive. 'He has amazing eyes,' you said."

"I saw him only a few months ago," said Thimiroi. "He handed me a cup of sweet red wine with his own hands, and recommended it, saying there certainly was nothing like it in my own land. He has a palace on Capri, nothing very grand—his stepson Tiberius, who was there also, would build a much greater one later on, so our guide told us—and he was there for the summer. We were guests under false pretenses, I suppose, ambassadors from a distant land, though he never would have guessed *how* distant. The year was—let me think—no, not the first century, not *your* first century, it was what you call B.C., the last century *before* the first century—I think the year was 19, the 19 *before*—such a muddle, these dating systems—"

"And in your country?" Christine asked. "What year is it now in your country, Thimiroi? 2600? 3100?"

He pondered that a moment. "We use a different system of reckoning. It is not at all analogous. The term would be meaningless to you."

"You can't tell me what year it is there?"

"Not in your kind of numbers, no. There was—a break in the pattern of numbering, long before our time. I could ask Kadro. He is our tour guide, Kadro. He knows how to compute the equivalencies."

She stared at him. "Couldn't you guess? Five hundred years? A thousand?"

"Perhaps it is something like that. But even if I knew, I would not tell you the exact span, Christine. It would be wrong. It is forbidden, absolutely forbidden." Thimiroi laughed. "Everything I have just told you is absolutely forbidden, do you know that? We must conceal the truth about ourselves to those we meet when we undertake The Travel. That is the rule. Of course, you don't believe a thing I've just been telling you, do you?"

Color flared in her cheeks. "Don't you think I do?" she cried.

Tenderly Thimiroi said, "There are two things they tell us about The Travel, Christine, before we set out for the first time. The first, they say, is that sooner or later you will feel some compulsion to reveal to a person of ancient times that you are a visitor from a future time. The second thing is that you will not be believed."

"But I believe you, Thimiroi!"

"Do you? Do you really?"

"Of course it all sounds so terribly strange, so fantastic—"

"Yes. Of course."

"But I want to believe you. And so I do believe you. The way you speak—the way you dress—the way you look—everything about you is *foreign*, Thimiroi, totally foreign beyond any ordinary kind of foreignness. It isn't Iran or India or Afghanistan that you come from, it has to be some other world, or some other time. Yes. Yes. Everything about you. The way you played the piano yesterday." She paused a moment. "The way you touch me in bed. You are like no man I have ever—like no man—" She faltered, reddened fiercely, looked away from him a moment. "Of course I believe that you are what you say you are. Of course I do!"

* * *

When he returned to the Montgomery House late that afternoon he went down the hall to Laliene's suite and rapped angrily at the door. Denvin opened it and peered out at him. He was dressed in peacock splendor, an outfit exceptional even for Denvin, a shirt with brilliant red stripes and golden epaulets, tight green trousers flecked with scarlet checks.

He gave Thimiroi a long cool malevolent glance and exclaimed, "Well! The prodigal returns!"

"How good to see you, Denvin. Am I interrupting anything?"

"Only a quiet little chat." Denvin turned. "Laliene! Our wandering poet is here!"

Laliene emerged from deeper within. Like Denvin she was elaborately clothed, wearing a pale topaz-hued gown fashioned of a myriad shimmering mirrors, shining metallic eye-shadow, gossamer finger-gloves. She looked magnificent. But for an instant, as her eyes met Thimiroi's, her matchless poise appeared to desert her, and she seemed startled, flustered, almost frightened. Then, regaining her equilibrium with a superb show of control, she gave him a cool smile and said, "So there you are. We tried to reach you before, but of course there was no finding you. Maitira, Antilimoin, and Fevra are here. We've just been with them. They've been holding open house all afternoon, and you were invited. I suppose it's still going on. Lesentru is due to arrive in about an hour, and Kuiane, and they say that Broyal and Hammin will be getting here tonight also."

"The whole clan," Thimiroi said. "That will be delightful. Laliene, may I speak with you privately?"

Again a flicker of distress from her. She glanced almost apologetically at Denvin.

"Well, excuse me!" Denvin said theatrically.

"Please," Laliene said. "For just a moment, Denvin."

"Certainly. Certainly, Laliene." He favored Thimiroi with a strange grimace as he went out.

"Very well," said Laliene, turning to face Thimiroi squarely. Her expression had hardened; she looked steely, now, and prepared for any sort of attack. "What is it, Thimiroi?"

He drew forth the little silvery pellet that he had found attached to the underside of the Sipulva table, and held it out to her in the palm of his hand.

"Do you know what this is, Laliene?"

"Some little broken toy, I assume. Why do you ask?"

"It's an erotic," he said. "I found it in my rooms, where someone had hidden it. It began broadcasting when I went to sleep last night. Sending out practically irresistible waves of sexual desire."

"How fascinating. I hope you were able to find someone to satisfy them with."

"The images I was getting, Laliene, were images of you. Standing naked next to my bed, whispering to me, inviting me to come down the hall and make love to you."

She smiled icily. "I had no idea you were still interested, Thimiroi!"

"Don't play games with me. Why did you plant this thing in my room, Laliene?"

"*I?*"

"I said, don't play games. You were in my room the other day. No one else of our group has been. The erotic was specifically broadcasting your image. How can there be any doubt that you planted it yourself, for the particular purpose of luring me into your bed?"

"You're being absurd, Thimiroi. Anyone could have planted it. Anyone. Do you think it's hard to get into these rooms? These people have no idea of security. You ask a chambermaid in the right way and you can enter anywhere. As for the images of me that were being broadcast to you, why, you know as well as I do that erotics don't broadcast images of specific individuals. They send out generalized waves of feeling, and the recipient supplies whatever image seems appropriate to him. In your case evidently it was my image that came up from your unconscious when—"

"Don't lie to me, Laliene."

Her eyes flashed. "I'm not lying. I deny planting anything in your room. Why on earth would I, anyway? Could going to bed with you, or anyone else, for that matter, possibly be that important to me that I would connive and sneak around and make use of some kind of mechanical amplifying device in order to achieve my purpose? Is that plausible, Thimiroi?"

"I don't know. What I do know is that what happened to me during the night happened to me, and that I found this when I searched my rooms." He thought for a moment to add, *And that you've been pressing yourself upon me ever since we began this trip, in the most embarrassing and irritating fashion.* But he did not have the heart to say that to her. "I believe that you hid this when you visited me for tea. What your reason may have been is something I can't begin to imagine."

"Of course you can't. Because I had no reason. And I didn't do it."

Thimiroi made no reply. Laliene's face was firmly set. Her gaze met his unwaveringly. She was certainly lying: he knew that beyond any question. But they were at an impasse. All he could do was accuse; he could not prove anything; he was stymied by her denial, and there was no way of carrying this further. She appeared to know that also. There was a long tense moment of silence between them, and then she said, "Are you finished with this, Thimiroi? Because there are more important things we should be discussing."

"Go ahead. What important things?"

"The plans for Friday night."

"Friday night," Thimiroi said, not understanding.

She looked at him scornfully. "Friday—tomorrow—is the last day of May. Or have you forgotten that?"

He felt a chill. "The meteor," he said.

"The meteor, yes. The event which we came to this place to see," Laliene said. "Do you recall?"

"So soon," Thimiroi said dully. "Tomorrow night."

"We will all assemble about midnight, or a little before, at the Sanciscos' house. The view will be best from there, according to Kadro. From their front rooms, upstairs. Kleph, Omerie, and Klia have invited everyone—everyone except Hollia and Hara, that is: Omerie is adamant about their not coming, because of something slippery that Hollia tried to do to him. Kleph would not discuss it, but I assume it had to do with trying to get the Sanciscos evicted, so that they could have the Wilson house for themselves. But all the rest of us will be there. And you are particularly included, Thimiroi. Kleph made a point of telling me that. Unless you have other plans for the evening, naturally."

"Is that what Kleph said? Or are you adding that part of it yourself, about my having other plans?"

"That is what Kleph said."

"I see."

"*Do* you have other plans?"

"What other plans could I possibly have, do you think? Where? With whom?"

* * *

CHRISTINE SEEMED STARTLED TO SEE him again so soon. She was still wearing an old pink robe that she had thrown on as he was leaving her house two hours before, and she looked rumpled and drowsy and confused. Behind him the sky held the pearl-gray of early twilight on this late spring evening, but she stood in the half-opened doorway blinking at him as though he had awakened her once again in the middle of the night.

"Thimiroi? You're back?"

"Let me in. Quickly, please."

"Is there something wrong? Are you in trouble?"

"Please."

He stepped past her into the vestibule and hastily pushed the door shut behind him. She gave him a baffled look. "I was just napping," she said. "I didn't think you'd be coming back this evening, and I had so little sleep last night, you know—"

"I know. We need to talk. This is urgent, Christine."

"Go into the parlor. I'll be with you in a moment."

She pointed to Thimiroi's left and vanished into the dim recesses at the rear of the entrance hall. Thimiroi went into the room she had indicated, a long, oppressively narrow chamber hung with heavy brocaded draperies and furnished with the sort of low-slung clumsy-looking couches and chairs, probably out of some even earlier era, that were everywhere in the house. He paced restlessly about the room. It was like being in a museum of forgotten styles. There was something eerie and almost hieratic about this mysterious furniture: the dark wood, the heavy legs jutting at curious angles, the coarse, intricately worked fabrics, the strange brass buttons running along the edges. Someone like Denvin would probably think it hideous. To him it was merely strange, powerful, haunting, wonderful in its way.

At last Christine appeared. She had been gone for what felt like hours: washing her face, brushing her hair, changing into a robe she evidently considered more seemly for receiving a visitor at nightfall. Her vanity was almost amusing. The world is about to come to an end, he thought, and she pauses to make herself fit for entertaining company.

But of course she could have no idea of why he was here.

He said, "Are you free tomorrow night?"

"Free? Tomorrow?" She looked uncertain. "Why—yes, yes, I suppose. Friday night. I'm free, yes. What did you have in mind, Thimiroi?"

"How well do you trust me, Christine?"

She did not reply for a moment. For the first time since that day they had had lunch together at the River Cafe, there was something other than fascination, warmth, even love for him, in her eyes. She seemed mystified, troubled, perhaps frightened. It was as if his sudden breathless arrival here this evening had reminded her of how truly strange their relationship was, and of how little she really knew about him.

"Trust you how?" she said finally.

"What I told you this afternoon, about Capri, about Canterbury, about The Travel—did you believe all that or not?"

She moistened her lips. "I suppose you're going to say that you were making it all up, and that you feel guilty now for having fed all that nonsense to a poor simple gullible woman like me."

"No."

"No what?"

"I wasn't making anything up. But do you believe that, Christine? Do you?"

"I said I did, this afternoon."

"But you've had a few hours to think about it. Do you still believe it?"

She made no immediate reply. At length she said, glancing at him warily, "I've been napping, Thimiroi. I haven't been thinking about anything at all. But since it seems to be so important to you: Yes. Yes, I think that what you told me, weird as it was, was the truth. There. If it was just a joke, I swallowed it. Does that make me a simpleton in your eyes?"

"So you trust me."

"Yes. I trust you."

"Will you go away with me, then? Leave here with me tomorrow, and possibly never come back?"

"*Tomorrow?*" The word seemed to have struck her like an explosion. She looked dazed. "Never—come—back—?"

"In all likelihood."

She put the palms of her hands together, rubbed them against each other, pressed them tight: a little ritual of hers, perhaps. When she looked up at him again her expression had changed: the confusion had cleared from her face and now she appeared merely puzzled, and even somewhat irritated.

In a sharp tone she said, "What is all this about, Thimiroi?"

He drew a deep breath. "Do you know why we chose the autumn of 1347 for our Canterbury visit?" he asked. "Because it was a season of extraordinarily fine weather, yes. But also because it was a peak time, looking down into a terrible valley, the last sweet moment before the coming of a great calamity. By the following summer the Black Death would be devouring England, and millions would die. We chose the timing of our visit to Augustus the same way. The year 19—19 B.C., it was—was the year he finally consolidated all imperial power in his grasp. Rome was his; he ruled it in a way that no one had ruled that nation before. After that there would be only anticlimax for him, and disappointments and losses; and indeed just after we went to him he would fall seriously ill, almost to the edge of death, and for a time it would seem to him that he had lost everything in the very moment of attaining it. But when we visited him in 19 B.C., it was the summit of his time."

"What does this have to do with—"

"This May, here, now, is another vintage season, Christine. This long golden month of unforgettable weather—it will end tomorrow, Christine, in terror, in destruction, a frightful descent from happiness into disaster, far steeper than either of the other two. That is why we are here, do you see? As spectators, as observers of the great irony—visiting your city at its happiest moment, and then, tomorrow, watching the catastrophe."

As he spoke, she grew pale and her lips began to quiver; and then color flooded into her face, as it will sometimes do when the full impact of terrible news arrives. Something close to panic was gleaming in her eyes.

"Are you saying that there's going to be nuclear war? That after all these years the bombs are finally going to go off?"

"Not war, no."

"What then?"

Without answering, Thimiroi drew forth his wallet and began to stack currency on the table in front of him, hundreds of dollars, perhaps thousands, all the strange little strips of green-and-black paper that they had supplied him with when he first had arrived here. Christine gaped in astonishment. He shoved the money toward her.

"Here," he said. "I'll get more tomorrow morning, and give you that too. Arrange a trip for us to some other country, France, Spain, England, wherever you'd like to go, it makes no difference which one, so long as it is far from here. You will understand how to do such things, with which I have had no experience. Buy airplane tickets—is that the right term, airplane tickets?—get us a hotel room, do whatever is necessary. But we must depart no later than this time tomorrow. When you pack, pack as though you may never return to this house: take your most precious things, the things you would not want to leave behind, but only as much as you can carry yourself. If you have money on deposit, take it out, or arrange for it to be transferred to some place of deposit in the country that we will be going to. Call me when everything is ready, and I'll come for you and we'll go together to the place where the planes take off."

Her expression was frozen, her eyes glazed, rigid. "You won't tell me what's going to happen?"

"I have already told you vastly too much. If I tell you more—and you tell others—and the news spreads widely, and the pattern of the future is greatly changed by the things that those people may do as a result of knowing what is to come—no. No. I do not dare, Christine. You are the only one I can save, and I can tell you no more than I have already told you. And you must tell no one else at all."

"This is like a dream, Thimiroi."

"Yes. But it is very real, I assure you."

Once again she stared. Her lips worked a moment before she could speak.

"I'm so terribly afraid, Thimiroi."

"I understand that. But you do believe me? Will you do as I ask? I swear to you, Christine, your only hope lies in trusting me. *Our* only hope."

"Yes," she said hesitantly.

"Then will you do as I ask?"

"Yes," she said, beginning the single syllable with doubt in her voice, and finishing it with sudden conviction. "But there's something I don't understand."

"What is that?"

"If something awful is going to happen here, why must we run off to England or Spain? Why not take me back to your own country, Thimiroi? Your own time."

"There is no way I can do that," he said softly.

"When you go back, then, what will happen to me?"

He took her hand in his. "I will not go back, Christine. I will stay here with you, in this era—in England, in France, wherever we may go—for the rest of my life. We will both be exiles. But we will be exiles together."

* * *

SHE ASKED HIM TO STAY with her at her house that night, and he refused. He could see that the refusal hurt her deeply; but there was much that he needed to do, and he could not do it there. They would have many other nights for spending together. Returning to his hotel, he went quickly to his rooms to contemplate the things that would have to be dealt with.

Everything that belonged to his own era, of course, packed and sent back via his suitcase: no question about that. He could keep some of his clothing with him here, perhaps, but none of the furniture, none of the artifacts, nothing that might betray the technology of a time yet unborn. The room would have to be bare when he left it. And he would have to requisition more twentieth-century money. He had no idea how much Christine might have above what he had already given her, nor how long it would last; but certainly they would need more as they began their new lives. As for the suitcase, his one remaining link to the epoch from which he came, he would have to destroy that. He would have to sever all ties. He would—

The telephone rang. The light jingling of its bell cut across his consciousness like a scream.

Christine, he thought. To tell him that she had reconsidered, that she saw now that this was all madness, that if he did not leave her alone she would call the police—

"Yes?" he said.

"Thimiroi! Oh, I *am* glad you're there." A warm, hearty, familiar masculine voice. "Laliene said I might have difficulty finding you, but I thought I'd ring your room anyway—"

"Antilimoin?"

"None other. We've just arrived. Ninth floor, the Presidential suite, whatever that may be. Maitira and Fevra are here with me, of course. Listen, old friend, we're having a tremendous blast tonight—oh, pardon me, that's a sick thing to say, isn't it?—a tremendous gathering, you know, a *soiree*, to enliven the night before the big night—do you think you can make it?"

"Well—"

"Laliene says you've been terribly standoffish lately, and I suppose she's right. But look, old friend, you can't spend the evening moping by yourself, you absolutely can't. Lesentru'll be here, do you know that? And Kuiane. Maybe even Broyal and Hammin, later on. And a rumor of Cenbe, too, though I suspect he won't show up until the very last minute, as usual. Listen, there are all sorts of stories to tell. You were in Canterbury, weren't you? And we've just done the Charlemagne thing. We have some splendid tips on what to see and what to avoid. You'll come, of course. Room 941, the end of the hall."

"I don't know if I—"

"Of course you will! Of course!"

Antilimoin's gusto was irresistible. It always was. The man was a ferociously social being: when he gave a party, attendance was never optional. And Thimiroi realized, after a moment, that it was better, perhaps, for him to go than to lurk here by himself, tensely awaiting the ordeals that tomorrow would bring. He had already brought more than enough suspicion upon himself. Antilimoin's party would be his farewell to his native time, to his friends, to everything that had been his life.

He spent a busy hour planning what had to be planned.

Then he dressed in his formal best—in the clothes, in fact, that he had planned to wear tomorrow night—and went upstairs. The party was going at full force. Antilimoin, dapper and elegant as always, greeted him with a hearty embrace, and Fevra and Maitira came gliding up from opposite sides of the room to kiss him, and Thimiroi saw, farther away, Lesentru and Kuiane deep in conversation with Lutheena, Denvin, and some others. Everyone seemed buoyant, excited, energetic. There was tension, too, the undercurrent of keen excitement that comes on the eve of a powerful experience.

Voices were pitched a little too high, gestures were a trifle too emphatic. A great screen on one wall was playing one of Cenbe's finest symphonias, but no one seemed to be watching or listening. Thimiroi glanced at it and shivered. Cenbe, of course: that connoisseur of disaster, assembling his masterpieces out of other people's tragedies—he was the perfect artist for this event. Doubtless he was in the city already, skulking around somewhere looking for the material he would need to complete his newest and surely finest work.

I will never see any of these people again after tonight, Thimiroi thought, and the concept was so difficult to accept that he repeated it to himself two or three more times, without being able to give it any more reality.

Laliene appeared beside him. There was no sign on her face of the earlier unpleasantness between them; her eyes were glowing and she was smiling warmly, even tenderly, as though they were lovers.

"I'm glad you came," she murmured. "I hoped you would."

"Antilimoin is very persuasive."

"You must have some tea. You look so tense, Thimiroi."

"Do I?"

"Is it because of our talk before?"

He shrugged. "Let's forget all about that, shall we?"

Laliene let the tips of her fingers rest lightly on his arm. "I should never have put that transmitter in your room. It was utterly stupid of me."

"It was, yes. But that's all ancient history."

Her face rose toward his. "Come have some tea with me."

"Laliene—"

Softly she said, "I wanted you to come to me so very badly. That was why I did it. You were ignoring me—you've ignored me ever since this trip began—oh, Thimiroi, Thimiroi, I'm trying to do the right thing, don't you see? And I want you to do the right thing too."

"What are you trying to tell me, Laliene?"

"Be careful, is what I'm trying to tell you."

"Careful of what?"

"Have some tea with me," she said.

"I'll have some tea," he told her. "But not, I think, with you."

Tears welled in her eyes. She turned her head to the side, but not so quickly that Thimiroi did not see them.

That was new, he thought. Tears in Laliene's eyes! He had never known her to be so overwrought. Too much euphoriac, he wondered?

She kept her grip on his arm for a long moment, and then, smiling sadly, she released him and moved away.

"Thimiroi!" Lesentru called, turning and grinning broadly at him and waving his long thin arms. "How absolutely splendid to see you! Come, come, let's sip a little together!" He crossed the room as if swimming through air. "You look so gloomy, man! That can't be allowed. Lutheena! Fevra! Everybody! We must cheer Thimiroi up! We can't let anyone go around looking as bleak as this, not tonight."

They swept toward him from every direction, six, eight, ten of them, laughing, whooping, embracing him, holding fragrant cups of euphoriac tea out at him. It began almost to seem that the party was in his honor. Why were they making such a fuss over him? He was starting to regret having come here at all. He drank the tea that someone put in his hand, and almost at once there was another cup there. He drank that too.

Laliene was at his side again. Thimiroi was having trouble focusing his eyes.

"What did you mean?" he asked. "When you said to be careful."

"I'm not supposed to say. It would be improperly influencing the flow of events."

"Be improper, then. But stop talking in riddles."

"Are they such riddles, then?"

"To me they are."

"I think you know what I'm talking about," Laliene said.

"I do?"

They might have been all alone in the middle of the room. I have had too much euphoriac, he told himself. But I can still hold my own. I can still hold my own, yes.

Laliene said in a low whisper, leaning close, her breath warm against his cheek, "Tomorrow—where are you going to go tomorrow, Thimiroi?"

He looked at her, astounded, speechless.

"I know," she said.

"Get away from me."

"I've known all along. I've been trying to save you from—"

"You're out of your mind, Laliene."

"No, Thimiroi. *You* are!"

She clung to him. Everyone was gaping at them.

Terror seized him. I have to get out of here, he thought.

Now. Go to Christine. Help her pack, and go with her to the airport. Right now. Whatever time it is, midnight, one in the morning, whatever. Before they can stop me. Before they *change* me.

"No, Thimiroi," Laliene cried. "Please—please—"

Furiously he pushed her away. She went sprawling to the floor, landing in a flurried heap at Antilimoin's feet. Everyone was yelling at once.

Laliene's voice came cutting through the confusion. "Don't do it, Thimiroi! *Don't do it!*"

He swung around and rushed toward the door, and through it, and wildly down the stairs, and through the quiet hotel lobby and out into the night. A brilliant crescent moon hung above him, and behind it the cold blaze of the stars in the clear darkness. Looking back, he saw no pursuers. He headed up the street toward Christine's, walking swiftly at first, then breaking into a light trot.

As he reached the corner, everything swirled and went strange around him. He felt a pang of inexplicable loss, and a sharp stab of wild fear, and a rush of anger without motive. The darkness closed bewilderingly around him, like a great glove. Then came a feeling of motion, swift and impossible to resist. He had a sense of being swept down a vast river toward an abyss that lay just beyond.

The effect lasted only a moment, but it was an endless moment, in which Thimiroi perceived the passage of time in sharp discontinuous segments, a burst of motion followed by a deep stillness and then another burst, and then stillness again. All color went from the world, even the muted colors of night: the sky was a startling blinding white, the buildings about him were black.

His eyes ached. His head was whirling.

He tried to move, but his movements were jerky and futile, as though he were fighting his way on foot through a deep tank of water. It must be the euphoriac, he told himself. I have had much too much. But I have had too much before, and I have never felt anything like—like—

Then the strangeness vanished as swiftly as it had come.

Everything was normal again, the whiteness gone from the sky, time flowing as it had always flowed, and he was running smoothly, steadily, down the street, like some sort of machine, arms and legs pumping, head thrown back.

Christine's house was dark. He rang the bell, and when there was no answer he hammered on the door.

"Christine! Christine, it's me, Thimiroi! Open the door, Christine! Hurry! Please!"

There was no response. He pounded on the door again.

This time a light went on upstairs.

"Here," he called. "I'm by the front door!"

Her window opened. Christine looked out and down at him.

"Who are you? What do you want? Do you know what time it is?"

"Christine!"

"Go away."

"But—Christine—"

"You have exactly two seconds to get away from here, whoever you are. Then I'm calling the police." Her voice was cold and angry. "They'll sober you up fast enough."

"Christine, I'm *Thimiroi.*"

"Who? What kind of name is that? I don't know anybody by that name. I've never seen you before in my life." The window slammed shut. The light went out above him. Thimiroi stood frozen, amazed, dumbstruck.

Then he began to understand.

* * *

Laliene said, "We all knew, yes. We were told before we ever came here. Nothing is secret to those who operate The Travel. How could it be? They move freely through all of time. They see everything. We were warned in Canterbury that you were going to try an intervention, and that there would be a counter-intervention if you did. So I tried to stop you. To prevent you from getting yourself into trouble."

"By throwing your body at me?" Thimiroi said bitterly.

"By getting you to fall in love with me," she said. "So that you wouldn't want to get involved with *her*."

He shook his head in wonder. "All along, throughout the whole trip. Everything you did, aimed at ensnaring me into a romance, just as I thought. What I didn't realize was that you were simply trying to save me from myself."

"Yes."

"I suppose you didn't try hard enough," Thimiroi said. "No. No, that isn't it. You tried too hard."

"Did I?"

"Perhaps that was it. At any rate I didn't want you, not at any point. I wanted her the moment I saw her. It couldn't have been avoided, I suppose."

"I'm sorry, Thimiroi."

"That you failed?"

"That you have done such harm to yourself."

He stood there wordlessly for a time. "What will happen to me now?" he asked finally.

"You'll be sent back for rehabilitation, Kadro says."

"When?"

"It's up to you. You can stay and watch the show with the rest of us—you've paid for it, after all. There's no harm, Kadro says, in letting you remain in this era another few hours. Or you can let them have you right now."

For an instant despair engulfed him. Then he regained his control.

"Tell Kadro that I think I'll go now," he said.

"Yes," said Laliene. "That's probably the wisest thing."

He said, "Will Kleph be punished too?"

"I don't think so."

He felt a surge of anger. "Why not? Why is what I did any different from what she did? All right, I had a twentieth-century lover. So did Kleph. You know that. That Wilson man."

"It was different, Thimiroi."

"Different? How?"

"For Kleph it was just a little diversion, an illicit adventure. What she was doing was wrong, but it didn't imperil the basic structure of things. She doesn't propose to save this Wilson. She isn't going to intervene with the pattern. You were going to run off with yours, weren't you? Live with her somewhere far from here, spare her from the calamity, possibly change all time to come? That couldn't be tolerated, Thimiroi. I'm astonished that you thought it would be. But of course you were in love."

Thimiroi was silent again. Then he said, "Will you do me one favor, at least?"

"What is that?"

"Send word to her. Her name's Christine Rawlins. She lives in the big old house right across the street from the one where the Sanciscos are. Tell her to go somewhere else tonight—to move into the Montgomery House, maybe, or even to leave the city. She can't stay where she is. Her house is almost certainly right in the path of—of—"

"I couldn't possibly do that," Laliene said quietly.

"No?"

"It would be intervention. It's the same thing you're being punished for."

"She'll die, though!" Thimiroi cried. "She doesn't deserve that. She's full of life, full of hopes, dreams—"

"She's been dead for hundreds of years," said Laliene coolly. "Giving her another day or two of life now won't matter. If the meteor doesn't get her, the plague will. You know that. You also know that I can't intervene for her. And you know that even if I tried, she'd never believe me. She'd have no reason to. No matter what you may have told her before, she knows nothing of it now. There's been a counter-intervention, Thimiroi. You understand that, don't you? She's never known you, now. Whatever may have happened between you and she has been unhappened."

Laliene's words struck him like knives.

"So you won't do a thing?"

“I can’t,” she said. “I’m sorry, Thimiroi. I tried to save you from this. For friendship’s sake. For love’s sake, even. But of course you wouldn’t be swerved at all.”

Kadro came into the room. He was dressed for the evening’s big event already.

“Well?” he said. “Has Laliene explained the arrangement? You can stay on through tonight, or you can go back now.”

Thimiroi looked at him, and back at Laliene, and to Kadro again. It was all very clear. He had gambled and lost. He had tried to do a foolish, romantic, impossible sort of thing, a twentieth-century sort of thing, for he was in many ways a twentieth-century sort of man; and it had failed, as of course, he realized now, it had been destined to do from the start. But that did not mean it had not been worth attempting. Not at all. Not at all.

“I understand,” Thimiroi said. “I’ll go back now.”

* * *

THE CHAIRS HAD ALL BEEN arranged neatly before the windows in the upstairs rooms. It was past midnight. There was euphoriac in the air, thick and dense. A quarter moon hung over the doomed city, but it was almost hidden now by the thickening clouds. The long season of clear skies was ending. The weather was changing, finally.

“It will be happening very soon now,” Omerie said.

Laliene nodded. “I feel almost as though I’ve lived through it several times already.”

“The same with me,” said Kleph.

“Perhaps we have,” said Klia, with a little laugh. “Who knows? We go round and round in time, and maybe we travel over the same paths more than once.”

Denvin said, “I wonder where Thimiroi is now. And what they’re doing to him.”

“Let’s not talk of Thimiroi,” Antilimoin said. “It’s too sad.”

“He won’t be able to Travel again, will he?” asked Maitira.

“Never again. Absolutely forbidden,” Omerie said. “But he’ll be lucky if that’s the worst thing they throw at him. What he did was unforgivable. Unforgivable!”

"Antilimoin's right," said Laliene. "Let's not talk of Thimiroi."

Kleph moved closer to her. "You love him, don't you?"

"Loved," Laliene said.

"Here. Some more tea."

"Yes. Yes." Laliene smiled grimly. "He wanted me to send a warning to that woman of his, do you know? She lives right across the way. Her house will be destroyed by the shock wave, almost certainly."

Lutheena said, looking shocked, "You didn't think of doing it, did you?"

"Of course not. But I feel so sad about it, all the same. He loved her, you know. And I loved him. And so, for his sake, entirely for his sake—" Laliene shook her head. "But of course it was inconceivable. I suppose she's asleep right at this minute, not even suspecting—"

"Better the meteor than the Blue Death that follows," said Omerie. "Quicker. The quick deaths are the good ones. What's the point of hiding from the meteor only to die of the plague?"

"This is too morbid," Klia said. "I almost wish we hadn't come here. We could have skipped it and just gone on to Charlemagne's coronation—"

"We'll be there soon enough," said Kleph. "But we're here, now. And it's going to be wonderful—wonderful—"

"Places, everybody!" Kadro called. "It's almost time! Ten—nine—eight—"

Laliene held her breath. This all seemed so familiar, she thought. As though she had been through it many times already. In a moment the impact, and the tremendous sound, and the first flames rising, and the first stunned cries from the city, and the dark shapes moving around in the distance, blind, bewildered—and then the lurid sky, red as blood, the long unending shriek coming as though from a single voice—

"Now," said Kadro.

There was an astounding stillness overhead. The onrushing meteor might almost have been sucking all sound from the city toward which it plummeted. And after the silence the cataclysmic crash, the incredible impact, the earth itself recoiling with the force of the collision.

Poor Thimiroi, Laliene thought. And that poor woman, too.

Her heart overflowed with love and sorrow, and her eyes filled with tears, and she turned away from the window, unable to watch, unable to see. Then came the cries. And then the flames.

TRAVELERS

Here's a story about a group of tourists very much like the sort of tourist I have been for more than six decades, wandering around the world gawking at interesting and unusual sights. The big difference is that of necessity I have been confined to the planet where I was born, whereas these people are touring the worlds of the universe, and imaginary worlds at that, since I made them all up for use in a novel called Star of Gypsies *that I wrote in the 1980s.* Star of Gypsies *spanned whole solar systems, and I invented I know not how many colorful planets for it—touching down on some of them just for the briefest of visits. I had left so much rich background behind me that now and again I would revisit one of them to use it in a completely unrelated story, as I did in this one, which I wrote in April, 1999 and which was published in the Summer, 1999 issue of the venerable, pioneering science fiction magazine* Amazing Stories.

"ARE WE ALL READY, *then*?" Nikomastir asks. He has fashioned a crown of golden protopetaloids for himself and gleaming scarlet baubles dangle from his ears: the bright translucent shells of galgalids, strung on slender strands of pure gold. His long pale arms wave in the air as though he is conducting a symphony orchestra.

"Our next destination is—" and he makes us wait for the announcement. And wait. And wait.

"Sidri Akrak," says Mayfly, giggling.

"How did you know?" cries Nikomastir. "Sidri Akrak! Yes! Yes! Set your coordinates, everybody! Off we go! Sidri Akrak it is!"

A faint yelp of dismay comes from Velimyle, and she shoots me a look of something that might almost have been fear, though perhaps there is a certain component of perverse delight in it also. I am not at all happy about the decision myself. Sidri Akrak is a nightmare world where gaudy monsters run screaming through the muddy streets. The people of Sidri Akrak are cold and dour and inhospitable; their idea of pleasure is to wallow in discomfort and ugliness. No one goes to Sidri Akrak if he can help it, no one.

But we must live by our rules; and this day Nikomastir holds the right of next choice. It is devilish of Mayfly to have put the idea of going to Sidri Akrak into his head. But she is like that, is Mayfly. And Nikomastir is terribly easily influenced.

Will we all perish on hideous Sidri Akrak, victims of Mayfly's casual frivolity?

I don't think so, however nasty the visit turns out to be. We often get into trouble, sometimes serious trouble, but we always get out of it. We lead charmed lives, we four travelers. Someday Mayfly will take one risk too many, I suppose, and I would like not to be there when she does. Most likely I will be, though. Mayfly is my mask-sister. Wherever she goes, I go. I must look after her: thoughtful, stolid, foolish me. I must protect her from herself as we four go traveling on and on, spinning giddily across the far-flung worlds.

Sidri Akrak, though—

The four of us have been to so many wondrous lovely places together: Elang-Lo and the floating isle of Vont, and Mikni and Chchikkikan, Heidoth and Thant, Milpar, Librot, Froidis, Smoor, Xamur and Iriarte and Nabomba Zom, and on and on and on. And now—Sidri Akrak? Sidri Akrak?

* * *

WE STAND IN A CIRCLE in the middle of a field of grass with golden blades, making ourselves ready for our relay-sweep departure from Galgala.

I wouldn't have minded remaining here a few months longer. A lovely world indeed is Galgala the golden, where myriads of auriferous microorganisms excrete atoms of gold as metabolic waste. It is everywhere on this planet, the lustrous pretty metal. It turns the rivers and streams to streaks of yellow flame and the seas to shimmering golden mirrors. Huge filters are deployed at the intake valve of Galgala's reservoirs to strain the silt of dissolved gold from the water supply. The plants of Galgala are turgid in every tissue, leaf and stem and root, with aureous particles. Gold dust, held in suspension in the air, transforms the clouds to golden fleece.

Therefore the once-precious stuff has grievously lost value throughout the galaxy since Galgala was discovered, and on Galgala itself a pound of gold is worth less than a pound of soap. But I understand very little about these economic matters and care even less. Only a miser could fail to rejoice in Galgala's luminous beauty. We have been here six weeks; we have awakened each morning to the tinkle of golden chimes, we have bathed in the golden rivers and come forth shining, we have wrapped our bodies round with delicate golden chains. Now, though, it is time for us to move along, and Nikomastir has decreed that our new destination is to be one of the universe's most disagreeable worlds. Unlike my companions I can see nothing amusing about going there. It strikes me as foolish and dangerous whimsy. But they are true sophisticates, untrammeled creatures made of air and light, and I am the leaden weight that dangles from their soaring souls. We will go to Sidri Akrak.

We all face Nikomastir. Smiling sweetly, he calls out the coordinate numbers for our journey, and we set our beacons accordingly and double-check the settings with care. We nod our readiness for departure to one another. Velimyle moves almost imperceptibly closer to me, Mayfly to Nikomastir.

I would have chosen a less flighty lover for her than Nikomastir if matters had been left to me. He is a slim elegant youth, high-spirited and shallow, a prancing fantastico with a taste for telling elaborate fanciful lies. And he is very young: only a single rebirth so far. Mayfly is on her fifth, as am I, and Velimyle claims three, which probably means four. Sembiran is Nikomastir's native world, a place of grand valleys and lofty snow-capped mountains and beautiful meadows and thriving cities, where his father is a minor aristocrat of some sort. Or so Nikomastir has said, although we have learned again and again that it is risky to take anything Nikomastir says at face value.

My incandescent mask-sister Mayfly, who is as small and fair as Nikomastir is tall and dark, encountered him while on a visit to Olej in the Lubrik system and was immediately captivated by his volatile impulsive nature, and they have traveled together ever since. Whither Mayfly goeth, thither go I: that is the pledge of the mask. So do I trudge along now from world to world with them, and therefore my winsome, sly, capricious Velimyle, whose psychosensitive paintings are sought by the connoisseurs of a hundred worlds but who belongs to me alone, has willy-nilly become the fourth member of our inseparable quartet.

Some people find relay-sweep transport unlikable and even frightening, but I have never minded it. What is most bothersome, I suppose, is that no starship is involved: you travel unprotected by any sort of tangible container, a mere plummeting parcel falling in frightful solitude through the interstices of the continuum. A journey-helmet is all that covers you, and some flimsy folds of coppery mesh. You set up your coordinates, you activate your beacon, and you stand and wait, you stand and wait, until the probing beam of some far-off sweep-station intersects your position and catches you and lifts you and carries you away. If you've done things right, your baggage will be picked up and transported at the same time. Most of the time that is so.

It is a stark and unluxurious mode of travel. The relay field wraps you in cocooning bands of force and shoots you off through one auxiliary space and another, kicking you through any convenient opening in the space-time lattice that presents itself, and while you wait to be delivered to your destination you drift like a bauble afloat in an infinite sea, helpless, utterly alone, bereft of all power to override the sweep. Your metabolic processes are suspended but the activity of your consciousness is not, so that your unsleeping mind ticks on and on in the most maddening way and there is nothing you can do to quiet its clamor. It is as though you must scratch your itching nose and your hands are tied behind your back.

Eventually you have no idea whether it has been an hour, a month, a century—you are plunked unceremoniously down into a relay station at the planet of your choice and there you are. Relay-sweep transport is ever so much more efficient than any system requiring vast vessels to plough the seas of space from world to world; but all the same it is a disquieting and somewhat degrading way to get around.

So now we depart. Mayfly is the first to be captured by the sweep-beam. Perhaps half an hour later Nikomastir disappears, and then, almost immediately after, Velimyle. My own turn does not arrive for many long hours, which leaves me fidgeting gloomily in that golden meadow, wondering when, if ever, I will be taken, and whether some disjunction in our routes will separate me forever from my three companions. There is that risk—not so much that we would fail to arrive on Sidri Akrak at all, but that we might get there many years apart. I find that a melancholy thought indeed. More than that: it is terrifying.

But finally the dazzling radiance of the sweep aura engulfs me and hurls me out into the Great Dark, and off I go, dropping freely through hundreds of light-years with nothing but an invisible sphere of force to protect me against the phantoms of the auxiliary spaces through which I fall.

I hang in total stasis in a realm of utter blackness for what feels like a thousand centuries, an infinity of empty space at my elbow, as I go my zigzag way through the wormholes of the adjacent continuua.

Within that terrible passivity my hyperactive mind ponders, as it all too often does, the deep questions of life—issues of honor, duty, justice, responsibility, the meaning of existence, subjects about which I have managed to learn nothing at all, basically, either in this life or the four that preceded it. I arrive at many profound conclusions during the course of my journey, but they fly away from me as fast as I construct them.

I begin to think the trip will never end, that I will be one of those few unfortunate travelers, the one out of a billion who is caught in some shunt malfunction and is left to dangle in the middle of nowhere for all eternity, or at least for the ten or twenty thousand realtime years it will take for his metabolically suspended body to die. Has this actually ever happened to anyone? There are only rumors, unfounded reports. But there comes a time in every sweep-jump when I am convinced that it has happened to me.

Then I see a glare of crimson and violet and azure and green, and my mask-sister Mayfly's voice purrs in my ear, saying, "Welcome to Sidri Akrak, darling, welcome, welcome, welcome!"

Nikomastir stands beside her. A moment later Velimyle materializes in a haze of color. The four of us have made a nearly simultaneous arrival, across who knows how many hundreds of light-years. We definitely do lead charmed lives, we four.

* * *

EVERYONE KNOWS ABOUT SIDRI AKRAK. The place was settled at least a thousand years ago and yet it still has the feel of a frontier world. Only the main streets of the half-dozen big cities are paved and all the rest are mere blue dirt that turn into rivers of mud during the rainy season. The houses are ramshackle slovenly things, lopsided and drafty, arrayed in higgledy-piggledy fashion as though they had been set down at random by their builders without any regard for logic or order. After all this time the planet is mostly jungle, a jungle that doesn't merely encroach on the settlements but comes right up into them. Wild animals of the most repellent sorts are permitted to rampage everywhere, wandering about as they please.

The Akrakikans simply don't care. They pretend the animals—monstrous, appalling—aren't there. The people of Sidri Akrak are a soulless bloodless bunch in the main, altogether indifferent to such things as comfort and beauty and proper sanitation. Primitive squalor is what they prefer, and if you don't care for it, well, you're quite free to visit some other world.

"Why, exactly, did we come here?" I ask.

It is a rhetorical question. I know perfectly well why: because Nikomastir, clueless about our next destination, had opened a void that Mayfly had mischievously filled with one of the most unappealing suggestions possible, just to see what Nikomastir would do with it, and Nikomastir had as usual given the matter about a thousandth of a second of careful consideration before blithely leaping headlong into the abyss, thereby taking the rest of us with him, as he has done so often before.

But Nikomastir has already rearranged the facts in what passes for his mind.

"I absolutely had to come here," he says. "It's a place I've always felt the need to see. My daddy was born on Sidri Akrak, you know. This is my ancestral world."

We know better than to challenge Nikomastir when he says things like that. What sense is there in arguing with him? He'll only defend himself by topping one whopper with another twice as wild, building such a towering edifice of spur-of-the-moment fantasy that he'll end up claiming to be the great-grandson of the Fourteenth Emperor, or perhaps the reincarnation of Julius Caesar.

Velimyle whispers at my side, "We'll just stay here two or three days and then we'll move along."

I nod. We all indulge Nikomastir in his whims, but only up to a point.

The sky of Sidri Akrak is a sort of dirty brown, broken by greasy, sullen green clouds. The sunlight is greenish too, pallid, tinged with undertones of dull gray. There is a sweet, overripe, mildly sickening flavor to the warm, clinging air, and its humidity is so intense that it is difficult to distinguish it from light rain. We have landed within some city, apparently—in a grassy open space that anywhere else might have been called a park, but which here seems merely to be a patch of land no one had bothered to use for anything, vaguely square and a couple of hundred meters across. To our left is an irregular row of bedraggled two-story wooden shacks; on our right is a dense clump of ungainly asymmetrical trees; before and behind us are ragged aggregations of unpainted buildings and scruffy unattractive shrubbery.

"Look," says Mayfly, pointing, and we have our first encounter with the famous wildlife of Sidri Akrak.

An ugly creature comes bounding toward us out of the trees: a bulky, round-bodied thing, dark and furry, that rises to a disconcerting height atop two scrawny hairless legs covered with bright yellow scales. Its face is something out of your worst dreams, bulging fiery eyes the size of saucers and dangling red wattles and jutting black fangs, and it is moving very quickly in our direction, howling ferociously.

We have weapons, of course. But it swiftly becomes apparent that the thing has no interest in us, that in fact it is fleeing an even more ghastly thing, a long bristle-covered many-legged monster built close to the ground, from whose spherical head emerge three long hornlike projections that branch and branch again, terminating in scores of writhing tendrils that are surely equipped with venomous stings. First one vile creature and then the other runs past us without seeming to notice us and they lose themselves in the shrubbery beyond. We can hear wild shrieking and hissing in there, and the sound of cracking branches.

Nikomastir is smiling benignly. All this must be delightful to him. Mayfly too looks entranced. Even Velimyle, who is closest to me in temperament, almost normal in her desires and amusements, claps her hands together in fascination. I alone seem to be troubled by the sight of such creatures running about unhindered on what is supposedly a civilized world.

But it is ever thus in our travels: I am fated always to stand a little to one side as I follow these three around the universe. Yet am I linked irrevocably to them all the same.

Mayfly was my lover once, two lives back. That was before we took the mask together. Now, of course, it would be unthinkable for anything carnal to happen between us, though I still cherish cheerful memories of her pixy breasts in my hands, her slim sleek thighs about my hips. Even if we have forsworn the sexual part of our friendship, the rest is deeper than ever, and in truth we are still profoundly a couple, Mayfly and I, despite the rich and rewarding relationship I maintain with Velimyle and the frothy, sportive one Mayfly has built with Nikomastir. Above and beyond all that, there is also the bond that links us all. The lines of attraction go this way and that. We are inseparables. They are my world; I am a citizen only of our little group. Wherever we go, we go together. Even unto Sidri Akrak.

* * *

In a little while two immigration officers show up to check us out. Sidri Akrak is an Imperium world and therefore the local immigration scanners have been automatically alerted to our arrival.

They come riding up in a sputtering little snub-nosed vehicle, a man and a woman in baggy brown uniforms, and begin asking us questions. Nikomastir does most of the answering. His charm is irresistible even to an Akrakikan.

The questioning, brusque and hard-edged, is done in Imperial, but from time to time the immigration officers exchange comments with each other in their own dialect, which sounds like static. The woman is swarthy and squat and flat-faced and the man is even less lovely, and they are not at all obliging; they seem to regard the arrival of tourists on their planet simply as an irritating intrusion. The discussion goes on and on—do we plan to remain here long, are we financially solvent, do we intend to engage in political activity in the course of our stay? Nikomastir meets every query with glib easy reassurances. During our interrogation a slimy rain begins to fall, oily pink stuff that coats us like grease, and a massive many-humped blue-green beast that looks like an ambulatory hill with purple eyes appears and goes lolloping thunderously past us with utter unconcern for our presence, leaving an odor of decay and corruption in its wake. After a time I stop listening to the discussion. But finally they flash bright lights in our faces—passports are validated retinally on Sidri Akrak—and Nikomastir announces that we have been granted six-month visas. Lodgings are available three streets away, they tell us.

The place they have sent us to turns out to be a dismal rickety hovel and our innkeeper is no more friendly than the immigration officials, but we are grudgingly allowed to rent the entire upper floor. The rooms I am to share with Velimyle face the rear garden, a patch of uncouth tangled wilderness where some slow-moving shaggy monster is sluggishly browsing about, nibbling on the shrubbery. It lifts its head in my direction and gives me a cold glare, as though to warn me away from the plants on which it's feeding. I signal it that it has nothing to worry about and turn away from the window. As I unpack I see a procession of glassy-shelled snail-like things with huge bulbous red eyes crawling diagonally across the bedroom wall. They too stare back at me. They seem almost to be smirking at me.

But Nikomastir and Mayfly claim to be delighted to be here, and Velimyle seems to have no complaints. I feel outnumbered by them. Velimyle announces that she would like to do a painting of Nikomastir in the hotel garden. She only paints when she's in a buoyant mood. Buoyant, here? They run off together downstairs, hand in hand like happy children. I watch from above as Velimyle sets up her easel outside and goes about the task of priming the psychosensitive surface of her canvas. She and Nikomastir are as untroubled as any Akrakikan by the shambling shaggy thing that grazes noisily nearby. How quickly they have acclimated.

"Are you very miserable here, darling?" Mayfly asks, running her fingertips lightly along my cheeks.

I give her a stoic smile. "I'll be all right. We'll find things to amuse us, I'm sure. It's all for the best that Nikomastir brought us to this place."

"You don't mean that, do you? Not really."

"Not really, no."

Yet in some sense I do. I often tell myself that it's important not to live as though life is just a perpetual holiday for us, even though in fact it is. It would be too easy to lose ourselves, if we aren't careful, in the nightmare that is perfection. This is an era when all things are possible. We have godlike existences. We have every imaginable comfort close at hand. Beauty and long life are ours for the asking; we are spared the whole dreary business of sagging flesh and spreading waistlines and blurry eyesight and graying hair and hardening arteries that afflicted our remote ancestors. And all the incredible richness of the galaxy lies open to us: key in your coordinates, snap your fingers, off you go, any world you choose to visit instantly available. Never in the history of the universe has any species lived such a life as ours.

I fear the terrible ease of this existence of ours. I think sometimes that we'll eventually be asked to pay a great price for it. That thought engulfs me in secret terror.

Mayfly, who knows me almost as well as I know myself, says, "Think of it this way, love. There's something to be learned even from ugliness. Isn't it true that what we're trying to get out of all this travel is experience that has meaning? If that's what we want, we can't just limit ourselves to the beautiful places. And maybe a horrid place like Sidri Akrak has something important to teach us."

Yes. She's right. Is she aware that she's voicing my own most private thoughts, or is she just being playful? Perhaps it's all self-delusion, but I do indeed seek for meaning as we travel, or at least think that I do. These furtive broodings in which I indulge in the hidden places of my soul are, so it seems to me, the thing that sets me apart from Nikomastir and Mayfly and Velimyle, who take life as it comes and ask no questions.

Velimyle and Nikomastir return from the garden a little while later. She puts the rolled canvas away without showing it to me. There is an uncharacteristically somber expression on Velimyle's face and even giddy Nikomastir seems troubled. Plainly something has gone awry.

I know better than to ask for details.

We eat at our hotel that night. The surly innkeeper slams the dishes down before us almost angrily: a thin greenish gruel, some sort of stewed shredded meat, a mess of overcooked vegetables. The meat tastes like cooked twine and the vegetables have a dank swampy flavor. I pretend we are back on Iriarte, where food is the highest art and every meal is a symphony. I pretend we have returned to Nabomba Zom, to that wondrous palatial hotel by the shore of the scarlet sea, the waters of which at dawn would reverberate as if struck by a hammer as the first blue rays of morning fell upon it.

But no, no, we are on Sidri Akrak. I lie sleepless through the night with Velimyle breathing gently beside me, listening to the fierce honkings and roarings and screechings of the wild beasts that roam the darkness beyond our windows. Now and again then the sounds of the lovemaking of Mayfly and Nikomastir come through the thin walls that separate our bedroom from theirs, giggles and gasps and long indrawn sighs of pleasure.

In the morning we go out exploring.

This city, we have learned, is called Periandros Andifang. It has a population of just under one hundred thousand, with not a single building of the slightest architectural distinction and a year-round climate of clamminess and drizzle. The plant life is, generally speaking, strikingly unsightly—a preponderance of gray leaves, black flowers—and the air is full of clouds of little stinging midges with malevolent purple beaks, and of course one has to deal with the fauna, too, the fiend's gallery of grisly monstrosities, seemingly no two alike, that greet you at every turn: huge beasts with beady eyes and slavering fangs and clacking claws, things with pockmarked pustulent skins or writhing furry tentacles or clutching many-jointed arms. Almost always they appear without warning, galloping out of some clump of trees uttering banshee shrieks or ground-shaking roars. I begin to understand now the tales of unwary travelers who have total mental breakdowns within an hour of their arrival on Sidri Akrak.

It quickly becomes clear to us, though, that none of these horrendous creatures has any interest in attacking us. The only real risk we run is that of getting trampled as they go charging past. Very likely it is the case that they find human flesh unpalatable, or indigestible, or downright poisonous. But encountering them is an unnerving business, and we encounter them again and again and again.

Nikomastir finds it all fascinating. Painstakingly he searches out the ill-favored, the misshapen, the feculent, the repulsive—not that they are hard to find. He drifts ecstatically from one eyesore of a building to the next, taking an infinite number of pictures. He adores the plants' sooty foul-smelling blossoms and sticky blighted-looking leaves. The rampaging animals give him even greater pleasure; whenever some particularly immense or especially abhorrent-looking loathsomeness happens to cross our path he cries out in boyish glee.

This starts to be very irritating. His callow idiocy is making me feel old.

"Remember, sweet, he's not even seventy yet," Mayfly reminds me, seeing my brows furrowing. "Surely you were like that yourself, once upon a time."

"Was I? I'd like to think that isn't so."

"And in any case," says Velimyle, "Can't you manage to find that enthusiasm of his charming?"

No. I can't. Perhaps it's getting to be time for my next rebirth, I think. Growing old, for us, isn't a matter so much of bodily decay—that is fended off by efficient processes of automatic bioenergetic correction—as of increasing inward rigidity, a creakiness of the soul, a corrugation of the psyche, a stiffening of the spiritual synapses. One starts to feel sour and petty and crabbed. Life loses its joy and its juice. By then you begin to become aware that it is time to clamber once more into the crystal tank where an intricate spiderweb of machinery will enfold you like a loving mother, and slip off into sweet oblivion for a while, and awaken to find yourself young again and ready to start all over. Which you can do over and over again, until eventually you arrive at the annoying point, after the eleventh or twelfth rebirth, where the buildup of solar poisons in your system has at last become ineradicable under any circumstances, and that is the end of you, alas. Even gods have to die eventually, it would seem.

Nikomastir is a young god, and I am, evidently, an aging one. I try to make allowances for that. But I find myself fervently hoping, all the same, that he will tire of this awful place very soon and allow us to go onward to some happier world.

* * *

HE DOES NOT TIRE OF it, though.

He loves it. He is in the grip of what some ancient poet once called the fascination of the abomination. He has gone up and down every street of the city, peering at this building and that one in unstinting admiration of their imperfections. For several days running he makes it clear that he is searching for some building in particular, and then he finds it: a rambling old ruin of great size and formidable ugliness at the very edge of town, standing apart from everything else in a sort of private park.

"Here it is!" he cries. "The ancestral mansion! The house where my father was born!"

So Nikomastir still clings to the claim that he is of Akrakikan descent. There is no way that this can be true; the natives of this world are a chilly bloodless folk with mean pinched hard souls, if they have souls at all and not just some clicking chattering robotic mechanisms inside their skulls. Indeed I have known robots with personalities far more appealing than anyone we have met thus far on Sidri Akrak. Nikomastir, bless him, is nothing at all like that. He may be silly and frivolous and empty-headed, but he also is sweet-natured and lively and amiable and vivacious, terms that have never yet been applied to any citizen of Sidri Akrak, and never will be.

Velimyle has tried to paint him again. Again the attempt was a failure. This time she is so distressed that I dare to breach the wall of privacy behind which she keeps her art and ask her what the difficulty is.

"Look," she says.

She unrolls the second canvas. Against the familiar swirling colors of a typical Velimyle background I see the slender, angular form of Nikomastir, imprinted there by the force of Velimyle's mental rapport with the psychosensitive fabric. But the features are all wrong. Nikomaster's perpetual easy smile has given way to a dreadful scowling grimace. His lip curls backward menacingly; his teeth are the teeth of some predatory beast. And his eyes—oh, Velimyle, those harsh, glaring eyes! Where is his cheerful sparkle? These eyes are hard, narrow, fierce, and above all else sad. The Nikomastir of Velimyle's painting stares out at the universe with tragic intensity. They are the eyes of a god, perhaps, but of a dying god, one who knows he must give up his life for the redemption of his race.

"The first one was almost as bad," Velimyle says. "Why is this happening? This isn't Nikomastir at all. I've never had something like this happen."

"Has he seen either of the paintings?"

"I wouldn't let him. All I told him was that they didn't come out right, that they would depress him if I showed them to him. And of course he didn't want to see them after that."

"Something about this planet must be shading your perceptions," I say. "Burn this, Velimyle. And the other one too. And forget about painting him until we've left here."

Nikomastir wants to have a look inside the crumbling, lurching pile that he says is his family's ancestral home. But the place, ruinous though it is, happens to be occupied by Akrakikans, a whole swarm of them, and when he knocks at the front door and grandly introduces himself to the major-domo of the house as Count Nikomastir of Sembiran, who has come here on a sentimental journey to his former paternal estate, the door is closed in his face without a word.

"How impolite," Nikomastir says, not seeming very surprised.

"But don't worry: I'll find a way of getting in."

That project gets tabled too. Over the next few days he leads us farther and farther afield, well out into the uninhabited countryside beyond the boundaries of Periandros Andifang. The land out here is swampy and uningratiating, and of course there are the animals to contend with, and the insects, and the humidity. I can tell that Mayfly and Velimyle are growing a little weary of Nikomastir's exuberance, but they both are as tolerant of his whims as ever and follow him loyally through these soggy realms. As do I—partly, I suppose, because we agreed long ago that we would journey everywhere as a single unit, and partly because I have been stung, evidently, by various hints of Mayfly's and Velimyle's that my recent crochetiness could mean I might be getting ready for my next rebirth.

Then he turns his attention once more to the old house that he imagines once belonged to his family. "My father once told me that there's a pool of fire behind it, a phosphorescent lake. He used to swim it when he was a boy, and he'd come up dripping with cool flame. I'm going to take a swim in it too, and then we can head off to the next planet. Whose turn is it to pick our next planet, any-way?"

"Mine," I say quickly. I have Marajo in mind—the sparkling sands, the City of Seven Pyramids. "If there's a lake behind that house,

Nikomastir, I advise you very earnestly to stay away from it. The people who live there don't seem to look favorably on trespassers. Besides, can't you imagine the kind of nastinesses that would live in a lake on this world?"

"My father went swimming in that one," Nikomastir replies, and gives me a defiant glare. "It's perfectly safe, I assure you."

I doubt, of course, that any such lake exists. If it's there, though, I hope he isn't fool enough to go swimming in it. My affection for the boy is real; I don't want him to come to harm.

But I let the matter drop. I've already said too much. The surest way to prod him into trouble, I know, is oppose him in one of his capricious fancies. My hope is that Nikomastir's attention will be diverted elsewhere in the next day or two and all thought of that dismal house, and of the fiery lake that may or may not be behind it, will fly out of his mind.

It's generally a good idea, when visiting a world you know very little about, to keep out of places of unknown chemical properties. When we toured Megalo Kastro, we stood at the edge of a cliff looking down into the famous living sea, that pink custardy mass that is in fact a single living organism of gigantic size, spreading across thousands of kilometers of that world. But it did not occur to us to take a swim in that sea, for we understood that in a matter of hours it would dissolve and digest us if we did.

And when we were on Xamur we went to see the Idradin crater, as everyone who goes to Xamur does. Xamur is the most perfect of worlds, flawless and serene, a paradise, air like perfume and water like wine, every tree in the ideal place, every brook, every hill. It has only one blemish—the Idradin, a huge round pit that reaches deep into the planet's primordial heart. It is a hideous place, that crater. Concentric rings of jagged cooled lava surround it, black and eroded and bleak. Stinking gases rise out of the depths, and yellow clouds of sulfuric miasma belch forth, and wild red shafts of roaring flame, and you peer down from the edge into a roiling den of hot surging magma. Everyone who goes to Xamur must visit the Idradin, for if you did not see perfect Xamur's one terrible flaw you could never be happy on any other world. And so we stared into it from above, and shivered with the horror we were expected to feel; but we were never at all tempted to clamber down the crater's sides and dip our toes into that realm of fire below.

It seems unlikely to me that Nikomastir will do anything so stupid here. But I have to be careful not to prod him in the wrong direction. I don't mention the lake to him again.

* * *

Our exploration of Sidri Akrak proceeds. We visit new swamps, new groves of fetid-smelling malproportioned trees, new neighborhoods of misshapen and graceless buildings. One drizzly disheartening day succeeds another, and finally I am unable to bear the sight of that brown sky and greenish sun any longer. Though it is a violation of our agreements, I stay behind at the hotel one morning and let the other three go off without me.

It is a quiet time. I spend the hours reflecting on our travels of years past, all the many worlds we have seen. Icy Mulano of the two suns, one yellow, one bloody red, and billions of ghostly electric lifeforms glimmering about you in the frigid air. Estrilidis, where the cats have two tails and the insects have eyes like blue diamonds. Zimbalou, the sunless nomad world, where the cities are buried deep below the frozen surface. Kalimaka, Haj Qaldun, Vietoris, Nabomba Zom—

So many places, so many sights. A lifetime of wonderful experiences; and yet what, I ask myself, has it all meant? How has it shaped me? What have I learned?

I have no answers, only to say that we will continue to go onward, ever onward. It is our life. It is what we do. We are travelers by choice, but also by nature, by destiny.

I am still lost in reverie when I hear Velimyle's voice outside my window, calling to me, telling me that I must come quickly. "Nikomastir—" she cries. "Nikomastir!"

"What about him?"

But she can only gesture and wave. Her eyes are wild. We run together through the muddy streets, paying no heed to the bulky and grotesque Akrakikan monstrosities that occasionally intersect our path. I realize after a time that Velimyle is leading me toward the tumbledown house at the edge of town that Nikomastir has claimed as his family's former home. A narrow grassy path leads around one side of it to the rear; and there, to my amazement, I see the phosphorescent lake of Nikomastir's fantasies, with Mayfly beside it, leaping up and down in agitation that verges on frenzy.

She points toward the water. "Out there—there—"

On this ugly world even a phosphorescent lake can somehow manage to be an unlovely sight. I saw one once on Darma Barma that flashed like heavenly fire in rippling waves of cobalt and amethyst, magenta and gold, aquamarine and emerald and jade. But from this lake emanates the most unradiant of radiances, a dull, prosaic, sickly gleam, dark-toned and dispiriting, except in one place off toward the farther shore where a disturbance of some sort is setting up whirlpools of glinting metallic effects, swirls of eye-jabbing bright sparkles, as though handfuls of iron filings are being thrown through a magnetic field.

The disturbance is Nikomastir. He—his body, rather—is tossing and heaving at the lake's surface, and all about him the denizens of the lake can be seen, narrow scaly jutting heads popping up by the dozens, hinged jaws snapping, sharp teeth closing on flesh. A widening pool of blood surrounds him. They, whatever they are, are ripping him to shreds.

"We have to get him out of there," Mayfly says, her voice congested with horror and fear.

"How?" I ask.

"I told him not to do it," says trembling Velimyle. "I told him, I told him, I told him. But he plunged right in, and when he was halfway across they began to break the surface, and then—then he began screaming, and—"

Mayfly plucks urgently at my sleeve. "What can we do? How can we rescue him?"

"He's beyond rescuing," I tell her hollowly.

"But if we can get his body back," she says, "there'll be a way to revive him, won't there? I know there is. Scientists can do anything nowadays." Velimyle, more tentatively, agrees. Some kind of scientific miracle, Nikomastir gathered up and repaired somehow by the regeneration of tissue—

But tissue is all that's left of him now, frayed sorry scraps, and the creatures of the lake, frantic now with blood-lust, are devouring even those in furious haste.

They want me to tell them that Nikomastir isn't really dead. But he is: really, really, really dead. Dead forever. What has been played out on this shore today was not a game. There is nothing that can be saved, no way to regenerate. I have never seen the death of a human being before. It is a dizzying thing to contemplate: the finality, the utterness. My mind is whirling; I have to fight back convulsions of shock and horror.

"Couldn't you have stopped him?" I ask angrily, when I am able to speak again.

"But he wanted so badly to do it," Mayfly replies. "We couldn't have stopped him, you know. Not even if we—"

She halts in midsentence.

"Not even if you had wanted to?" I say. "Is that it?" Neither of them can meet my furious gaze. "But you didn't want to, did you? You thought it would be fun to see Nikomastir swim across the phosphorescent lake. Fun. Am I right? Yes. I know that I am. What could you have been thinking, Mayfly? Velimyle?"

There is no sign of Nikomastir at the surface any longer. The lake is growing still again. Its phosphorescence has subsided to a somber tarnished glow.

For a long time, minutes, hours, weeks, none of us is capable of moving. Silent, pale, stunned, we stand with bowed heads by the shore of that frightful lake, scarcely even able to breathe.

We are in the presence of incontrovertible and permanent death, which to us is a novelty far greater even than the living sea of Megalo Kastro or the blue dawn of Nabomba Zom, and the immense fact of it holds us rooted to the spot. Was this truly Nikomastir's ancestral world? Was his father actually born in that great old falling-down house, and did he really once swim in this deadly lake? And if none of that was so, how did Nikomastir know that the lake was there? We will never be able to answer those questions. Whatever we do not know about Nikomastir that we have already learned, we will never come to discover now. That is the meaning of death: the finality of it, the severing of communication, the awful unanswerable power of the uncompromising curtain that descends like a wall of steel. We did not come to Sidri Akrak to learn about such things, but that is what we have learned on Sidri Akrak, and we will take it with us wherever we go henceforth, pondering it, examining it.

"Come," I say to Mayfly and Velimyle, after a time. "We need to get away from here."

* * *

So, THEN. NIKOMASTIR WAS FOOLISH. He was bold. He has had his swim and now he is dead. And why? Why? For what? What was he seeking, on this awful world? What were we? We know what we found, yes, but not what it was that we were looking for. I wonder if we will ever know.

He has lived his only life, has Nikomastir, and he has lost it in the pursuit of idle pleasure. There is a lesson in that, for me, for Velimilye, for Mayfly, for us all. And one day I will, I hope, understand what it is.

All I do know after having lived these hundreds of years is that the universe is very large and we are quite small. We live godlike lives these days, flitting as we do from world to world, but even so we are not gods. We die: some sooner, some later, but we do die. Only gods live forever. Nikomastir hardly lived at all.

So be it. We have learned what we have learned from Nikomastir's death, and now we must move on. We are travelers by nature and destiny, and we will go forward into our lives. Tomorrow we leave for Marajo. The shining sands, the City of Seven Pyramids. Marajo will teach us something, as Xamur once did, and Nabomba Zom, and Galgala. And also Sidri Akrak. Something. Something. Something.

CHIP RUNNER

Not all voyages are journeys into the remote regions of the galaxy. Here is one that covers hardly any distance at all, and yet is infinite in scope.

In the summer of 1987 the energetic publisher and book packager Byron Preiss, having produced a pair of magnificent illustrated anthologies to which I had been a contributor—*The Planets* and *The Universe*—now turned his attention the other way, to the world of the infinitely small. *The Microverse* was his new project, and Byron asked me to write something for this one too.

The scientific part of the story was easy enough to put together: required by the theme of the book to deal with the universe on the subatomic level, I rummaged about in my file of *Scientific American* to see what the current state of thinking about electrons and protons and such might be. In the course of my rummaging I stumbled upon something about microchip technology, and that led me to the fictional component of the story. All about me in the San Francisco Bay Area where I live are bright boys and girls with a deep, all-consuming, and spooky passion for computers. I happen to know something, also, about the prevalence of such eating disorders as anorexia and bulimia in Bay Area adolescents—disorders mainly involving girls, but not exclusively so. Everything fit together swiftly: an anorexic computer kid who has conceived the wild idea of entering the subatomic world by starving down to it. The rest was a matter of orchestrating theme and plot and style—of writing the story, that is. Byron had Ralph McQuarrie illustrate it with a fine, terrifying painting when he published it in *The Microverse* in 1989. Gardner Dozois bought the story also for the November, 1989 issue of Isaac *Asimov's Science Fiction Magazine* and Donald A. Wollheim selected it for his annual *World's Best SF* anthology.

He was fifteen, and looked about ninety, and a frail ninety at that. I knew his mother and his father, separately—they were Silicon Valley people, divorced, very important in their respective companies—and separately they had asked me to try to work with him. His skin was blue-gray and tight, drawn cruelly close over the jutting bones of his face. His eyes were gray too, and huge, and they lay deep within their sockets. His arms were like sticks. His thin lips were set in an angry grimace.

The chart before me on my desk told me that he was five feet eight inches tall and weighed 71 pounds. He was in his third year at one of the best private schools in the Palo Alto district. His I.Q. was 161. He crackled with intelligence and intensity. That was a novelty for me right at the outset. Most of my patients are depressed, withdrawn, uncertain of themselves, elusive, shy: virtual zombies. He wasn't anything like that. There would be other surprises ahead.

"So you're planning to go into the hardware end of the computer industry, your parents tell me," I began. The usual let's-build-a-relationship procedure.

He blew it away instantly with a single sour glare. "Is that your standard opening? 'Tell me all about your favorite hobby, my boy'? If you don't mind I'd rather skip all the bullshit, doctor, and then we can both get out of here faster. You're supposed to ask me about my eating habits."

It amazed me to see him taking control of the session this way within the first thirty seconds. I marveled at how different he was from most of the others, the poor sad wispy creatures who force me to fish for every word.

"Actually I do enjoy talking about the latest developments in the world of computers, too," I said, still working hard at being genial.

"But my guess is you don't talk about them very often, or you wouldn't call it 'the hardware end.' Or 'the computer industry.' We don't use mondo phrases like those any more." His high thin voice sizzled with barely suppressed rage. "Come on, doctor. Let's get right down to it. You think I'm anorexic, don't you?"

"Well—"

"I know about anorexia. It's a mental disease of girls, a vanity thing. They starve themselves because they want to look beautiful and they can't bring themselves to realize that they're not too fat. Vanity isn't the issue for me. And I'm not a girl, doctor. Even you ought to be able to see that right away."

"Timothy—"

"I want to let you know right out front that I don't have an eating disorder and I don't belong in a shrink's office. I know exactly what I'm doing all the time. The only reason I came today is to get my mother off my back, because she's taken it into her head that I'm trying to starve myself to death. She said I had to come here and see you. So I'm here. All right?"

"All right," I said, and stood up. I am a tall man, deep-chested, very broad through the shoulders. I can loom when necessary. A flicker of fear crossed Timothy's face, which was the effect I wanted to produce. When it's appropriate for the therapist to assert authority, simple-minded methods are often the most effective. "Let's talk about eating, Timothy. What did you have for lunch today?"

He shrugged. "A piece of bread. Some lettuce."

"That's all?"

"A glass of water."

"And for breakfast?"

"I don't eat breakfast."

"But you'll have a substantial dinner, won't you?"

"Maybe some fish. Maybe not. I think food is pretty gross."

I nodded. "Could you operate your computer with the power turned off, Timothy?"

"Isn't that a pretty condescending sort of question, doctor?"

"I suppose it is. Okay, I'll be more direct. Do you think you can run your body without giving it any fuel?"

"My body runs just fine," he said, with a defiant edge.

"Does it? What sports do you play?"

"Sports?" It might have been a Martian word.

"You know, the normal weight for someone of your age and height ought to be—"

"There's nothing normal about me, doctor. Why should my weight be any more normal than the rest of me?"

"It was until last year, apparently. Then you stopped eating. Your family is worried about you, you know."

"I'll be okay," he said sullenly.

"You want to stay healthy, don't you?"

He stared at me for a long chilly moment. There was something close to hatred in his eyes, or so I imagined.

"What I want is to disappear," he said.

* * *

THAT NIGHT I DREAMED I was disappearing. I stood naked and alone on a slab of gray metal in the middle of a vast empty plain under a sinister coppery sky and I began steadily to shrink. There is often some carryover from the office to a therapist's own unconscious life: we call it counter-transference. I grew smaller and smaller. Pores appeared on the surface of the metal slab and widened into jagged craters, and then into great crevices and gullies. A cloud of luminous dust shimmered about my head. Grains of sand, specks, mere motes, now took on the aspect of immense boulders. Down I drifted, gliding into the darkness of a fathomless chasm. Creatures I had not noticed before hovered about me, astonishing monsters, hairy, many-legged. They made menacing gestures, but I slipped away, downward, downward, and they were gone. The air was alive now with vibrating particles, inanimate, furious, that danced in frantic zigzag patterns, veering wildly past me, now and again crashing into me, knocking my breath from me, sending me ricocheting for what seemed like miles. I was floating, spinning, tumbling with no control. Pulsating waves of blinding light pounded me. I was falling into the infinitely small, and there was no halting my descent. I would shrink and shrink and shrink until I slipped through the realm of matter entirely and was lost. A mob of contemptuous glowing things—electrons and protons, maybe, but how could I tell?—crowded close around me, emitting fizzy sparks that seemed to me like jeers and laughter. They told me to keep moving along, to get myself out of their kingdom, or I would meet a terrible death. "To see a world in a grain of sand," Blake wrote. Yes. And Eliot wrote, "I will show you fear in a handful of dust." I went on downward, and downward still. And then I awoke gasping, drenched in sweat, terrified, alone.

* * *

Normally the patient is uncommunicative. You interview parents, siblings, teachers, friends, anyone who might provide a clue or an opening wedge. Anorexia is a life-threatening matter. The patients—girls, almost always, or young women in their twenties—have lost all sense of normal body-image and feel none of the food-deprivation prompts that a normal body gives its owner. Food is the enemy. Food must be resisted. They eat only when forced to, and then as little as possible. They are unaware that they are frighteningly gaunt. Strip them and put them in front of a mirror and they will pinch their sagging empty skin to show you imaginary fatty bulges. Sometimes the process of self-skeletonization is impossible to halt, even by therapy. When it reaches a certain point the degree of organic damage becomes irreversible and the death-spiral begins.

"He was always tremendously bright," Timothy's mother said. She was fifty, a striking woman, trim, elegant, almost radiant, vice president for finance at one of the biggest Valley companies. I knew her in that familiarly involuted California way: her present husband used to be married to my first wife. "A genius, his teachers all said. But strange, you know? Moody. Dreamy. I used to think he was on drugs, though of course none of the kids do that anymore." Timothy was her only child by her first marriage. "It scares me to death to watch him wasting away like that. When I see him I want to take him and shake him and force ice cream down his throat, pasta, milkshakes, anything. And then I want to hold him, and I want to cry."

"You'd think he'd be starting to shave by now," his father said. Technical man, working on nanoengineering projects at the Stanford AI lab. We often played racquetball together. "I was. You too, probably. I got a look at him in the shower, three or four months ago. Hasn't even reached puberty yet. Fifteen and not a hair on him. It's the starvation, isn't it? It's retarding his physical development, right?"

"I keep trying to get him to like eat something, anything," his step-brother Mick said. "He lives with us, you know, on the weekends, and most of the time he's downstairs playing with his computers, but sometimes I can get him to go out with us, and we buy like a chili dog for him, or, you know, a burrito, and he goes, Thank you, thank you, and pretends to eat it, but then he throws it away when he thinks we're not looking. He is *so* weird, you know? And scary. You look at him with those ribs and all and he's like something out of a horror movie."

"What I want is to disappear," Timothy said.

* * *

He came every Tuesday and Thursday for one-hour sessions. There was at the beginning an undertone of hostility and suspicion to everything he said. I asked him, in my layman way, a few things about the latest developments in computers, and he answered me in monosyllables at first, not at all bothering to hide his disdain for my ignorance and my innocence. But now and again some question of mine would catch his interest and he would forget to be irritated, and reply at length, going on and on into realms I could not even pretend to understand. Trying to find things of that sort to ask him seemed my best avenue of approach. But of course I knew I was unlikely to achieve anything of therapeutic value if we simply talked about computers for the whole hour.

He was very guarded, as was only to be expected, when I would bring the conversation around to the topic of eating. He made it clear that his eating habits were his own business and he would rather not discuss them with me, or anyone. Yet there was an aggressive glow on his face whenever we spoke of the way he ate that called Kafka's hunger artist to my mind: he seemed proud of his achievements in starvation, even eager to be admired for his skill at shunning food.

Too much directness in the early stages of therapy is generally counterproductive where anorexia is the problem. The patient *loves* her syndrome and resists any therapeutic approach that might deprive her of it. Timothy and I talked mainly of his studies, his classmates, his step-brothers. Progress was slow, circuitous, agonizing. What was most agonizing was my realization that I didn't have much time. According to the report from his school physician he was already running at dangerously low levels, bones weakening, muscles degenerating, electrolyte balance cockeyed, hormonal systems in disarray. The necessary treatment before long would be hospitalization, not psychotherapy, and it might almost be too late even for that.

He was aware that he was wasting away and in danger. He didn't seem to care.

I let him see that I wasn't going to force anything on him. So far as I was concerned, I told him, he was basically free to starve himself to death if that was what he was really after. But as a psychologist whose role it is to help people, I said, I had some scientific interest in finding out what made him tick—not particularly for his sake, but for the sake of other patients who might be more interested in being helped. He could relate to that. His facial expressions changed. He became less hostile. It was the fifth session now, and I sensed that his armor might be ready to crack. He was starting to think of me not as a member of the enemy but as a neutral observer, a dispassionate investigator. The next step was to make him see me as an ally. You and me, Timothy, standing together against *them*. I told him a few things about myself, my childhood, my troubled adolescence: little nuggets of confidence, offered by way of trade.

"When you disappear," I said finally, "where is it that you want to go?"

* * *

THE MOMENT WAS RIPE AND the breakthrough went beyond my highest expectations.

"You know what a microchip is?" he asked.

"Sure."

"I go down into them."

Not I *want* to go down into them. But I *do* go down into them.

"Tell me about that," I said.

"The only way you can understand the nature of reality," he said, "is to take a close look at it. To really and truly take a look, you know? Here we have these fantastic chips, a whole processing unit smaller than your little toenail with fifty times the data-handling capacity of the old mainframes. What goes on inside them? I mean, what *really* goes on? I go into them and I look. It's like a trance, you know? You sharpen your concentration and you sharpen it and sharpen it and then you're moving downward, inward, deeper and deeper." He laughed harshly. "You think this is all mystical ka-ka, don't you? Half of you thinks I'm just a crazy kid mouthing off, and the other half thinks here's a kid who's smart as hell, feeding you a line of malarkey to keep you away from the real topic. Right, doctor? Right?"

"I had a dream a couple of weeks ago about shrinking down into the infinitely small," I said. "A nightmare, really. But a fascinating one. Fascinating and frightening both. I went all the way down to the molecular level, past grains of sand, past bacteria, down to electrons and protons, or what I suppose were electrons and protons."

"What was the light like, where you were?"

"Blinding. It came in pulsing waves."

"What color?"

"Every color all at once," I said.

He stared at me. "No shit!"

"Is that the way it looks for you?"

"Yes. No." He shifted uneasily. "How can I tell if you saw what I saw? But it's a stream of colors, yes. Pulsing. And—all the colors at once, yes, that's how you could describe it—"

"Tell me more."

"More what?"

"When you go downward—tell me what it's like, Timothy."

He gave me his lofty look, his pedagogic look. "You know how small a chip is? A MOSFET, say?"

"MOSFET?"

"Metal-oxide-silicon field-effect-transistor," he said. "The newest ones have a minimum feature size of about a micrometer. Ten to the minus sixth meters. That's a millionth of a meter, all right? Small. It isn't down there on the molecular level, no. You could fit 200 amoebas into a MOSFET channel one micrometer long. Okay? Okay? Or a whole army of viruses. But it's still plenty small. That's where I go. And run, down the corridors of the chips, with electrons whizzing by me all the time. Of course I can't see them. Even a lot smaller, you can't see electrons, you can only compute the probabilities of their paths. But you can feel them. *I* can feel them. And I run among them, everywhere, through the corridors, through the channels, past the gates, past the open spaces in the lattice. Getting to know the territory. Feeling at home in it."

"What's an electron like, when you feel it?"

"You dreamed it, you said. You tell me."

"Sparks," I said. "Something fizzy, going by in a blur."

"You read about that somewhere, in one of your journals?"

"It's what I saw," I said. "What I felt, when I had that dream."

"But that's it! That's it exactly!" He was perspiring. His face was flushed. His hands were trembling. His whole body was ablaze with a metabolic fervor I had not previously seen in him. He looked like a skeleton who had just trotted off a basketball court after a hard game. He leaned toward me and said, looking suddenly vulnerable in a way that he had never allowed himself to seem with me before, "Are you sure it was only a dream? Or do you go there too?"

* * *

Kafka had the right idea. What the anorexic wants is to demonstrate a supreme ability. "Look," she says. "I am a special person. I have an extraordinary gift. I am capable of exerting total control over my body. By refusing food I take command of my destiny. I display supreme force of will. Can you achieve that sort of discipline? Can you even begin to understand it? Of course you can't. But I can." The issue isn't really one of worrying about being too fat. That's just a superficial problem. The real issue is one of exhibiting strength of purpose, of proving that you can accomplish something remarkable, of showing the world what a superior person you really are. So what we're dealing with isn't merely a perversely extreme form of dieting. The deeper issue is one of gaining control—over your body, over your life, even over the physical world itself.

* * *

He began to look healthier. There was some color in his cheeks now, and he seemed more relaxed, less twitchy. I had the feeling that he was putting on a little weight, although the medical reports I was getting from his school physician didn't confirm that in any significant way—some weeks he'd be up a pound or two, some weeks down, and there was never any net gain. His mother reported that he went through periods when he appeared to be showing a little interest in food, but these were usually followed by periods of rigorous fasting or at best his typical sort of reluctant nibbling. There was nothing in any of this that I could find tremendously encouraging, but I had the definite feeling that I was starting to reach him, that I was beginning to win him back from the brink.

* * *

Timothy said, "I have to be weightless in order to get there. I mean, literally weightless. Where I am now, it's only a beginning. I need to lose all the rest."

"Only a beginning," I said, appalled, and jotted a few quick notes.

"I've attained takeoff capability. But I can never get far enough. I run into a barrier on the way down, just as I'm entering the truly structural regions of the chip."

"Yet you do get right into the interior of the chip."

"Into it, yes. But I don't attain the real understanding that I'm after. Perhaps the problem's in the chip itself, not in me. Maybe if I tried a quantum-well chip instead of a MOSFET I'd get where I want to go, but they aren't ready yet, or if they are I don't have any way of getting my hands on one. I want to ride the probability waves, do you see? I want to be small enough to grab hold of an electron and stay with it as it zooms through the lattice." His eyes were blazing. "Try talking about this stuff with my brother. Or anyone. The ones who don't understand think I'm crazy. So do the ones who do."

"You can talk here, Timothy."

"The chip, the integrated circuit—what we're really talking about is transistors, microscopic ones, maybe a billion of them arranged side by side. Silicon or germanium, doped with impurities like boron, arsenic, sometimes other things. On one side are the N-type charge carriers, and the P-type ones are on the other, with an insulating layer between; and when the voltage comes through the gate, the electrons migrate to the P-type side, because it's positively charged, and the holes, the zones of positive charge, go to the N-type side. So your basic logic circuit—" He paused. "You following this?"

"More or less. Tell me about what you feel as you start to go downward into a chip."

* * *

IT BEGINS, HE SAID, WITH a rush, an upward surge of almost ecstatic force: he is not descending but floating. The floor falls away beneath him as he dwindles. Then comes the intensifying of perception, dust-motes quivering and twinkling in what had a moment before seemed nothing but empty air, and the light taking on strange new refractions and shimmerings. The solid world begins to alter. Familiar shapes—the table, a chair, the computer before him—vanish as he comes closer to their essence. What he sees now is detailed structure, the intricacy of surfaces: no longer a forest, only trees. Everything is texture and there is no solidity. Wood and metal become strands and webs and mazes. Canyons yawn. Abysses open. He goes inward, drifting, tossed like a feather on the molecular breeze.

It is no simple journey. The world grows grainy. He fights his way through a dust-storm of swirling granules of oxygen and nitrogen, an invisible blizzard battering him at every step. Ahead lies the chip he seeks, a magnificent thing, a gleaming radiant Valhalla. He begins to run toward it, heedless of obstacles. Giant rainbows sweep the sky: dizzying floods of pure color, hammering down with a force capable of deflecting the wandering atoms. And then—then—the chip stands before him like some temple of Zeus rising on the Athenian plain. Giant glowing columns—yawning gateways—dark beckoning corridors—hidden sanctuaries, beyond access, beyond comprehension. It glimmers with light of many colors. A strange swelling music fills the air. He feels like an explorer taking the first stumbling steps into a lost world. And he is still shrinking. The intricacies of the chip swell, surging like metal fungi filling with water after a rain: they spring higher and higher, darkening the sky, concealing it entirely. Another level downward and he is barely large enough to manage the passage across the threshold, but he does, and enters. Here he can move freely.

He is in a strange canyon whose silvery walls, riven with vast fissures, rise farther than he can see. He runs. He runs. He has infinite energy; his legs move like springs. Behind him the gates open, close, open, close. Rivers of torrential current surge through, lifting him, carrying him along. He senses, does not see, the vibrating of the atoms of silicon or boron; he senses, does not see, the electrons and the not-electrons flooding past, streaming toward the sides, positive or negative, to which they are inexorably drawn.

But there is more. He runs on and on and on. There is infinitely more, a world within this world, a world that lies at his feet and mocks him with its inaccessibility. It swirls before him, a whirlpool, a maelstrom. He would throw himself into it if he could, but some invisible barrier keeps him from it. This is as far as he can go. This is as much as he can achieve. He yearns to reach out as an electron goes careening past, and pluck it from its path, and stare into its heart. He wants to step inside the atoms and breathe the mysterious air within their boundaries. He longs to look upon their hidden nuclei. He hungers for the sight of mesons, quarks, neutrinos. There is more, always more, an unending series of worlds within worlds, and he is huge, he is impossibly clumsy, he is a lurching reeling mountainous titan, incapable of penetrating beyond this point—

So far, and no farther—no farther—

* * *

HE LOOKED UP AT ME from the far side of the desk. Sweat was streaming down his face and his light shirt was clinging to his skin. That sallow cadaverous look was gone from him entirely. He looked transfigured, aflame, throbbing with life: more alive than anyone I had ever seen, or so it seemed to me in that moment. There was a Faustian fire in his look, a world-swallowing urgency. Magellan must have looked that way sometimes, or Newton, or Galileo. And then in a moment more it was gone, and all I saw before me was a miserable scrawny boy, shrunken, feeble, pitifully frail.

* * *

I WENT TO TALK TO a physicist I knew, a friend of Timothy's father who did advanced research at the university. I said nothing about Timothy to him.

"What's a quantum well?" I asked him.

He looked puzzled. "Where'd you hear of those?"

"Someone I know. But I couldn't follow much of what he was saying."

"Extremely small switching device," he said. "Experimental, maybe five, ten years away. Less if we're very lucky. The idea is that you use two different semiconductive materials in a single crystal lattice, a superlattice, something like a three-dimensional checkerboard. Electrons tunneling between squares could be made to perform digital operations at tremendous speeds."

"And how small would this thing be, compared with the sort of transistors they have on chips now?"

"It would be down in the nanometer range," he told me. "That's a billionth of a meter. Smaller than a virus. Getting right down there close to the theoretical limits for semiconductivity. Any smaller and you'll be measuring things in angstroms."

"Angstroms?"

"One ten-billionth of a meter. We measure the diameter of atoms in angstrom units."

"Ah," I said. "All right. Can I ask you something else?"

He looked amused, patient, tolerant.

"Does anyone know much about what an electron looks like?"

"*Looks* like?"

"Its physical appearance. I mean, has any sort of work been done on examining them, maybe even photographing them—"

"You know about the Uncertainty Principle?" he asked.

"Well—not much, really—"

"Electrons are very damned tiny. They've got a mass of—ah—about nine times ten to the minus twenty-eighth grams. We need light in order to see, in any sense of the word. We see by receiving light radiated by an object, or by hitting it with light and getting a reflection. The smallest unit of light we can use, which is the photon, has such a long wavelength that it would completely hide an electron from view, so to speak. And we can't use radiation of shorter wavelength—gammas, let's say, or x-rays—for making our measurements, either, because the shorter the wavelength the greater the energy, and so a gamma ray would simply kick any electron we were going to inspect to hell and gone. So we can't 'see' electrons. The very act of determining their position imparts new velocity to them, which alters their position. The best we can do by way of examining electrons is make an enlightened guess, a probabilistic determination, of where they are and how fast they're moving. In a very rough way that's what we mean by the Uncertainty Principle."

"You mean, in order to look an electron in the eye, you'd virtually have to be the size of an electron yourself? Or even smaller?"

He gave me a strange look. "I suppose that question makes sense," he said. "And I suppose I could answer yes to it. But what the hell are we talking about, now?"

* * *

I DREAMED AGAIN THAT NIGHT: a feverish, disjointed dream of gigantic grotesque creatures shining with a fluorescent glow against a sky blacker than any night. They had claws, tentacles, eyes by the dozens. Their swollen asymmetrical bodies were bristling with thick red hairs. Some were clad in thick armor, others were equipped with ugly shining spikes that jutted in rows of ten or twenty from their quivering skins. They were pursuing me through the airless void. Wherever I ran there were more of them, crowding close. Behind them I saw the walls of the cosmos beginning to shiver and flow. The sky itself was dancing. Color was breaking through the blackness: eddying bands of every hue at once, interwoven like great chains. I ran, and I ran, and I ran, but there were monsters on every side, and no escape.

* * *

TIMOTHY MISSED AN APPOINTMENT. FOR some days now he had been growing more distant, often simply sitting silently, staring at me for the whole hour out of some hermetic sphere of unapproachability. That struck me as nothing more than predictable passive-aggressive resistance, but when he failed to show up at all I was startled: such blatant rebellion wasn't his expectable mode. Some new therapeutic strategies seemed in order: more direct intervention, with me playing the role of a gruff, loving older brother, or perhaps family therapy, or some meetings with his teachers and even classmates. Despite his recent aloofness I still felt I could get to him in time. But this business of skipping appointments was unacceptable. I phoned his mother the next day, only to learn that he was in the hospital; and after my last patient of the morning I drove across town to see him. The attending physician, a chunky-faced resident, turned frosty when I told him that I was Timothy's therapist, that I had been treating him for anorexia. I didn't need to be telepathic to know that he was thinking, *You didn't do much of a job with him, did you?* "His parents are with him now," he told me. "Let me find out if they want you to go in. It looks pretty bad."

Actually they were all there, parents, step-parents, the various children by the various second marriages. Timothy seemed to be no more than a waxen doll. They had brought him books, tapes, even a laptop computer, but everything was pushed to the corners of the bed. The shrunken figure in the middle barely raised the level of the coverlet a few inches. They had him on an IV unit and a whole webwork of other lines and cables ran to him from the array of medical machines surrounding him. His eyes were open, but he seemed to be staring into some other world, perhaps that same world of rampaging bacteria and quivering molecules that had haunted my sleep a few nights before. He seemed perhaps to be smiling.

"He collapsed at school," his mother whispered.

"In the computer lab, no less," said his father, with a nervous ratcheting laugh. "He was last conscious about two hours ago, but he wasn't talking coherently."

"He wants to go inside his computer," one of the little boys said. "That's crazy, isn't it?" He might have been seven.

"Timothy's going to die, Timothy's going to die," chanted somebody's daughter, about seven.

"Christopher! Bree! Shhh, both of you!" said about three of the various parents, all at once.

I said, "Has he started to respond to the IV?"

"They don't think so. It's not at all good," his mother said. "He's right on the edge. He lost three pounds this week. We thought he was eating, but he must have been sliding the food into his pocket, or something like that." She shook her head. "You can't be a policeman."

Her eyes were cold. So were her husband's, and even those of the step-parents. Telling me, *This is your fault, we counted on you to make him stop starving himself.* What could I say? You can only heal the ones you can reach. Timothy had been determined to keep himself beyond my grasp. Still, I felt the keenness of their reproachful anger, and it hurt.

"I've seen worse cases than this come back under medical treatment," I told them. "They'll build up his strength until he's capable of talking with me again. And then I'm certain I'll be able to lick this thing. I was just beginning to break through his defenses when—when he—"

Sure. It costs no more to give them a little optimism. I gave them what I could: experience with other cases of severe food deprivation, positive results following a severe crisis of this nature, et cetera, et cetera, the man of science dipping into his reservoir of experience. They all began to brighten as I spoke. They even managed to convince themselves that a little color was coming into Timothy's cheeks, that he was stirring, that he might soon be regaining consciousness as the machinery surrounding him pumped the nutrients into him that he had so conscientiously forbidden himself to have.

"Look," this one said, or that one. "Look how he's moving his hands! Look how he's breathing. It's better, isn't it!"

I actually began to believe it myself.

But then I heard his dry thin voice echoing in the caverns of my mind. *I can never get far enough. I have to be weightless in order to get there. Where I am now, it's only a beginning. I need to lose all the rest.*

I want to disappear.

* * *

THAT NIGHT, A THIRD DREAM, vivid, precise, concrete. I was falling and running at the same time, my legs pistoning like those of a marathon runner in the twenty-sixth mile, while simultaneously I dropped in free fall through airless dark toward the silver-black surface of some distant world. And fell and fell and fell, in utter weightlessness, and hit the surface easily and kept on running, moving not forward but downward, the atoms of the ground parting for me as I ran. I became smaller as I descended, and smaller yet, and even smaller, until I was a mere phantom, a running ghost, the bodiless idea of myself. And still I went downward toward the dazzling heart of things, shorn now of all impediments of the flesh.

I phoned the hospital the next morning. Timothy had died a little after dawn.

* * *

Did I fail with him? Well, then, I failed. But I think no one could possibly have succeeded. He went where he wanted to go; and so great was the force of his will that any attempts at impeding him must have seemed to him like the mere buzzings of insects, meaningless, insignificant.

So now his purpose is achieved. He has shed his useless husk. He has gone on, floating, running, descending: downward, inward, toward the core, where knowledge is absolute and uncertainty is unknown. He is running among the shining electrons, now. He is down there among the angstrom units at last.

LOOKING FOR THE FOUNTAIN

Then there are the voyages not into space or time but into alternative realities, worlds parallel to our own, separated from ours by some small fork in the path that has led to ever-widening differences. In the early months of 1991 my friend Gregory Benford told me that in conjunction with the redoubtable anthologist Martin H. Greenberg he would be editing another in their series of alternative-history anthologies under the title, *What Might Have Been*, and asked me to contribute to it. I had already written stories ("To the Promised Land" and "A Sleep and a Forgetting") for the first two volumes of the series, a couple of years earlier. Somehow I missed Volume Three, but now a fourth was being assembled—stories of Alternate Americas—and, calling on my knowledge of the exploration narratives of the Spanish conquistadores in the New World and throwing in a speculation about a vagrant band of Crusaders, I came up with this one, which saw print first in the May, 1992 issue of *Isaac Asimov's Science Fiction Magazine* before making its way into the anthology for which it was written.

My name is Francisco de Ortega and by the grace of God I am 89 years old and I have seen many a strange thing in my time, but nothing so strange as the Indian folk of the island called Florida, whose great dream it is to free the Holy Land from the Saracen conquerors that profane it.

It was fifty years ago that I encountered these marvelous people, when I sailed with his excellency the illustrious Don Juan Ponce de Leon on his famous and disastrous voyage in quest of what is wrongly called the Fountain of Youth. It was not a Fountain of Youth at all that he sought, but a Fountain of Manly Strength, which is somewhat a different thing. Trust me: I was there, I saw and heard everything, I was by Don Juan Ponce's side when his fate overtook him. I know the complete truth of this endeavor and I mean to set it all down now so there will be no doubt; for I alone survive to tell the tale, and as God is my witness I will tell it truthfully now, here in my ninetieth year, all praises be to Him and to the Mother who bore Him.

* * *

The matter of the Fountain, first.

Commonly, I know, it is called the Fountain of Youth. You will read that in many places, such as in the book about the New World which that Italian wrote who lived at Seville, Peter Martyr of Anghiera, where he says, "The governor of the Island of Borinquena, Juan Ponce de Leon, sent forth two caravels to seek the Islands of Boyuca in which the Indians affirmed there to be a fountain or spring whose water is of such marvelous virtue, that when it is drunk it makes old men young again."

This is true, so far as it goes. But when Peter Martyr talks of "making old men young again," his words must be interpreted in a poetic way.

Perhaps long life is truly what that Fountain really provides, along with its other and more special virtue—who knows? For I have tasted of that Fountain's waters myself, and here I am nearly 90 years of age and still full of vigor, I who was born in the year of our Lord 1473, and how many others are still alive today who came into the world then, when Castile and Aragon still were separate kingdoms? But I tell you that what Don Juan Ponce was seeking was not strictly speaking a Fountain of Youth at all, but rather a Fountain that offered a benefit of a very much more intimate kind. For I was there, I saw and heard everything. And they have cowardly tongues, those who say it was a Fountain of Youth, for it would seem that out of shame they choose not to speak honestly of the actual nature of the powers that the Fountain which we sought was supposed to confer.

It was when we were in the island of Hispaniola that we first heard of this wonderful Fountain, Don Juan Ponce and I. This was, I think, in the year 1504. Don Juan Ponce, a true nobleman and a man of high and elegant thoughts, was governor then in the province of Higuey of that island, which was ruled at that time by Don Nicolas de Ovando, successor to the great Admiral Cristobal Colon. There was in Higuey then a certain Indian cacique or chieftain of remarkable strength and force, who was reputed to keep seven wives and to satisfy each and every one of them each night of the week. Don Juan Ponce was curious about the great virility of this cacique, and one day he sent a certain Aurelio Herrera to visit him in his village.

"He does indeed have many wives," said Herrera, "though whether there were five or seven or fifty-nine I could not say, for there were women surrounding me all the time I was there, coming and going in such multitudes that I was unable to make a clear count, and swarms of children also, and from the looks of it the women were his wives and the children were his children."

"And what sort of manner of man is this cacique?" asked Don Juan Ponce.

"Why," said Herrera, "he is a very ordinary man, narrow of shoulders and shallow of chest, whom you would never think capable of such marvels of manhood, and he is past middle age besides. I remarked on this to him, and he said that when he was young he was easily exhausted and found the manly exercises a heavy burden. But then he journeyed to Boyuca, which is an island to the north of Cuba that is also called Bimini, and there he drank of a spring that cures the debility of sex. Since then, he asserts, he has been able to give pleasure to any number of women in a night without the slightest fatigue."

I was there. I saw and heard everything. *El enflaquecimiento del sexo* was the phrase that Aurelio Herrera used, "the debility of sex." The eyes of Don Juan Ponce de Leon opened wide at this tale, and he turned to me and said, "We must go in search of this miraculous fountain some day, Francisco, for there will be great profit in the selling of its waters."

Do you see? Not a word had been spoken about long life, but only about the curing of *el enflaquecimiento del sexo.* Nor was Don Juan Ponce in need of any such cure for himself, I assure you, for in the year 1504 he was just thirty years old, a lusty and aggressive man of fiery and restless spirit, and red-haired as well, and you know what is said about the virility of red-haired men. As for me, I will not boast, but I will say only that since the age of thirteen I have rarely gone a single night without a woman's company, and have been married four times, on the fourth occasion to a woman fifty years younger than myself. And if you find yourself in the province of Valladolid where I live and come to pay a call on me I can show you young Diego Antonio de Ortega whom you would think was my great-grandson, and little Juana Maria de Ortega who could be my great-granddaughter, for the boy is seven and the girl is five, but in truth they are my own children, conceived when I was past eighty years of age; and I have had many other sons and daughters too, some of whom are old people now and some are dead.

So it was not to heal our own debilities that Don Juan Ponce and I longed to find this wonderful Fountain, for of such shameful debilities we had none at all, he and I. No, we yearned for the Fountain purely for the sake of the riches we might derive from it: for each year saw hundreds or perhaps thousands of men come from Spain to the New World to seek their fortunes, and some of these were older men who no doubt suffered from a certain *enflaquecimiento.* In Spain I understand they use the powdered horn of the unicorn to cure this malady, or the crushed shells of a certain insect, though I have never had need of such things myself. But those commodities are not to be found in the New World, and it was Don Juan Ponce's hope that great profit might be made by taking possession of Bimini and selling the waters of the Fountain to those who had need of such a remedy. This is the truth, whatever others may claim.

* * *

BUT THE PURSUIT OF GOLD comes before everything, even the pursuit of miraculous Fountains of Manly Strength. We did not go at once in search of the Fountain because word came to Don Juan Ponce in Hispaniola that the neighboring island of Borinquen was rich in gold, and thereupon he applied to Governor Ovando for permission to go there and conquer it. Don Juan Ponce already somewhat knew that island, having seen its western coast briefly in 1493 when he was a gentleman volunteer in the fleet of Cristobal Colon, and its beauty had so moved him that he had resolved someday to return and make himself master of the place.

With one hundred men, he sailed over to this Borinquen in a small caravel, landing there on Midsummer Day, 1506, at the same bay he had visited earlier aboard the ship of the great Admiral. Seeing us arrive with such force, the cacique of the region was wise enough to yield to the inevitable and we took possession with very little fighting.

So rich did the island prove to be that we put the marvelous Fountain of which we had previously heard completely out of our minds. Don Juan Ponce was made governor of Borinquen by royal appointment and for several years the natives remained peaceful and we were able to obtain a great quantity of gold indeed. This is the same island that Cristobal Colon called San Juan Bautista and which people today call Puerto Rico.

All would have been well for us there but for the stupidity of a certain captain of our forces, Cristobal de Sotomayor, who treated the natives so badly that they rose in rebellion against us. This was in the year of our Lord 1511. So we found ourselves at war; and Don Juan Ponce fought with all the great valor for which he was renowned, doing tremendous destruction against our pagan enemies. We had among us at that time a certain dog, called Bercerillo, of red pelt and black eyes, who could tell simply by smell alone whether an Indian was friendly to us or hostile, and could understand the native speech as well; and the Indians were more afraid of ten Spaniards with this dog, than of one hundred without him. Don Juan Ponce rewarded Bercerillo's bravery and cleverness by giving the dog a full share of all the gold and slaves we captured, as though he were a crossbowman; but in the end the Indians killed him. I understand that a valiant pup of this Bercerillo, Leoncillo by name, went with Nunez de Balboa when he crossed the Isthmus of Panama and discovered the great ocean beyond.

During this time of our difficulties with the savages of Puerto Rico, Don Diego Colon, the son of the great Admiral, was able to take advantage of the trouble and make himself governor of the island in the place of Don Juan Ponce. Don Juan Ponce thereupon returned to Spain and presented himself before King Ferdinand, and told him the tale of the fabulous Fountain that restores manly power. King Ferdinand, who was greatly impressed by Don Juan Ponce's lordly bearing and noble appearance, at once granted him a royal permit to seek and conquer the isle of Bimini where this Fountain was said to be. Whether this signifies that His Most Catholic Majesty was troubled by debilities of a sexual sort, I would not dare to say. But the king was at that time a man of sixty years and it would not be unimaginable that some difficulty of that kind had begun to perplex him.

Swiftly Don Juan Ponce returned to Puerto Rico with the good news of his royal appointment, and on the third day of March of the year of our Lord 1513 we set forth from the Port of San German in three caravels to search for Bimini and its extraordinary Fountain.

I should say at this point that it was a matter of course that Don Juan Ponce should have asked me to take part in the quest for this Fountain. I am a man of Tervas de San Campos in the province of Valladolid, where Don Juan Ponce de Leon also was born less than one year after I was, and he and I played together as children and were friends all through our youth. As I have said, he first went to the New World in 1493, when he was nineteen years of age, as a gentleman aboard the ship of Admiral Cristobal Colon, and after settling in Hispaniola he wrote to me and told me of the great wealth of the New World and urged me to join him there. Which I did forthwith; and we were rarely separated from then until the day of his death.

Our flagship was the *Santiago*, with Diego Bermudez as its master—the brother to the man who discovered the isle of Bermuda—and the famous Anton de Alaminos as its pilot. We had two Indian pilots too, who knew the islands of that sea. Our second ship was the *Santa Maria de Consolacion*, with Juan Bono de Quexo as its captain, and the third was the *San Cristobal.* All of these vessels were purchased by Don Juan Ponce himself out of the riches he had laid by in the time when he was governor of Puerto Rico.

I have to tell you that there was not one priest in our company, not that we were ungodly men but only that it was not our commander's purpose on this voyage to bring the word of Jesus to the natives of Bimini. We did have some few women among us, including my own wife Beatriz, who had come out from Spain to be with me, and grateful I was to have her by my side; and my wife's young sister Juana was aboard the ship also, that I could better look after her among these rough Spaniards of the New World.

Northward we went. After ten days we halted at the isle of San Salvador to scrape weeds from the bottom of one of our ships. Then we journeyed west-northwest, passing the isle of Ciguateo on Easter Sunday, and, continuing onward into waters that ran ever shallower, we caught sight on the second day of April of a large delightful island of great and surpassing beauty, all blooming and burgeoning with a great host of wildflowers whose delectable odors came wafting to us on the warm gentle breeze. We named this isle La Florida, because Easter is the season when things flower and so we call that time of year in our language *Pascua Florida.* And we said to one another at once, seeing so beautiful a place, that this island of Florida must surely be the home of the wondrous Fountain that restores men to their fleshly powers and grants all their carnal desires to the fullest.

* * *

Of the loveliness of Florida I could speak for a day and a night and a night and a day, and not exhaust its marvels. The shallowing green waters give way to white crests of foam that fall upon beaches paved hard with tiny shells; and when you look beyond the beach you see dunes and marshes, and beyond those a land altogether level, not so much as a hillock upon it, where glistening sluggish lagoons bordered brilliantly with rushes and sedges show the way to the mysterious forests of the interior.

Those forests! Palms and pines, and gnarled gray trees whose names are known only to God! Trees covered with snowy beards! Trees whose leaves are like swords! Flowers everywhere, dizzying us with their perfume! We were stunned by the fragrance of jasmine and honeyflower. We heard the enchanting songs of a myriad of birds. We stared in wonder at the bright blooms. We doffed our helmets and dropped to our knees to give thanks to God for having led us to this most beautiful of shores.

Don Juan Ponce was the first of us to make his way to land, carrying with him the banner of Castile and Leon. He thrust the royal standard into the soft sandy soil and in the name of God and Spain took possession of the place. This was at the mouth of a river which he named in honor of his patron, the blessed San Juan. Then, since there were no Indians thereabouts who might lead us to the Fountain, we returned to our vessels and continued along the coast of that place.

Though the sea looked gentle we found the currents unexpectedly strong, carrying us northward so swiftly that we feared we would never see Puerto Rico again. Therefore did Don Juan Ponce give orders for us to turn south; but although we had a fair following wind the current was so strong against us that we could make no headway, and at last we were compelled to anchor in a cove. Here we spent some days, with the ships straining against their cables; and during that time the little *San Cristobal* was swept out to sea and we lost sight of her altogether, though the day was bright and the weather fair. But within two days by God's grace she returned to us.

At this time we saw our first Indians, but they were far from friendly. Indeed they set upon us at once and two of our men were wounded by their little darts and arrows, which were tipped with sharp points made of bone. When night came we were able to withdraw and sail on to another place that we called the Rio de la Cruz, where we collected wood and water; and here we were attacked again, by sixty Indians, but they were driven off. And so we continued for many days, until in latitude 28 degrees 15 minutes we did round a cape, which we called Cabo de los Corrientes on account of the powerful currents, which were stronger than the wind.

Here it was that we had the strangest part of our voyage, indeed the strangest thing I have ever seen in all my ninety years. Which is to say that we encountered at this time in this remote and hitherto unknown land the defenders of the Christian Faith, the sworn foes of the Saracens, the last sons of the Crusades, whose great dream it was, even now, to wrest the Holy Land of our Savior's birth from those infidel followers of Muhammad who seized it long ago and rule it today.

We suspected nothing of any of what awaited us when we dropped our anchors near an Indian town on the far side of Cabo de los Corrientes. Cautiously, for we had received such a hostile reception farther up the coast, we made our landfall a little way below the village and set about the task of filling our water casks and cutting firewood. While this work was being carried out we became aware that the Indians had left their village and had set out down the shore to encounter us, for we heard them singing and chanting even before we could see them; and we halted in our labors and made ourselves ready to deal with another attack.

After a short while the Indians appeared, still singing as they approached. Wonder of wonders, they were clothed, though all the previous natives that we had seen were naked, or nearly so, as these savages usually are. Even more marvelous was the nature of their clothing, which was of a kind not very different from that which Christians wear, jerkins and doublets and tunics, and such things. And—marvel of marvel—every man of them wore upon his chest a white garment that bore the holy cross of Jesus painted brightly in red! We could not believe our eyes. But if we had any doubt that these were Christian men, it was eradicated altogether when we saw that in the midst of the procession came certain men wearing the dark robes of priests, who carried great wooden crosses held high aloft.

Were these indeed Indians? Surely not! Surely they must be Spaniards like ourselves! We might almost have been in Toledo, or Madrid, or Seville, and not on the shore of some strange land of the Indies! But indeed we saw without doubt now that the marchers were men of the sort that is native to the New World, with the ruddy skins and black hair and sharp features of their kind, Christian though they might be in dress, and carrying the cross itself in their midst.

When they were close enough so that we could hear distinctly the words of their song, it sounded to some of us that they might be Latin words, though Latin of a somewhat barbarous kind. Could that be possible? We doubted the evidence of our ears. But then Pedro de Plasencia, who had studied for the priesthood before entering the military, crossed himself most vigorously and said to us in wonder, "Do you hear that? They are singing the *Gloria in excelsis Deo*!" And in truth we could tell that hymn was what they sang, now that Pedro de Plasencia had picked out the words of it for us. Does that sound strange to you, that Indians of an unknown isle should be singing in Latin? Yes, it is strange indeed. But doubt me at your peril. I was there; I saw and heard everything myself.

"Surely," said Diego Bermudez, "there must have been Spaniards here before us, who have instructed these people in the way of God."

"That cannot be," said our pilot, Anton de Alaminos. "For I was with Cristobal Colon on his second voyage and have been on every voyage since of any note that has been made in these waters, and I can tell you that no white man has set foot on this shore before us."

"Then how came these Indians by their crosses and their holy hymns?" asked Diego Bermudez. "Is it a pure miracle of the saints, do you think?"

"Perhaps it is," said Don Juan Ponce de Leon, with some heat, for it looked as if there might be a quarrel between the master and the pilot. "Who can say? Be thankful that these folk are our Christian friends and not our enemy, and leave off your useless speculations."

And in the courageous way that was his nature, Don Juan Ponce went forward and raised his arms to the Indians, and made the sign of the cross in the air, and called out to them, saying, "I am Don Juan Ponce de Leon of Valladolid in the land of Spain, and I greet you in the name of the Father, and of the Son, and of the Holy Ghost." All of which he said clearly and loudly in his fine and beautiful Castilian, which he spoke with the greatest purity. But the Indians, who by now had halted in a straight line before us, showed no understanding in their eyes. Don Juan Ponce spoke again, once more in Spanish, saying that he greeted them also in the name of His Most Catholic Majesty King Ferdinand of Aragon and Castile. This too produced no sign that it had been understood.

One of the Indians then spoke. He was a man of great presence and bearing, who wore chains of gold about his chest and carried a sword of strange design at his side, the first sword I had ever seen a native of these islands to have. From these indications it was apparent that he was the cacique.

He spoke long and eloquently in a language that I suppose was his own, for none of us had ever heard it before, not even the two Indian pilots we had brought with us. Then he said a few words that had the sound and the ring of French or perhaps Catalan, though we had a few men of Barcelona among us who leaned close toward him and put their hands to their ears and even they could make no sense out of what they heard.

But then finally this grand cacique spoke words which we all could understand plainly, garbled and thick-tongued though his speaking of them was: for what he said was, and there could be no doubt of it however barbarous his accent, "*In nomine Patris, et Filii, et Spiritus Sancti,*" and he made the sign of the cross over his chest as any good Christian man would do. To which Don Juan replied, "*Amen. Dominus vobiscum.*" Whereupon the cacique, exclaiming, "*Et cum spiritu tuo,*" went forthrightly to the side of Don Juan Ponce, and they embraced with great love, likewise as any Christian men might do, here on this remote beach in this strange and lovely land of Florida.

* * *

THEY BROUGHT US THEN TO their village and offered a great feast for us, with roasted fish and the meat of tortoises and sweet fruits of many mysterious kinds, and made us presents of the skins of animals. For our part we gave them such trinkets as we had carried with us, beads and bracelets and little copper daggers and the like, but of all the things we gave them they were most eager to receive the simple figurines of Jesus on the cross that we offered them, and passed them around amongst themselves in wonder, showing such love for them as if they were made of the finest gold and studded with emeralds and rubies. And we said privately to each other that we must be dreaming, to have met with Indians in this land who were of such great devotion to the faith.

We tried to speak with them again in Spanish, but it was useless, and so too was speaking in any of the native tongues of Hispaniola or Puerto Rico that we knew. In their turn they addressed us in their own language, which might just as well have been the language of the people of the Moon for all we comprehended it, and also in that tantalizing other tongue which seemed almost to be French or Catalan. We could not make anything of that, try though we did. But Pedro de Plasencia, who was the only one of us who could speak Latin out loud like a priest, sat down with the cacique after the meal and addressed him in that language. I mean not simply saying things like the Pater Noster and the Ave Maria, which any child can say, but speaking to him as if Latin was a real language with words and sentences of common meaning, the way it was long ago. To which the cacique answered, though he seemed to be framing his words with much difficulty; and Pedro answered him again, just as hesitatingly; and so they went on, talking to each other in a slow and halting way, far into the night, nodding and smiling most jubilantly whenever one of them reached some understanding of the other's words, while we looked on in astonishment, unable to fathom a word of what they were saying.

At last Pedro rose, looking pale and exhausted like a man who has carried a bull on his back for half a league, and came over to us where we were sitting in a circle.

"Well?" Don Juan Ponce demanded at once.

Pedro de Plasencia shook his head wearily. "It was all nonsense, what the cacique said. I understood nothing. Nothing at all! It was mere incomprehensible babble and no more than that." And he picked up a leather sack of wine that lay near his feet and drank from it as though he had a thirst that no amount of drinking ever could quench.

"You appeared to comprehend, at times," said Don Juan Ponce. "Or so it seemed to me as I watched you."

"Nothing. Not a word. Let me sleep on it, and perhaps it will come clear to me in the morning."

I thought Don Juan Ponce would pursue him on the matter. But Don Juan Ponce, though he was an impatient and high-tempered man, was also a man of great sagacity, and he knew better than to press Pedro further at a time when he seemed so troubled and fatigued. So he dismissed the company and we settled down in the huts that the Indians had given us for lodging, all except those of us who were posted as sentries during the night to guard against treachery.

I rose before dawn. But I saw that Don Juan Ponce and Pedro de Plasencia were already awake and had drawn apart from the rest of us and were talking most earnestly. After a time they returned, and Don Juan Ponce beckoned to me.

"Pedro has told me something of his conversation with the cacique," he said.

"And what is it that you have learned?"

"That these Indians are indeed Christians."

"Yes, that seems to be the plain truth, strange though it seems," I said. "For they do carry the cross about, and sing the *Gloria,* and honor the Father and the Son."

"There is more."

I waited.

He continued, "Unless Pedro much mistook what the cacique told him, the greatest hope in which these people live is that of wresting the Holy Land from the Saracen, and restoring it to good Christian pilgrims."

At that I burst out into such hearty laughter that Don Juan Ponce, for all his love of me, looked at me with eyes flashing with reproof. Yet I could not withhold my mirth, which poured from me like a river.

I said at last, when I had mastered myself, "But tell me, Don Juan, what would these savages know of the Holy Land, or of Saracens, or any such thing? The Holy Land is thousands of leagues away, and has never been spoken of so much as once in this New World by any man, I think; nor does anyone speak of the Crusade any longer in this age, neither here nor at home."

"It is very strange, I agree," replied Don Juan Ponce. "Nevertheless, so Pedro swears, the cacique spoke to him of *Terra Sancta, Terra Sancta,* and of infidels, and the liberation of the city of Jerusalem."

"And how does it come to pass," I asked, "that they can know of such things, in this remote isle, where no white man has ever visited before?"

"Ah," said Don Juan Ponce, "that is the great mystery, is it not?"

* * *

In time we came to understand the solution to this mystery, though the tale was muddled and confused, and emerged only after much travail, and long discussions between Pedro de Plasencia and the cacique of the Indians. I will tell you the essence of it, which was this:

Some three hundred years ago, or perhaps it was four hundred, while much of our beloved Spain still lay under the Moorish hand, a shipload of Frankish warriors set sail from the port of Genoa, or perhaps it was Marseilles, or some other city along the coast of Provence. This was in the time when men still went crusading, to make war for Jesus' sake in the Holy Land against the followers of Muhammad who occupied that place.

But the voyage of these Crusaders miscarried; for when they entered the great Mar Mediterraneo, thinking to go east they were forced west by terrible storms and contrary winds, and swept helpless past our Spanish shores, past Almeria and Malaga and Tarifa, and through the narrow waist of the Estrecho de Gibraltar and out into the vastness of the Ocean Sea.

Here, having no sound knowledge as we in our time do of the size and shape of the African continent, they thought to turn south and then east below Egypt and make their voyage yet to the Holy Land. Of course this would be impossible, except by rounding the Buena Fortuna cape and traveling up past Arabia, a journey almost beyond our means to this day. But being unaware of that, these bold but hapless men made the attempt, coasting southerly and southerly and southerly, and the land of course not only not ending but indeed carrying them farther and farther outward into the Ocean Sea, until at last, no doubt weary and half dead of famine, they realized that they had traveled so far to the west that there was no hope of returning eastward again, nor of turning north and making their way back into the Mediterraneo. So they yielded to the westerly winds that prevail near the Canary Isles, and allowed themselves to be blown clear across the sea to the Indies. And so after long arduous voyaging they made landfall in this isle we call Florida. Thus these men of three hundred years ago were the first discoverers of the New World, although I doubt very greatly that they comprehended what it was that they had achieved.

You must understand that we received few of these details from our Indian hosts: only the tale that men bound to Terra Sancta departing from a land in the east were blown off course some hundreds of years previous and were brought after arduous sailing to the isle of Florida and to this very village where our three caravels had made their landfall. All the rest did we conclude for ourselves, that they were Crusaders and so forth, after much discussing of the matter and recourse to the scholarship that the finest men among us possessed.

And what befell these men of the Crusade, when they came to this Florida? Why, they offered themselves to the mercies of the villagers, who greeted them right honorably and took them to dwell amongst them, and married them to their daughters! And for their part the seafarers offered the word of Jesus to the people of the village and thereby gave them hope of Heaven; and taught these kindly savages the Latin tongue so well that it remained with them after a fashion hundreds of years afterward, and also some vestiges of the common speech that the seafaring men had had in their own native land.

But most of all did the strangers from the sea imbue in the villagers the holy desire to rid the birthplace of Jesus of the dread hand of the Mussulman; and ever, in years after, did the Christian Indians of this Florida village long to put to sea, and cross the great ocean, and wield their bows and spears valiantly amidst the paynim enemy in the defense of the True Faith. Truly, how strange are the workings of God Almighty, how far beyond our comprehension, that He should make Crusaders out of the naked Indians in this far-off place!

You may ask what became of those European men who landed there, and whether we saw anyone who plainly might mark his descent from them. And I will tell you that those ancient Crusaders, who intermarried with the native women since they had brought none of their own, were wholly swallowed up by such intermarrying and were engulfed by the fullness of time. For they were only forty or fifty men among hundreds, and the passing centuries so diluted the strain of their race that not the least trace of it remained, and we saw no pale skin or fair hair or blue eyes or other marks of European men here. But the ideas that they had fetched to this place did survive, that is, the practicing of the Catholic faith and the speaking of a debased and corrupt sort of Latin and the wearing of a kind of European clothes, and such. And I tell you it was passing strange to see these red savages in their surplices and cassocks, and in their white tunics bearing the great emblem of our creed, and other such ancient marks of our civilization, and to hear them chanting the *Kyrie eleison* and the *Confiteor* and the *Sanctus, Sanctus, Sanctus Dominus Deus Sabaoth* in that curious garbled way of theirs, like words spoken in a dream.

Nay, I have spoken untruthfully, for the men of that lost voyage did leave other remnants of themselves among the villagers beside our holy faith, which I have neglected to mention here, but which I will tell you of now.

For after we had been in that village several days, the cacique led us through the close humid forest along a tangled trail to a clearing nearby just to the north of the village, and here we saw certain tangible remains of the voyagers: a graveyard with grave markers of white limestone, and the rotting ribs and strakes and some of the keel of a seafaring vessel of an ancient design, and the foundation walls of a little wooden church. All of which things were as sad a sight as could be imagined, for the gravestones were so weathered and worn that although we could see the faint marks of names we could not read the names themselves, and the vessel was but a mere sorry remnant, a few miserable decaying timbers, and the church was only a pitiful fragment of a thing.

We stood amidst these sorry ruins and our hearts were struck into pieces by pity and grief for these brave men, so far from home and lonely, who in this strange place had nevertheless contrived to plant the sacred tree of Christianity. And the noble Don Juan Ponce de Leon went down on his knees before the church and bowed his head and said, "Let us pray, my friends, for the souls of these men, as we hope that someday people will pray for ours."

* * *

WE SPENT SOME DAYS AMONGST these people in feasting and prayer, and replenishing our stock of firewood and water. And then Don Juan Ponce gave new thought to the primary purpose of our voyage, which was, to find the miraculous Fountain that renews a man's energies. He called Pedro de Plasencia to his side and said, "Ask of the cacique, whether he knows such a Fountain."

"It will not be easy, describing such things in my poor Latin," answered Pedro. "I had my Latin from the Church, Don Juan, and what I learned there is of little use here, and it was all so very long ago."

"You must try, my friend. For only you of all our company has the power to speak with him and be understood."

Whereupon Pedro went to the cacique; but I could see even at a distance that he was having great difficulties. For he would speak a few halting words, and then he would act out his meaning with gestures, like a clown upon a stage, and then he would speak again. There would be silence; and then the cacique would reply, and I would see Pedro leaning forward most intently, trying to catch the meaning of the curious Latin that the cacique spoke. They did draw pictures for each other also in the sand, and point to the sky and sweep their arms to and fro, and do many another thing to convey to each other the sense of their words, and so it went, hour after hour.

At length Pedro de Plasencia returned to where we stood, and said, "There does appear to be a source of precious water that they cherish on this island, which they call the Blue Spring."

"And is this Blue Spring the Fountain for which we search?" Don Juan Ponce asked, all eagerness.

"Ah, of that I am not certain."

"Did you tell him that the water of it would allow a man to take his pleasure with women all day and all night, and never tire of it?"

"So I attempted to say."

"With many women, one after another?"

"These are Christian folk, Don Juan!"

"Yes, so they are. But they are Indians also. They would understand such a thing, just as any man of Estremadura or Galicia or Andalusia would understand such a thing, Christian though he be."

Pedro de Plasencia nodded. "I told him what I could, about the nature of the Fountain for which we search. And he listened very close, and he said, Yes, yes, you are speaking of the Blue Spring."

"So he understood you, then?"

"He understood something of what I said, Don Juan, so I do firmly believe. But whether he understood it all, that is only for God to know."

I saw the color rise in Don Juan Ponce's face, and I knew that that restless choleric nature of his was coming to the fore, which had always been his great driving force and also his most perilous failing.

He said to Pedro de Plasencia, "And will he take us to this Blue Spring of his, do you think?"

"I think he will," said Pedro. "But first he wishes to enact a treaty with us, as the price of transporting us thither."

"A treaty."

"A treaty, yes. He wants our aid and assistance."

"Ah," said Don Juan Ponce. "And how can we be of help to these people, do you think?"

"They want us to show them how to build seafaring ships," said Pedro. "So that they can sail across the Ocean Sea, and go to the rescue of the Holy Land, and free it from the paynim hordes."

* * *

THERE WAS MUCH MORE OF back and forth, and forth and back, in these negotiations, until Pedro de Plasencia grew weary indeed, and there was not enough wine in our sacks to give him the rest he needed, so that we had to send a boat out to fetch more from one of our ships at anchor in the harbor. For it was a great burden upon him to conduct these conversations, he remembering only little patches of Church Latin from his boyhood, and the cacique speaking a language that could be called Latin only by great courtesy. I sat with them as they talked, on several occasions, and not for all my soul could I understand a thing that they said to each other. From time to time Pedro would lose his patience and speak out in Spanish, or the cacique would begin to speak in his savage tongue or else in that other language, somewhat like Provencal, which must have been what the seafaring Crusaders spoke amongst themselves. But none of that added to the understanding between the two men, which I think was a very poor understanding indeed.

It became apparent after a time that Pedro had misheard the cacique's terms of treaty: what he wished us to do was not to teach them how to build ships but to give them one of ours in which to undertake their Crusade.

"It cannot be," replied Don Juan Ponce, when he had heard. "But tell him this, that I will undertake to purchase ships for him with my own funds, in Spain. Which I will surely do, after we have received the proceeds from the sale of the water from the Fountain."

"He wishes to know how many ships you will provide," said Pedro de Plasencia, after another conference.

"Two," said Don Juan Ponce. "No: three. Three fine caravels."

Which Pedro duly told the cacique; but his way of telling him was to point to our three ships in the harbor, which led the cacique into thinking that Don Juan Ponce meant to give him those three actual ships then and now, and that required more hours of conferring to repair. But at length all was agreed on both sides, and our journey toward the Blue Spring was begun.

The cacique himself accompanied us, and the three priests of the tribe, carrying the heavy wooden crosses that were their staffs of office, and perhaps two dozen of the young men and girls of the village. In our party there were ten men, Don Juan Ponce and Pedro and I, and seven ordinary seamen carrying barrels in which we meant to store the waters of the Fountain. My wife Beatriz and her sister Juana accompanied us also, for I never would let them be far from me.

Some of the ordinary seamen among us were rough men of Estremadura, who spoke jestingly and with great licentiousness of how often they would embrace the girls of the native village after they had drunk of the Fountain. I had to silence them, reminding them that my wife and her sister could overhear their words. Yet I wondered privately what effects the waters would have on my own manhood: not that it had ever been lacking in any aspect, but I could not help asking myself if I would find it enhanced beyond its usual virtue, for such curiosity is but a natural thing to any man, as you must know.

We journeyed for two days, through hot close terrain where insects of great size buzzed among the flowers and birds of a thousand colors astounded our eyes. And at last we came to a place of bare white stone, flat like all other places in this isle of Florida, where clear cool blue water gushed up out of the ground with wondrous force.

The cacique gestured grandly, with a great sweep of his arms.

"It is the Blue Spring," said Pedro de Plasencia.

Our men would have rushed forward at once to lap up its waters like greedy dogs at a pond; but the cacique cried out, and Don Juan Ponce also in that moment ordered them to halt. There would be no unseemly haste here, he said. And it was just as well he did, for we very soon came to see that this spring was a holy place to the people of the village, and it would have been profaned by such an assault on it, to our possible detriment and peril.

The cacique came forward, with his priests beside him, and gestured to Don Juan Ponce to kneel and remove his helmet. Don Juan

Ponce obeyed; and the cacique took his helmet from him, and passed it to one of the priests, who filled it with water from the spring and poured it down over Don Juan Ponce's face and neck, so that Don Juan Ponce laughed out loud. The which laughter seemed to offend the Indians, for they showed looks of disapproval, and Don Juan Ponce at once grew silent.

The Indians spoke words which might almost have been Latin words, and there was much elevating of their crosses as the water was poured down over Don Juan Ponce, after which he was given the order to rise.

And then one by one we stepped forth, and the Indians did the same to each of us.

"It is very like a rite of holy baptism, is it not?" said Aurelio Herrera to me.

"Yes, very much like a baptism," I said to him.

And I began to wonder: How well have we been understood here? Is it a new access of manly strength that these Indians are conferring upon us, or rather the embrace of the Church? For surely there is nothing about this rite that speaks of anything else than a religious enterprise. But I kept silent, since it was not my place to speak.

When the villagers were done dousing us with water, and speaking words over us and elevating their crosses, which made me more sure than ever that we were being taken into the congregation of their faith, we were allowed to drink of the spring—they did the same—and to fill our barrels. Don Juan Ponce turned to me after we had drunk, and winked at me and said, "Well, old friend, this will serve us well in later years, will it not? For though we have no need of such invigoration now, you and I, nevertheless time will have its work with us as it does with all men."

"If it does," I said, "why, then, we are fortified against it now indeed."

But in truth I felt no change within. The water was pure and cool and good, but it had seemed merely to be water to me, with no great magical qualities about it; and when I turned and looked upon my wife Beatriz, she seemed pleasing to me as she always had, but no more than that. Well, so be it, I thought; this may be the true Fountain or maybe it is not, and only time will tell; and we began our return to the village, carrying the casks of water with us; and the day of our return, Pedro de Plasencia drew up a grand treaty on a piece of bark from a tree, in which we pledged our sacred honor and our souls to do all in our power to supply this village with good Spanish ships so that the villagers would be able to fulfill their pledge to liberate the Holy Land.

"Which we will surely do for them," said Don Juan Ponce with great conviction. "For I mean to come back to this place as soon as I am able, with many ships of our own as well as the vessels I have promised them from Spain; and we will fill our holds with cask upon cask of this virtuous water from the Fountain, and replenish our fortunes anew by selling that water to those who need its miraculous power. Moreover we ourselves will benefit from its use in our declining days. And also we will bring this cacique some priests, who will correct him in his manner of practicing our faith, and guide him in his journey to Jerusalem. All of which I will swear by a great oath upon the Cross itself, in the presence of the cacique, so that he may have no doubt whatsoever of our kindly Christian purposes."

* * *

AND SO WE DEPARTED, FILLED with great joy and no little wonder at all that we had seen and heard.

Well, and none of the brave intentions of Don Juan Ponce were fulfilled, as you surely must know, inasmuch as the valiant Don Juan Ponce de Leon never saw Spain again, nor did he live to enjoy the rejuvenations of his body that he hoped the water of the Fountain would bring him in his later years. For when we left the village of the Indian Crusaders, we continued on our way along the coast of the isle of Florida a little further in a southerly direction, seeking to catch favorable winds and currents that would carry us swiftly back to Puerto Rico; and on the 23rd of May we halted in a pleasing bay to gather wood and water—for we would not touch the water of our casks from the Fountain!—and to careen the *San Cristobal*, the hull of which was fouled with barnacles. And as we did our work there, a party of Indians came forth out of the woods.

"Hail, brothers in Christ!" Don Juan Ponce called to them with great cheer, for the cacique had told him that his people had done wonderful things in bringing their neighbors into the embrace of Jesus, and he thought now that surely all the Indians of this isle had been converted to the True Faith by those Crusading men of long ago.

But he was wrong in that; for these Indians were no Christians at all, but only pagan savages like most of their kind, and they replied instantly to Don Juan Ponce's halloos with a volley of darts and arrows that struck five of us dead then and there before we were able to drive them off. And among those who took his mortal wound that day was the valiant and noble Don Juan Ponce de Leon of Valladolid, in the thirty-ninth year of his life.

I knelt beside him on the beach in his last moments, and said the last words with him. And he looked up at me and smiled—for death had never been frightening to him—and he said to me, almost with his last breath, "There is only one thing that I regret, Francisco. And that is that I will never know, now, what powers the water of that Fountain would have conferred upon me, when I was old and greatly stricken with the frailty of my years." With that he perished.

What more can I say? We made our doleful way back to Puerto Rico, and told our tale of Crusaders and Indians and cool blue waters. But we were met with laughter, and there were no purchasers for the contents of our casks, and our fortunes were greatly depleted. All praise be to God, I survived that dark time and went on afterward to join the magnificent Hernando Cortes in his conquest of the land of Mexico, which today is called New Spain, and in the fullness of time I returned to my native province of Valladolid with much gold in my possession, and here I live in health and vigor to this day.

Often do I think of the isle of Florida and those Christian Indians we found there. It is fifty years since that time. In those fifty years the cacique and his people have rendered most of Florida into Christians by now, as we now know, and I tell you what is not generally known, that this expansion of their nation was brought about the better to support their Crusade against the Mussulman once the ships that Don Juan Ponce promised them had arrived.

So there is a great warlike Christian kingdom in Florida today, filling all that land and spreading over into adjacent isles, against which we men of Spain so far have struggled in vain as we attempt to extend our sway to those regions. I think it was poor Don Juan Ponce de Leon, in his innocent quest for a miraculous Fountain, who without intending it caused them to become so fierce, by making them a promise which he could not fulfill, and leaving them thinking that they had been betrayed by false Christians. Better that they had remained forever in the isolation in which they lived when we found them, singing the *Gloria* and the *Credo* and the *Sanctus*, and waiting with Christian patience for the promised ships that are to take them to the reconquest of the Holy Land. But those ships did not come; and they see us now as traitors and enemies.

I often think also of the valiant Don Juan Ponce, and his quest for the wondrous Fountain. Was the Blue Spring indeed the Fountain of legend? I am not sure of that. It may be that those Indians misunderstood what Pedro de Plasencia was requesting of them, and that they were simply offering us baptism—us, good Christians all our lives!—when what we sought was something quite different from that.

But if the Fountain was truly the one we sought, I feel great sorrow and pity for Don Juan Ponce. For though he drank of its waters, he died too soon to know of its effects. Whereas here I am, soon to be ninety years old, and the father of a boy of seven and a girl of five.

Was it the Fountain's virtue that has given me so long and robust a life, or have I simply enjoyed the favor of God? How can I say? Whichever it is, I am grateful; and if ever there is peace between us and the people of the isle of Florida, and you should find yourself in the vicinity of that place, you could do worse, I think, than to drink of that Blue Spring, which will do you no harm and may perhaps bring you great benefit. If by chance you go to that place, seek out the Indians of the village nearby, and tell them that old Francisco de Ortega remembers them, and cherishes the memory, and more than once has said a Mass in their praise despite all the troubles they have caused his countrymen, for he knows that they are the last defenders of the Holy Land against the paynim infidels.

This is my story, and the story of Don Juan Ponce de Leon and the miraculous Fountain, which the ignorant call the Fountain of Youth, and of the Christian Indians of Florida who yearn to free the Holy Land. You may wonder about the veracity of these things, but I beg you, have no doubt on that score. All that I have told you is true. For I was there. I saw and heard everything.

SHIP-SISTER, STAR-SISTER

At the time I wrote this story—November, 1972—I was going through a prolonged period of skepticism about the value and merit of science fiction. I was having difficulties making myself believe in the classic furnishings of s-f: all those starships, telepaths, galactic empires, and time machines, all the stuff I had been dealing with as reader and writer for twenty-plus years, had become monstrously unreal, implausible, impossible to me.

That seemed like an unhealthy attitude for a science fiction writer to hold; and so, when that hyperactive anthology editor Roger Elwood asked me for a longish story for a book called *Tomorrow's Alternatives*, I took a deep breath and reached for one of the most far-out Stapledonian concepts in my science fiction idea file, a voyage of the strangest sort into the most remote regions of the galaxy, figuring that if I could write that with some conviction, I'd be able to handle less audacious themes without any problem afterward. Somehow it worked. While I was writing "Ship-Sister" I made myself believe in half a dozen different astonishments at once, long enough (five weeks) for me to bring off this story in, I hope, fairly convincing manner.

When I wrote an introduction to "Ship-Sister" in 1992 for an earlier collection of my stories, I concluded by saying, "The material of this story still fascinates me and I have a feeling that I may return to it some day and deal with it at book length." Indeed so. I did just that very thing a couple of years later, expanding the original novelette into the novel *Starborne*, which was published in 1996.

SIXTEEN LIGHT-YEARS FROM EARTH TODAY, in the fifth month of the voyage, and the silent throb of acceleration continues to drive the velocity higher. Three games of Go are in progress in the ship's lounge. The year-captain stands at the entrance to the lounge, casually watching the players: Roy and Sylvia, Leon and Chiang, Heinz and Elliot. Go has been a craze aboard ship for weeks. The players —some eighteen or twenty members of the expedition have caught the addiction by now—sit hour after hour, contemplating strategies, devising variations, grasping the smooth black or white stones between forefinger and second finger, putting the stones down against the wooden board with the proper smart sharp clacking sound. The year-captain himself does not play, though the game once interested him to the point of obsession, long ago; he finds his responsibilities so draining that an exercise in simulated territorial conquest does not attract him now. He comes here often to watch, however, remaining five or ten minutes, then going on about his duties.

The best of the players is Roy, the mathematician, a large, heavy man with a soft sleepy face. He sits with his eyes closed, awaiting in tranquility his turn to play. "I am purging myself of the need to win," he told the year-captain yesterday when asked what occupies his mind while he waits. Purged or not, Roy wins more than half of his games, even though he gives most of his opponents a handicap of four or five stones.

He gives Sylvia a handicap of only two. She is a delicate woman, fine-boned and shy, a geneticist, and she plays well although slowly. She makes her move. At the sound of it Roy opens his eyes. He studies the board, points, and says, *"Atari,"* the conventional way of calling to his opponent's attention the fact that her move will enable him to capture several of her stones. Sylvia laughs lightly and retracts her move. After a moment she moves again. Roy nods and picks up a white stone, which he holds for nearly a minute before he places it.

The year-captain would like to speak with Sylvia about one of her experiments, but he sees she will be occupied with the game for another hour or more. The conversation can wait. No one hurries aboard this ship. They have plenty of time for everything: a lifetime, maybe, if no habitable planet can be found. The universe is theirs. He scans the board and tries to anticipate Sylvia's next move. Soft footsteps sound behind him. The year-captain turns. Noelle, the ship's communicator, is approaching the lounge. She is a slim sightless girl with long dark hair, and she customarily walks the corridors unaided: no sensors for her, not even a cane. Occasionally she stumbles, but usually her balance is excellent and her sense of the location of obstacles is superb. It is a kind of arrogance for the blind to shun assistance, perhaps. But also it is a kind of desperate poetry.

As she comes up to him she says, "Good morning, year-captain."

Noelle is infallible in making such identifications. She claims to be able to distinguish members of the expedition by the tiny characteristic sounds they make: their patterns of breathing, their coughs, the rustling of their clothing. Among the others there is some skepticism about this. Many aboard the ship believe that Noelle is reading their minds. She does not deny that she possesses the power of telepathy; but she insists that the only mind to which she has direct access is that of her twin sister Yvonne, far away on Earth.

He turns to her. His eyes meet hers: an automatic act, a habit. Hers, dark and clear, stare disconcertingly through his forehead. He says, "I'll have a report for you to transmit in about two hours."

"I'm ready whenever." She smiles faintly. She listens a moment to the clacking of the Go stones. "Three games being played?" she asks.

"Yes."

"How strange that the game hasn't begun to lose its hold on them by this time."

"Its grip is powerful," the year-captain says.

"It must be. How good it is to be able to give yourself so completely to a game."

"I wonder. Playing Go consumes a great deal of valuable time."

"Time?" Noelle laughs. "What is there to do with time, except to consume it?" After a moment she says, "Is it a difficult game?"

"The rules are simple enough. The application of the rules is another matter entirely. It's a deeper and more subtle game than chess, I think."

Her blank eyes wander across his face and suddenly lock into his. "How long would it take for me to learn how to play?"

"You?"

"Why not? I also need amusement, year-captain."

"The board has hundreds of intersections. Moves may be made at any of them. The patterns formed are complex and constantly changing. Someone who is unable to see—"

"My memory is excellent," Noelle says. "I can visualize the board and make the necessary corrections as play proceeds. You need only tell me where you put down your stones. And guide my hand, I suppose, when I make my moves."

"I doubt that it'll work, Noelle."

"Will you teach me anyway?"

* * *

THE SHIP IS SLEEK, TAPERED, graceful: a silver bullet streaking across the universe at a velocity that has at this point come to exceed a million kilometers per second. No. In fact the ship is no bullet at all, but rather something squat and awkward, as clumsy as any ordinary spacegoing vessel, with an elaborate spidery superstructure of extensor arms and antennas and observation booms and other externals. Yet because of its incredible speed the year-captain persists in thinking of it as sleek and tapered and graceful. It carries him without friction through the vast empty gray cloak of nospace at a velocity greater than that of light. He knows better, but he is unable to shake that streamlined image from his mind.

Already the expedition is sixteen light-years from Earth. That isn't an easy thing for him to grasp. He feels the force of it, but not the true meaning. He can tell himself, *Already we are sixteen kilometers from home,* and understand that readily enough. *Already we are sixteen hundred kilometers from home*—yes, he can understand that too. What about *Already we are sixteen million kilometers from home?* That much strains comprehension—a gulf, a gulf, a terrible empty dark gulf—but he thinks he is able to understand even so great a distance, after a fashion. Sixteen light-years, though? How can he explain that to himself? Brilliant stars flank the tube of nospace through which the ship now travels, and he knows that his gray-flecked beard will have turned entirely white before the light of those stars glitters in the night sky of Earth. Yet only a few months have elapsed since the departure of the expedition. How miraculous it is, he thinks, to have come so far so swiftly.

Even so, there is a greater miracle. He will ask Noelle to relay a message to Earth an hour after lunch, and he knows that he will have an acknowledgment from Control Central in Brazil before dinner. That seems an even greater miracle to him.

* * *

HER CABIN IS NEAT, AUSTERE, underfurnished: no paintings, no light-sculptures, nothing to please the visual sense, only a few small sleek bronze statuettes, a smooth oval slab of green stone, and some objects evidently chosen for their rich textures—a strip of nubby fabric stretched across a frame, a sea-urchin's stony test, a collection of rough sandstone chunks. Everything is meticulously arranged. Does someone help her keep the place tidy? She moves serenely from point to point in the little room, never in danger of a collision; her confidence of motion is unnerving to the year-captain, who sits patiently waiting for her to settle down. She is pale, precisely groomed, her dark hair drawn tightly back from her forehead and held by an intricate ivory clasp. Her lips are full, her nose is rounded. She wears a soft flowing robe. Her body is attractive: he has seen her in the baths and knows of her high full breasts, her ample curving hips, her creamy perfect skin. Yet so far as he has heard she has had no shipboard liaisons. Is it because she is blind? Perhaps one tends not to think of a blind person as a potential sexual partner. Why should that be? Maybe because one hesitates to take advantage of a blind person in a sexual encounter, he suggests, and immediately catches himself up, startled, wondering why he should think of any sort of sexual relationship as "taking advantage." Well, then, possibly compassion for her handicap gets in the way of erotic feeling; pity too easily becomes patronizing and kills desire. He rejects that theory: glib, implausible. Could it be that people fear to approach her, suspecting that she is able to read their inmost thoughts? She has repeatedly denied any ability to enter minds other than her sister's. Besides, if you have nothing to hide, why be put off by her telepathy? No, it must be something else, and now he thinks he has isolated it: that Noelle is so self-contained, so serene, so much wrapped up in her blindness and her mind-power and her unfathomable communion with her distant sister, that no one dares to breach the crystalline barricades that guard her inner self. She is unapproached because she seems unapproachable; her strange perfection of soul sequesters her, keeping others at a distance the way extraordinary physical beauty can sometimes keep people at a distance. She does not arouse desire because she does not seem at all human. She gleams. She is a flawless machine, an integral part of the ship.

He unfolds the text of today's report to Earth. "Not that there's anything new to tell them," he says, "but I suppose we have to file the daily communiqué all the same."

"It would be cruel if we didn't. We mean so much to them."

"I wonder."

"Oh, yes. Yvonne says they take our messages from her as fast as they come in, and send them out on every channel. Word from us is terribly important to them."

"As a diversion, nothing more. As the latest curiosity. Intrepid explorers venturing into the uncharted wilds of interstellar nospace." His voice sounds harsh to him, his rhythms of speech coarse and blurting. His words surprise him. He had not known he felt this way about Earth. Still, he goes on. "That's all we represent: a novelty, vicarious adventure, a moment of amusement."

"Do you mean that? It sounds so awfully cynical."

He shrugs. "Another six months and they'll be completely bored with us and our communiqués. Perhaps sooner than that. A year and they'll have forgotten us."

She says, "I don't see you as a cynical man. Yet you often say such"—she falters—"such—"

"Such blunt things? I'm a realist, I guess. Is that the same as a cynic?"

"Don't try to label yourself, year-captain."

"I only try to look at things realistically."

"You don't know what real is. You don't know what you are, year-captain."

The conversation is suddenly out of control: much too charged, much too intimate. She has never spoken like this before. It is as if there is a malign electricity in the air, a prickly field that distorts their normal selves, making them unnaturally tense and aggressive. He feels panic. If he disturbs the delicate balance of Noelle's consciousness, will she still be able to make contact with far-off Yvonne?

He is unable to prevent himself from parrying: "Do *you* know what I am, then?"

She tells him, "You're a man in search of himself. That's why you volunteered to come all the way out here."

"And why did you volunteer to come all the way out here, Noelle?" he asks helplessly.

She lets the lids slide slowly down over her unseeing eyes and offers no reply. He tries to salvage things a bit by saying more calmly into her tense silence, "Never mind. I didn't intend to upset you. Shall we transmit the report?"

"Wait."

"All right."

She appears to be collecting herself. After a moment she says less edgily, "How do you think they see us at home? As ordinary human beings doing an unusual job or as superhuman creatures engaged in an epic voyage?"

"Right now, as superhuman creatures, epic voyage."

"And later we'll become more ordinary in their eyes?"

"Later we'll become nothing to them. They'll forget us."

"How sad." Her tone tingles with a grace note of irony. She may be laughing at him. "And you, year-captain? Do you picture yourself as ordinary or as superhuman?"

"Something in between. Rather more than ordinary, but no demigod."

"I regard myself as quite ordinary except in two respects," she says sweetly.

"One is your telepathic communication with your sister and the other—" He hesitates, mysteriously uncomfortable at naming it. "The other is your blindness."

"Of course," she says. Smiles. Radiantly. "Shall we do the report now?"

"Have you made contact with Yvonne?"

"Yes. She's waiting."

"Very well, then." Glancing at his notes, he begins slowly to read: "Ship-day 117. Velocity . . . Apparent location . . . "

* * *

SHE NAPS AFTER EVERY TRANSMISSION. They exhaust her. She was beginning to fade even before he reached the end of today's message; now, as he steps into the corridor, he knows she will be asleep before he closes the door. He leaves, frowning, troubled by the odd outburst of tension between them and by his mysterious attack of "realism." By what right does he say Earth will grow jaded with the voyagers? All during the years of preparation for his first interstellar journey the public excitement never flagged, indeed spurred the voyagers themselves on at times when their interminable training routines threatened *them* with boredom. Earth's messages, relayed by Yvonne to Noelle, vibrate with eager queries; the curiosity of the home-world has been overwhelming since the start. Tell us, tell us, tell us!

But there is so little to tell, really, except in that one transcendental area where there is so much. And how, really, can any of that be told?

How can *this*—

He pauses by the viewplate in the main transit corridor, a rectangular window a dozen meters long that gives direct access to the external environment. The pearl-gray emptiness of nospace, dense and pervasive, presses tight against the skin of the ship. During the training period the members of the expedition had been warned to anticipate nothing in the way of outside inputs as they crossed the galaxy; they would be shuttling through a void of infinite length, a matter-free tube, and there would be no sights to entertain them, no backdrop of remote nebulae, no glittering stars, no stray meteors, not so much as a pair of colliding atoms yielding the tiniest momentary spark, only an external sameness, like a blank wall. They had been taught methods of coping with that: turn inward, demand no delights from the universe beyond the ship, make the ship itself your universe. And yet, and yet, how misguided those warnings had been! Nospace was not a wall but rather a window. It was impossible for those on Earth to understand what revelations lay in that seeming emptiness. The year-captain, head throbbing from his encounter with Noelle, now revels in his keenest pleasure. A glance at the viewplate reveals that place where the immanent becomes the transcendent: the year-captain sees once again the infinite reverberating waves of energy that sweep through the grayness. What lies beyond the ship is neither a blank wall nor an empty tube; it is a stunning profusion of interlocking energy fields, linking everything to everything; it is music that also is light, it is light that also is music, and those aboard the ship are sentient particles wholly enmeshed in that vast all-engulfing reverberation, that radiant song of gladness that is the universe. The voyagers journey joyously toward the center of all things, giving themselves gladly into the care of cosmic forces far surpassing human control and understanding. He presses his hands against the cool glass. He puts his face close to it. *What do I see, what do I feel, what am I experiencing?* It is instant revelation, every time. It is almost, *almost!*—the sought after oneness. Barriers remain, but yet he is aware of an altered sense of space and time, a knowledge of the awesome something that lurks in the vacancies between the spokes of the cosmos, something majestic and powerful; he knows that that something is part of himself, and he is part of it. When he stands at the viewplate he yearns to open the ship's great hatch and tumble into the eternal. But not yet, not yet. Barriers remain. The voyage has only begun. They grow closer every day to that which they seek, but the voyage has only begun.

How could we convey any of this to those who remain behind? How could we make them understand?

Not with words. Never with words.

Let them come out here and see for themselves—

He smiles. He trembles and does a little shivering wriggle of delight. He turns away from the viewplate, drained, ecstatic.

* * *

NOELLE LIES IN UNEASY DREAMS. She is aboard a ship, an archaic three-master struggling in an icy sea. The rigging sparkles with fierce icicles, which now and again snap free in the cruel gales and smash with little tinkling sounds against the deck. The deck wears a slippery shiny coating of thin hard ice, and footing is treacherous. Great eroded bergs heave wildly in the gray water, rising, slapping the waves, subsiding. If one of those bergs hits the hull, the ship will sink. So far they have been lucky about that, but now a more subtle menace is upon them. The sea is freezing over. It congeals, coagulates, becomes a viscous fluid, surging sluggishly. Broad glossy plaques toss on the waves: new ice floes, colliding, grinding, churning; the floes are at war, destroying one another's edges, but some are making treaties, uniting to form a single implacable shield. When the sea freezes altogether the ship will be crushed. And now it is freezing. The ship can barely make headway. The sails belly out uselessly, straining at their lines. The wind makes a lyre out of the rigging as the ice-coated ropes twang and sing. The hull creaks like an old man; the grip of the ice is heavy. The timbers are yielding. The end is near. They will all perish. They will all perish. Noelle emerges from her cabin, goes above, seizes the railing, sways, prays, wonders when the wind's fist will punch through the stiff frozen canvas of the sails. Nothing can save them. But now! Yes, yes! A glow overhead! Yvonne! Yvonne! She comes. She hovers like a goddess in the black star-pocked sky. Soft golden light streams from her. She is smiling, and her smile thaws the sea. The ice relents. The air grows gentle. The ship is freed. It sails on, unhindered, toward the perfumed tropics.

* * *

In late afternoon Noelle drifts silently, wraithlike, into the control room where the year-captain is at work; she looks so weary and drawn that she is almost translucent; she seems unusually vulnerable, as though a harsh sound would shatter her. She has brought the year-captain Earth's answer to this morning's transmission. He takes from her the small, clear data-cube on which she has recorded her latest conversation with her sister. As Yvonne speaks in her mind, Noelle repeats the message aloud into a sensor disc, and it is captured on the cube. He wonders why she looks so wan. "Is anything wrong?" he asks. She tells him that she has had some difficulty receiving the message; the signal from Earth was strangely fuzzy. She is perturbed by that.

"It was like static," she says.

"Mental static?"

She is puzzled. Yvonne's tone is always pure, crystalline, wholly undistorted. Noelle has never had an experience like this before.

"Perhaps you were tired," he suggests. "Or maybe she was."

He fits the cube into the playback slot, and Noelle's voice comes from the speakers. She sounds unfamiliar, strained and ill at ease; she fumbles words frequently and often asks Yvonne to repeat. The message, what he can make out of it, is the usual cheery stuff, predigested news from the home-world—politics, sports, the planetary weather, word of the arts and sciences, special greetings for three or four members of the expedition, expressions of general good wishes—everything light, shallow, amiable. The static disturbs him. What if the telepathic link should fail? What if they were to lose contact with Earth altogether? He asks himself why that should trouble him so. The ship is self-sufficient; it needs no guidance from Earth in order to function properly, nor do the voyagers really have to have daily information about events on the mother planet. Then why care if silence descends? Why not accept the fact that they are no longer earthbound in any way, that they have become virtually a new species as they leap, faster than light, outward into the stars? No. He cares. The link matters. He decides that it has to do with what they were experiencing in relation to the intense throbbing grayness outside, that interchange of energies, that growing sense of universal connection. They are making discoveries every day, not astronomical but—well, spiritual—and, the year-captain thinks, what a pity if none of this can ever be communicated to those who have remained behind. We must keep the link open.

"Maybe," he says, "we ought to let you and Yvonne rest for a few days."

* * *

THEY LOOK UPON ME AS some sort of nun because I'm blind and special. I hate that, but there's nothing I can do to change it. I am what they think I am. I lie awake imagining men touching my body. The year-captain stands over me. I see his face clearly, the skin flushed and sweaty, the eyes gleaming. He strokes my breasts. He puts his lips to my lips. Suddenly, terribly, he embraces me and I scream. Why do I scream?

* * *

"YOU PROMISED TO TEACH ME how to play," she says, pouting a little. They are in the ship's lounge. Four games are under way: Elliot with Sylvia, Roy and Paco, David and Heinz, Mike and Bruce. Her pout fascinates him: such a little-girl gesture, so charming, so human. She seems to be in much better shape today, even though there was trouble again in the transmission, Yvonne complaining that the morning report was coming through indistinctly and noisily. Noelle has decided that the noise is some sort of local phenomenon, something like a sunspot effect, and will vanish once they are far enough from this sector of nospace. He is not as sure of this as she is, but she probably has a better understanding of such things than he. "Teach me, year-captain," she prods. "I really do want to know how to play. Have faith in me."

"All right," he says. The game may prove valuable to her, a relaxing pastime, a timely distraction. "This is the board. It has nineteen horizontal lines, nineteen vertical lines. The stones are played on the intersections of these lines, not on the squares that they form." He takes her hand and traces, with the tip of her fingers, the pattern of intersecting lines. They have been printed with a thick ink, easily discernible against the flatness of the board. "These nine dots are called stars," he tells her. "They serve as orientation points." He touches her fingertips to the nine stars. "We give the lines in this direction numbers, from one to nineteen, and we give the lines in the other direction letters, from A to T, leaving out 1. Thus we can identify positions on the board. This is B10, this is D18, this is J4, do you follow?" He feels despair. How can she ever commit the board to memory? But she looks untroubled as she runs her hand along the edges of the board, murmuring, "A, B, C, D . . . "

The other games have halted. Everyone in the lounge is watching them. He guides her hand toward the two trays of stones, the white and the black, and shows her the traditional way of picking up a stone between two fingers and clapping it down against the board. "The stronger player uses the white stones," he says. "Black always moves first. The players take turns placing stones, one at a time, on any unoccupied intersection. Once a stone is placed it is never moved unless it is captured, when it is removed at once from the board."

"And the purpose of the game?" she asks.

"To control the largest possible area with the smallest possible number of stones. You build walls. The score is reckoned by counting the number of vacant intersections within your walls, plus the number of prisoners you have taken." Methodically he explains the technique of play to her: the placing of stones, the seizure of territory, the capture of opposing stones. He illustrates by setting up simulated situations on the board, calling out the location of each stone as he places it: "Black holds P12, Q12, R12, S12, T12, and also P11, P10, P9, Q8, R8, S8, T8. White holds—" Somehow she visualizes the positions; she repeats the patterns after him, and asks questions that show she sees the board clearly in her mind. Within twenty minutes she understands the basic ploys. Several times, in describing maneuvers to her, he gives her an incorrect coordinate—the board, after all, is not marked with numbers and letters, and he misgauges the point occasionally—but each time she corrects him, gently, saying, "N13? Don't you mean N12?"

At length she says, "I think I follow everything now. Would you like to play a game?"

* * *

Consider your situation carefully. You are twenty years old, female, sightless. You have never married or even entered into a basic pairing. Your only real human contact is your twin sister, who is like yourself blind and single. Her mind is fully open to yours. Yours is to hers. You and she are two halves of one soul, inexplicably embedded in separate bodies. With her, only with her, do you feel complete. Now you are asked to take part in a voyage to the stars, without her, a voyage that is sure to cut you off from her forever. You are told that if you leave Earth aboard the starship there is no chance that you will ever see your sister again. You are also told that your presence is important to the success of the voyage, for without your help it would take decades or even centuries for news of the starship to reach Earth, but if you are aboard it will be possible to maintain instantaneous communication across any distance. What should you do? Consider. Consider.

You consider. And you volunteer to go, of course. You are needed: how can you refuse? As for your sister, you will naturally lose the opportunity to touch her, to hold her close, to derive direct comfort from her presence. Otherwise you will lose nothing. Never "see" her again? No. You can "see" her just as well, certainly, from a distance of a million light-years as you can from the next room. There can be no doubt of that.

* * *

The morning transmission. Noelle, sitting with her back to the year-captain, listens to what he reads her and sends it coursing over a gap of more than sixteen light-years. "Wait," she says. "Yvonne is calling for a repeat. From *'metabolic.'"* He pauses, goes back, reads again: *"Metabolic balances remain normal, although, as earlier reported, some of the older members of the expedition have begun to show trace deficiencies of manganese and potassium. We are taking appropriate corrective steps, and—"* Noelle halts him with a brusque gesture. He waits, and she bends forward, forehead against the table, hands pressed tightly to her temples. "Static again," she says. "It's worse today."

"Are you getting through at all?"

"I'm getting through, yes. But I have to push, to push, to push. And still Yvonne asks for repeats. I don't know what's happening, year-captain."

"The distance—"

"No."

"Better than sixteen light-years."

"No," she says. "We've already demonstrated that distance effects aren't a factor. If there's no falling off of signal after a million kilometres, after one light-year, after ten light-years—no perceptible drop in clarity and accuracy whatever—then there shouldn't be any qualitative diminution suddenly at sixteen light-years. Don't you think I've thought about this?"

"Noelle—"

"Attenuation of signal is one thing, and interference is another. An attenuation curve is a gradual slope. Yvonne and I have had perfect contact from the day we left Earth until just a few days ago. And now—no, year-captain, it can't be attenuation. It has to be some sort of interference. A local effect."

"Yes, like sunspots, I know. But—"

"Let's start again. Yvonne's calling for signal. Go on from *'manganese and potassium.'*"

"—manganese and potassium. We are taking appropriate corrective steps—"

* * *

Playing Go seems to ease her tension. He has not played in years, and he is rusty at first, but within minutes the old associations return and he finds himself setting up chains of stones with skill. Although he expects her to play poorly, unable to remember the patterns on the board after the first few moves, she proves to have no difficulty keeping the entire array in her mind. Only in one respect has she overestimated herself: for all her precision of coordination, she is unable to place the stones exactly, tending rather to disturb the stones already on the board as she makes her moves. After a little while she admits failure and thenceforth she calls out the plays she desires—M17, Q6, P6, R4, C11—and he places the stones for her. In the beginning he plays unaggressively, assuming that as a novice she will be haphazard and weak, but soon he discovers that she is adroitly expanding and protecting her territory while pressing a sharp attack against his, and he begins to devise more cunning strategies. They play for two hours and he wins by sixteen points, a comfortable margin but nothing to boast about, considering that he is an experienced and adept player and that this is her first game.

The others are skeptical of her instant ability. "Sure she plays well," Heinz mutters. "She's reading your mind, isn't she? She can see the board through your eyes and she knows what you're planning."

"The only mind open to her is her sister's," the year-captain says vehemently.

"How can you be sure she's telling the truth?"

The year-captain scowls. "Play a game with her yourself. You'll see whether it's skill or mind-reading that's at work."

Heinz, looking sullen, agrees. That evening he challenges Noelle; later he comes to the year-captain, abashed. "She plays well. She almost beat me, and she did it fairly."

The year-captain plays a second game with her. She sits almost motionless, eyes closed, lips compressed, offering the coordinates of her moves in a quiet bland monotone, like some sort of game-playing mechanism. She rarely takes long to decide on a move and she makes no blunders that must be retracted. Her capacity to devise game patterns has grown astonishingly; she nearly shuts him off from the center, but he recovers the initiative and manages a narrow victory. Afterward she loses once more to Heinz, but again she displays an increase of ability, and in the evening she defeats Chiang, a respected player. Now she becomes invincible. Undertaking two or three matches every day, she triumphs over Heinz, Sylvia, the year-captain, and Leon; Go has become something immense to her, something much more than a mere game, a simple test of strength; she focuses her energy on the board so intensely that her playing approaches the level of a religious discipline, a kind of meditation. On the fourth day she defeats Roy, the ship's champion, with such economy that everyone is dazzled. Roy can speak of nothing else. He demands a rematch and is defeated again.

* * *

NOELLE WONDERED, AS THE SHIP was lifting from Earth, whether she really would be able to maintain contact with Yvonne across the vast span of interstellar space. She had nothing but faith to support her belief that the power that joined their minds was wholly unaffected by distance. They had often spoken to each other without difficulty from opposite sides of the planet, yes, but would it be so simple when they were half a galaxy apart? During the early hours of the voyage she and Yvonne kept up a virtually continuous linking, and the signal remained clear and sharp, with no perceptible falling off of reception, as the ship headed outward. Past the orbit of the moon, past the million-kilometer mark, past the orbit of Mars: clear and sharp, clear and sharp. They had passed the first test: clarity of signal was not a quantitative function of distance. But Noelle remained unsure of what would happen once the ship abandoned conventional power and shunted into nospace in order to attain faster-than-light velocity. She would then be in a space apart from Yvonne; in effect she would be in another universe; would she still be able to reach her sister's mind? Tension rose in her as the moment of the shunt approached, for she had no idea what life would be like for her in the absence of Yvonne. To face that dreadful silence, to find herself thrust into such terrible isolation—but it did not happen. They entered nospace and her awareness of Yvonne never flickered. *Here we are, wherever we are,* she said, and moments later came Yvonne's response, a cheery greeting from the old continuum. Clear and sharp, clear and sharp. Nor did the signal grow more tenuous in the weeks that followed. Clear and sharp, clear and sharp, until the static began.

* * *

The year-captain visualizes the contact between the two sisters as an arrow whistling from star to star, as fire speeding through a shining tube, as a river or pure force coursing down a celestial wave guide. He sees the joining of those two minds as a stream of pure light binding the moving ship to the far-off mother world. Sometimes he dreams of Yvonne and Noelle, Noelle and Yvonne, and the glowing bond that stretches between the sisters gives off so brilliant a radiance that he stirs and moans and presses his forehead into the pillow.

* * *

The interference grows worse. Neither Noelle nor Yvonne can explain what is happening; Noelle clings without conviction to her sunspot analogy. They still manage to make contact twice daily, but it is increasingly a strain on the sisters' resources, for every sentence must be repeated two or three times, and whole blocks of words now do not get through at all. Noelle has become thin and haggard. Go refreshes her, or at least diverts her from this failing of her powers. She has become a master of the game, awarding even Roy a two-stone handicap; although she occasionally loses, her play is always distinguished, extraordinarily original in its sweep and design. When she is not playing she tends to be remote and aloof. She is in all respects a more elusive person than she was before the onset of this communications crisis.

* * *

Noelle dreams that her blindness has been taken from her. Sudden light surrounds her, and she opens her eyes, sits up, looks about in awe and wonder, saying to herself, This is a table, this is a chair, this is how my statuettes look, this is what my sea urchin is like. She is amazed by the beauty of everything in her room. She rises, goes forward, stumbling at first, groping, then magically gaining poise and balance, learning how to walk in this new way, judging the positions of things not by echoes and air currents but rather by using her eyes. Information floods her. She moves about the ship, discovering the faces of her ship-mates. You are Roy, you are Sylvia, you are Heinz, you are the year-captain. They look, surprisingly, very much as she had imagined them: Roy fleshy and red-faced, Sylvia fragile, the year-captain lean and fierce, Heinz like this, Elliot like that, everyone matching expectations. Everyone beautiful. She goes to the window of which the others all talk, and looks out into the famous grayness. Yes, yes, it is as they say it is: a cosmos of wonders, a miracle of complex pulsating tones, level after level of incandescent reverberation sweeping outward toward the rim of the boundless universe. For an hour she stands before that dense burst of rippling energies, giving herself to it and taking it into herself, and then, and then, just as the ultimate moment of illumination is coming over her, she realizes that something is wrong. Yvonne is not with her. She reaches out and does not reach Yvonne. She has somehow traded her power for the gift of sight. Yvonne? Yvonne? All is still. Where is Yvonne? Yvonne is not with her. This is only a dream, Noelle tells herself, and I will soon awaken. But she cannot awaken. In terror she cries out. "It's all right," Yvonne whispers. "I'm here, love, I'm here, I'm here, just as always." Yes. Noelle feels the closeness. Trembling, she embraces her sister. Looks at her. I can see, Yvonne! I can see! Noelle realizes that in her first rapture she quite forgot to look at herself, though she rushed about looking at everything else. Mirrors have never been part of her world. She looks at Yvonne, which is like looking at herself, and Yvonne is beautiful, her hair dark and silken and lustrous, her face smooth and pale, her features fine of outline, her eyes—her blind eyes—alive and sparkling. Noelle tells Yvonne how beautiful she is, and Yvonne nods, and they laugh and hold one another close, and they begin to weep with pleasure and love, and Noelle awakens, and the world is dark around her.

* * *

"I HAVE THE NEW COMMUNIQUÉ to send," the year-captain says wearily. "Do you feel like trying again?"

"Of course I do." She gives him a ferocious smile. "Don't even hint at giving up, year-captain. There absolutely has to be some way around this interference."

"Absolutely," he says. He rustles his papers restlessly. "Okay, Noelle. Let's go. Ship-day 128. Velocity . . . "

"Give me another moment to get ready," Noelle says.

He pauses. She closes her eyes and begins to enter the transmitting state. She is conscious, as ever, of Yvonne's presence. Even when no specific information is flowing between them, there is perpetual low-level contact, there is the sense that the other is near, that warm proprioceptive awareness such as one has of one's own arm or leg or lip. But between that impalpable subliminal contact and the actual transmission of specific content lie several key steps. Yvonne and Noelle are human biopsychic resonators constituting a long-range communications network; there is a tuning procedure for them as for any transmitters and receivers. Noelle opens herself to the radiant energy spectrum, vibratory, pulsating, that will carry her message to her earthbound sister. As the transmitting circuit in this interchange she must be the one to attain maximum energy flow. Quickly, intuitively, she activates her own energy centers, the one in the spine, the one in the solar plexus, the one at the top of the skull; energy pours from her and instantaneously spans the galaxy. But today there is an odd and troublesome splashback effect: monitoring the circuit, she is immediately aware that the signal has failed to reach Yvonne. Yvonne is there, Yvonne is tuned and expectant, yet something is jamming the channel and nothing gets through, not a single syllable. "The interference is worse than ever," she tells the year-captain. "I feel as if I could put my hand out and touch Yvonne. But she's not reading me and nothing's coming back from her." With a little shake of her shoulders Noelle alters the sending frequency; she feels a corresponding adjustment at Yvonne's end of the connection; but again they are thwarted, again there is total blockage. Her signal is going forth and is being soaked up by—what? How can such a thing happen?

Now she makes a determined effort to boost the output of the system. She addresses herself to the neural center in her spine, exciting its energies, using them to drive the next center to a more intense vibrational tone, harnessing that to push the highest center of all to its greatest harmonic capacity. Up and down the energy bands she roves. Nothing. Nothing. She shivers; she huddles; she is physically emptied by the strain. "I can't get through," she murmurs. "She's there, I can feel her there, I know she's working to read me. But I can't transmit any sort of intelligible coherent message."

* * *

ALMOST SEVENTEEN LIGHT-YEARS FROM EARTH and the only communication channel is blocked. The year-captain is overwhelmed by frosty terrors. The ship, the self-sufficient autonomous ship, has become a mere gnat blowing in a hurricane. The voyagers hurtle blindly into the depths of an unknown universe, alone, alone, alone. He was so smug about not needing any link to Earth, but now that the link is gone he shivers and cowers. Everything has been made new. There are no rules. Human beings have never been this far from home. He presses himself against the viewplate and the famous grayness just beyond, swirling and eddying, mocks him with its immensity. Leap into me, it calls, leap, leap, leap, lose yourself in me, drown in me.

Behind him: the sound of soft footsteps. Noelle. She touches his hunched, knotted shoulders. "It's all right," she whispers. "You're overreacting. Don't make such a tragedy out of it." But it is. Her tragedy, more than anyone's, hers and Yvonne's. But also his, theirs, everybody's. Cut off. Lost in a foggy silence.

Down in the lounge people are singing. Boisterous voices, Elliot, Chiang, Leon.

> Travelin' Dan was a spacefarin' man
> He jumped in the nospace tube.

The year-captain whirls, seizes Noelle, pulls her against him. Feels her trembling. Comforts her, where a moment before she had been comforting him. "Yes, yes, yes, yes," he murmurs. With his arm around her shoulders he turns, so that both of them are facing the viewplate. As if she could see. Nospace dances and churns an inch from his nose. He feels a hot wind blowing through the ship, the khamsin, the sirocco, the simoom, the leveche, a sultry wind, a killing wind coming out of the grey strangeness, and he forces himself not to fear that wind. It is a wind of life, he tells himself, a wind of joy, a cool sweet wind, the mistral, the tramontana. Why should he think there is anything to fear in the realm beyond the viewplate? How beautiful it is out there how ecstatically beautiful! How sad that we can never tell anyone about it, now, except one another. A strange peace unexpectedly descends on him. Everything is going to be all right, he insists. No harm will come of what has happened. And perhaps some good. And perhaps some good. Benefits lurk in the darkest places.

* * *

SHE PLAYS GO OBSESSIVELY, BEATING everyone. She seems to live in the lounge twenty hours a day. Sometimes she takes on two opponents at once—an incredible feat, considering that she must hold the constantly changing intricacies of both boards in her memory—and defeats them both: two days after losing verbal-level contact with Yvonne, she simultaneously triumphs over Roy and Heinz before an audience of thirty. She looks animated and buoyant; the sorrow she must feel over the snapping of the link she takes care to conceal. She expresses it, the others suspect, only by her manic Go-playing. The year-captain is one of her most frequent adversaries, taking his turn at the board in the time he would have devoted to composing and dictating the communiqués for Earth. He had thought Go was over for him years ago, but he too is playing obsessively now, building walls and the unassailable fortresses known as eyes. There is reassurance in the rhythmic clacking march of the black and white stones. Noelle wins every game against him. She covers the board with eyes.

* * *

WHO CAN EXPLAIN THE INTERFERENCE? No one believes that the problem is a function of anything so obvious as distance. Noelle has been quite convincing on that score: a signal that propagates perfectly for the first sixteen light-years of a journey ought not suddenly to deteriorate. There should at least have been prior sign of attenuation, and there was no attenuation, only noise interfering with and ultimately destroying the signal. Some force is intervening between the sisters. But what can it be? The idea that it is some physical effect analogous to sunspot static, that it is the product of radiation emitted by some giant star in whose vicinity they have lately been traveling, must in the end be rejected. There is no energy interface between realspace and nospace, no opportunity for any kind of electromagnetic intrusion. That much had been amply demonstrated long before any manned voyages were undertaken. The nospace tube is an impermeable wall. Nothing that has mass or charge can leap the barrier between the universe of accepted phenomena and the cocoon of nothingness that the ship's drive mechanism has woven about them, nor can a photon get across, nor even a slippery neutrino.

Many speculations excite the voyagers. The one force that can cross the barrier, Roy points out, is thought: intangible, unmeasurable, limitless. What if the sector of realspace corresponding to this region of the nospace tube is inhabited by beings of powerful telepathic capacity whose transmissions, flooding out over a sphere with a radius of many light-years, are able to cross the barrier just as readily as those of Yvonne? The alien mental emanations, Roy supposes, are smothering the signal from Earth.

Heinz extends this theory into a different possibility: that the interference is caused by denizens of nospace. There is a seeming paradox in this, since it has been shown mathematically that the nospace tube must be wholly matter-free except for the ship that travels through it; otherwise a body moving at speeds faster than light would generate destructive resonances as its mass exceeds infinity. But perhaps the equations are imperfectly understood. Heinz imagines giant incorporeal beings as big as asteroids, as big as planets, masses of pure energy or even pure mental force that drift freely through the tube. These beings may be sources of biopsychic transmissions that disrupt the Yvonne-Noelle circuit, or maybe they are actually feeding on the sisters' mental output, Heinz postulates. "Angels," he calls them. It is an implausible but striking concept that fascinates everyone for several days. Whether the "angels" live within the tube as proposed by Heinz, or on some world just outside it as pictured by Roy, is unimportant at the moment; the consensus aboard the ship is that the interference is the work of an alien intelligence, and that arouses wonder in all.

What to do? Leon, inclining toward Roy's hypothesis, moves that they leave nospace immediately and seek the world or worlds where the "angels" dwell. The year-captain objects, noting that the plan of the voyage obliges them to reach a distance of one hundred light-years from Earth before they begin their quest for habitable planets. Roy and Leon argue that the plan is merely a guide, arbitrarily conceived, and not received scriptural writ; they are free to depart from it if some pressing reason presents itself. Heinz, supporting the year-captain, remarks that there is no need actually to leave nospace regardless of the source of the alien transmissions; if the thoughts of these creatures can come in from beyond the tube, then Noelle's thoughts can surely go outward through the tube to them, and contact can be established without the need of deviating from the plan. After all, if the interference is the work of beings sharing the tube with them, and the voyagers seek them in vain outside the tube, it may be impossible to find them again once the ship returns to nospace. This approach seems reasonable, and the question is put to Noelle: Can you attempt to open a dialogue with these beings?

She laughs. "I make no guarantees. I've never tried to talk to angels before. But I'll try, my friends, I'll try."

* * *

SHE HAS NEVER DONE ANYTHING like this before. It seems almost an act of infidelity, this opening of her mind to something or someone who is not Yvonne. But it must be done. She extends a tenuous tendril of thought that probes like a rivulet of quicksilver. Through the wall of the ship, into the surrounding grayness, upward, outward, toward, toward——angels?—

Angels. Oh. Brightness. Strength. Magnetism. Yes. Awareness now of a fierce roiling mass of concentrated energy close by. A mass in motion, laying a terrible stress on the fabric of the cosmos: the angel has angular momentum. It tumbles ponderously on its colossal axis. Who would have thought an angel could be so huge? Noelle is oppressed by the shifting weight of it as it makes its slow heavy axial swing. She moves closer. Oh. She is dazzled. *Too much light! Too much power!* She draws back, overwhelmed by the intensity of the other being's output. Such a mighty mind: she feels dwarfed. If she touches it with her mind she will be destroyed. She must step down the aperture, establish some kind of transformer to shield herself against the full blast of power that comes from it. It requires time and discipline. She works steadily, making adjustments, mastering new techniques, discovering capacities she had not known she possessed. And now. Yes. Try again. Slowly, slowly, slowly, with utmost care. Outward goes the tendril.

Yes.

Approaching the angel.

See? Here am I. Noelle. Noelle. Noelle. I come to you in love and fear. Touch me lightly. Just touch me—

Just a touch—

Touch—

Oh. Oh.

I see you. The light—eye of crystal—fountains of lava—oh, the light—your light—I see—I see—

Oh, like a god—

—and Semele wished to behold Zeus in all his brightness, and Zeus would have discouraged her, but Semele insisted and Zeus who loved her could not refuse her; so Zeus came upon her in full majesty and Semele was consumed by his glory, so that only the ashes of her remained, but the son she had conceived by Zeus, the boy Dionysus, was not destroyed, and Zeus saved Dionysus and took him away sealed in his thigh, bringing him forth afterward and bestowing godhood upon him—

—Oh God I am Semele—

She withdraws again. Rests, regroups her powers. The force of this being is frightening. But there are ways of insulating herself against destruction, of letting the overflow of energy dissipate itself. She will try once more. She knows she stands at the brink of wonders. Now. Now. The questing mind reaches forth.

I am Noelle. I come to you in love, angel.

Contact.

The universe is burning. Bursts of wild silver light streak across the metal dome of the sky. Words turn to ash. Walls smolder and burst into flames. There is contact. A dancing solar flare—a stream of liquid fire—a flood tide of brilliant radiance, irresistible, unendurable, running into her, sweeping over her, penetrating her. Light everywhere.

—Semele.

The angel smiles and she quakes. *Open to me,* cries the vast tolling voice, and she opens and the force enters fully, sweeping through her.

* * *

She has been in a coma for days, wandering in delirium. Troubled, fearful, the year-captain keeps a somber vigil at her bedside. Sometimes she seems to rise toward consciousness; intelligible words, even whole sentences, bubble dreamily from her lips. She talks of light, of a brilliant unbearable white glow, of arcs of energy, of intense solar eruptions. A star holds me, she mutters. She tells him that she has been conversing with a star. How poetic, the year-captain thinks: what a lovely metaphor. Conversing with a star. But where is she, what is happening to her? Her face is flushed; her eyes move about rapidly, darting like trapped fish beneath her closed lids, Mind to mind, she whispers, the star and I, mind to mind. She begins to hum—an edgy whining sound, climbing almost toward inaudibility, a high-frequency keening. It pains him to hear it: hard aural radiation. Then she is silent.

Her body goes rigid. A convulsion of some sort? No. She is awakening. He sees lightning bolts of perception flashing through her quivering musculature; the galvanized frog, twitching at the end of its leads. Her eyelids tremble. She makes a little moaning noise.

She looks up at him.

The year-captain says gently, "Your eyes are open. I think you can see me now, Noelle. Your eyes are tracking me, aren't they?"

"I can see you, yes." Her voice is hesitant, faltering, strange for a moment, a foreign voice, but then it becomes more like its usual self as she asks, "How long was I away?"

"Eight ship-days. We were worried."

"You look exactly as I thought you would," she says. "Your face is hard. But not a dark face. Not a hostile face."

"Do you want to talk about where you went, Noelle?"

She smiles. "I talked with the . . . angel."

"Angel?"

"Not really an angel, year-captain. Not a physical being, either, not any kind of alien species. More like the energy creatures Heinz was discussing. But bigger. Bigger. I don't know what it was, year-captain."

"You told me you were talking with a star."

"—a star!"

"In your delirium. That's what you said."

Her eyes blaze with excitement. "A star! Yes! Yes, year-captain! I think I was, yes!"

"But what does that mean: talking to a star?"

She laughs. "It means talking to a star, year-captain. A great ball of fiery gas, year-captain, and it has a mind, it has a consciousness. I think that's what it was. I'm sure now. I'm sure!"

"But how can a—"

The light goes abruptly from her eyes. She is traveling again; she is no longer with him. He waits beside her bed. An hour, two hours, half a day. What bizarre realm has she penetrated? Her breathing is a distant, impersonal drone. So far away from him now, so remote from any place he comprehends. At last her eyelids flicker. She looks up. Her face seems transfigured. To the year-captain she still appears to be partly in that other world beyond the ship. "Yes," she says. "Not an angel, year-captain. A sun. A living intelligent sun." Her eyes are radiant. "A sun, a star, a sun," she murmurs. "I touched the consciousness of a sun. Do you believe that, year-captain? I found a network of stars that live, that think, that have minds, that have souls. That communicate. The whole universe is alive."

"A star," he says dully. "The stars have minds."

"Yes."

"All of them? Our own sun too?"

"All of them. We came to the place in the galaxy where this star lives, and it was broadcasting on my wavelength, and its output began overriding my link with Yvonne. That was the interference, year-captain. The big star broadcasting."

This conversation has taken on for him the texture of a dream. He says quietly, "Why didn't Earth's sun override you and Yvonne when you were on Earth?"

She shrugs. "It isn't old enough. It takes—I don't know, billions of years—until they're mature, until they can transmit. Our sun isn't old enough, year-captain. None of the stars close to Earth is old enough. But out here—"

"Are you in contact with it now?"

"Yes. With it and with many others. And with Yvonne."

"Yvonne too?"

"She's back in the link with me. She's in the circuit." Noelle pauses. "I can bring others into the circuit. I could bring you in, year-captain."

"Me?"

"You. Would you like to touch a star with your mind?"

"What will happen to me? Will it harm me?"

"Did it harm me, year-captain?"

"Will I still be me afterward?"

"Am I still me, year-captain?"

"I'm afraid."

"Open to me. Try. See what happens."

"I'm afraid."

"Touch a star, year-captain."

He puts his hand on hers. "Go ahead," he says, and his soul becomes a solarium.

* * *

Afterward, with the solar pulsations still reverberating in the mirrors of his mind, with blue-white sparks leaping in his synapses, he says, "What about the others?"

"I'll bring them in too."

He feels a flicker of momentary resentment. He does not want to share the illumination. But in the instant that he conceives his resentment, he abolishes it. *Let them in.*

"Take my hand," Noelle says.

They reach out together. One by one they touch the others. Roy. Sylvia. Heinz. Elliot. He feels Noelle surging in tandem with him, feels Yvonne, feels greater presences, luminous, eternal. All are joined. Ship-sister, star-sister: all become one. The year-captain realizes that the days of playing Go have ended. They are one person; they are beyond games.

"And now," Noelle whispers, "now we reach toward Earth. We put our strength into Yvonne, and Yvonne—"

Yvonne draws Earth's seven billion into the network.

* * *

THE SHIP HURTLES THROUGH THE nospace tube. Soon the year-captain will initiate the search for a habitable planet. If they discover one, they will settle there. It not, they will go on, and it will not matter at all, and the ship and its seven billion passengers will course onward forever, warmed by the light of the friendly stars.

THE CHANGELING

In Memoriam: PKD

A trip across the boundaries of reality, into an alternative world. The scene is mysterious Mexico, a country I have visited many times. Pre-Columbian darkness is endlessly fascinating to me. I went there in March of 1982 to wander around amidst the ancient stone monuments of Tenochtitlan and Oaxaca and to revel in the multitude of weird succulent plants. Soon after my return, George Scithers of *Amazing Stories* asked me for a new short story, and when I told him what such slick magazines as *Playboy* and *Omni* were currently paying me, he unhesitatingly offered me a price matching theirs. (It was a heady time for some of us, then!) A few days later the great science fiction writer Philip K. Dick, whom I had known very well, died. With my head full of the strangeness of Mexico, I sat down and wrote a story which, while not at all done in the Philip K. Dick style, played with reality somewhat in the fashion that Dick had made his specialty, and I dedicated it to him. Scithers ran it in his November, 1982 issue.

Just as the startling facade of the Temple of Quetzalcoatl came into view on the far side of the small pyramid, Hilgard felt a sudden touch of vertigo and swayed for a moment, as though a little earthquake had rippled through the Teotihuacan archeological zone. He leaned against a railing until the worst of the queasiness and confusion had passed. The heat? The altitude? Last night's fiery dinner exacting its price? Down here in Mexico a tourist learned to expect that some kind of internal upset could strike at any time.

But the discomfort vanished as quickly as it had come, and Hilgard looked up in awe, at the great stone staircase of the temple. The jutting heads of the feathered serpents burst like the snouts of dinosaurs from the massive blocks. Traces of the original frescoes, perhaps fifteen hundred years old, glinted here and there. Hilgard took eight or nine photos. But he was too hot and dusty and weary to explore the wondrous building with any real vigor, and he still felt a little shaky from that dizzy spell a moment ago. The pressure of time was on him also: he had promised to meet his driver at two o'clock at the main parking lot for the return trip to Mexico City. It was nearly two now, and the parking area was at least a mile to the north, along the searing, shadeless thoroughfare known as the Avenue of the Dead. He wished now that he had started his tour here at the awesome Quetzalcoatl Temple instead of consuming his morning's energy scrambling around on the two huge pyramids at the other end.

Too late to do anything about that. Hilgard trudged quickly toward the parking lot, pausing only to buy a tepid beer from a vendor midway along the path. By quarter past two he was in the lot, sweaty and puffing. There was no sign of his driver and the battered black cab. Still at lunch, probably, Hilgard thought, relieved at not having to feel guilty about his own tardiness but annoyed by yet another example of Mexican punctuality. Well, now he had time to get a few more shots of the Pyramid of the Sun while he waited, and maybe—

"Señor? Señor!"

Hilgard turned. A driver—not his—had emerged from a shiny little Volkswagen cab and was waving to him.

"Your wife, *señor,* she will be here in two more minutes. She is taking more pictures on the top of the big pyramid, and she says to please wait, she will not be long."

"I think you want someone else," Hilgard said.

The driver looked baffled. "But you are her husband, *señor.*"

"Sorry. I am not anybody's husband."

"Is a joke? I am not understanding." The driver grinned uncertainly. "A blonde woman, dark glasses. I pick you and she up in front of the Hotel Century, Zona Rosa, ten o'clock this morning, you remember? She said to me, ten minutes ago, tell my husband wait a little, I go take more pyramid pictures, just a few minutes. And—"

"I'm staying at the Hotel Presidente," Hilgard said. "I'm not married. I drove out here this morning in a black Ford cab. The driver's name was Chucho."

The Mexican's grin, earnest and ingratiating, stayed on his face, but it grew ragged, and something hostile came into his eyes, as though he was beginning to think he was being made the butt of some incomprehensible gringo prank. Slowly he said, "I know Chucho, yes. He took some American people down to Xochimilco this morning. Maybe he was your driver yesterday."

"He met me outside the Presidente. We arranged it last night. The fare was seventeen hundred pesos." Hilgard glanced around, wishing the man would show up before things got even more muddled. "You must be mistaking me for a different American. I'm traveling alone. I wouldn't mind meeting an interesting blonde, I guess, but I don't happen to be married to one, and I really am certain that you're not the driver I was with this morning. I'm very sorry if—"

"There is your wife, *señor,*" said the Mexican coolly.

Hilgard turned. A trim, attractive woman in her late thirties, with short golden hair and an alert, open face, was making her way through the clutter of souvenir stands at the entrance to the parking area. "Ted!" she called. "Here I am!"

He stared blankly. He had never seen her before. As she drew closer he forced a smile and held it in a fixed and rigid way. But what was he supposed to say to her? He didn't even know her name. *Excuse me, ma'am, I'm not actually your husband.* Eh? Was there a television program, he wondered, that went to elaborate lengths to stage complicated hoaxes with hapless, unsuspecting victims, and was he at the center of it? Would they shower him with home appliances and cruise tickets once they were done bewildering him?

Pardon me, ma'am, but I'm not really Ted Hilgard. I'm just someone else of the same name and face. Yes? No.

She came up to him and said, "You should have climbed it with me. You know what they've been doing up there for the past half hour? They're celebrating the spring equinox with some kind of Aztec rite. Incense, chanting, green boughs, two white doves in a cage that they just liberated. Fascinating stuff, and I got pictures of the whole thing. Hold this for me for a minute, will you?" she said casually, slipping her heavy camera bag from her shoulder and pushing it into his hands. "God, it's hot today! Did you have fun at the other temple? I just didn't feel like hiking all the way down there, but I hope I didn't miss—"

The driver, standing to one side, now said mildly, "It is getting late, Missus. We go back to the city now?"

"Yes. Of course." She tucked a stray shirttail back into her slacks, took the camera bag from Hilgard and followed the driver toward the Volkswagen cab. Hilgard, mystified, stayed where he was, scanning the parking lot hopelessly for Chucho and the old black Ford and trying to construct some plausible course of action. After a moment the blonde woman looked back, frowning, and said, "Ted? What's the matter?"

He made an inarticulate sound and fluttered his hands in confusion. Possibly, he told himself, he was having some sort of psychotic episode of fugue. Or perhaps that moment of dizziness at the Temple of Quetzalcoatl had in fact been a light stroke that had scrambled his memory. Could she really be his wife? He felt quite certain that he had been single all his life, except for those eight months a dozen years ago with Beverly. He could clearly envision his bachelor flat on Third Avenue, the three neat rooms, the paintings, the little cabinet of pre-Columbian statuettes. He saw himself at his favorite restaurants with his several lovers, Judith or Janet or Denise. This brisk, jaunty blonde woman fit nowhere into those images. But yet—yet—

He had no idea what to do. His fingers began to tremble and his feet felt like blocks of frozen mud, and he started to walk in a numbed, dazed way toward the Volkswagen. The driver, holding the door open for him, gave him the sort of venomous look of contempt that Hilgard imagined was generally given to gringos who were so drunk at midday that they were unable to remember they were married. But Hilgard was not drunk.

The woman chattered pleasantly as they zipped back toward Mexico City. Evidently they were planning to visit the Museum of Anthropology in Chapultepec Park that afternoon, and tomorrow morning they would move on either to Cuernavaca or Guadalajara, depending on which one of them won a low-keyed disagreement that had evidently been going on for several days. Hilgard faked his way through the conversation answering vaguely and remotely and eventually withdrawing from it altogether by pleading fatigue, a touch of the sun. Before long, gray tendrils of smog were drifting toward them: they were at the outskirts of Mexico City. In the relatively light Sunday traffic, the driver roared flamboyantly down the broad Paseo de la Reforma and cut sharply into the Zona Rosa district to deposit there in front of the slender black-and-white tower of the Hotel Century. "Give him a nice tip, darling," the woman said to Hilgard. "We've kept him out longer than we were supposed to."

Hilgard offered the glowering driver a pair of thousand-peso notes, waved away the change, and they went into the hotel. In the small lobby she said, "Get the key, will you? I'll ring for the elevator." Hilgard approached the desk and looked imploringly at the clerk, who said in fluent English, "Good afternoon, Mr. Hilgard. Did you find the pyramids interesting?" and handed him, without being asked, the key to room 177.

This is not happening. Hilgard told himself, thinking of his comfortable room on the seventh floor of the glossy Hotel Presidente. This is a dream. This is a hallucination. He joined the blonde woman in the elevator; she pressed 17 and it began to ascend slowly, pausing dismayingly for a fraction of a second between the tenth and eleventh floors as the power sagged. Room 177 was compact, efficient, with a semicircular double bed and a little bar unit stocked with miniature bottles of liquor, mixers, and such. The woman took a brandy from it and said to him, "Shall I get you a rum, Ted?"

"No. Thank you." He wandered the room. Feminine things all over the bathroom sink, makeup and lotions and whatnot. Matching his-and-hers luggage in the closet. A man's jacket and shirts hanging neatly—not his, but the sort of things he might have owned—a book on the night-table, the new Updike novel. He had read it a few months ago, but in some other edition, apparently, for this had a red jacket and he remembered it as blue.

"I'm going to grab a shower," she said. "Then we go out to get lunch and head over to the museum, okay?"

He looked up. She padded past him to the bathroom, naked; he had a sudden surprising glimpse of small round breasts and dimpled buttocks, and then the door closed. Hilgard waited until he heard the water running, and took her wallet from her open purse. In it he saw the usual credit cards, some travelers' checks, a thick wad of well-worn Mexican banknotes. And a driver's license: Celia Hilgard, thirty-six years old, five feet five, blond hair, blue eyes, 124 pounds, married. *Married.* An address on East 85th Street. A card in the front of the wallet declared that in case of emergency Theodore Hilgard was to be notified, either at the East 85th Street address or at the offices of Hilgard & Hilgard on West 57th Street. Hilgard studied the card as though it were written in Sanskrit. His apartment was on East 62nd Street, his gallery two blocks south of it. He was sure of that. He could see himself quite sharply as he walked down Third every morning, glancing toward Bloomingdale's, turning east on 60th—

Two Ted Hilgards? With the same face?

"What are you looking for?" Celia asked, stepping from the bathroom and toweling herself dry.

Hilgard's cheeks reddened. Guiltily he tucked her wallet back in her purse. "Ah—just checking to see how many pesos you have left. I thought we might want to cash some travelers' checks when the banks open tomorrow."

"I cashed some on Friday. Don't you remember?"

"Slipped my mind, I guess."

"Do you want some of my pesos?"

"I've got enough for now," he said.

They had lunch at the hotel. For Hilgard it was like sitting across the table from a keg of dynamite. He was not yet ready to admit that he had gone insane, but very little that he could say to her was likely to make any sense, and eventually she was bound to challenge him. He felt like someone who had come into a movie in the middle and was trying to figure out what was going on, but this was worse, much worse, because he was not merely watching the movie, he was starring in it. And found himself lunching with a total stranger to whom he had been married, it seemed, for years. But people who have been married for years have little new to say to one another at lunch, usually. He was grateful for the long silences. When she did speak, he answered cautiously and briefly. Once he allowed himself the luxury of calling her by name, just to show that he knew her name; but his "Celia" provoked a quick frown in her that puzzled him. Was he supposed to have used some pet name instead? Or was there a name other than Celia by which everybody called her—Cee, perhaps, or Cele, or Charley? He was altogether lost. Lingering over his coffee, he thought again of that dizzying moment at the Temple of Quetzalcoatl, when everything had swayed and swirled in his head. Was there such a thing as a stroke that affected one's memory without causing any sort of paralysis of the body? Well, maybe. But he wasn't suffering merely from amnesia; he had a complete and unblurred set of memories of a life without Celia, as a contented single man running a successful art gallery, living a fulfilling existence, friends, lovers, travel. Arriving in Mexico City three days ago, looking forward to a week of cheerful solitude, warm weather, spicy food, perhaps some interesting new pieces for his collection. How could a stroke build all that into his mind? With such detail, too: the black Ford cab, Chucho the amiable driver, the seventh-floor room at the Hotel Presidente—

"I've left something upstairs," he told Celia. "I'll just run up for it, and then we can go."

From the room he dialed the Presidente. "Mr. Hilgard, please."

"One moment." A long pause. Then: "Please repeat the name."

"Hilgard. Theodore Hilgard. I think he's in room 770." A longer pause.

"I'm sorry, sir. We have no one by that name."

"I see," Hilgard said, not seeing at all, and put the phone down. He stared at himself in the mirror, searching for signs of a stroke, the drooping eyelid, the sagging cheek. Nothing. Nothing. But his face was gray. He looked a thousand years old.

They hailed a cab outside the hotel and went to the Museum of Anthropology. He had been there several times, most recently yesterday afternoon. But from what Celia said it was apparent she had never seen it, which was a new awkwardness for him: he had to pretend he had no familiarity with that very familiar place. As they wandered through it he did his best to feign fresh responses to objects he had known for years, the great Olmec stone heads, the terrifying statue of the goddess Coatlicue, the jade-encrusted masks. Sometimes it was not necessary to feign it. In the Aztec room there was an immense marble stela just to the left of the calendar stone that he could not recall from yesterday's visit, and there was a case of amazing little Olmec figurines of polished jade absolutely new to him, and the Mayan room seemed arranged in an entirely different way. Hilgard found all that impossible to comprehend. Even the huge umbrella-shaped fountain in the museum courtyard was subtly different, with golden spokes now sprouting from it. The cumulative effect of the day's little strangenesses was making him feel giddy, almost feverish: Celia several times asked if he was getting ill.

They had dinner that night at an outdoor café a few blocks from their hotel, and strolled for a long time afterward, returning to their room a little before midnight. As they undressed Hilgard felt new dismay. Was she expecting him to make love? The thought horrified him. Not that she was unattractive, far from it. But he had never been able to go to bed with strangers. A prolonged courtship, a feeling of ease with the other person, of closeness, of real love—that was what he preferred, indeed what he required. Aside from all that, how could he pretend with any success to be this woman's husband? No two men make love quite the same way; in two minutes she'd realize that he was an impostor, or else she'd wonder what he thought he was up to. All the little sexual rituals and adjustments that a couple evolves and permanently establishes were unknown to him. She would be confused or annoyed or possibly frightened if he betrayed complete ignorance of her body's mechanisms.

And until he understood what had happened to him, he was terrified of revealing his sense of displacement from what he still regarded as his real life. Luckily she seemed not to be in an amorous mood. She gave him a quick kiss, a light friendly embrace, and rolled over, pressing her rump against him. He lay awake a long time, listening to her soft breathing and feeling weirdly adulterous in this bed with another man's wife. Even though she was Mrs. Ted Hilgard, all the same—all the same—

He ruled out the stroke theory. It left too much unexplained. Sudden insanity? But he didn't *feel* crazy. The events around him were crazy; but inside his skull he still seemed calm, orderly, precise. Surely true madness was something wilder and more chaotic. If he had not suffered any disruption of his brain or some all-engulfing delusional upheaval, though, what was going on? It was as though some gateway between worlds had opened for him at Teotihuacan, he thought, and in that instant of dizziness he had stepped through into the other Ted Hilgard's universe, and that other Hilgard had stumbled past him into his own world. That sounded preposterous. But what he was experiencing was preposterous, too.

In the morning Celia said, "I've got a solution to the argument over Cuernavaca versus Guadalajara. Let's go to Oaxaca instead."

"Wonderful!" Hilgard cried. "I *love* Oaxaca. We ought to phone the Presidente Convento to see if they've got a room—that's such a splendid hotel, with those old courtyards and—"

She was staring strangely at him. "When were you in Oaxaca, Ted?"

Hesitantly he said, "Why—I suppose—long ago, before we were married—"

"I thought this was the first time you'd ever been in Mexico."

"Did I say that?" His cheeks were reddening. "I don't know what I could have been thinking of. I must have meant this was *our* first trip to Mexico. I mean, I barely remember the Oaxaca trip, years and years and years ago, but I did go there, just for a weekend once—"

It sounded terribly lame. A trip that was only a vague memory, though the mere mention of Oaxaca had made him glow with recollections of a lovely hotel? Celia had registered the inconsistency, but she chose not to probe it. He was grateful for that. But he knew she must be adding up all the little contradictions and false notes in the things he was saying, and sooner or later she was apt to demand an explanation.

Within an hour they had everything arranged, and that afternoon they flew down to Oaxaca. As they checked in at the hotel, Hilgard had a sudden horrified fear that the clerk, remembering him from two years ago, would greet him by name, but that did not happen. Sitting by poolside before dinner, Hilgard and Celia leafed through their guidebooks, planning their Oaxaca excursions—a drive to the ruins at Monte Albán, a trip out to the Mitla site, a visit to the famous Saturday morning market—and once again he found it necessary to pretend little knowledge of a place he knew quite well. He wondered how convincing he was. They had dinner that night at a splendid Basque restaurant on a balcony overlooking the main plaza, and afterward they strolled back slowly to their hotel. The night air was soft and fragrant, and music floated toward them from the plaza bandstand. When they were halfway back, Celia reached for his hand. He forced himself not to pull away, though even that innocent little contact between them made him feel monstrously fraudulent. At the hotel he suggested stopping in the bar for a nightcap, but she shook her head and smiled. "It's late," she said softly. "Let's just go upstairs." At dinner they had had a carafe of sangria and then a bottle of red Mexican wine, and he felt loose-jointed and tranquil, but not so tranquil that he did not fear the confrontation that lay just ahead. He halted a moment on the landing, looking toward the glittering pool. By moonlight the heavy purple clusters of bougainvillea climbing the ancient stone walls of the courtyard seemed almost black. Huge hibiscus blossoms were strewn everywhere on the lawn and strange spiky flowers rose from a border of large bizarre succulents. Celia touched his elbow. "Come," she said. He nodded. They went into their room. She turned on a lamp and began to undress. Hilgard's eyes met hers and he saw a host of expressions cross her face in an instant—affection, desire, apprehension, perplexity. She knew something was wrong. Give it a try, Hilgard told himself fiercely. Fake it. Fake it. He ran his hand timidly along her hips, her thighs. No.

"Ted?" she said. "Ted, what's going on?"

"I can't explain. I think I'm losing my mind."

"You've been so strange. Since yesterday."

He took a deep breath. "Yesterday is the first time I ever laid eyes on you in my life."

"Ted?"

"It's true. I'm not married. I run a gallery at 60th near Second. I came to Mexico alone last Thursday and I was staying at the Presidente."

"What are you saying, Ted?"

"Yesterday at Teotihuacan I started to walk past the Temple of Quetzalcoatl and I felt a peculiar sensation in my forehead and since then I seem to be somebody else of the same name. I'm sorry, Celia. Do I sound incoherent? I don't think I do. But I know I'm not making any real sense."

"We've been married nine years. We're partners in a marketing research firm, Hilgard & Hilgard, on 57th and Sixth."

"Marketing research. How strange. Do we have children?"

"No. We live in a co-op on 85th, and in the summers we—oh, Ted! *Ted?"*

"I'm so sorry, Celia."

Her eyes in the moonlit darkness were fixed, bright, terrified. There was the acrid smell of fear-sweat in the room, hers, his. She said huskily, "You don't remember any of our life together? Not a thing? In January we went to San Francisco. We stayed at the Stanford Court and it rained all the time and you bought three ivory carvings at a little place across the street from Ghirardelli Square. Last month we got the contract for the Bryce account and you said, 'Fine, let's celebrate by going to Mexico. We've always wanted to go to Mexico and there's no better time than this.' In April we have a big presentation to do in Atlanta, and in May—Ted? Nothing. Ted?"

"Nothing. It's all a blank."

"How scary that is. Hold me, Ted."

"I'm so sorry."

"You don't remember us in bed either?"

"The first time I saw you was two o'clock yesterday afternoon."

"We'll have to fly home tomorrow. There's got to be some kind of therapy—a drug treatment, or maybe even shock—we'll talk to Judith Rose first thing—"

Hilgard felt a shiver of surprise. "Who?"

"You don't remember her either?"

"That's just it. I do. I know a Judith Rose. Tall handsome olive-skinned woman with curly black hair, professor of neurobiology at Rockefeller University—"

"At New York Medical," Celia said. "All the rest is right. You see? You haven't forgotten everything! You still remember Judith!"

"She's at Rockefeller," said Hilgard. "I've known her four or five years. She and I were supposed to take this trip to Mexico together, but at the last moment she had to cancel because she got tied up on a grant proposal, and it looked like she'd be busy with that for weeks and weeks, so we decided that I would come down here by myself, and—"

"What are you saying?" Celia asked, amazed.

"Why, Judith and I are lovers, Celia."

She began to laugh. "Oh, no! No, that's too much. You and Judith—"

"We both see other people. But Judith has the priority. Neither one of us is the marrying sort, but we have an excellent relationship of its kind, and—"

"Stop it, Ted."

"I'm not trying to hurt you. I'm just telling you how it is between me and Judith."

"If you want to tell me you've had affairs, I can handle it. I wouldn't even be immensely surprised. But not with Judith. That's too absurd. Nothing's ever certain in this world, but one thing I'm positive of is that Judith doesn't have any lovers. She and Ron are still like honeymooners. She must be the most faithful woman in the world."

"Ron?"

"Ron Wolff," Celia said. "Judith's husband."

He turned away and stared through the window. Hollowly he said, "In the world I live in, Judith is single and so am I, and she's at Rockefeller University, and I don't know any Ron Wolffs. Or any Celias. And I don't do marketing research. I don't know anything about marketing research. I'm forty-two years old and I went to Harvard and I majored in art history, and I was married to someone named Beverly once for a little while and it was a very bad mistake that I didn't intend to make twice, and I feel sorry as hell for spoiling your vacation and screwing up your life but I simply don't know who you are or where you came from. Do you believe any of that?"

"I believe that you need a great deal of help. And I'll do whatever I have to do to see that you get it, Ted. Whatever has happened to you can be cured, I'm sure, with love and patience and time and money."

"I don't think I'm crazy, Celia."

"I didn't use that word. You're the one who talked of losing your mind. You've had some kind of grotesque mental accident, you've undergone a disturbance of—"

"No," Hilgard said. "I don't think it's anything mental at all. I have another theory now. Suppose that in front of the Temple of Quetzalcoatl there's a mystery place, a—a whirlpool in the structure of the universe, let's say—a gateway, a vortex, whatever you want to call it. Thousands of people walk through at and nothing ever happens to them. But I was the victim of a one-in-a-trillion shot. I went to Mexico in my world and the Ted Hilgard of your world went there at the same time, and we were both at Teotihuacan at the same time, and some immense coincidence brought us both to the whirlpool place simultaneously, and we both went through the gateway and changed places. It could only have happened because our two worlds were touching and he and I were identical enough to be interchangeable."

"That does sound crazy, Ted."

"Does it? Not as crazy as any other theory. Things are different in this world. You, Judith, Ron. The Updike book has a red jacket here. I'm in marketing research instead of art. The museum has a different kind of fountain. Maybe it costs twenty cents to mail a letter instead of eighteen. Everything's *almost* the same, but not quite, and the longer I look, the more differences I see. I have a complete and vivid picture in my mind of the world on the other side of the gateway, down to the littlest details. That can't be just a mental aberration. No aberration is that detailed. How much does it cost to mail a letter?"

"Twenty cents."

"In my world it's eighteen. You see? You see?"

"I don't see anything," Celia said tiredly. "If you can delude yourself into thinking you're entirely different from who you are, you can also very sincerely believe that the postage rate is eighteen cents. They keep changing it all the time anyway. What does that prove? Listen, Ted, we'll go back to New York. We'll try to get you help for this. I want to repair you. I love you. I want you back, Ted. Do you understand that? We've had a wonderful marriage. I don't want it vanishing like a dream."

"I'm so damn sorry, Celia."

"We'll work something out."

"Maybe. Maybe."

"Let's get some sleep now. We're both exhausted."

"That's a fine idea," he said. He touched his hand lightly to her forearm and she stiffened, as though anticipating his caress to be an initiation of lovemaking. But all he was doing was clutching at her as at a rescue line at sea. He squeezed her arm briefly, let go, rolled to the far side of the bed. Tired as he was, he found it hard to fall asleep, and he lay alert a long time. Once he heard her quietly sobbing. When sleep came to him, it was deep and nearly dreamless.

Hilgard would have liked to roam Oaxaca for a few days, enjoying its clear air, lovely old streets, and easy, unhurried pace, but Celia was insistent that they start at once on the task of restoring his memory. They flew back to Mexico City on the 11:00 A.M. flight. At the airport Celia learned that there was a flight to New York in mid-afternoon, but Hilgard shook his head. "We'll stay over in Mexico City tonight and take the first plane out in the morning," he said.

"Why?"

"I want to go back to Teotihuacan."

She gasped. "For Christ's sake, Ted!"

"Humor me. I won't leave Mexico without making certain."

"You think you're just going to walk back into another world?"

"I don't know what I think. I just want to check it out."

"And you expect the other Ted Hilgard to come strolling out from behind a pyramid as you vanish?"

She was starting to sound distraught. Calmly he said, "I don't expect anything. It's just an investigation."

"What if you do? What if you vanish into that whirlpool of yours, and he *doesn't* come out, and I'm left without either of you? Answer me that, Ted."

"I think you're beginning to believe my theory—"

"Oh, no, Ted, no. But—"

"Look," he said, "if the theory's crazy, then nothing will happen. If it isn't, maybe I'll go back where I belong and the right me will return to this world. Nobody knows. But I can't go to New York until I've checked. Grant me that much. I want you to humor me, Celia. Will you do that?"

In the end she had to yield, of course, and they checked their baggage at the airport and booked a hotel room for the night and a flight for the morning, and then they hired a cab to take them to Teotihuacan. The driver spoke little English and it was hard to make him understand that they did not intend to spend all afternoon at the pyramids, but only half an hour or less. That seemed unthinkable to him: why would anyone, even two rich gringos, bother driving an hour and a half each way for a half-hour visit? But finally he accepted the idea. He parked at the southernmost parking lot, near the museum, and Celia and Hilgard waked quickly across the road to the Temple of Quetzalcoatl. His throat was dry and his heart was pounding, and she looked equally tense and drawn. He tried to retrace his steps exactly. "I came through this way," he said, "and just around this corner, as I got my first glimpse of the facade—"

"Ted, please don't. Please."

"Do you want to try? Maybe you'll go through it after him."

"Please. Let's not."

"I have to," he said. Frowning, he made his way along the paved walkway, paused as the facade and its fierce serpent-snouts emerged in sight, caught his breath, plunged onward, waiting for the moment of vertigo, that sensation as of a highly localized earthquake. Nothing. He looked back. Celia, pale, grim, arms folded, was staring at him. Hilgard returned and tried it again. "Maybe I was just six inches off that time. A little to the left—" Nothing. Nothing the third time, or the fourth. A few other tourists passed by, staring oddly at him. Back and forth he went, covering every inch. The pathway was narrow; there were only a few possible routes. He felt no vertigo. No gateway in space opened for him. He did not tumble trough into his rightful world.

"Please, Ted. Enough."

"Once more."

"This is embarrassing. You look so damned obsessive."

"I want to go where I belong," Hilgard said.

Back and forth. Back and forth. He was beginning to feel embarrassed too. Perhaps she was right: this was mere madness that had possessed his soul. There are no gateways. He could not walk back and forth in front of those horrendous stone faces all afternoon. "Once more," he said, and nothing happened and he turned away. "It doesn't work," he told her. "Or else it works only when one's counterpart is passing through it at the same instant. And that would be impossible to arrange. If I could send him a message—tie it to a rock, toss it through the gateway, tell him to be here tomorrow at nine sharp—"

"Let's go," Celia said.

"All right. Yes." Defeated, dejected, he let her lead him across the dry hot temple courtyard to the waiting taxi. They returned to Mexico City in the full madness of the evening rush hour, saying little to each other. Their hotel room turned out to have two single beds instead of a double. Just as well, Hilgard thought. He felt an immense airless distance between himself and this woman who believed she was his wife. They had a bleak dinner at a Zona Rosa restaurant and went to sleep early, and before daybreak they were up and out and on their way to the airport.

"Maybe when you're in your own home," she said, "you'll begin to get pieces of your memory back."

"Maybe," he said.

But the co-op on East 85th meant nothing to him. It was a handsome apartment, thirty stories up, obviously worth a fortune, and it was furnished beautifully, but it was someone else's house, with someone else's books and clothes and treasures in it. The books included a good many that he also owned, and the clothes fit him, and some of the paintings and primitive artifacts were quite in accordance with his own taste. It was like being in one's twin brother's home, perhaps. But he wandered helplessly and in growing panic from room to room, wondering where his files were, his little hoard of boyhood things, his first editions, his Peruvian pottery collection. Delusions? Phantom memories of a nonexistent life? He was cut off from everything that he thought to be real, and it terrified him. The Manhattan phone book listed no Theodore Hilgard on Third Avenue, and no Hilgard Galleries, either. The universe had swallowed that Ted Hilgard.

"I phoned Judith," Celia said, "and told her something of what happened. She wants to see you first thing tomorrow."

He had been to Judith's Rockefeller University office often enough, just a few blocks east of his gallery. But this was a different Judith and her office was at New York Medical, uptown at the edge of Spanish Harlem. Hilgard walked over to Fifth and caught a bus, wondering if he had to pay his fare with some sort of token in this world, wondering if the Metropolitan Museum was where he remembered it, wondering about Judith. He negotiated the bus problem without difficulty. The gray bulk of the museum still crouched on the flank of Central Park. Upper Fifth Avenue looked more or less untransformed, the Frick Collection building just as dignified as ever, the Guggenheim spiral as peculiar as ever. And Judith was untransformed also: elegant, beautiful, warm, with the light of that wonderful intelligence gleaming in her eyes. The only thing missing was that certain mischievous sparkle, that subliminal aura of shared intimacies, that acknowledged that they had long been lovers. She greeted him as a friend and nothing more than a friend.

"What in God's name has been going on with you?" she asked at once.

He smiled ruefully. "Between one moment and the next I seem to have had a total identity transplant. I used to be a bachelor with an art gallery down the block from Bloomingdale's. Now I'm a married man with a marketing research company on 57th Street. And so on. A burst of dizziness at the ruins of Teotihuacan and everything in my life got switched around."

"You don't remember Celia?"

"It isn't just amnesia, if that's where you're heading. I don't remember Celia or anything else having to do with my life here. But I *do* remember a million other things that don't seem to exist any more, a complete reality substructure: phone numbers, addresses, biographical details. You, for instance. The Judith I know is with Rockefeller University. She's single and lives at 382 East 61st Street and her phone number is—you see what I mean? As a matter of fact, you may be the only link between my old life and this one. Somehow I got to know you in both identities. Figure the odds against that."

Judith looked at him with intense, somber concern. "We'll arrange a full battery of neurological tests right away. This sounds like the damnedest mental short circuit I've ever heard of, though I suspect I'll turn up some similar cases in the literature. People who experienced sudden drastic dissociative reactions leading to complete disruption of personality patterns."

"Some sort of schizoid break, is that what you're saying?"

"We don't use terms like schizophrenia or paranoia much any more, Ted. They've been corrupted by popular misconceptions, and they're too imprecise anyway. We know now that the brain is an enormously complex instrument that has capabilities far beyond our rational understanding—I mean freakish stuff like being able to multiply ten-digit numbers in your head—and it's entirely possible that given the right stimulus it can manufacture a perfectly consistent surrogate identity, which—"

"In layman's terms, I'm crazy."

"If you want to use layman's terms," Judith said, "you're suffering from delusions of an extraordinarily vivid kind."

Hilgard nodded. "Among those delusions, you should know, is that you and I were lovers for the past four years."

She smiled. "I'm not at all surprised. You've been carrying on a lovely little flirtation with me from the moment we met."

"Have we ever been to bed together?"

"Of course not, Ted."

"Have I ever seen you naked?"

"Not unless you've been spying on me."

He wondered how much this Judith differed from his. Risking it, he said, "Then how do I know you have a small surgical scar on your left breast?"

Shrugging, she said, "I had a little benign tumor removed years ago. Celia might have mentioned that to you."

"And I'd know which breast?"

"You might."

"I can tell you six or seven other things about your body that only somebody who's plenty familiar with it would know. I can tell you what your favorite lovemaking position is, and why. I can imitate the sound you make at your climax."

"Oh? Can you?"

"Listen," he said, and did his best to duplicate that strange whining passionate cry he had heard so many times. Judith's playful, challenging smile disappeared. Her lips grew taut and her eyes narrowed and splotches of color came to her cheeks. She glanced away from him.

Hilgard said, "I didn't have a tape recorder under your bed. I haven't been discussing your sexual idiosyncrasies with Ron. I wouldn't even know Ron if I tripped over him in the street. And I'm not reading your mind. How do I know all these things, then?"

She was silent. She moved papers about randomly on her desk. Her hands appeared to be shaking.

"Maybe you're the one with dissociative reactions," he said. "You've forgotten all about our affair."

"You know that's nonsense."

"You're right. Because the Judith Rose I've been to bed with is at Rockefeller University. But I've been to bed with a Judith Rose who's very much like you. Do you doubt that now?"

She made no reply. She was staring at him in an astounded way, and there seemed to be something else in her look, a volatility, an excitement, that led him to think he had somehow reached across the barrier of his lost world to touch her, *this* Judith, to arouse her and kindle in her some simulacrum of the love and passion that he knew they had had in another existence. A sudden wild fantasy erupted in him—getting free of Celia, getting Judith free of Ron, and reconstructing in this unfamiliar world the relationship that had been taken from him. But the idea faded as quickly as it had come. It was foolishness; it was nonsense; it was an impossibility.

She said finally, "Describe what you think happened to you?"

He told her in all the detail he could muster—the vertigo, the feeling of passing through a gateway, the gradual discovery of the wrongness of everything. "I want to believe this is all just a mental illness and that six lithium pills will make everything be right again. But I don't think that's how it is. I think what happened to me may be a lot wilder than a mere schizoid break. But I don't want to believe that. I want to think it's just a dissociative reaction."

"Yes. I'm sure you do."

"What do you think it is, Judith?"

"My opinion doesn't matter, does it? What matters is proof."

"Proof?"

She said, "What were you carrying on you when you experienced your moment of vertigo?"

"My camera." He thought. "And my wallet."

"Which had credit cards, driver's license, all that stuff?"

"Yes," he said, beginning to understand. He felt a stab of fear, cold, intense. Pulling his wallet out, he said, "Here—here—" He drew forth his driver's license. It had the Third Avenue address. He took out his Diner's Club card. Judith laid her own next to it. The cards were of different designs. He produced a twenty-dollar bill. She peered at the signatures on it and shook her head. Hilgard closed his eyes an instant and had a flashing vision of the Temple of Quetzalcoatl, the great heavy snouts of the serpents, the massive stone steps. Judith's face was dark and grim, and Hilgard knew she had forced him to confront the final proof, and he had a sense of a mighty gate swinging shut forever behind him. He was not the victim of any psychosis. He had actually made the crossing, and it was irrevocable. His other life was gone—it was dead. Bitterly he said, "I forged all this stuff, right? While I was down in Mexico City I had it all printed up, counterfeit money, a fake driver's license, to make the hoax look really convincing. Right? Right?" He remembered something else and went burrowing for it in his wallet and found it after a frantic search—Judith's own business card, with Department of Neurobiology, Rockefeller University on it in shining engraved letters. The card was old and worn and creased. She looked at it as though he had put a basilisk in her hand. When she stared at him again, it was with a sad and tender look of pity.

At length she said, "Ted, I'll give you all the help I can."

"What kind of help?"

"Making the adaptation. Learning your role here. Celia and I, between us, ought to be able to fill you in on who you're supposed to be. It's the only thing I can imagine doing now. You're right that lithium won't fix anything."

"No," Hilgard said. "Don't involve Celia."

"We have to."

"No," he said. "She thinks I'm her husband and that I'm suffering from an unfortunate dissociative reaction, or whatever you call it. If she comes to realize I'm the complete stranger I've been insisting I am, I'm lost. She'll throw me out and try to find ways of getting him back. And I have no way to function in this world except in the identity of Theodore Hilgard."

"You *are* Theodore Hilgard."

"Yes, and I intend to go on being him. Doing marketing research and living with Celia and signing my name to checks. You'll help me adapt, yes. You'll have a couple of sessions of therapy with me every week, and you'll tell me where I went to college and what the names of my friends are and who the presidents have been in this world, if they have presidents here. So far as everyone else will know, you're helping me recover from a mysterious mental fog. You won't tell a soul that I don't belong here. And sooner or later I *will* belong here. All right, Judith? You see, I've got no choice. There's no way for me to get back across the barrier. I've managed to prove to one other human being that I'm not crazy, and now I've got to put that behind me and start living the life I've been handed. Will you help me?"

"One condition," she said.

"Which is?"

"You're in love with me. I see that, and I don't blame you because I know you can't help thinking I'm *your* Judith. I'm not. I'm Ron's. Go on flirting with me, go on having fantasies about me, but don't give me any moves, ever. All right? Because you might open up in me something that I don't want opened, do you understand? We remain *friends*. Co-conspirators, even. That's all. Is that agreed?"

Hilgard looked at her unhappily. It was a long while before he could bring himself to say it.

"Agreed," he told her at last.

* * *

CELIA SAID, "JUDITH PHONED WHILE you were on the way back. She talked to me for twenty minutes. Oh, Ted—my poor Ted—"

"I'm going to be okay. It'll take time."

"She says these amnesias, these detailed delusions, are extraordinarily rare. You're going to be a textbook case."

"Wonderful. I'm going to need a lot of help from you, Celia."

"Whatever I can do."

"I'm a blank. I don't know who our friends are, I don't know how to practice my profession, I don't even know who *you* are. Everything's wiped out. I'll have to rebuild it all. Judith will do as much as she can, but the real burden, day by day, hour by hour, is going to fall on you."

"I'm prepared for that."

"Then we'll start all over—from scratch. We'll make a go of it. Tonight we'll eat at one of our special restaurants—you'll have to tell me which our special restaurants are—and we'll have the best wine in the house, or maybe a bottle or two of champagne, and then we'll come back here—we'll be like newlyweds, Celia, it'll be like a wedding night. All right?"

"Of course," she said softly.

"And then tomorrow the hard work begins. Fitting me back into the real world."

"Everything will come back, Ted. Don't worry. And I'll give you all the help you need. I love you, Ted. No matter what's happened to you, that hasn't changed. I love you."

He nodded. He took her hands in his. Falteringly, guiltily, with a thick tongue and a numbed heart, he forced himself to get the words out, the words that were his only salvation now, the words that gave him his one foothold on the shores of an unknown continent. "And I love you, Celia," he told the absolute stranger who was his wife.

WE ARE FOR THE DARK

Where do story ideas come from? the non-writer often asks. And the writer's usual answer is a bemused shrug. But in this instance I can reply very precisely.

My wife and I were visiting London in September of 1987 and we were spending virtually every evening at the theatre and some afternoons besides. On the next to last day of our stay we were at the National Theatre, on the south side of the Thames, to see Anthony Hopkins and Judi Dench in *Antony and Cleopatra*, a wondrous, magical matinee performance. Act Five came around, Cleopatra's great catastrophe, and her serving-maid Iras signaled the beginning of the final act with lines long familiar to me:

Finish, good lady; the bright day is done. And we are for the dark.

A mysterious shiver ran through me at those words, *we are for the dark*. I had seen the play half a dozen times or more over the years, and they had never seemed unusual to me before; but, hearing them now, I suddenly saw great vistas of black space opening before me. Later that splendid afternoon, strolling back across the bridge toward the heart of the city under brilliant summer sunshine, I found myself continuing to dwell on the vistas that Shakespeare's five words had evoked for me, and soon I was taking notes for a story that had absolutely nothing to do with the travails of Cleopatra or Antony.

That was the engendering point. The other details followed quickly enough, all but the mechanism of the matter-transmission system around which the interstellar venture of the story was to be built. That had to wait until January of the following year. Now I was in Los Angeles, resting and reading before going out to dinner, and suddenly I found myself scribbling down stuff about the spontaneous conversion of matter into antimatter and a necessary balancing conversion in the opposite direction. Whether any such thing is actually the case is beyond my own scientific expertise, though I suspect it's nonsense, but at least the idea seemed plausible enough to work with, and very quickly I had built an entire method of faster-than-light travel out of it—one which is probably utterly unfeasible in the real universe but would serve well enough in my fictional one. I wrote the story in March of 1988 and Gardner Dozois published it in the October, 1988 *Isaac Asimov's Science Fiction Magazine*. I include it in this book of voyages because it is a story of voyaging, all right: vast voyaging indeed. For me it has some of the sweep and grandeur that first had drawn me to science fiction as a reader more than forty years before, and it pleases me greatly on that account .

GREAT WARMTH COMES FROM HIM, golden cascades of bright, nurturing energy. The Master is often said to be like a sun, and so he is, a luminous creature, a saint, a sun indeed. But warmth is not the only thing that emanates from suns. They radiate at many frequencies of the spectrum, hissing and crackling and glaring like furnaces as they send forth the angry power that withers, the power that kills. The moment I enter the Master's presence I feel that other force, that terrible one, flowing from him. The air about him hums with it, though the warmth of him, the benevolence, is evident also. His power is frightful. And yet all he is is a man, a very old one at that, with a smooth round hairless head and pale, mysteriously gentle eyes. Why should I fear him? My faith is strong. I love the Master. We all love him.

This is only the fifth time I have met him. The last was seven years ago, at the time of the Altair launch. We of the other House rarely have reason to come to the Sanctuary, or they to us. But he recognizes me at once, and calls me by name, and pours cool clear golden wine for me with his own hand. As I expect, he says nothing at first about his reason for summoning me. He talks instead of his recent visit to the Capital, where great swarms of ragged hungry people trotted tirelessly alongside his palanquin as he was borne in procession, begging him to send them into the Dark. "Soon, soon, my children," is what he tells me now that he told them then. "Soon we will all go to our new dwelling-places in the stars." And he wept, he says, for sheer joy, feeling the intensity of their love for him, feeling their longing for the new worlds to which we alone hold the keys. It seems to me that he is quietly weeping now, telling me these things.

Behind his desk is a star-map of extraordinary vividness and detail, occupying the rear wall of his austere chamber. Indeed, it *is* the rear wall: a huge curving shield of some gleaming dark substance blacker than night, within which I can see our galaxy depicted, its glittering core, its spiraling arms. Many of the high-magnitude stars shine forth clearly in their actual colors. Beyond, sinking into the depths of the dark matrix in a way that makes the map seem to stretch outward to infinity, are the neighboring galaxies, resting in clouds of shimmering dust. More distant clusters and nebulae are visible still farther from the map's center. As I stare, I feel myself carried on and on to the outermost ramparts of the universe. I compliment him on the ingenuity of the map, and on its startling realism.

But that seems to be a mistake. "Realism? This map?" the Master cries, and the energies flickering around him grow fierce and sizzling once again. "This map is nothing: a crazy hodgepodge. A lunacy. Look, this star sent us its light twelve billion years ago, and that one six billion years ago, and this other one twenty-three years ago, and we're seeing them all at once. But this one didn't even exist when that one started beaming its light at us. And this one may have died five billion years ago, but we won't know it for five billion more." His voice, usually so soft, is rising now and there is a dangerous edge on it. I have never seen him this angry. "So what does this map actually show us? Not the absolute reality of the universe but only a meaningless ragbag of subjective impressions. It shows the stars as they happen to appear to us just at this minute and we pretend that that is the actual cosmos, the true configuration." His face has grown flushed. He pours more wine. His hand is trembling, suddenly, and I think he will miss the rim of the glass, but no: his control is perfect. We drink in silence. Another moment and he is calm again, benign as the Buddha, bathing me in the glow and lustre of his spirit.

"Well, we must do the best we can within our limitations," he says gently. "For the closer spans the map is not so useless." He touches something on his desk and the star-map undergoes a dizzying shift, the outer clusters dropping away and the center of our own galaxy coming up until it fills the whole screen. Another flick of his finger and the inner realm of the galaxy stands out in bright highlighting: that familiar sphere, a hundred light-years in diameter, which is the domain of our Mission. A network of brilliant yellow lines cuts across the heart of it from star to star, marking the places where we have chosen to place our first receiver stations. It is a pattern I could trace from memory, and, seeing it now, I feel a sense of comfort and well-being, as though I am looking at a map of my native city.

Now, surely, he will begin to speak of Mission matters, he will start working his way round to the reason for my being here. But no, no, he wants to tell me of a garden of aloes he has lately seen by the shores of the Mediterranean, twisted spiky green rosettes topped by flaming red torches of blooms, and then of his visit to a lake in East Africa where pink flamingos massed in millions, so that all the world seemed pink, and then of a pilgrimage he has undertaken in the highest passes of the Sierra Nevada, where gnarled little pines ten thousand years old endure the worst that winter can hurl at them. As he speaks, his face grows more animated, his eyes taken on an eager sparkle. His great age drops away from him: he seems younger by thirty, forty, fifty years. I had not realized he was so keen a student of nature. "The next time you are in my country," I tell him, "perhaps you will allow me to show you the place along the southern shore where the fairy penguins come to nest in summer. In all the world I think that is the place I love the best."

He smiles. "You must tell me more about that some time." But his tone is flat, his expression has gone slack. The effort of this little talk must have exhausted him. "This Earth of ours is so beautiful," he says. "Such marvels, such splendors."

What can he mean by that? Surely he knows that only a few scattered islands of beauty remain, rare fortunate places rising above the polluted seas or sheltered from the tainted air, and that everything else is soiled, stained, damaged, corroded beyond repair by one sort of human folly or another.

"Of course," he says, "I would leave it in a moment, if duty beckoned me into the Dark. I would not hesitate. That I could never return would mean nothing to me." For a time he is silent. Then he draws a disk from a drawer of his desk and slides it toward me. "This music has given me great pleasure. Perhaps it will please you also. We'll talk again in a day or two."

The map behind him goes blank. His gaze, though it still rests on me, is blank now also.

So the audience is over, and I have learned nothing. Well, indirection has always been his method. I understand now that whatever has gone wrong with the Mission—for surely something has, why else would I be here?—is not only serious enough to warrant calling me away from my House and my work, but is so serious that the Master feels the need of more than one meeting to convey its nature to me. Of course I am calm. Calmness is inherent in the character of those who serve the Order. Yet there is a strangeness about all this that troubles me as I have never been troubled before in the forty years of my service.

Outside, the night air is warm, and still humid from earlier rain. The Master's lodge sits by itself atop a lofty stepped platform of pink granite, with the lesser buildings of the Order arrayed in a semi-circle below it on the side of the great curving hill. As I walk toward the hostelry where I am staying, novitiates and even some initiates stare at me as though they would like to prostrate themselves before me. They revere me as I revere the Master. They would touch the hem of my robe, if they could. I nod and smile. Their eyes are hungry, God-haunted, star-haunted.

"Lord Magistrate," they murmur. "God be with you, your grace. God be with you." One novitiate, a gaunt boy, all cheekbones and eyebrows, dares to run to my side and ask me if the Master is well. "Very well," I tell him. A girl, quivering like a bowstring, says my name over and over as though it alone can bring her salvation. A plump monkish-looking man in a gray robe much too heavy for this hot climate looks toward me for a blessing, and I give him a quick gesture and walk swiftly onward, sealing my attention now inward and heavenward to free myself of their supplications as I stride across the terraced platform to my lodging.

There is no moon tonight, and against the blackness of the highlands sky the stars shine forth resplendently by the tens of thousands. I feel those stars in all their multitudes pressing close about me, enclosing me, enfolding me, and I know that what I feel is the presence of God. I imagine even that I see the distant nebulas, the far-off island universes. I think of our little ships, patiently sailing across the great Dark toward the remote precincts of our chosen sphere of settlement, carrying with them the receivers that will, God willing, open all His heavens to us. My throat is dry. My eyes are moist. After forty years I have lost none of my ability to feel the wonder of it.

In my spacious and lavishly appointed room in the hostelry I kneel and make my devotions, and pray, as ever, to be brought ever closer to Him. In truth I am merely the vehicle by which others are allowed to approach Him, I know: the bridge through which they cross to Him. But in my way I serve God also, and to serve Him is to grow closer to Him. My task for these many years has been to send voyagers to the far worlds of His realm. It is not for me to go that way myself: that is my sacrifice, that is my glory. I have no regret over remaining Earthbound: far from it! Earth is our great mother. Earth is the mother of us all. Troubled as she is, blighted as she now may be, dying, even, I am content to stay here, and more than content. How could I leave? I have my task, and the place of my task is here, and here I must remain.

I meditate upon these things for a time.

Afterward I oil my body for sleep and pour myself a glass of the fine brandy I have brought with me from home. I go to the wall dispenser and allow myself thirty seconds of ecstasy. Then I remember the disk the Master gave me, and decide to play it before bed. The music, if that is what it is, makes no impression on me whatever. I hear one note, and the next, and the one after that, but I am unable to put them together into any kind of rhythmic or melodic pattern. When it ends I play it again. Again I can hear only random sound, neither pleasant nor unpleasant, merely incomprehensible.

* * *

THE NEXT MORNING THEY CONDUCT me on a grand tour of the Sanctuary complex to show me everything that has been constructed here since my last visit. The tropical sunlight is brilliant, dazzling, so strong that it bleaches the sky to a matte white, against which the colorful domes and pavilions and spires of the complex stand out in strange clarity and the lofty green bowl of surrounding hills, thick and lush with flowering trees bedecked in yellow and purple, takes on a heavy, looming quality.

Kastel, the Lord Invocator, is my chief guide, a burly, redfaced man with small, shrewd eyes and a deceptively hearty manner. With us also are a woman from the office of the Oracle and two subAdjudicators. They hurry me, though with the utmost tact, from one building to the next. All four of them treat me as though I were something extremely fragile, made of the most delicate spun glass—or, perhaps, as though I were a bomb primed to explode at the touch of a breath.

"Over here on the left," says Kastel, "is the new observatory, with the finest scanning equipment ever devised, providing continuous input from every region of the Mission. The scanner itself, I regret to say, Lord Magistrate, is out of service this morning. There, of course, is the shrine of the blessed Haakon. Here we see the computer core, and this, behind it under the opaque canopy, is the recently completed stellarium."

I see leaping fountains, marble pavements, alabaster walls, gleaming metallic facades. They are very proud of what they have constructed here. The House of the Sanctuary has evolved over the decades, and by now has come to combine in itself aspects of a pontifical capital, a major research facility, and the ultimate sybaritic resort. Everything is bright, shining, startlingly luxurious. It is at once a place of great symbolic power, a potent focus of spiritual authority as overwhelming in its grandeur as any great ceremonial center of the past—ranking with the Vatican, the Potala, the shrine at Delphi, the grand temple of the Aztecs—and an efficient command post for the systematic exploration of the universe. No one doubts that the Sanctuary is the primary House of the Order—how could it be anything else?—but the splendors of this mighty eyrie underscore that primacy beyond all question. In truth I prefer the starker, more disciplined surroundings of my own desert domain, ten thousand kilometers away. But the Sanctuary is certainly impressive in its way.

"And that one down there?" I ask, more for politeness' sake than anything else. "The long flat-roofed building near that row of palms?"

"The detention center, Lord Magistrate," replies one of the subAdjudicators.

I give him a questioning look.

"People from the towns below constantly come wandering in here," he explains. "Trespassers, I mean." His expression is cold. Plainly the intruders of which he speaks are annoyances to him; or is it my question that bothers him? "They hope they can talk us into shipping them out, you understand. Or think that the actual transmitters are somewhere on the premises and they can ship themselves out when nobody's looking. We keep them for a while, so that they'll learn that trying to break in here isn't acceptable. Not that it does much good. They keep on coming. We've caught at least twenty so far this week."

Kastel laughs. "We try to teach them a thing or two, all right! But they're too stupid to learn."

"They have no chance of getting past the perimeter screen," says the woman from the Oracle's office. "We pick them up right away. But as Joseph says, they keep on coming all the same." She shivers. "They look so dirty! And mean, and frightening. I don't think they want to be shipped out at all. I think they're just bandits who come up here to try to steal from us, and when they're caught they give us a story about wanting to be colonists. We're much too gentle with them, let me tell you. If we started dealing with them like the thieves they are, they wouldn't be so eager to come creeping around in here."

I find myself wondering just what does happen to the detainees in the detention center. I suspect that they are treated a good deal less gently than the woman from the Oracle's office thinks, or would have me believe. But I am only a guest here. It's not my place to make inquiries into their security methods.

It is like another world up here above the clouds. Below is the teeming Earth, dark and troubled, cult-ridden, doom-ridden, sweltering and stewing in its own corruption and decay; while in this airy realm far above the crumbling and sweltering cities of the plain these votaries of the Order, safe behind their perimeter screen, go quietly about their task of designing and clarifying the plan that is carrying mankind's best outward into God's starry realm. The contrast is vast and jarring: pink marble terraces and fountains here, disease and squalor and despair below.

And yet, is it any different at my own headquarters on the Australian plains? In our House we do not go in for these architectural splendors, no alabaster, no onyx, just plain green metal shacks to house our equipment and ourselves. But we keep ourselves apart from the hungry sweaty multitudes in hieratic seclusion, a privileged caste, living simply but well, undeniably well, as we perform our own task of selecting those who are to go to the stars and sending them forth on their unimaginable journeys. In our own way we are as remote from the pressures and torments of mankind as these coddled functionaries of the Sanctuary. We know nothing of the life beyond our own Order. Nothing. Nothing.

* * *

The Master says, "I was too harsh yesterday, and even blasphemous." The map behind him is aglow once again, displaying the inner sphere of the galaxy and the lines marking the network of the Mission, as it had the day before. The Master himself is glowing too, his soft skin ruddy as a baby's, his eyes agleam. How old is he? A hundred fifty? Two hundred? "The map, after all, shows us the face of God," he says. "If the map is inadequate, it simply reveals the inadequacies of our own perceptions. But should we condemn it, then? Hardly, any more than we should condemn ourselves for not being gods. We should revere it, rather, flawed though it may be, because it is the best approximation that we can ever make of the reality of the Divine."

"The face of God?"

"What is God, if not the Great Totality? And how can we expect to see and comprehend the Totality of the Totality in a single glance?" The Master smiles. These are not thoughts that he has just had for the first time, nor can his complete reversal of yesterday's outburst be a spontaneous one. He is playing with me. "God is eternal motion through infinite space. He is the cosmos as it was twelve billion years ago and as it was twelve billion years from now, all in the same instant. This map you see here is our pitiful attempt at a representation of something inherently incapable of being represented; but we are to be praised for making an attempt, however foredoomed, at doing that which cannot be done."

I nod. I stare. What could I possibly say?

"When we experience the revelation of God," the Master continues softly, "what we receive is not the communication of a formula about a static world, which enables us to be at rest, but rather a sense of the power of the Creator, which sets us in motion even as He is in motion."

I think of Dante, who said, "In His will is our peace." Is there a contradiction here? How can "motion" be "peace"? Why is the Master telling me all this? Theology has never been my specialty, nor the specialty of my House in general, and he knows that. The abstruse nature of this discussion is troublesome to me. My eyes rest upon the Master, but their focus changes, so that I am looking beyond him, to red Antares and blue Rigel and fiery blue-white Vega, blazing at me from the wall.

The Master says, "Our Mission, you must surely agree, is an aspect of God's great plan. It is His way of enabling us to undertake the journey toward Him."

"Of course."

"Then whatever thwarts the design of the Mission must be counter to the will of God, is that not so?"

It is not a question. I am silent again, waiting.

He gestures toward the screen. "I would think that you know this pattern of lights and lines better than you do that of the palm of your hand."

"So I do."

"What about this one?"

The Master touches a control. The pattern suddenly changes: the bright symmetrical network linking the inner stars is sundered, and streaks of light now skid wildly out of the center toward the far reaches of the galaxy, like errant particles racing outward in a photomicrograph of an atomic reaction. The sight is a jarring one: balance overthrown, the sky untuned, discordancy triumphant. I wince and lean back from it as though he has slapped my face.

"Ah. You don't like it, eh?"

"Your pardon. It seems like a desecration."

"It is," he says. "Exactly so."

I feel chilled. I want him to restore the screen to its proper state. But he leaves the shattered image where it is.

He says, "This is only a probability projection, you understand. Based on early fragmentary reports from the farther outposts, by way of the Order's relay station on Lalande 21185. We aren't really sure what's going on out there. What we hope, naturally, is that our projections are inaccurate and that the plan is being followed after all. Harder data will be here soon."

"Some of those lines must reach out a thousand light-years!"

"More than that."

"Nothing could possibly have gotten so far from Earth in just the hundred years or so that we've been—"

"These are projections. Those are vectors. But they seem to be telling us that some carrier ships have been aimed beyond the predetermined targets, and are moving through the Dark on trajectories far more vast than anything we intend."

"But the plan—the Mission—"

His voice begins to develop an edge again. "Those whom we, acting through your House, have selected to implement the plan are very far from home, Lord Magistrate. They are no longer subject to our control. If they choose to do as they please once they're fifty light-years away, what means do we have of bringing them into check?"

"I find it very hard to believe that any of the colonists we've sent forth would be capable of setting aside the ordinances of Darklaw," I say, with perhaps too much heat in my voice.

What I have done, I realize, is to contradict him. Contradicting the Master is never a good idea. I see the lightnings playing about his head, though his expression remains mild and he continues to regard me benignly. Only the faintest of flushes on his ancient face betrays his anger. He makes no reply. I am getting into deep waters very quickly.

"Meaning no disrespect," I say, "but if this is, as you say, only a probability projection—"

"All that we have devoted our lives to is in jeopardy now," he says quietly. "What are we to do? What are we to do, Lord Magistrate?"

* * *

We have been building our highway to the stars for a century now and a little more, laying down one small paving-block after another. That seems like a long time to those of us who measure our spans in tens of years, and we have nibbled only a small way into the great darkness; but though we often feel that progress has been slow, in fact we have achieved miracles already, and we have all of eternity to complete our task.

In summoning us toward Him, God did not provide us with magical chariots. The inflexible jacket of the relativistic equations constrains us as we work. The speed of light remains our limiting factor while we establish our network. Although the Velde Effect allows us to deceive it and in effect to sidestep it, we must first carry the Velde receivers to the stars, and for that we can use only conventional space-going vehicles. They can approach the velocity of light, they may virtually attain it, but they can never exceed it: a starship making the outward journey to a star forty light-years from Earth must needs spend some forty years, and some beyond, in the doing of it. Later, when all the sky is linked by our receivers, that will not be a problem. But that is later.

The key to all that we do is the matter/antimatter relationship. When He built the universe for us, He placed all things in balance. The basic constituents of matter come in matched pairs: for each kind of particle there is an antiparticle, identical in mass but otherwise wholly opposite in all properties, mirror images in such things as electrical charge and axis of spin. Matter and antimatter annihilate one another upon contact, releasing tremendous energy. Conversely, any sufficiently strong energy field can bring about the creation of pairs of particles and antiparticles in equal quantities, though mutual annihilation will inevitably follow, converting the mass of the paired particles back into energy.

Apparently there is, and always has been since the Creation, a symmetry of matter and antimatter in the universe, equal quantities of each—a concept that has often been questioned by physicists, but which we believe now to be God's true design. Because of the incompatibility of matter and antimatter in the same vicinity, there is very little if any antimatter in our galaxy, which leads us to suppose that if symmetry is conserved, it must be through the existence of entire galaxies of antimatter, or even clusters of galaxies, at great distances from our own. Be that as it may: we will probably have no way of confirming or denying that for many thousands of years.

But the concept of symmetry is the essential thing. We base our work on Velde's Theorem, which suggests that the spontaneous conversion of matter into antimatter may occur at any time—though in fact it is an event of infinitesimal probability—but it must inescapably be accompanied by a simultaneous equal decay of antimatter into matter somewhere else, anywhere else, in the universe. About the same time that Velde offered this idea—that is, roughly a century and a half ago—Wilf demonstrated the feasibility of containment facilities capable of averting the otherwise inevitable mutual annihilation of matter and antimatter, thus making possible the controlled transformation of particles into their antiparticles. Finally came the work of Simtow, linking Wilf's technical achievements with Velde's theoretical work and giving us a device that not only achieved controlled matter/antimatter conversion but also coped with the apparent randomness of Velde symmetry-conservation.

Simtow's device tunes the Velde Effect so that conversion of matter into antimatter is accompanied by the requisite balancing transformation of antimatter into matter, not at some random site anywhere in the universe, *but at a designated site.* Simtow was able to induce particle decay at one pole of a closed system in such a way that a corresponding but opposite decay occurs at the other. Wilf containment fields were employed at both ends of the system to prevent annihilation of the newly converted particles by ambient particles of the opposing kind.

The way was open now, though it was some time before we realized it, for the effective instantaneous transmission of matter across great distances. That was achieved by placing the receiving pole of a Simtow transformer at the intended destination. Then an intricate three-phase cycle carried out the transmission.

In the first phase, matter is converted into antimatter at the destination end in an untuned reaction, and stored in a Wilf containment vessel. This, following Velde's conservation equations, presumably would induce spontaneous transformation of an equivalent mass of antimatter into matter in one of the unknown remote antimatter galaxies, where it would be immediately annihilated.

In the second phase, matter is converted to antimatter at the transmitting end, this time employing Simtow tuning so that the corresponding Velde-law transformation of the previously stored antimatter takes place not at some remote and random location but within the Wilf field at the designated receiving pole, which may be situated anywhere in the universe. What this amounts to, essentially, is the instantaneous particle-by-particle duplication of the transmitted matter at the receiving end.

The final step is to dispose of the unwanted antimatter that has been created at the transmission end. Since it is unstable outside the

Wilf containment vessel, its continued existence in an all-matter system is pointless as well as untenable. Therefore it is annihilated under controlled circumstances, providing a significant release of energy that can be tapped to power a new cycle of the transmission process.

What is accomplished by all this? A certain quantity of matter at the transmission end of the system is destroyed; an exact duplicate of it is created, essentially simultaneously, at the receiving end. It made no difference, the early experimenters discovered, what was being put through the system: a stone, a book, a potted geranium, a frog. Whatever went in here came out there, an apparently perfect replica, indistinguishable in all respects from the original. Whether the two poles were situated at opposite ends of the same laboratory, or in different continents, or on Earth and Mars, the transmission was instant and total. What went forth alive came out alive. The geranium still bloomed and set seed; the frog still stared and leaped and gobbled insects. A mouse was sent, and thrived, and went on to live and die a full mouse-life. A pregnant cat made the journey and was delivered, three weeks later, of five healthy kittens. A dog—an ape—a man—

A man, yes. Has anyone ever made a bolder leap into the darkness than God's great servant Haakon Christiansen, the blessed Haakon whom we all celebrate and revere? He gambled everything on one toss of the dice, and won, and by his victory made himself immortal and gave us a gift beyond price.

His successful voyage opened the heavens. All we needed to do now was set up receiving stations. The Moon, Mars, the moons of Jupiter and Saturn, were only an eyeblink away. And then? Then? Why, of course, what remained but to carry our receivers to the stars?

* * *

For hours I wander the grounds of the Sanctuary, alone, undisturbed, deeply troubled. It is as if a spell of silence and solitude surrounds and protects me. No one dares approach me, neither as a supplicant of some sort nor to offer obeisance nor merely to see if I am in need of any service. I suppose many eyes are studying me warily from a distance, but in some way it must be obvious to all who observe me that I am not to be intruded upon. I must cast a forbidding aura today. In the brilliance of the tropic afternoon a darkness and a chill have settled over my soul. It seems to me that the splendid grounds are white with snow as far as I can see, snow on the hills, snow on the lawns, snow piled high along the banks of the sparkling streams, a sterile whiteness all the way to the rim of the world.

I am a dour man, but not a melancholy or tormented one. Others mistake my disciplined nature for something darker, seeing in me an iciness of spirit, a somberness, a harshness that masks some pervasive anguish of the heart. It is not so. If I have renounced the privilege of going to the stars, which could surely have been mine, it is not because I love the prospect of ending my days on this maimed and ravaged world of ours, but because I feel that God demands this service of me, that I remain here and help others to go forth. If I am hard and stern, it is because I can be nothing else, considering the choices I have made in shaping my course: I am a priest and a magistrate and a soldier of sorts, all in one. I have passed a dedicated and cloistered life. Yet I understand joy. There is a music in me. My senses are fully alive, all of them. From the outside I may appear unyielding and grim, but it is only because I have chosen to deny myself the pleasure of being ordinary, of being slothful, of being unproductive. There are those who misunderstand that in me, and see me as some kind of dismal monastic, narrow and fanatical, a gloomy man, a desolate man, one whom the commonplace would do well to fear and to shun. I think they are wrong. Yet this day, contemplating all that the Master has just told me and much that he has only implied, I am swept with such storms of foreboding and distress that I must radiate a frightful bleakness which warns others away. At any rate for much of this afternoon they all leave me alone to roam as I please.

The Sanctuary is a self-sufficient world. It needs nothing from outside. I stand near the summit of the great hill, looking down on children playing, gardeners setting out new plantings, novitiates sitting cross-legged at their studies on the lawn. I look toward the gardens and try to see color, but all color has leached away. The sun has passed beyond the horizon, here at this high altitude, but the sky is luminous. It is like a band of hot metal, glowing white. It devours everything: the edges of the world are slowly being engulfed by it. Whiteness is all, a universal snowy blanket.

For a long while I watch the children. They laugh, they shriek, they run in circles and fall down and rise again, still laughing. Don't they feel the sting of the snow? But the snow, I remind myself, is not there. It is illusionary snow, metaphorical snow, a trick of my troubled soul, a snowfall of the spirit. For the children there is no snow. I choose a little girl, taller and more serious than the others, standing somewhat to one side, and pretend that she is my own child. A strange idea, myself as a father, but pleasing. I could have had children. It might not have meant a very different life from the one I have had. But it was not what I chose. Now I toy with the fantasy for a time, enjoying it. I invent a name for the girl; I picture her running to me up the grassy slope; I see us sitting quietly together, poring over a chart of the sky. I tell her the names of the stars, I show her the constellations. The vision is so compelling that I begin to descend the slope toward her. She looks up at me while I am still some distance from her. I smile. She stares, solemn, uncertain of my intentions. Other children nudge her, point, and whisper. They draw back, edging away from me. It is as if my shadow has fallen upon them and chilled them as they played. I nod and move on, releasing them from its darkness.

A path strewn with glossy green leaves takes me to an overlook point at the cliff's edge, where I can see the broad bay far below, at the foot of Sanctuary Mountain. The water gleams like a burnished shield, or perhaps it is more like a huge shimmering pool of quicksilver. I imagine myself leaping from the stone balcony where I stand and soaring outward in a sharp smooth arc, striking the water cleanly, knifing down through it, vanishing without a trace.

Returning to the main Sanctuary complex, I happen to glance downslope toward the long narrow new building that I have been told is the detention center. A portcullis at its eastern end has been hoisted and a procession of prisoners is coming out. I know they are prisoners because they are roped together and walk in a sullen, slack way, heads down, shoulders slumped.

They are dressed in rags and tatters, or less than that. Even from fairly far away I can see cuts and bruises and scabs on them, and one has his arm in a sling, and one is bandaged so that nothing shows of his face but his glinting eyes. Three guards walk alongside them, carelessly dangling neural truncheons from green lanyards. The ropes that bind the prisoners are loosely tied, a perfunctory restraint. It would be no great task for them to break free and seize the truncheons from the captors. But they seem utterly beaten down; for them to make any sort of move toward freedom is probably as unlikely as the advent of an army of winged dragons swooping across the sky.

They are an incongruous and disturbing sight, these miserable prisoners plodding across this velvet landscape. Does the Master know that they are here, and that they are so poorly kept? I start to walk toward them. The Lord Invocator Kastel, emerging suddenly from nowhere as if he had been waiting behind a bush, steps across my path and says, "God keep you, your grace. Enjoying your stroll through the grounds?"

"Those people down there—"

"They are nothing, Lord Magistrate. Only some of our thieving rabble, coming out for a little fresh air."

"Are they well? Some of them look injured."

Kastel tugs at one ruddy fleshy jowl. "They are desperate people. Now and then they try to attack their guards. Despite all precautions we can't always avoid the use of force in restraining them."

"Of course. I quite understand," I say, making no effort to hide my sarcasm. "Is the Master aware that helpless prisoners are being beaten within a thousand meters of his lodge?"

"Lord Magistrate—!"

"If we are not humane in all our acts, what are we, Lord Invocator Kastel? What example do we set for the common folk?"

"It's these common folk of yours," Kastel says sharply—I have not heard that tone from him before—"who ring this place like an army of filthy vermin, eager to steal anything they can carry away and destroy everything else. Do you realize, Lord Magistrate, that this mountain rises like a towering island of privilege above a sea of hungry people? That within a sixty-kilometer radius of these foothills there are probably thirty million empty bellies? That if our perimeter defenses were to fail, they'd sweep through here like locusts and clean the place out? And probably slaughter every last one of us, up to and including the Master."

"God forbid."

"God created them. He must love them. But if this House is going to carry out the work God intended for us, we have to keep them at bay. I tell you, Lord Magistrate, leave these grubby matters of administration to us. In a few days you'll go flying off to your secluded nest in the Outback, where your work is undisturbed by problems like these. Whereas we'll still be here, in our pretty little mountain paradise, with enemies on every side. If now and then we take some action that you might not consider entirely humane, I ask you to remember that we guard the Master here, who is the heart of the Mission." He allows me, for a moment, to see the contempt he feels for my qualms. Then he is all affability and concern again. In a completely different tone he says, "The observatory's scanning equipment will be back in operation again tonight. I want to invite you to watch the data come pouring in from every corner of space. It's an inspiring sight, Lord Magistrate."

"I would be pleased to see it."

"The progress we've made, Lord Magistrate—the way we've moved out and out, always in accordance with the divine plan—I tell you, I'm not what you'd call an emotional man, but when I see the track we're making across the Dark my eyes begin to well up, let me tell you. My eyes begin to well up."

His eyes, small and keen, study me for a reaction.

Then he says, "Everything's all right for you here?"

"Of course, Lord Invocator."

"Your conversations with the Master—have they met with your expectations?"

"Entirely so. He is truly a saint."

"Truly, Lord Magistrate. Truly."

"Where would the Mission be without him?"

"Where will it be," says Kastel thoughtfully, "when he is no longer here to guide us?"

"May that day be far from now."

"Indeed," Kastel says. "Though I have to tell you, in all confidence, I've started lately to fear—"

His voice trails off.

"Yes?"

"The Master," he whispers. "Didn't he seem different to you, somehow?"

"Different?"

"I know it's years since you last saw him. Perhaps you don't remember him as he was."

"He seemed lucid and powerful to me, the most commanding of men," I reply.

Kastel nods. He takes me by the arm and gently steers me toward the upper buildings of the Sanctuary complex, away from those ghastly prisoners, who are still shuffling about like walking corpses in front of their jail. Quietly he says, "Did he tell you that he thinks someone's interfering with the plan? That he has evidence that some of the receivers are being shipped far beyond the intended destinations?"

I look at him, wide-eyed.

"Do you really expect me to violate the confidential nature of the Master's audiences with me?"

"Of course not! Of course not, Lord Magistrate. But just between you and me—and we're both important men in the Order, it's essential that we level with each other at all times—I can admit to you that I'm pretty certain what the Master must have told you. Why else would he have sent for you? Why else pull you away from your House and interrupt what is now the key activity of the Mission? He's obsessed with this idea that there have been deviations from the plan. He's reading God knows what into the data. But I don't want to try to influence you. It's absurd to think that a man of your supreme rank in the second House of the Order can't analyze the situation unaided. You come tonight, you look at what the scanner says, you make up your own mind. That's all I ask. All right, Lord Magistrate? All right?"

He walks away, leaving me stunned and shocked. The Master insane? Or the Lord Invocator disloyal? Either one is unthinkable.

I will go to the observatory tonight, yes.

Kastel, by approaching me, seems to have broken the mysterious spell of privacy that has guarded me all afternoon. Now they come from all sides, crowding around me as though I am some archangel—staring, whispering, smiling hopefully at me. They gesture, they kneel. The bravest of them come right up to me and tell me their names, as though I will remember them when the time comes to send the next settlers off to the worlds of Epsilon Eridani, of Castor C, of Ross 154, of Wolf 359. I am kind with them, I am gracious, I am warm. It costs me nothing; it gives them happiness. I think of those bruised and slump-shouldered prisoners sullenly parading in front of the detention center. For them I can do nothing; for these, the maids and gardeners and acolytes and novitiates of the Sanctuary, I can at least provide a flicker of hope. And, smiling at them, reaching my hands toward them, my own mood lightens. All will be well. God will prevail, as ever. The Kastels of this world cannot dismay me.

I see the little girl at the edge of the circle, the one whom I had taken, for a strange instant, to be my daughter. Once again I smile at her. Once again she gives me a solemn stare, and edges away. There is laughter. "She means no disrespect," a woman says. "Shall I bring her to you, your grace?" I shake my head. "I must frighten her," I say. "Let her be." But the girl's stare remains to haunt me, and I see snow about me once more, thickening in the sky, covering the lush gardens of the Sanctuary, spreading to the rim of the world and beyond.

* * *

In the observatory they hand me a polarizing helmet to protect my eyes. The data flux is an overpowering sight: hot pulsing flares, like throbbing suns. I catch just a glimpse of it while still in the vestibule. The world, which has thawed for me, turns to snow yet again. It is a total white-out, a flash of photospheric intensity that washes away all surfaces and dechromatizes the universe.

"This way, your grace. Let me assist you."

Soft voices. Solicitous proximity. To them, I suppose, I am an old man. Yet the Master was old before I was born. Does he ever come here?

I hear them whispering: "The Lord Magistrate—the Lord Magistrate—"

The observatory, which I have never seen before, is one huge room, an eight-sided building as big as a cathedral, very dark and shadowy within, massive walls of some smooth moist-looking greenish stone, vaulted roof of burnished red metal, actually not a roof at all but an intricate antenna of colossal size and complexity, winding round and round and round upon itself. Spidery catwalks run everywhere to link the various areas of the great room. There is no telescope. This is not that sort of observatory. This is the central gathering-point for three rings of data-collectors, one on the Moon, one somewhere beyond the orbit of Jupiter, one eight light-years away on a world of the star Lalande 21185. They scan the heavens and pump a stream of binary digits toward this building, where the data arrives in awesome convulsive actinic spurts, like thunderbolts hurled from Olympus.

There is another wall-sized map of the Mission here, the same sort of device that I saw in the Master's office, but at least five times as large. It too displays the network of the inner stars illuminated in bright yellow lines. But it is the old pattern, the familiar one, the one we have worked with since the inception of the program. This screen shows none of the wild divagations and bizarre trajectories that marked the image the Master showed me in my last audience with him.

"The system's been down for four days," a voice at my elbow murmurs: one of the astronomers, a young one, who evidently has been assigned to me. She is dark-haired, snub-nosed, bright-eyed, a pleasant-faced girl. "We're just priming it now, bringing it up to real-time level. That's why the flares are so intense. There's a terrific mass of data backed up in the system and it's all trying to get in here at once."

"I see."

She smiles. "If you'll move this way, your grace—"

She guides me toward an inner balcony that hangs suspended over a well-like pit perhaps a hundred meters deep. In the dimness far below I see metal arms weaving in slow patterns, great gleaming disks turning rapidly, mirrors blinking and flashing. My astronomer explains that this is the main focal limb, or some such thing, but the details are lost on me. The whole building is quivering and trembling here, as though it is being pounded by a giant's hand. Colors are changing: the spectrum is being tugged far off to one side. Gripping the rail of the balcony, I feel a terrible vertigo coming over me. It seems to me that the expansion of the universe has suddenly been reversed, that all the galaxies are converging on this point, that I am standing in a vortex where floods of ultraviolet light, x-rays, and gamma rays come rushing in from all points of the cosmos at once. "Do you notice it?" I hear myself asking. "The violet-shift? Everything running backwards toward the center?"

"What's that, your grace?"

I am muttering incoherently. She has not understood a word, thank God! I see her staring at me, worried, perhaps shocked. But I pull myself together, I smile, I manage to offer a few rational-sounding questions. She grows calm. Making allowances for my age, perhaps, and for my ignorance of all that goes on in this building. I have my own area of technical competence, she knows—oh, yes, she certainly knows that!—but she realizes that it is quite different from hers.

From my vantage point overlooking the main focal limb I watch with more awe than comprehension as the data pours in, is refined and clarified, is analyzed, is synthesized, is registered on the various display units arrayed on the walls of the observatory. The young woman at my side keeps up a steady whispered flow of commentary, but I am distracted by the terrifying patterns of light and shadow all about me, by sudden and unpredictable bursts of high-pitched sound, by the vibrations of the building, and I miss some of the critical steps in her explanations and rapidly find myself lost. In truth I understand almost nothing of what is taking place around me. No doubt it is significant. The place is crowded with members of the Order, and high ones at that, everyone at least an initiate, several wearing the armbands of the inner levels of the primary House, the red, the green, even a few amber. Lord Invocator Kastel is here, smiling smugly, embracing people like a politician, coming by more than once to make sure I appreciate the high drama of this great room. I nod, I smile, I assure him of my gratitude.

Indeed it is dramatic. Now that I have recovered from my vertigo I find myself looking outward rather than down, and my senses ride heavenward as though I myself am traveling to the stars.

This is the nerve-center of our Mission, this is the grand sensorium by which we keep track of our achievement.

The Alpha Centauri system was the starting-point, of course, when we first began seeding the stars with Velde receivers, and then Barnard's Star, Wolf 359, Lalande 21185, and so on outward and outward, Sirius, Ross 154, Epsilon Indi—who does not know the names?—to all the stars within a dozen light-years of Earth. Small unmanned starships, laser-powered robot drones, unfurling great lightsails and gliding starward on the urgent breath of photonic winds that we ourselves stirred up. Light was their propulsive force, and its steady pressure afforded constant acceleration, swiftly stepping up the velocity of our ships until it approached that of light.

Then, as they neared the stars that were their destinations, scanning for planets by one method or another, plotting orbital deviations or homing in on infrared radiation or measuring Doppler shifts—finding worlds, and sorting them to eliminate the unlivable ones, the gas giants, the ice-balls, the formaldehyde atmospheres—

One by one our little vessels made landfall on new Earths. Silently opened their hatches. Sent forth the robots who would set up the Velde receivers that would be our gateways. One by one, opening the heavens.

And then—the second phase, the fabricating devices emerging, going to work, tiny machines seeking out carbon, silicon, nitrogen, oxygen, and the rest of the necessary building-blocks, stacking up the atoms in the predesignated patterns, assembling new starships, new laser banks, new Velde receivers. Little mechanical minds giving the orders, little mechanical arms doing the work. It would take some fifteen years for one of our ships to reach a star twelve light-years away. But it would require much less than that for our automatic replicators to construct a dozen twins of that ship at the landing point and send them in a dozen directions, each bearing its own Velde receiver to be established on some farther star, each equipped to replicate itself just as quickly and send more ships onward. Thus we built our receiver network, spreading our highway from world to world across a sphere that by His will and our choice would encompass only a hundred light-years in the beginning. Then from our transmitters based on Earth we could begin to send—instantly, miraculously—the first colonists to the new worlds within our delimited sphere.

And so have we done. Standing here with my hands gripping the metal rail of the observatory balcony, I can in imagination send my mind forth to our colonies in the stars, to those tiny far-flung outposts peopled by the finest souls Earth can produce, men and women whom I myself have helped to choose and prepare and hurl across the gulf of night, pioneers sworn to Darklaw, bound by the highest of oaths not to repeat in the stars the errors we have made on Earth. And, thinking now of everything that our Order has achieved and all that we will yet achieve, the malaise that has afflicted my spirit since I arrived at the Sanctuary lifts, and a flood of joy engulfs me, and I throw my head back, I stare toward the maze of data-gathering circuitry far above me, I let the full splendor of the Project invade my soul.

It is a wondrous moment, but short-lived. Into my ecstasies come intrusive sounds: mutterings, gasps, the scurrying of feet. I snap to attention. All about me, there is sudden excitement, almost a chaos. Someone is sobbing. Someone else is laughing. It is a wild, disagreeable laughter that is just this side of hysteria. A furious argument has broken out across the way: the individual words are blurred by echo but the anger of their inflection is unmistakable.

"What's happening?" I ask the astronomer beside me.

"The master chart," she says. Her voice has become thick and hoarse. There is a troubled gleam in her eyes. "It's showing the update now—the new information that's just come in—"

She points. I stare at the glowing star-map. The familiar pattern of the Mission network has been disrupted, now, and what I see, what they all see, is that same crazy display of errant tracks thrusting far out beyond our designated sphere of colonization that I beheld on the Master's own screen two days before.

* * *

THE MOST TACTFUL THING I can do, in the difficult few days that follow, is to withdraw to my quarters and wait until the Sanctuary people have begun to regain their equilibrium. My being here among them now must be a great embarrassment for them. They are taking this apparent deviation from the Mission's basic plan as a deep humiliation and a stinging rebuke upon their House. They find it not merely profoundly disquieting and improper, as I do, but a mark of shame, a sign that God himself has found inadequate the plan of which they are the designers and custodians, and has discarded it. How much more intense their loss of face must be for all this to be coming down upon them at a time when the Lord Magistrate of the Order's other high House is among them to witness their disgrace.

It would be even more considerate of me, perhaps, to return at once to my own House's headquarters in Australia and let the Sanctuary people sort out their position without my presence to distract and reproach them. But that I cannot do. The Master wants me here. He has called me all the way from Australia to be with him at the Sanctuary in this difficult time. Here I must stay until I know why.

So I keep out of the way. I ask for my meals in my chambers instead of going to the communal hall. I spend my days and nights in prayer and meditation and reading. I sip brandy and divert myself with music. I take pleasure from the dispenser when the need comes over me. I stay out of sight and await the unfolding of events.

But my isolation is shortlived. On the third day after my retreat into solitude Kastel comes to me, pale and shaken, all his hearty condescension gone from him now.

"Tell me," he says hoarsely, "what do you make of all this? Do you think the data's genuine?"

"What reason do I have to think otherwise?"

"But suppose"—he hesitates, and his eyes do not quite meet mine—"suppose the Master has rigged things somehow so that we're getting false information?"

"Would that be possible? And why would he do such a monstrous thing in the first place?"

"I don't know."

"Do you really have so little regard for the Master's honesty? Or is it his sanity that you question?"

He turns crimson.

"God forbid, either one!" he cries. "The Master is beyond all censure. I wonder only whether he has embarked upon some strange plan beyond our comprehension, absolutely beyond our understanding, which in the execution of his unfathomable purpose requires him to deceive us about the true state of things in the heavens."

Kastel's cautious, elaborately formal syntax offends my ear. He did not speak to me in such baroque turns and curlicues when he was explaining why it was necessary to beat the prisoners in the detention center. But I try not to let him see my distaste for him. Indeed he seems more to be pitied than detested, a frightened and bewildered man.

"Why don't you ask the Master?" I say.

"Who would dare? But in any case the Master has shut himself away from us all since the other night."

"Ah. Then ask the Oracle."

"The Oracle offers only mysteries and redundancies, as usual."

"I can't offer anything better," I tell him. "Have faith in the Master. Accept the data of your own scanner until you have solid reason to doubt it. Trust God."

Kastel, seeing I can tell him nothing useful, and obviously uneasy now over having expressed these all but sacrilegious suppositions about the Master to me, asks a blessing of me, and I give it, and he goes. But others come after him, one by one—hesitantly, even fearfully, as though expecting me to turn them away in scorn. High and low, haughty and humble, they seek audiences with me. I understand now what is happening. With the Master in seclusion, the community is leaderless in this difficult moment. On him they dare not intrude under any circumstances, if he has given the sign that he is not to be approached. I am the next highest ranking member of the hierarchy currently in residence at the Sanctuary. That I am of another House, and that between the Master and me lies an immense gulf of age and primacy, does not seem to matter to them just now. So it is to me that they come, asking for guidance, comfort, whatever. I give them what I can—platitudes, mainly—until I begin to feel hollow and cynical. Toward evening the young astronomer comes to me, she who had guided me through the observatory on the night of the great revelation. Her eyes are red and swollen, with dark rings below them. By now I have grown expert at offering these Sanctuary people the bland reassurances that are the best I can provide for them, but as I launch into what has become my standard routine I see that it is doing more harm to her than good—she begins to tremble, tears roll down her cheeks, she shakes her head and looks away, shivering—and suddenly my own facade of spiritual authority and philosophical detachment crumbles, and I am as troubled and confused as she is. I realize that she and I stand at the brink of the same black abyss. I begin to feel myself toppling forward into it. We reach for each other and embrace in a kind of wild defiance of our fears. She is half my age. Her skin is smooth, her flesh is firm. We each grasp for whatever comfort we can find. Afterward she seems stunned, numbed, dazed. She dresses in silence.

"Stay," I urge her. "Wait until morning."

"Please, your grace—no—no—"

But she manages a faint smile. Perhaps she is trying to tell me that though she is amazed by what we have done she feels no horror and perhaps not even regret. I hold the tips of her fingers in my hands for a moment, and we kiss quickly, a dry, light, chaste kiss, and she goes.

Afterward I experience a strange new clarity of mind. It is as if this unexpected coupling has burned away a thick fog of the soul and allowed me to think clearly once again.

In the night, which for me is a night of very little sleep, I contemplate the events of my stay at the House of Sanctuary and I come to terms, finally, with the obvious truth that I have tried to avoid for days. I remember the Master's casual phrase at my second audience with him, as he told me of his suspicion that certain colonists must be deviating from the tenets of Darklaw: "Those whom we, *acting through your House,* have selected . . . " Am I being accused of some malfeasance? Yes. Of course. I am the one who chose the ones who have turned away from the plan. It has been decided that the guilt is to fall upon me. I should have seen it much earlier, but I have been distracted, I suppose, by troublesome emotions. Or else I have simply been unwilling to see.

* * *

I DECIDE TO FAST TODAY. When they bring me my morning meal-tray they will find a note from me, instructing them not to come to me again until I notify them.

I tell myself that this is not so much an act of penitence as one of purgation. Fasting is not something that the Order asks of us. For me it is a private act, one which I feel brings me closer to God. In any case my conscience is clear; it is simply that there are times when I think better on an empty stomach, and I am eager now to maintain and deepen that lucidity of perception that came upon me late the previous evening. I have fasted before, many times, when I felt a similar need. But then, when I take my morning shower, I dial it cold. The icy water burns and stings and flays; I have to compel myself to remain under it, but I do remain, and I hold myself beneath the shower head much longer than I might ordinarily have stayed there. That can only be penitence. Well, so be it. But penitence for what? I am guilty of no fault. Do they really intend to make me the scapegoat? Do I intend to offer myself to expiate the general failure? Why should I? Why do I punish myself now?

All that will be made known to me later. If I have chosen to impose a day of austerity and discomfort upon myself, there must be a good reason for it, and I will understand in good time.

Meanwhile I wear nothing but a simple linen robe of a rough texture, and savor the roughness against my skin. My stomach, by midmorning, begins to grumble and protest, and I give it a glass of water, as though to mock its needs. A little later the vision of a fine meal assails me, succulent grilled fish on a shining porcelain plate, cool white wine in a sparkling crystal goblet. My throat goes dry, my head throbs. But instead of struggling against these tempting images I encourage them, I invite my traitor mind to do its worst: I add platters of gleaming red grapes to the imaginary feast, cheeses, loaves of bread fresh from the oven. The fish course is succeeded by roast lamb, the lamb by skewers of beef, the wine in the glass is now a fine red Coonawarra, there is rare old port to come afterward. I fantasize such gluttonies that they become absurd, and I lose my appetite altogether.

The hours go by and I begin to drift into the tranquility that for me is the first sign of the presence of God close at hand. Yet I find myself confronting a barrier. Instead of simply accepting His advent and letting Him engulf me, I trouble myself with finicky questions. Is He approaching me, I wonder? Or am I moving toward Him? I tell myself that the issue is an empty one. He is everywhere. It is the power of God which sets us in motion, yes, but He is motion incarnate. It is pointless to speak of my approaching Him, or His approaching me: those are two ways of describing the same thing. But while I contemplate such matters my mind itself holds me apart from Him.

I imagine myself in a tiny ship, drifting toward the stars. To make such a voyage is not what I desire; but it is a useful focus for my reverie. For the journey to the stars and the journey toward God are one thing and the same. It is the journey into reality.

Once, I know, these things were seen in a different light. But it was inevitable that as we began to penetrate the depths of space we would come to see the metaphysical meaning of the venture on which we had embarked. And if we had not, we could not have proceeded. The curve of secular thought had extended as far as it could reach, from the seventeenth century to the twenty-first, and had begun to crack under its own weight; just when we were beginning to believe that *we* were God, we rediscovered the understanding that we were not. The universe was too huge for us to face alone. That new ocean was so wide, and our boats so very small.

I urge my little craft onward. I set sail at last into the vastness of the Dark. My voyage has begun. God embraces my soul. He bids me be welcome in His kingdom. My heart is eased.

Under the Master's guidance we have all come to know that in our worldly lives we see only distortions—shadows on the cave wall. But as we penetrate the mysteries of the universe we are permitted to perceive things as they really are. The entry into the cosmos is the journey into the sublime, the literal attainment of heaven. It is a post-Christian idea: voyages must be undertaken, motion must never cease, we must seek Him always. In the seeking is the finding.

Gradually, as I reflect on these things yet again, the seeking ends for me and the finding begins, and my way becomes clear. I will resist nothing. I will accept everything. Whatever is required of me, that will I do, as always.

It is night, now. I am beyond any hunger and I feel no need for sleep. The walls of my chamber seem transparent to me and I can cast my vision outward to all the world, the heavy surging seas and the close blanket of the sky, the mountains and valleys, the rivers, the fields. I feel the nearness of billions of souls. Each human soul is a star: it glows with unique fire, and each has its counterpart in the heavens. There is one star that is the Master, and one that is Kastel, and one that is the young astronomer who shared my bed. And somewhere there is a star that is me. My spirit goes outward at last, it roves the distant blackness, it journeys on and on, to the ends of the universe. I soar above the Totality of the Totality. I look upon the face of God.

When the summons comes from the Master, shortly before dawn, I go to him at once. The rest of the House of Sanctuary sleeps. All is silent. Taking the garden path uphill, I experience a marvelous precision of sight: as though by great magnification I perceive the runnels and grooves on each blade of grass, the minute jagged teeth left by the mower as it bit it short, the glistening droplets of dew on the jade surface. Blossoms expand toward the pale new light now streaming out of the east as though they are coming awake. On the red earth of the path, strutting like dandies in a summer parade, are little shining scarlet-backed beetles with delicate black legs that terminate in intricate hairy feet. A fine mist rises from the ground. Within the silence I hear a thousand tiny noises.

The Master seems to be bursting with youthful strength, vitality, a mystic energy. He sits motionless, waiting for me to speak. The star-screen behind him is darkened, an ebony void, infinitely deep. I see the fine lines about his eyes and the corners of his mouth. His skin is pink, like a baby's. He could be six weeks old, or six thousand years.

His silence is immense.

"You hold me responsible?" I say at last.

He stares for a long while. "Don't you?"

"I am the Lord Magistrate of Senders. If there has been a failure, the fault must be mine."

"Yes. The fault must be yours."

He is silent again.

It is very easy, accepting this, far easier than I would have thought only the day before.

He says after a time, "What will you do?"

"You have my resignation."

"From your magistracy?"

"From the Order," I say. "How could I remain a priest, having been a Magistrate?"

"Ah. But you must."

The pale gentle eyes are inescapable.

"Then I will be a priest on some other world," I tell him. "I could never stay here. I respectfully request release from my vow of renunciation."

He smiles. I am saying exactly the things he hoped I would say.

"Granted."

It is done. I have stripped myself of rank and power. I will leave my House and my world; I will go forth into the Dark, although long ago I had gladly given that great privilege up. The irony is not lost on me.

For all others it is heart's desire to leave Earth, for me it is merely the punishment for having failed the Mission. My penance will be my exile and my exile will be my penance. It is the defeat of all my work and the collapse of my vocation. But I must try not to see it that way. This is the beginning of the next phase of my life, nothing more. God will comfort me. Through my fall He has found a way of calling me to Him.

I wait for a gesture of dismissal, but it does not come.

"You understand," he says after a time, "that the Law of Return will hold, even for you?"

He means the prime tenet of Darklaw, the one that no one has ever violated. Those who depart from Earth may not come back to it. Ever. The journey is a one-way trip.

"Even for me," I say. "Yes. I understand."

* * *

I STAND BEFORE A VELDE doorway like any other, one that differs in no way from the one that just a short time before had carried me instantaneously halfway around the world, home from Sanctuary to the House of Senders. It is a cubicle of black glass, four meters high, three meters wide, three meters deep. A pair of black-light lenses face each other like owlish eyes on its inner sides. From the rear wall jut the three metal cones that are the discharge points.

How many journeys have I made by way of transmitting stations such as this one? Five hundred? A thousand? How many times have I been scanned, measured, dissected, stripped down to my component baryons, replicated: annihilated *here*, created *there*, all within the same moment? And stepped out of a receiver, intact, unchanged, at some distant point, Paris, Karachi, Istanbul, Nairobi, Dar-esSalaam?

This doorway is no different from the ones through which I stepped those other times. But this journey will be unlike all those others. I have never left Earth before, not even to go to Mars, not even to the Moon. There has been no reason for it. But now I am to leap to the stars. Is it the scope of the leap that I fear? But I know better. The risks are not appreciably greater in a journey of twenty light-years than in one of twenty kilometers.

Is it the strangeness of the new worlds which I will confront that arouses this uneasiness in me? But I have devoted my life to building those worlds. What is it, then? The knowledge that once I leave this House I will cease to be Lord Magistrate of the Senders, and become merely a wandering pilgrim?

Yes. Yes, I think that that is it. My life has been a comfortable one of power and assurance, and now I am entering the deepest unknown, leaving all that behind, leaving everything behind, giving up my House, relinquishing my magistracy, shedding all that I have been except for my essence itself, from which I can never be parted. It is a great severance. Yet why do I hesitate? I have asked so many others, after all, to submit to that severance. I have bound so many others, after all, by the unbending oaths of Darklaw. Perhaps it takes more time to prepare oneself than I have allowed. I have given myself very short notice indeed.

But the moment of uneasiness passes. All about me are friendly faces, men and women of my House, come to bid me a safe journey. Their eyes are moist, their smiles are tender. They know they will never see me again. I feel their love and their loyalty, and it eases my soul.

Ancient words drift through my mind.

> *Into thy hands, O Lord, I commend my spirit.*

Yes. And my body also.

> *Lord, thou hast been our refuge: from one generation to another. Before the mountains were brought forth, or ever the earth and the world were made: thou art God from everlasting, and world without end.*

Yes. And then:

> *The heavens declare the glory of God: and the firmament showeth His handiwork.*

* * *

THERE IS NO SENSATION OF transition. I was there; now I am here. I might have traveled no further than from Adelaide to Melbourne, or from Brisbane to Cairns. But I am very far from home now. The sky is amber, with swirls of blue. On the horizon is a great dull warm red mass, like a gigantic glowing coal, very close by. At the zenith is a smaller and brighter star, much more distant.

This world is called Cuchulain. It is the third moon of the subluminous star Gwydion, which is the dark companion of Lalande 21185. I am eight light-years from Earth. Cuchulain is the Order's prime outpost in the stars, the home of Second Sanctuary. Here is where I have chosen to spend my years of exile. The fallen magistrate, the broken vessel.

The air is heavy and mild. Crazy whorls of thick green ropy vegetation entangle everything, like a furry kelp that has infested the land. As I step from the Velde doorway I am confronted by a short, crisp little man in dark priestly robes. He is tonsured and wears a medallion of high office, though it is an office two or three levels down from the one that had been mine.

He introduces himself as Procurator-General Guardiano. Greeting me by name, he expresses his surprise at my most unexpected arrival in his diocese. Everyone knows that those who serve at my level of the Order must renounce all hope of emigration from Earth.

"I have resigned my magistracy," I tell him. "No," I say. "Actually I've been dismissed. For cause. I've been reassigned to the ordinary priesthood."

He stares, plainly shocked and stunned.

"It is still an honor to have you here, your grace," he says softly, after a moment.

I go with him to the chapter house, not far away. The gravitational pull here is heavier than Earth's, and I find myself leaning forward as I walk and pulling my feet after me as though the ground is sticky. But such incidental strangenesses as this are subsumed, to my surprise, by a greater familiarity: this place is not as alien as I had expected. I might merely be in some foreign land, and not on another world. The full impact of my total and final separation from Earth, I know, will not hit me until later.

We sit together in the refectory, sipping glass after glass of a sweet strong liqueur. Procurator-General Guardiano seems flustered by having someone of my rank appear without warning in his domain, but he is handling it well. He tries to make me feel at home. Other priests of the higher hierarchy appear—the word of my arrival must be traveling fast—and peer into the room. He waves them away. I tell him, briefly, the reasons for my downfall. He listens gravely and says, "Yes. We know that the outer worlds are in rebellion against Darklaw."

"Only the outer worlds?"

"So far, yes. It's very difficult for us to get reliable data."

"Are you saying that they've closed the frontier to the Order?"

"Oh, no, nothing like that. There's still free transit to every colony, and chapels everywhere. But the reports from the outer worlds are growing increasingly mysterious and bizarre. What we've decided is that we're going to have to send an Emissary Plenipotentiary to some of the rebel worlds to get the real story."

"A spy, you mean?"

"A spy? No. Not a spy. A teacher. A guide. A prophet, if you will. One who can bring them back to the true path." Guardiano shakes his head. "I have to tell you that all this disturbs me profoundly, this repudiation of Darklaw, these apparent breaches of the plan. It begins to occur to me—though I know the Master would have me strung up for saying any such thing—that we may have been in error from the beginning." He gives me a conspiratorial look. I smile encouragingly. He goes on, "I mean, this whole elitist approach of ours, the Order maintaining its monopoly over the mechanism of matter transmission, the Order deciding who will go to the stars and who will not, the Order attempting to create new worlds in our own image—" He seems to be talking half to himself. "Well, apparently it hasn't worked, has it? Do I dare say it? They're living just as they please, out there. We can't control them at long range. Your own personal tragedy is testimony to that. And yet, and yet—to think that we would be in such a shambles, and that a Lord Magistrate would be compelled to resign, and go into exile—exile, yes, that's what it is!—"

"Please," I say. His ramblings are embarrassing; and painful, too, for there may be seeds of truth in them. "What's over is over. All I want now is to live out my years quietly among the people of the Order on this world. Just tell me how I can be of use. Any work at all, even the simplest—"

"A waste, your grace. An absolute shameful waste."

"Please."

He fills my glass for the fourth or fifth time. A crafty look has come into his eyes. "You would accept any assignment I give you?"

"Yes. Anything."

"Anything?" he says.

I see myself sweeping the chapel house stairs, polishing sinks and tables, working in the garden on my knees.

"Even if there is risk?" he says. "Discomfort?"

"Anything."

He says, "You will be our Plenipotentiary, then."

* * *

THERE ARE TWO SUNS IN the sky here, but they are not at all like Cuchulain's two, and the frosty air has a sharp sweet sting to it that is like nothing I have ever tasted before, and everything I see is haloed by a double shadow, a rim of pale red shading into deep, mysterious azure. It is very cold in this place. I am fourteen light-years from Earth.

A woman is watching me from just a few meters away. She says something I am unable to understand.

"Can you speak Anglic?" I reply.

"Anglic. All right." She gives me a chilly, appraising look. "What are you? Some kind of priest?"

"I was Lord Magistrate of the House of Senders, yes."

"Where?"

"Earth."

"On *Earth*? Really?"

I nod. "What is the name of this world?"

"Let me ask the questions," she says. Her speech is odd, not so much a foreign accent as a foreign intonation, a curious singsong, vaguely menacing. Standing face to face just outside the Velde station, we look each other over. She is thick-shouldered, deep-chested, with a flat-featured face, close-cropped yellow hair, green eyes, a dusting of light red freckles across her heavy cheekbones. She wears a heavy blue jacket, fringed brown leggings, blue leather boots, and she is armed. Behind her I see a muddy road cut through a flat snowy field, some low rambling metal buildings with snow piled high on their roofs, and a landscape of distant jagged towering mountains whose sharp black spires are festooned with double-shadowed glaciers. An icy wind rips across the flat land. We are a long way from those two suns, the fierce blue-white one and its cooler crimson companion. Her eyes narrow and she says, "Lord Magistrate, eh? The House of Senders. Really?"

"This was my cloak of office. This medallion signified my rank in the Order."

"I don't see them."

"I'm sorry. I don't understand."

"You have no rank here. You hold no office here."

"Of course," I say. "I realize that. Except such power as Darklaw confers on me."

"Darklaw?"

I stare at her in some dismay. "Am I beyond the reach of Darklaw so soon?"

"It's not a word I hear very often. Shivering, are you? You come from a warmer place?"

"Earth," I say. "South Australia. It's warm there, yes."

"Earth. South Australia." She repeats the words as though they are mere noises to her. "We have some Earthborn here, still. Not many. They'll be glad to see you, I suppose. The name of this world is Zima."

"Zima." A good strong sound. "What does that mean?"

"Mean?"

"The name must mean something. This planet wasn't named Zima just because someone liked the way it sounded."

"Can't you see why?" she asks, gesturing toward the far-off ice-shrouded mountains.

"I don't understand."

"Anglic is the only language you speak?"

"I know some Español and some Deutsch."

She shrugs. "Zima is Russkiye. It means Winter."

"And this is wintertime on Winter?"

"It is like this all the year round. And so we call the world Zima."

"Zima," I say. "Yes."

"We speak Russkiye here, mostly, though we know Anglic too. Everybody knows Anglic, everywhere in the Dark. It is necessary. You really speak no Russkiye?"

"Sorry."

"Ty shto, s pizdy sarvalsa?" she says, staring at me.

I shrug and am silent.

"Bros' dumat' zhopay!"

I shake my head sadly.

"Idi v zhopu!"

"No," I say. "Not a word."

She smiles, for the first time. "I believe you."

"What were you saying to me in Russkiye?"

"Very abusive things. I will not tell you what they were. If you understood, you would have become very angry. They were filthy things, mockery. At least you would have laughed, hearing such vile words. I am named Marfa Ivanovna. You must talk with the boyars. If they think you are a spy, they will kill you."

I try to hide my astonishment, but I doubt that I succeed. *Kill?* What sort of world have we built here? Have these Zimans reinvented the middle ages?

"You are frightened?" she asks.

"Surprised," I say.

"You should lie to them, if you are a spy. Tell them you come to bring the Word of God, only. Or something else that is harmless. I like you. I would not want them to kill you."

A spy? No. As Guardiano would say, I am a teacher, a guide, a prophet, if you will. Or as I myself would say, I am a pilgrim, one who seeks atonement, one who seeks forgiveness.

"I'm not a spy, Marfa Ivanovna," I say.

"Good. Good. Tell them that." She puts her fingers in her mouth and whistles piercingly, and three burly bearded men in fur jackets appear as though rising out of the snowbanks. She speaks with them a long while in Russkiye. Then she turns to me. "These are the boyars Ivan Dimitrovich, Pyotr Pyotrovich, and Ivan Pyotrovich. They will conduct you to the voivode Ilya Alexandrovich, who will examine you. You should tell the voivode the truth."

"Yes," I say. "What else is there to tell?"

* * *

GUARDIANO HAD TOLD ME BEFORE I left Cuchulain, of course, that the world I was going to had been settled by emigrants from Russia. It was one of the first to be colonized, in the early years of the Mission. One would expect our Earthly ways to begin dropping away, and something like an indigenous culture to have begun evolving, in that much time. But I am startled, all the same, by how far they have drifted. At least Marfa Ivanova—who is, I imagine, a third-generation Ziman—knows what Darklaw is. But is it observed? They have named their world Winter, at any rate, and not New Russia or New Moscow or something like that, which Darklaw would have forbidden. The new worlds in the stars must not carry such Earthly baggage with them. But whether they follow any of the other laws, I cannot say. They have reverted to their ancient language here, but they know Anglic as well, as they should. The robe of the Order means something to her, but not, it would seem, a great deal. She speaks of spies, of killing. Here at the outset of my journey I can see already that there will be many surprises for me as I make my way through the Dark.

The voivode Ilya Alexandrovich is a small, agile-looking man, brown-faced, weather-beaten, with penetrating blue eyes and a great shock of thick, coarse white hair. He could be any age at all, but from his vigor and seeming reserves of power I guess that he is about forty. In a harsh climate the face is quickly etched with the signs of age, but this man is probably younger than he looks.

Voivode, he tells me, means something like "mayor," or "district chief." His office, brightly lit and stark, is a large ground-floor room in an unassuming two-story aluminum shack that is, I assume, the town hall. There is no place for me to sit. I stand before him, and the three husky boyars, who do not remove their fur jackets, stand behind me, arms folded ominously across their breasts.

I see a desk, a faded wall map, a terminal. The only other thing in the room is the immense bleached skull of some alien beast on the floor beside his desk. It is an astounding sight, two meters long and a meter high, with two huge eye-sockets in the usual places and a third set high between them, and a pair of colossal yellow tusks that rise straight from the lower jaw almost to the ceiling. One tusk is chipped at the tip, perhaps six centimeters broken off. He sees me staring at it. "You ever see anything like that?" he asks, almost belligerently.

"Never. What is it?"

"We call it a bolshoi. Animal of the northern steppe, very big. You see one five kilometers away and you shit your trousers, I tell you for true." He grins. "Maybe we send one back to Earth some day to show them what we have here. Maybe."

His Anglic is much more heavily accented than Marfa Ivanovna's, and far less fluent. He seems unable to hold still very long. The district that he governs, he tells me, is the largest on Zima. It looks immense indeed on his map, a vast blue area, a territory that seems to be about the size of Brazil. But when I take a closer look I see three tiny dots clustered close together in the center of the blue zone. They are, I assume, the only villages. He follows my gaze and strides immediately across the room to tap the map. "This is Tyomni," he says. "That is this village. This one here, it is Doch. This one, Sin. In this territory we have six thousand people altogether. There are two other territories, here and here." He points to regions north and south of the blue zone. A yellow area and a pink one indicate the other settlements, each with two towns. The whole human population of this planet must be no more than ten thousand.

Turning suddenly toward me, he says, "You are big priest in the Order?"

"I was Lord Magistrate, yes. The House of Senders."

"Senders. Ah. I know Senders. The ones who choose the colonists. And who run the machinery, the transmitters."

"That's right."

"And you are the bolshoi Sender? The big man, the boss, the captain?"

"I was, yes. This robe, this medallion, those are signs of my office."

"A very big man. Only instead of sending, you are sent."

"Yes," I say.

"And you come here, why? Nobody from Earth comes here in ten, fifteen years." He no longer makes even an attempt to conceal his suspicions, or his hostility. His cold eyes flare with anger. "Being boss of Senders is not enough for you? You want to tell us how to run Zima? You want to run Zima yourself?"

"Nothing of that sort, believe me."

"Then what?"

"Do you have a map of the entire Dark?"

"The Dark," he says, as though the word is unfamiliar to him. Then he says something in Russkiye to one of the boyars. The man leaves the room and returns, a few moments later, with a wide, flat black screen that turns out to be a small version of the wall screen in the Master's office. He lights it and they all look expectantly at me.

The display is a little different from the one I am accustomed to, since it centers on Zima, not on Earth, but the glowing inner sphere that marks the location of the Mission stars is easy enough to find. I point to that sphere and I remind them, apologizing for telling them what they already know, that the great plan of the Mission calls for an orderly expansion through space from Earth in a carefully delimited zone a hundred light-years in diameter. Only when that sphere has been settled are we to go farther, not because there are any technical difficulties in sending our carrier ships a thousand light-years out, or ten thousand, but because the Master has felt from the start that we must assimilate our first immense wave of outward movement, must pause and come to an understanding of what it is like to have created a galactic empire on so vast a scale, before we attempt to go onward into the infinity that awaits us. Otherwise, I say, we risk falling victim to a megalomaniacal centrifugal dizziness from which we may never recover. And so Darklaw forbids journeys beyond the boundary.

They watch me stonily throughout my recital of these overfamiliar concepts, saying nothing.

I go on to tell them that Earth now is receiving indications that voyages far beyond the hundred-light-year limit have taken place.

Their faces are expressionless.

"What is that to us?" the voivode asks.

"One of the deviant tracks begins here," I say.

"Our Anglic is very poor. Perhaps you can say that another way."

"When the first ship brought the Velde receiver to Zima, it built replicas of itself and of the receiver, and sent them onward to other stars farther from Earth. We've traced the various trajectories that lead beyond the Mission boundaries, and one of them comes out of a world that received its Velde equipment from a world that got its equipment from here. A granddaughter world, so to speak."

"This has nothing to do with us, nothing at all," the voivode says coolly.

"Zima is only my starting point," I say. "It may be that you are in contact with these outer worlds, that I can get some clue from you about who is making these voyages, and why, and where he's setting out from."

"We have no knowledge of any of this."

I point out, trying not to do it in any overbearing way, that by the authority of Darklaw vested in me as a Plenipotentiary of the Order he is required to assist me in my inquiry. But there is no way to brandish the authority of Darklaw that is not overbearing, and I see the voivode stiffen at once, I see his face grow black, I see very clearly that he regards himself as autonomous and his world as independent of Earth.

That comes as no surprise to me. We were not so naive, so innocent of historical precedent, as to think we could maintain control over the colonies. What we wanted was quite the opposite, new Earths free of our grasp—cut off, indeed, by an inflexible law forbidding all contact between mother world and colony once the colony has been established—and free, likewise, of the compulsion to replicate the tragic mistakes that the old Earth had made. But because we had felt the hand of God guiding us in every way as we led mankind forth into the Dark, we believed that God's law as we understood it would never be repudiated by those whom we had given the stars. Now, seeing evidence that His law is subordinate out here to the will of willful men, I fear for the structure that we have devoted our lives to building.

"If this is why you really have come," the voivode says, "then you have wasted your time. But perhaps I misunderstand everything you say. My Anglic is not good. We must talk again." He gestures to the boyars and says something in Russkiye that is unmistakably a dismissal. They take me away and give me a room in some sort of dreary lodging-house overlooking the plaza at the center of town. When they leave, they lock the door behind them. I am a prisoner.

* * *

IT IS A HARSH LAND. In the first few days of my internment there is a snowstorm every afternoon. First the sky turns metal-gray, and then black. Then hard little pellets of snow, driven by the rising wind, strike the window. Then it comes down in heavy fluffy flakes for several hours. Afterwards machines scuttle out and clear the pathways. I have never before been in a place where they have snow. It seems quite beautiful to me, a kind of benediction, a cleansing cover.

This is a very small town, and there is wilderness all around it. On the second day and again on the third, packs of wild beasts go racing through the central plaza. They look something like huge dogs, but they have very long legs, almost like those of horses, and their tails are tipped with three pairs of ugly-looking spikes. They move through the town like a whirlwind, prowling in the trash, butting their heads against the closed doors, and everyone gets quickly out of their way.

Later on the third day there is an execution in the plaza, practically below my window. A jowly, heavily bearded man clad in furs is led forth, strapped to a post, and shot by five men in uniforms. For all I can tell, he is one of the three boyars who took me to the voivode on my first day. I have never seen anyone killed before, and the whole event has such a strange, dreamlike quality for me that the shock and horror and revulsion do not strike me until perhaps half an hour later.

It is hard for me to say which I find the most alien, the snowstorms, the packs of fierce beasts running through the town, or the execution.

My food is shoved through a slot in the door. It is rough, simple stuff, stews and soups and a kind of gritty bread. That is all right. Not until the fourth day does anyone come to see me. My first visitor is Marfa Ivanovna, who says, "They think you're a spy. I told you to tell them the truth."

"I did."

"Are you a spy?"

"You know that I'm not."

"Yes," she says. "I know. But the voivode is troubled. He thinks you mean to overthrow him."

"All I want is for him to give me some information. Then I'll be gone from here and won't ever return."

"He is a very suspicious man."

"Let him come here and pray with me, and see what my nature is like. All I am is a servant of God. Which I hope is true of the voivode as well."

"He is thinking of having you shot," Marfa Ivanovna says.

"Let him come to me and pray with me," I tell her.

* * *

THE VOIVODE COMES TO ME, not once but three times. We do no praying—in truth, any mention of God, or Darklaw, or even the Mission, seems to make him uncomfortable—but gradually we begin to understand each other. We are not that different. He is a hard, dedicated, cautious man governing a harsh troublesome land. I have been called hard and dedicated and cautious myself. My nature is not as suspicious as his, but I have not had to contend with snowstorms and wild beasts and the other hazards of this place. Nor am I Russian. They seem to be suspicious from birth, these Russians. And they have lived apart from Earth a long while. That too is Darklaw: we would not have the new worlds contaminated with our plagues of the spirit or of the flesh, nor do we want alien plagues of either kind carried back from them to us. We have enough of our own already.

I am not going to be shot. He makes that clear. "We talked of it, yes. But it would be wrong."

"The man who was? What did he do?"

"He took that which was not his," says the voivode, and shrugs. "He was worse than a beast. He could not be allowed to live among us."

Nothing is said of when I will be released. I am left alone for two more days. The coarse dull food begins to oppress me, and the solitude. There is another snowstorm, worse than the last. From my window I see ungainly birds something like vultures, with long naked yellow necks and drooping reptilian tails, circling in the sky. Finally the voivode comes a second time, and simply stares at me as though expecting me to blurt out some confession. I look at him in puzzlement, and after long silence he laughs explosively and summons an aide, who brings in a bottle of a clear fiery liquor. Two or three quick gulps and he becomes expansive, and tells me of his childhood. His father was voivode before him, long ago, and was killed by a wild animal while out hunting. I try to imagine a world that still has dangerous animals roaming freely. To me it is like a world where the gods of primitive man are real and alive, and go disguised among mortals, striking out at them randomly and without warning.

Then he asks me about myself, wanting to know how old I was when I became a priest of the Order, and whether I was as religious as a boy as I am now. I tell him what I can, within the limits placed on me by my vows. Perhaps I go a little beyond the limits, even. I explain about my early interest in technical matters, my entering the Order at seventeen, my life of service.

The part about my religious vocation seems odd to him. He appears to think I must have undergone some sudden conversion midway through my adolescence. "There has never been a time when God has not been present at my side," I say.

"How very lucky you are," he says.

"Lucky?"

He touches his glass to mine.

"Your health," he says. We drink. Then he says, "What does your Order really want with us, anyway?"

"With you? We want nothing with you. Three generations ago we gave you your world; everything after that is up to you."

"No. You want to dictate how we shall live. You are people of the past, and we are people of the future, and you are unable to understand our souls."

"Not so," I tell him. "Why do you think we want to dictate to you? Have we interfered with you up till now?"

"You are here now, though."

"Not to interfere. Only to gain information."

"Ah. Is this so?" He laughs and drinks. "Your health," he says again.

He comes a third time a couple of days later. I am restless and irritable when he enters; I have had enough of this imprisonment, these groundless suspicions, this bleak and frosty world; I am ready to be on my way. It is all I can do to keep from bluntly demanding my freedom. As it is I am uncharacteristically sharp and surly with him, answering in quick snarling monosyllables when he asks me how I have slept, whether I am well, is my room warm enough. He gives me a look of surprise, and then one of thoughtful appraisal, and then he smiles. He is in complete control, and we both know it.

"Tell me once more," he says, "why you have come to us."

I calm myself and run through the whole thing one more time. He nods. Now that he knows me better, he tells me, he begins to think that I may be sincere, that I have not come to spy, that I actually would be willing to chase across the galaxy this way in pursuit of an ideal. And so on in that vein for a time, both patronizing and genuinely friendly almost in the same breath.

Then he says, "We have decided that it is best to send you onward."

"Where?"

"The name of the world is Entrada. It is one of our daughter worlds, eleven light-years away, a very hot place. We trade our precious metals for their spices. Someone came from there not long ago and told us of a strange man named Oesterreich, who passed through Entrada and spoke of undertaking journeys to new and distant places. Perhaps he can provide you with the answers that you seek. If you can find him."

"Oesterreich?"

"That is the name, yes."

"Can you tell me any more about him than that?"

"What I have told you is all that I know."

He stares at me truculently, as if defying me to show that he is lying. But I believe him.

"Even for that much assistance, I am grateful," I say.

"Yes. Never let it be said that we have failed to offer aid to the Order." He smiles again. "But if you ever come to this world again, you understand, we will know that you were a spy after all. And we will treat you accordingly."

* * *

MARFA IVANOVNA IS IN CHARGE of the Velde equipment. She positions me within the transmitting doorway, moving me about this way and that to be certain that I will be squarely within the field. When she is satisfied, she says, "You know, you ought not ever come back this way."

"I understand that."

"You must be a very virtuous man. Ilya Alexandrovitch came very close to putting you to death, and then he changed his mind. This I know for certain. But he remains suspicious of you. He is suspicious of everything the Order does."

"The Order has never done anything to injure him or anyone else on this planet, and never will."

"That may be so," says Marfa Ivanovna. "But still, you are lucky to be leaving here alive. You should not come back. And you should tell others of your sort to stay away from Zima too. We do not accept the Order here."

I am still pondering the implications of that astonishing statement when she does something even more astonishing. Stepping into the cubicle with me, she suddenly opens her fur-trimmed jacket, revealing full round breasts, very pale, dusted with the same light red freckles that she has on her face. She seizes me by the hair and presses my head against her breasts, and holds it there a long moment. Her skin is very warm. It seems almost feverish.

"For luck," she says, and steps back. Her eyes are sad and strange. It could almost be a loving look, or perhaps a pitying one, or both. Then she turns away from me and throws the switch.

* * *

ENTRADA IS TORRID AND MOIST, a humid sweltering hothouse of a place so much the antithesis of Zima that my body rebels immediately against the shift from one world to the other. Coming forth into it, I feel the heat rolling toward me like an implacable wall of water. It sweeps up and over me and smashes me to my knees. I am sick and numb with displacement and dislocation. It seems impossible for me to draw a breath. The thick, shimmering, golden-green atmosphere here is almost liquid; it crams itself into my throat, it squeezes my lungs in an agonizing grip. Through blurring eyes I see a tight green web of jungle foliage rising before me, a jumbled vista of corrugated-tin shacks, a patch of sky the color of shallow sea-water, and, high above, a merciless, throbbing, weirdly elongated sun shaped like no sun I have ever imagined. Then I sway and fall forward and see nothing more.

I lie suspended in delirium a long while. It is a pleasing restful time, like being in the womb. I am becalmed in a great stillness, lulled by soft voices and sweet music. But gradually consciousness begins to break through. I swim upward toward the light that glows somewhere above me, and my eyes open, and I see a serene friendly face, and a voice says, "It's nothing to worry about. Everyone who comes here the way you did has a touch of it, the first time. At your age I suppose it's worse than usual."

Dazedly I realize that I am in mid-conversation.

"A touch of what?" I ask.

The other, who is a slender gray-eyed woman of middle years wearing a sort of Indian sari, smiles and says, "Of the Falling. It's a lambda effect. But I'm sorry. We've been talking for a while, and I thought you were awake. Evidently you weren't."

"I am now," I tell her. "But I don't think I've been for very long."

Nodding, she says, "Let's start over. You're in Traveler's Hospice. The humidity got you, and the heat, and the lightness of the gravity. You're all right now."

"Yes."

"Do you think you can stand?"

"I can try," I say.

She helps me up. I feel so giddy that I expect to float away. Carefully she guides me toward the window of my room. Outside I see a veranda and a close-cropped lawn. Just beyond, a dark curtain of dense bush closes everything off. The intense light makes everything seem very near; it is as if I could put my hand out the window and thrust it into the heart of that exuberant jungle.

"So bright—the sun—" I whisper.

In fact there are two whitish suns in the sky, so close to each other that their photospheres overlap and each is distended by the other's gravitational pull, making them nearly oval in shape. Together they seem to form a single egg-shaped mass, though even the one quick dazzled glance I can allow myself tells me that this is really a binary system, discrete bundles of energy forever locked together.

Awed and amazed, I touch my fingertips to my cheek in wonder, and feel a thick coarse beard there that I had not had before.

The woman says, "Two suns, actually. Their centers are only about a million and a half kilometers apart, and they revolve around each other every seven and a half hours. We're the fourth planet out, but we're as far from them as Neptune is from the Sun."

But I have lost interest for the moment in astronomical matters. I rub my face, exploring its strange new shagginess. The beard covers my cheeks, my jaws, much of my throat.

"How long have I been unconscious?" I ask.

"About three weeks."

"Your weeks or Earth weeks?"

"We use Earth weeks here."

"And that was just a light case? Does everybody who gets the Falling spend three weeks being delirious?"

"Sometimes much more. Sometimes they never come out of it."

I stare at her. "And it's just the heat, the humidity, the lightness of the gravity? They can knock you down the moment you step out of the transmitter and put you under for weeks? I would think it should take something like a stroke to do that."

"It *is* something like a stroke," she says. "Did you think that traveling between stars is like stepping across the street? You come from a low-lambda world to a high-lambda one without doing your adaptation drills and of course the change is going to knock you flat right away. What did you expect?"

High-lambda? Low-lambda?

"I don't know what you're talking about," I say.

"Didn't they tell you on Zima about the adaptation drills before they shipped you here?"

"Not a thing."

"Or about lambda differentials?"

"Nothing," I say.

Her face grows very solemn. "Pigs, that's all they are. They should have prepared you for the jump. But I guess they didn't care whether you lived or died."

I think of Marfa Ivanovna, wishing me luck as she reached for the switch. I think of that strange sad look in her eyes. I think of the voivode Ilya Alexandrovitch, who might have had me shot but decided instead to offer me a free trip off his world, a one-way trip. There is much that I am only now beginning to understand, I see, about this empire that Earth is building in what we call the Dark. We are building it in the dark, yes, in more ways than one.

"No," I say. "I guess they didn't care."

* * *

THEY ARE FRIENDLIER ON ENTRADA, no question of that. Interstellar trade is important here and visitors from other worlds are far more common than they are on wintry Zima. Apparently I am free to live at the hospice as long as I wish. The weeks of my stay have stretched now into months, and no one suggests that it is time for me to be moving along.

I had not expected to stay here so long. But gathering the information I need has been a slow business, with many a maddening detour and delay.

At least I experience no further lambda problems. Lambda, they tell me, is a planetary force that became known only when Velde jumps between solar systems began. There are high-lambda worlds and low-lambda worlds, and anyone going from one kind to the other without proper preparation is apt to undergo severe stress. It is all news to me. I wonder if the Order on Earth is aware at all of these difficulties. But perhaps they feel that matters which may arise during journeys *between* worlds of the Dark are of no concern to us of the mother world.

They have taken me through the adaptation drills here at the hospice somehow while I was still unconscious, and I am more or less capable now of handling Entradan conditions. The perpetual steambath heat, which no amount of air conditioning seems really to mitigate, is hard to cope with, and the odd combination of heavy atmosphere and light gravity puts me at risk of nausea with every breath, though after a time I get the knack of pulling shallow nips of air. There are allergens borne on every breeze, too, pollen of a thousand kinds and some free-floating alkaloids, against which I need daily medication. My face turns red under the force of the double sun, and the skin of my cheeks gets strangely soft, which makes my new beard an annoyance. I rid myself of it. My hair acquires an unfamiliar silver sheen, not displeasing, but unexpected. All this considered, though, I can manage here.

Entrada has a dozen major settlements and several hundred thousand people. It is a big world, metal-poor and light, on which a dozen small continents and some intricate archipelagoes float in huge warm seas. The whole planet is tropical, even at the poles: distant though it is from its suns, it would probably be inhospitable to human life if it were very much closer. The soil of Entrada has the lunatic fertility that we associate with the tropics, and agriculture is the prime occupation here. The people, drawn from many regions of Earth, are attractive and outgoing, with an appealingly easy manner.

It appears that they have not drifted as far from Darklaw here as the Zimans have.

Certainly the Order is respected. There are chapels everywhere and the people use them. Whenever I enter one there is a little stir of excitement, for it is generally known that I was Lord Magistrate of the

Senders during my time on Earth, and that makes me a celebrity, or a curiosity, or both. Many of the Entradans are Earthborn themselves—emigration to this world was still going on as recently as eight or ten years ago—and the sight of my medallion inspires respect and even awe in them. I do not wear my robe of office, not in this heat. Probably I will never wear it again, no matter what climate I find myself in when I leave here. Someone else is Lord Magistrate of the House of Senders now, after all. But the medallion alone is enough to win me a distinction here that I surely never had on Zima.

I think, though, that they pick and choose among the tenets of Darklaw to their own satisfaction on Entrada, obeying those which suit them and casting aside anything that seems too constricting. I am not sure of this, but it seems likely. To discuss such matters with anyone I have come to know here is, of course, impossible. The people I have managed to get to know so far, at the hospice, at the chapel house in town, at the tavern where I have begun to take my meals, are pleasant and sociable. But they become uneasy, even evasive, whenever I speak of any aspect of Earth's migration into space. Let me mention the Order, or the Master, or anything at all concerning the Mission, and they begin to moisten their lips and look uncomfortable. Clearly things are happening out here, things never envisioned by the founders of the Order, and they are unwilling to talk about them with anyone who himself wears the high medallion.

It is a measure of the changes that have come over me since I began this journey that I am neither surprised nor dismayed by this.

Why should we have believed that we could prescribe a single code of law that would meet the needs of hundreds of widely varying worlds? Of course they would modify our teachings to fit their own evolving cultures, and some would probably depart entirely from that which we had created for them. It was only to be expected. Many things have become clear to me on this journey that I did not see before, that, indeed, I did not so much as pause to consider. But much else remains mysterious.

* * *

I AM AT THE BUSY waterfront esplanade, leaning over the rail, staring out toward Volcano Isle, a dim gray peak far out to sea. It is mid-morning, before the full heat of noon has descended. I have been here long enough so that I think of this as the cool time of the day.

"Your grace?" a voice calls. "Lord Magistrate?"

No one calls me those things here.

I glance down to my left. A dark-haired man in worn seaman's clothes and a braided captain's hat is looking up at me out of a rowboat just below the sea-wall. He is smiling and waving. I have no idea who he is, but he plainly wants to talk with me, and anything that helps me break the barrier that stands between me and real knowledge of this place is to be encouraged.

He points to the far end of the harbor, where there is a ramp leading from the little beach to the esplanade, and tells me in pantomime that he means to tie up his boat and go ashore. I wait for him at the head of the ramp, and after a few moments he comes trudging up to greet me. He is perhaps fifty years old, trim and sun-bronzed, with a lean weather-beaten face.

"You don't remember me," he says.

"I'm afraid not."

"You personally interviewed me and approved my application to emigrate, eighteen years ago. Sandys. Lloyd Sandys." He smiles hopefully, as though his name alone will open the floodgates of my memory.

When I was Lord Magistrate I reviewed five hundred emigrant dossiers a week, and interviewed ten or fifteen applicants a day myself, and forgot each one the moment I approved or rejected them. But for this man the interview with the Lord Magistrate of the Senders was the most significant moment of his life.

"Sorry," I say. "So many names, so many faces—"

"I would have recognized you even if I hadn't already heard you were here. After all these years, you've hardly changed at all, your grace." He grins. "So now you've come to settle on Entrada yourself?"

"Only a short visit."

"Ah." He is visibly disappointed. "You ought to think of staying. It's a wonderful place, if you don't mind a little heat. I haven't regretted coming here for a minute."

He takes me to a seaside tavern where he is obviously well known, and orders lunch for both of us: skewers of small corkscrew-shaped creatures that look and taste a little like squid, and a flask of a strange but likable emerald-colored wine with a heavy, musky, spicy flavor. He tells me that he has four sturdy sons and four strapping daughters, and that he and his wife run a harbor ferry, short hops to the surrounding islands of this archipelago, which is Entrada's main population center. There still are traces of Melbourne in his accent. He seems very happy. "You'll let me take you on a tour, won't you?" he asks. "We've got some very beautiful islands out there, and you can't get to see them by Velde jumps."

I protest that I don't want to take him away from his work, but he shrugs that off. Work can always wait, he says. There's no hurry, on a world where anyone can dip his net in the sea and come up with a good meal. We have another flask of wine. He seems open, genial, trustworthy. Over cheese and fruit he asks me why I've come here.

I hesitate.

"A fact-finding mission," I say.

"Ah. Is that really so? Can I be of any help, d'ye think?"

* * *

It is several more winy lunches, and a little boat-trip to some nearby islands fragrant with masses of intoxicating purple blooms, before I am willing to begin taking Sandys into my confidence. I tell him that the Order has sent me into the Dark to study and report on the ways of life that are evolving on the new worlds. He seems untroubled by that, though Ilya Alexandrovitch might have had me shot for such an admission.

Later, I tell him about the apparent deviations from the planned scope of the Mission that are the immediate reason for my journey.

"You mean, going out beyond the hundred-light-year zone?"

"Yes."

"That's pretty amazing, that anyone would go there."

"We have indications that it's happening."

"Really," he says.

"And on Zima," I continue, "I picked up a story that somebody here on Entrada has been preaching ventures into the far Dark. You don't know anything about that, do you?"

His only overt reaction is a light frown, quickly erased. Perhaps he has nothing to tell me. Or else we have reached the point, perhaps, beyond which he is unwilling to speak.

But some hours later he revives the topic himself. We are on our way back to harbor, sunburned and a little tipsy from an outing to one of the prettiest of the local islands, when he suddenly says, "I remember hearing something about that preacher you mentioned before."

I wait, not saying anything.

"My wife told me about him. There was somebody going around talking about far voyages, she said." New color comes to his face, a deep red beneath the bronze. "I must have forgotten about it when we were talking before." In fact he must know that I think him disingenuous for withholding this from me all afternoon. But I make no attempt to call him on that. We are still testing each other.

I ask him if he can get more information for me, and he promises to discuss it with his wife. Then he is absent for a week, making a circuit of the outer rim of the archipelago to deliver freight. When he returns, finally, he brings with him an unusual golden brandy from one of the remote islands as a gift for me, but my cautious attempt to revive our earlier conversation runs into a familiar sort of Entradan evasiveness. It is almost as though he doesn't know what I'm referring to.

At length I say bluntly, "Have you had a chance to talk to your wife about that preacher?"

He looks troubled. "In fact, it slipped my mind."

"Ah."

"Tonight, maybe—"

"I understand that the man's name is Oesterreich," I say.

His eyes go wide.

"You know that, do you?"

"Help me, will you, Sandys? I'm the one who sent you to this place, remember? Your whole life here wouldn't exist but for me."

"That's true. That's very true."

"Who's Oesterreich?"

"I never knew him. I never had any dealings with him."

"Tell me what you know about him."

"A crazy man, he was."

"Was?"

"He's not here any more."

I uncork the bottle of rare brandy, pour a little for myself, a more generous shot for Sandys.

"Where'd he go?" I ask.

He sips, reflectively. After a time he says, "I don't know, your grace. That's God's own truth. I haven't seen or heard of him in a couple of years. He chartered one of the other captains here, a man named Feraud, to take him to one of the islands, and that's the last I know."

"Which island?"

"I don't know."

"Do you think Feraud remembers?"

"I could ask him," Sandys says.

"Yes. Ask him. Would you do that?"

"I could ask him, yes," he says.

* * *

So it goes, slowly. Sandys confers with his friend Feraud, who hesitates and evades, or so Sandys tells me; but eventually Feraud finds it in him to recall that he had taken Oesterreich to Volcano Isle, three hours' journey to the west. Sandys admits to me, now that he is too deep in to hold back, that he himself actually heard Oesterreich speak several times, that Oesterreich claimed to be in possession of some secret way of reaching worlds immensely remote from the settled part of the Dark.

"And do you believe that?"

"I don't know. He seemed crazy to me."

"Crazy how?"

"The look in his eye. The things he said. That it's our destiny to reach the rim of the universe. That the Order holds us back out of its own timidity. That we must follow the Goddess Avatar, who beckons us onward to—"

"*Who?*"

His face flushes bright crimson. "The Goddess Avatar. I don't know what she is, your grace. Honestly. It's some cult he's running, some new religion he's made up. I told you he's crazy. I've never believed any of this."

There is a pounding in my temples, and a fierce ache behind my eyes. My throat has gone dry and not even Sandys' brandy can soothe it.

"Where do you think Oesterreich is now?"

"I don't know." His eyes are tormented. "Honestly. Honestly. I think he's gone from Entrada."

"Is there a Velde transmitter station on Volcano Isle?"

He thinks for a moment. "Yes. Yes, there is."

"Will you do me one more favor?" I ask. "One thing, and then I won't ask any more."

"Yes?"

"Take a ride over to Volcano Isle tomorrow. Talk with the people who run the Velde station there. See if you can find out where they sent Oesterreich."

"They'll never tell me anything like that."

I put five shining coins in front of him, each one worth as much as he can make in a month's ferrying.

"Use these," I say. "If you come back with the answer, there are five more for you."

"Come with me, your grace. You speak to them."

"No."

"You ought to see Volcano Isle. It's a fantastic place. The center of it blew out thousands of years ago, and people live up on the rim, around a lagoon so deep nobody's been able to find the bottom. I was meaning to take you there anyway, and—"

"You go," I say. "Just you."

After a moment he pockets the coins. In the morning I watch him go off in one of his boats, a small hydrofoil skiff. There is no word from him for two days, and then he comes to me at the hospice, looking tense and unshaven.

"It wasn't easy," he says.

"You found out where he went?"

"Yes."

"Go on," I urge, but he is silent, lips working but nothing coming out. I produce five more of the coins and lay them before him. He ignores them. This is some interior struggle.

He says, after a time, "We aren't supposed to reveal anything about anything of this. I told you what I've already told you because I owe you. You understand that?"

"Yes."

"You mustn't ever let anyone know who gave you the information."

"Don't worry," I say.

He studies me for a time. Then he says, "The name of the planet where Oesterreich went is Eden. It's a seventeen-light-year hop. You won't need lambda adjustment, coming from here. There's hardly any differential. All right, your grace? That's all I can tell you." He stares at the coins and shakes his head. Then he runs out of the room, leaving them behind.

* * *

EDEN TURNS OUT TO BE no Eden at all. I see a spongy, marshy landscape, a gray sodden sky, a raw, half-built town. There seem to be two suns, a faint yellow-white one and a larger reddish one. A closer look reveals that the system here is like the Lalande one: the reddish one is not really a star but a glowing substellar mass about the size of Jupiter. Eden is one of its moons. What we like to speak of in the Order as the new Earths of the Dark are in fact scarcely Earthlike at all, I am coming to realize: all they have in common with the mother world is a tolerably breathable atmosphere and a manageable gravitational pull. How can we speak of a world as an Earth when its sun is not yellow but white or red or green, or there are two or three or even four suns in the sky all day and all night, or the primary source of warmth is not even a sun but a giant planet-like ball of hot gas?

"Settler?" they ask me, when I arrive on Eden.

"Traveler," I reply. "Short-term visit."

They scarcely seem to care. This is a difficult world and they have no time for bureaucratic formalities. So long as I have money, and I do—at least these strange daughter worlds of ours still honor our currency—I am, if not exactly welcome, then at least permitted.

Do they observe Darklaw here? When I arrive I am wearing neither my robe of office nor my medallion, and it seems just as well. The Order appears not to be in favor, this far out. I can find no sign of our chapels or other indications of submission to our rule. What I do find, as I wander the rough streets of this jerry-rigged town on this cool, rainswept world, is a chapel of some other kind, a white geodesic dome with a mysterious symbol—three superimposed six-pointed stars—painted in black on its door.

"Goddess save you," a woman coming out says brusquely to me, and shoulders past me in the rain.

They are not even bothering to hide things, this far out on the frontier.

I go inside. The walls are white and an odd, disturbing mural is painted on one of them. It shows what seems to be a windowless ruined temple drifting in blue starry space, with all manner of objects and creatures floating near it, owls, skulls, snakes, masks, golden cups, bodiless heads. It is like a scene viewed in a dream. The temple's alabaster walls are covered with hieroglyphics. A passageway leads inward and inward and inward, and at its end I can see a tiny view of an eerie landscape like a plateau at the end of time.

There are half a dozen people in the room, each facing in a different direction, reading aloud in low murmurs. A slender dark-skinned man looks up at me and says, "Goddess save you, father. How does your journey go?"

"I'm trying to find Oesterreich. They said he's here."

A couple of the other readers look up. A woman with straw-colored hair says, "He's gone Goddessward."

"I'm sorry. I don't under—"

Another woman, whose features are tiny and delicately modeled in the center of a face vast as the map of Russia, breaks in to tell me, "He was going to stop off on Phosphor first. You may be able to catch up with him there. Goddess save you, father."

I stare at her, at the mural of the stone temple, at the other woman.

"Thank you," I say. "Goddess save you," my voice adds.

* * *

I BUY PASSAGE TO PHOSPHOR. It is sixty-seven light-years from Earth. The necessary lambda adjustment costs nearly as much as the transit fee itself, and I must spend three days going through the adaptation process before I can leave.

Then, Goddess save me, I am ready to set out from Eden for whatever greater strangeness awaits me beyond.

As I wait for the Simtow reaction to annihilate me and reconstruct me in some unknown place, I think of all those who passed through my House over the years as I selected the outbound colonists—and how I and the Lord Magistrates before me had clung to the fantasy that we were shaping perfect new Earths out there in the Dark, that we were composing exquisite symphonies of human nature, filtering out all of the discordances that had marred all our history up till now. Without ever going to the new worlds ourselves to view the results of our work, of course, because to go would mean to cut ourselves off forever, by Darklaw's own constricting terms, from our House, from our task, from Earth itself. And now, catapulted into the Dark in a moment's convulsive turn, by shame and guilt and the need to try to repair that which I had evidently made breakable instead of imperishable, I am learning that I have been wrong all along, that the symphonies of human nature that I had composed were built out of the same old tunes, that people will do what they will do unconstrained by abstract regulations laid down for them *a priori* by others far away.

The tight filter of which the House of Senders is so proud is no filter at all. We send our finest ones to the stars and they turn their backs on us at once. And, pondering these things, it seems to me that my soul is pounding at the gates of my mind, that madness is pressing close against the walls of my spirit—a thing which I have always dreaded, the thing which brought me to the cloisters of the Order in the first place.

Black light flashes in my eyes and once more I go leaping through the Dark.

* * *

"He isn't here," they tell me on Phosphor. There is a huge cool red sun here, and a hot blue one a couple of hundred solar units away, close enough to blaze like a brilliant beacon in the day sky. "He's gone on to Entropy. Goddess save you."

"Goddess save you," I say.

There are triple-triangle signs on every doorfront in Phosphor's single city. The city's name is Jerusalem. To name cities or worlds for places on Earth is forbidden. But I know that I have left Darklaw far behind here.

Entropy, they say, is ninety-one light-years from Earth. I am approaching the limits of the sphere of settlement.

* * *

Oesterreich has a soft, insinuating voice. He says, "You should come with me. I really would like to take a Lord Magistrate along when I go to her."

"I'm no longer a Lord Magistrate."

"You can't ever stop being a Lord Magistrate. Do you think you can take the Order off just by putting your medallion in your suitcase?"

"Who is she, this Goddess Avatar everybody talks about?"

Oesterreich laughs. "Come with me and you'll find out."

He is a small man, very lean, with broad, looming shoulders that make him appear much taller than he is when he is sitting down. Maybe he is forty years old, maybe much older. His face is paper-white, with perpetual bluish stubble, and his eyes have a black troublesome gleam that strikes me as a mark either of extraordinary intelligence or of pervasive insanity, or perhaps both at once. It was not difficult at all for me to find him, only hours after my arrival on Entropy. The planet has a single village, a thousand settlers. The air is mild here, the sun yellow-green. Three huge moons hang just overhead in the daytime sky, as though dangling on a clothesline.

I say, "Is she real, this goddess of yours?"

"Oh, she's real, all right. As real as you or me."

"Someone we can walk up to and speak with?"

"Her name used to be Margaret Benevente. She was born in Geneva. She emigrated to a world called Three Suns about thirty years ago."

"And now she's a goddess."

"No. I never said that."

"What is she, then?"

"She's the Goddess Avatar."

"Which means what?"

He smiles. "Which means she's a holy woman in whom certain fundamental principles of the universe have been incarnated. You want to know any more than that, you come with me, eh? Your grace."

"And where is she?"

"She's on an uninhabited planet about five thousand light-years from here right now."

I am dealing with a lunatic, I tell myself. That gleam is the gleam of madness, yes.

"You don't believe that, do you?" he asks.

"How can it be possible?"

"Come with me and you'll find out."

"Five thousand light-years—" I shake my head. "No. No."

He shrugs. "So don't go, then."

There is a terrible silence in the little room. I feel impaled on it. Thunder crashes outside, finally, breaking the tension. Lightning has been playing across the sky constantly since my arrival, but there has been no rain.

"Faster-than-light travel is impossible," I say inanely. "Except by way of Velde transmission. You know that. If we've got Velde equipment five thousand light-years from here, we would have had to start shipping it out around the time the Pyramids were being built in Egypt."

"What makes you think we get there with Velde equipment?" Oesterreich asks me.

* * *

HE WILL NOT EXPLAIN. FOLLOW me and you'll see, he tells me. Follow me and you'll see.

The curious thing is that I like him. He is not exactly a likable man—too intense, too tightly wound, the fanaticism carried much too close to the surface—but he has a sort of charm all the same. He travels from world to world, he tells me, bringing the new gospel of the Goddess Avatar. That is exactly how he says it, "the new gospel of the Goddess Avatar," and I feel a chill when I hear the phrase. It seems absurd and frightening both at once. Yet I suppose those who brought the Order to the world a hundred fifty years ago must have seemed just as strange and just as preposterous to those who first heard our words.

Of course, we had the Velde equipment to support our philosophies.

But these people have—what? The strength of insanity? The clear cool purposefulness that comes from having put reality completely behind them?

"You were in the Order once, weren't you?" I ask him.

"You know it, your grace."

"Which House?"

"The Mission," he says.

"I should have guessed that. And now you have a new mission, is that it?"

"An extension of the old one. Mohammed, you know, didn't see Islam as a contradiction of Judaism and Christianity. Just as the next level of revelation, incorporating the previous ones."

"So you would incorporate the Order into your new belief?"

"We would never repudiate the Order, your grace."

"And Darklaw? How widely is that observed, would you say, in the colony worlds?"

"I think we've kept much of it," Oesterreich says. "Certainly we keep the part about not trying to return to Earth. And the part about spreading the Mission outward."

"Beyond the boundaries decreed, it would seem."

"This is a new dispensation," he says.

"But not a repudiation of the original teachings?"

"Oh, no," he says, and smiles. "Not a repudiation at all, your grace."

He has that passionate confidence, that unshakable assurance, that is the mark of the real prophet and also of the true madman. There is something diabolical about him, and irresistible. In these conversations with him I have so far managed to remain outwardly calm, even genial, but the fact is that I am quaking within. I really do believe he is insane. Either that or an utter fraud, a cynical salesman of the irrational and the unreal, and though he is flippant he does not seem at all cynical. A madman, then. Is his condition infectious? As I have said, the fear of madness has been with me all my life; and so my harsh discipline, my fierce commitment, my depth of belief. He threatens all my defenses.

"When do you set out to visit your Goddess Avatar?" I ask.

"Whenever you like, your grace."

"You really think I'm going with you?"

"Of course you are. How else can you find out what you came out here to learn?"

"I've learned that the colonies have fallen away from Darklaw. Isn't that enough?"

"But you think we've all gone crazy, right?"

"When did I say that?"

"You didn't need to say it."

"If I send word to Earth of what's happened, and the Order chooses to cut off all further technical assistance and all shipments of manufactured goods—?"

"They won't do that. But even if they do—well, we're pretty much self-sufficient out here now, and getting more so every year—"

"And further emigration from Earth?"

"That would be your loss, not ours, your grace. Earth needs the colonies as a safety valve for her population surplus. We can get along without more emigrants. We know how to reproduce, out here." He grins at me. "This is foolish talk. You've come this far. Now go the rest of the way with me."

I am silent.

"Well?"

"Now, you mean?"

"Right now."

* * *

THERE IS ONLY ONE VELDE station on Entropy, about three hundred meters from the house where I have been talking with Oesterreich. We go to it under a sky berserk with green lightning. He seems not even to notice.

"Don't we have to do lambda drills?" I ask.

"Not for this hop," Oesterreich says. "There's no differential between here and there." He is busy setting up coordinates.

"Get into the chamber, your grace."

"And have you send me God knows where by myself?"

"Don't be foolish. Please."

It may be the craziest thing I have ever done. But I am the servant of the Order; and the Order has asked this of me. I step into the chamber. No one else is with us. He continues to press keys, and I realize that he is setting up an automatic transfer, requiring no external operator. When he is done with that he joins me, and there is the moment of flash.

We emerge into a cool, dry world with an Earthlike sun, a sea-green sky, a barren, rocky landscape. Ahead of us stretches an empty plateau broken here and there by small granite hillocks that rise like humped islands out of the flatness.

"Where are we?" I ask.

"Fifty light-years from Entropy, and about eighty-five light-years from Earth."

"What's the name of this place?"

"It doesn't have one. Nobody lives here. Come, now we walk a little."

We start forward. The ground has the look that comes of not having felt rain for ten or twenty years, but tough little tussocks of a grayish jagged-looking grass are pushing up somehow through the hard, stony red soil. When we have gone a hundred meters or so the land begins to drop away sharply on my left, so that I can look down into a broad, flat valley about three hundred meters below us. A solitary huge beast, somewhat like an elephant in bulk and manner, is grazing quietly down there, patiently prodding at the ground with its rigid two-pronged snout.

"Here we are," Oesterreich says.

We have reached the nearest of the little granite islands. When we walk around it, I see that its face on the farther side is fissured and broken, creating a sort of cave. Oesterreich beckons and we step a short way into it.

To our right, against the wall of the cave, is a curious narrow three-sided framework, a kind of tapering doorway, with deep darkness behind it. It is made of an odd glossy metal, or perhaps a plastic, with a texture that is both sleek and porous at the same time. There are hieroglyphs inscribed on it that seem much like those I saw on the wall of the stone temple in the mural in the Goddess-chapel on Phosphor, and to either side of it, mounted in the cave wall, are the triple six-pointed stars that are the emblem of Oesterreich's cult.

"What is this here?" I say, after a time.

"It's something like a Velde transmitter."

"It isn't anything like a Velde transmitter."

"It works very much like a Velde transmitter," he says. "You'll see when we step into its field. Are you ready?"

"Wait."

He nods. "I'm waiting."

"We're going to let this thing send us somewhere?"

"That's right, your grace."

"What is it? Who built it?"

"I've already told you what it is. As for who built it, I don't have any idea. Nobody does. We think it's five or ten million years old, maybe. It could be older than that by a factor of ten. Or a factor of a hundred. We have no way of judging."

After a long silence I say, "You're telling me that it's an alien device?"

"That's right."

"We've never discovered any sign of intelligent alien life anywhere in the galaxy."

"There's one right in front of you," Oesterreich says. "It isn't the only one."

"You've found aliens?"

"We've found their matter-transmitters. A few of them, anyway. They still work. Are you ready to jump now, your grace?"

I stare blankly at the three-sided doorway.

"Where to?"

"To a planet about five hundred light-years from here, where we can catch the bus that'll take us to the Goddess Avatar."

"You're actually serious?"

"Let's go, your grace."

"What about lambda effects?"

"There aren't any. Lambda differentials are a flaw in the Velde technology, not in the universe itself. This system gets us around without any lambda problems at all. Of course, we don't know how it works. Are you ready?"

"All right," I say helplessly.

He beckons to me and together we step toward the doorway and simply walk through it, and out the other side into such astonishing beauty that I want to fall down and give praise. Great feathery trees rise higher than sequoias, and a milky waterfall comes tumbling down the flank of an ebony mountain that fills half the sky, and the air quivers with a diamond-bright haze. Before me stretches a meadow like a scarlet carpet, vanishing into the middle distance.

There is a Mesozoic richness of texture to everything: it gleams, it shimmers, it trembles in splendor.

A second doorway, identical to the first, is mounted against an enormous boulder right in front of us. It too is flanked by the triple star emblem.

"Put your medallion on," Oesterreich tells me.

"My medallion?" I say, stupidly.

"Put it on. The Goddess Avatar will wonder why you're with me, and that'll tell her."

"Is she here?"

"She's on the next world. This is just a way station. We had to stop here first. I don't know why. Nobody does. Ready?"

"I'd like to stay here longer."

"You can come back some other time," he says. "She's waiting for you. Let's go."

"Yes," I say, and fumble in my pocket and find my medallion, and put it around my throat. Oesterreich winks and puts his thumb and forefinger together approvingly. He takes my hand and we step through.

* * *

SHE IS A LEAN, LEATHERY-LOOKING woman of sixty or seventy years with hard bright blue eyes. She wears a khaki jacket, an olive-drab field hat, khaki shorts, heavy boots. Her graying hair is tucked behind her in a tight bun. Standing in front of a small tent, tapping something into a hand terminal, she looks like an aging geology professor out on a field trip in Wyoming. But next to her tent the triple emblem of the Goddess is displayed on a sandstone plaque.

This is a Mesozoic landscape too, but much less lush than the last one: great red-brown cliffs sparsely peppered with giant ferns and palms, four-winged insects the size of dragons zooming overhead, huge grotesque things that look very much like dinosaurs warily circling each other in a stony arroyo out near the horizon. I see some other tents out there too. There is a little colony here. The sun is reddish-yellow, and large.

"Well, what do we have here?" she says. "A Lord Magistrate, is it?"

"He was nosing around on Zima and Entrada, trying to find out what was going on."

"Well, now he knows." Her voice is like flint. I feel her contempt, her hostility, like something palpable. I feel her strength, too, a cold, harsh, brutal power. She says, "What was your house, Lord Magistrate?"

"Senders."

She studies me as if I were a specimen in a display case. In all my life I have known only one other person of such force and intensity, and that is the Master. But she is nothing like him.

"And now the Sender is sent?"

"Yes," I say. "There were deviations from the plan. It became necessary for me to resign my magistracy."

"We weren't supposed to come out this far, were we?" she asks. "The light of that sun up there won't get to Earth until the seventy-third century, do you know that? But here we are. Here we are!" She laughs, a crazed sort of cackle. I begin to wonder if they intend to kill me. The aura that comes from her is terrifying. The geology professor I took her for at first is gone: what I see now is something strange and fierce, a prophet, a seer. Then suddenly the fierceness vanishes too and something quite different comes from her: tenderness, pity, even love. The strength of it catches me unawares and I gasp at its power. These shifts of hers are managed without apparent means; she has spoken only a few words, and all the rest has been done with movement, with posture, with expression. I know that I am in the presence of some great charismatic. She walks over to me and with her face close to mine says, "We spoiled your plan, I know. But we too follow the divine rule. We discovered things that nobody had suspected, and everything changed for us. Everything."

"Do you need me, Lady?" Oesterreich asks.

"No. Not now." She touches the tips of her fingers to my medallion of office, rubbing it lightly as though it is a magic talisman. Softly she says, "Let me take you on a tour of the galaxy, Lord Magistrate."

One of the alien doorways is located right behind her tent. We step through it hand in hand, and emerge on a dazzling green hillside looking out over a sea of ice. Three tiny blue-white suns hang like diamonds in the sky. In the trembling air they look like the three six-pointed stars of the emblem. "One of their capital cities was here once," she says. "But it's all at the bottom of that sea now. We ran a scan on it and saw the ruins, and some day we'll try to get down there." She beckons and we step through again, and out onto a turbulent desert of iron-hard red sand, where heavily armored crabs the size of footballs go scuttling sullenly away as we appear. "We think there's another city under here," she says. Stooping, she picks up a worn shard of gray pottery and puts it in my hand. "That's an artifact millions of years old. We find them all over the place." I stare at it as if she has handed me a small fragment of the core of a star. She touches my medallion again, just a light grazing stroke, and leads me on into the next doorway, and out onto a world of billowing white clouds and soft dewy hills, and onward from there to one where trees hang like ropes from the sky, and onward from there, and onward from there— "How did you find all this?" I ask, finally.

"I was living on Three Suns. You know where that is? We were exploring the nearby worlds, trying to see if there was anything worthwhile, and one day I stepped out of a Velde unit and found myself looking at a peculiar three-sided kind of doorway right next to it, and I got too close and found myself going through into another world entirely. That was all there was to it."

"And you kept on going through one doorway after another?"

"Fifty of them. I didn't know then how to tune for destination, so I just kept jumping, hoping I'd get back to my starting point eventually. There wasn't any reason in the world why I should. But after six months I did. The Goddess protects me."

"The Goddess," I say.

She looks at me as though awaiting a challenge. But I am silent.

"These doorways link the whole galaxy together like the Paris Metro," she says after a moment. "We can go everywhere with them. *Everywhere.*"

"And the Goddess? Are the doorways Her work?"

"We hope to find that out some day."

"What about this emblem?" I ask, pointing to the six-pointed stars beside the gateway. "What does that signify?"

"Her presence," she says. "Come. I'll show you."

We step through once more, and emerge into night. The sky on this world is the blackest black I have ever seen, with comets and shooting stars blazing across it in almost comic profusion. There are two moons, bright as mirrors. A dozen meters to one side is the white stone temple of the chapel mural I saw on Eden, marked with the same hieroglyphs that are shown on the painting there and that are inscribed on all the alien doorways. It is made of cyclopean slabs of white stone that look as if they were carved billions of years ago. She takes my arm and guides me through its squared-off doorway into a high-vaulted inner chamber where the triple six-pointed triangle, fashioned out of the glossy doorway material, is mounted on a stone altar.

"This is the only building of theirs we've ever found," she says. Her eyes are gleaming. "It must have been a holy place. Can you doubt it? You can feel the power."

"Yes."

"Touch the emblem."

"What will happen to me if I do?"

"Touch it," she says. "Are you afraid?"

"Why should I trust you?"

"Because the Goddess has used me to bring you to this place. Go on. Touch."

I put my hand to the smooth cool alien substance, and instantly I feel the force of revelation flowing through me, the unmistakable power of the Godhead. I see the multiplicity of worlds, an infinity of them circling an infinity of suns. I see the Totality. I see the face of God clear and plain. It is what I have sought all my life and thought that I had already found; but I know at once that I am finding it for the first time. If I had fasted for a thousand years, or prayed for ten thousand, I could not have felt anything like that. It is the music out of which all things are built. It is the ocean in which all things float. I hear the voice of every god and goddess that ever had worshippers, and it is all one voice, and it goes coursing through me like a river of fire.

After a moment I take my hand away. And step back, trembling, shaking my head. This is too easy. One does not reach God by touching a strip of smooth plastic.

She says, "We mean to find them. They're still alive somewhere. How could they not be? And who could doubt that we were meant to follow them and find them? And kneel before them, for they are Whom we seek. So we'll go on and on, as far as we need to go, in search of them. To the farthest reaches, if we have to. To the rim of the universe and then beyond. With these doorways there are no limits. We've been handed the key to everywhere. We are for the Dark, all of it, on and on and on, not the little hundred-light-year sphere that your Order preaches, but the whole galaxy and even beyond. Who knows how far these doorways reach? The Magellanic Clouds? Andromeda? M33? They're waiting for us out there. As they have waited for a billion years."

So she thinks she can hunt Him down through doorway after doorway. Or Her. Whichever. But she is wrong. The One who made the universe made the makers of the doorways also.

"And the Goddess—?" I say.

"The Goddess is the Unknown. The Goddess is the Mystery toward which we journey. You don't feel Her presence?"

"I'm not sure."

"You will. If not now, then later. She'll greet us when we arrive. And embrace us, and make us all gods."

I stare a long while at the six-pointed stars. It would be simple enough to put forth my hand again and drink in the river of revelation a second time. But there is no need. That fire still courses through me. It always will, drawing me onward toward itself. Whatever it may be, there is no denying its power.

She says, "I'll show you one more thing, and then we'll leave here."

We continue through the temple and out the far side, where the wall has toppled. From a platform amid the rubble we have an unimpeded view of the heavens. An immense array of stars glitters above us, set out in utterly unfamiliar patterns. She points straight overhead, where a Milky Way in two whirling strands spills across the sky.

"That's Earth right up there," she says. "Can you see it? Going around that little yellow sun, only a hundred thousand light-years away? I wonder if they ever paid us a visit. We won't know, will we, until we turn up one of their doorways somewhere in the Himalayas, or under the Antarctic ice, or somewhere like that. I think that when we finally reach them, they'll recognize us. It's interesting to think about, isn't it." Her hand rests lightly on my wrist. "Shall we go back now, Lord Magistrate?"

* * *

So we return, in two or three hops, to the world of the dinosaurs and the giant dragonflies. There is nothing I can say. I feel storms within my skull. I feel myself spread out across half the universe.

Oesterreich waits for me now. He will take me back to Phosphor, or Entropy, or Entrada, or Zima, or Cuchulain, or anywhere else I care to go.

"You could even go back to Earth," the Goddess Avatar says. "Now that you know what's happening out here. You could go back home and tell the Master all about it."

"The Master already knows, I suspect. And there's no way I can go home. Don't you understand that?"

She laughs lightly. "Darklaw, yes. I forgot. The rule is that no one goes back. We've been catapulted out here to be cleansed of original sin, and to return to Mother Earth would be a crime against the laws of thermodynamics. Well, as you wish. You're a free man."

"It isn't Darklaw," I say. "Darklaw doesn't bind anyone any more."

I begin to shiver. Within my mind shards and fragments are falling from the sky: the House of Senders, the House of the Sanctuary, the whole Order and all its laws, the mountains and valleys of Earth, the body and fabric of Earth. All is shattered; all is made new; I am infinitely small against the infinite greatness of the cosmos. I am dazzled by the light of an infinity of suns.

And yet, though I must shield my eyes from that fiery glow, though I am numbed and humbled by the vastness of that vastness, I see that there are no limits to what may be attained, that the edge of the universe awaits me, that I need only reach and stretch, and stretch and reach, and ultimately I will touch it.

I see that even if she has made too great a leap of faith, even if she has surrendered herself to assumptions without basis, she is on the right path. The quest is unattainable because its goal is infinite. But the way leads ever outward. There is no destination, only a journey. And she has traveled farther on that journey than anyone.

And me? I had thought I was going out into the stars to spin out the last of my days quietly and obscurely, but I realize now that my pilgrimage is nowhere near its end. Indeed it is only beginning. This is not any road that I ever thought I would take. But this is the road that I am taking, all the same, and I have no choice but to follow it, though I am not sure yet whether I am wandering deeper into exile or finding my way back at last to my true home.

What I cannot help but see now is that our Mission is ended and that a new one has begun; or, rather, that this new Mission is the continuation and culmination of ours. Our Order has taught from the first that the way to reach God is to go to the stars. So it is. And so we have done. We have been too timid, limiting ourselves to that little ball of space surrounding Earth. But we have not failed. We have made possible everything that is to follow after.

I hand her my medallion. She looks at it the way I looked at that bit of alien pottery on the desert world, and then she starts to hand it back to me, but I shake my head.

"For you," I say. "A gift. An offering. It's of no use to me now."

She is standing with her back to the great reddish-yellow sun of this place, and it seems to me that light is streaming from her as it does from the Master, that she is aglow, that she is luminous, that she is herself a sun.

"Goddess save you, Lady," I say quietly.

All the worlds of the galaxy are whirling about me. I will take this road and see where it leads, for now I know there is no other.

"Goddess save you," I say. "Goddess save you, Lady."

THE TROUBLE WITH SEMPOANGA

This was one of those odd jobs that come a professional writer's way every now and then. A magazine called *Beyond* was getting started, published out of Los Angeles, and intended, I think, for distribution entirely on college campuses. They wanted to publish a science fiction story by a well-known writer in each issue. My friend, the writer Harlan Ellison, put its editor, Judith Sims, in touch with me in September of 1981; a good price was being offered and I was then in the midst of the rush of creative activity that in recent months had produced the *Majipoor Chronicles* short stories and four or five others; after doing a short story for *Playboy* I sat right down and wrote "The Trouble With Sempoanga" for this new magazine. At this late date it may seem to have been inspired by the AIDS epidemic, but in fact AIDS had not yet surfaced as a major problem in 1981 and if there was any kind of real-world inspiration for this little story, it was the epidemic of genital herpes that then was a big topic of conversation in the United States.

At any rate, I wrote the story and *Beyond* published it in its second issue (I think the magazine lasted four issues altogether) and that was that. I haven't given that ephemeral magazine a thought for decades. Even Google seems to know nothing about it and I'm not sure where my file copy is. But I did get a nice nasty story out of the project. Tourism, as I note here, does have its risks as well as its benefits.

When Helmut Schweid decided to go to Sempoanga for his holiday, he knew the risks, but of course he assumed they didn't apply to him. "You'll pick up a dose of *zanjak* and never get out of quarantine," his friends told him. Helmut laughed. He was a careful man, especially with his body. He would avoid getting *zanjak* by avoiding going to bed with women who had *zanjak*: that was simple enough to manage, wasn't it?

By common agreement Sempoanga was the most beautiful planet in the galaxy. See one sunrise on Sempoanga, everyone said, and you won't care if you never see anything else anywhere. The trouble with Sempoanga was the dismal parasite its humanoid natives harbored. There was only one way to transmit that parasite—by making love. Since the natives of Sempoanga are a good deal less attractive to humans than its sunrises, it is not easy to understand how any human could ever have caught it, but somehow someone had, and it had adapted nicely to human bodies, thriving and multiplying and making itself remarkably contagious, and in the past few years a good many human visitors to Sempoanga had passed it around to one another, with horrendous results. Biologists were working on a cure and hoped they might see results in just a few more years. But meanwhile no one went home from Sempoanga without undergoing tests and if you caught *zanjak*, you stayed quarantined there indefinitely, because the parasite's effect on the human reproductive system was so startling that the future of the entire species might be in jeopardy if it were allowed to spread to the other civilized worlds.

For his first few days on Sempoanga Helmut was so busy experiencing the gorgeous planet itself that he was in no danger of catching any kind of venereal disease, neither the old standbys nor the exotic local specialty. His own world, Waldemar, was a frosty place with a planet-wide winter for three-quarters of the year, and on Sempoanga he erupted with great gusto into eternal tropical summer. From dawn to midnight he toured the wonders—Hargillin Falls, where the water is the color of red wine, and Stinivong Chute, a flawless mountain of obsidian at the edge of a lake of phosphorescent pink gas, and The Bubbles, where subterranean psychedelic vapors percolate upward through a shield of porous yellow rock with delightful effect. He ran naked through a grove of voluptuous ferns that wrapped him in their fleshy fronds. He swam in crystalline rivers, eye to eye with vast harmless turtles the size of small islands. And each night he staggered back to his hotel, wonderfully weary, to collapse into his solitary sleep-tube for a few hours.

But after those early greedy gulps of natural marvels, his normal social instincts reasserted themselves. On the fourth day he saw a striking-looking radium-blonde from one of the Rigel worlds at the gravity-ball court. She met his tentative grin with a dazzling one of her own and quickly agreed to have dinner with him. Everything was going beautifully until she excused herself for a moment late in the meal, and the waiter who was bringing the brandies paused to whisper to Helmut, "Watch out for that one. *Zanjak.*"

He was stunned. Was she trying to hide it from him, then? No, give her more credit than that: as they strolled through the garden under the light of the five moons she said, "I'd like to spend the night with you. But only if you're already carrying. I am, you know." So that was that. He walked her to her room and kissed her sadly and warmly goodnight, and trembled for a moment as her soft elegant body moved close against his; but he managed to escape without doing anything foolish.

The next night, sitting alone in the hotel cocktail lounge and beginning to feel more than lonely, he noticed another woman noticing him. She was dark-haired and long-legged and perhaps two or three years younger than he was. They exchanged glances and then smiles and he tapped his empty glass and she nodded and they rose and went to the bar and ritualistically bought each other drinks. Her name was Marbella and she had been on holiday here since last month, escaping from a collapsed six-group on the planet of Tlon. "The divorce is going to take *years,*" she told him. "It's a universal-option planet, the six of us come from four different worlds and everybody's home-world laws apply, some of the lawyers aren't even *human*—"

"And you plan to hide out on Sempoanga until it's all over?"

"Can you imagine a better place?"

"Except for—"

"Well, yes, there's *that.* But every paradise has its little snake, after all." Quickly she shifted topics. "I saw you this morning at the puff-glider field. You looked like you wanted to try it."

"How is it done?" he asked. Helmut had watched hotel guests clambering into huge fungoid puff-balls, which immediately broke free of their moorings and went drifting out across golden Lake Mangalole in what looked like guided flight.

"Would you like me to teach you? It's a matter of controlling the puffer's hydrogen-synthesis. Stroke it one way and it gets more buoyant, another and it sinks. And you learn how to ride the thermals and all. Where did you say you were from?"

"Waldemar."

"Brr," she said. "Are you free for dinner tonight?"

He liked her forthright, aggressive ways. They arranged to meet for dinner and to try the puff-gliders in the morning. What might happen in between was left undiscussed, but once again Helmut found himself confronting the problem of *zanjak.* She had been here more than long enough to pick up an infection, and, coming out of a turbulent marriage, it was hardly likely that she had been chaste in this sensuous place. On the other hand, if she did carry the parasite, she would certainly tell him about it ahead of time, as the other woman had. There was bound to be an etiquette about such things.

Over dinner they spoke of her complex marriage and his simpler, but ultimately just as disastrous, one, and briefly of his work and hers and of his planet and hers, and then of the splendors of Sempoanga. He liked her very much. And the gleam in her eyes told him he was making the right impression.

When he invited her to his room, though, she turned him down—warmly and graciously and with what seemed like genuine regret, explaining that this was the last night of her five-day contraceptive holiday; she was fertile as a mink just now and feared giving way to temptation. She seemed sincere. "There'll be other nights, you know," she said, and her smile left him with no doubts.

In the morning they met at the puff glider field and she taught him quickly and expertly how to control the great organisms. Within an hour they were off and soaring. They crossed the lake, landed on the slopes of jag-toothed Mount Monolang for a lunch of sun-grilled fish and wineberries and ran laughing toward a glistening stream for a dip. Later, when they lay sunning themselves on shelves of glassy rock, he studied her bare body as surreptitiously as possible for signs of *zanjak*—some swelling around the thighs, perhaps, or maybe little puckered red marks below the navel, anything at all that seemed irregular. Nothing visible, at any rate. The pamphlet on *zanjak* that the hotel had thoughtfully left beside his bed had told him there were no external symptoms, but he was uneasy all the same.

It would have been simple enough to drift into lovemaking on this secluded hillside, but his uncertainties held him back, nor did she try to take the initiative. Eventually they dressed and resumed their glider-journey. They halted again to visit a village of natives—flat-faced warty creatures with furry moth-like antennae, so ugly that Helmut wondered what sort of tourist could have been desperate enough to catch the original parasite from one of *them*—and then in late afternoon, strolling hand in hand in fields of mildly aphrodisiac blossoms, they slipped into one of those low-toned, earnest, intimate conversations that only people who are about to become lovers engage in. "What a lovely day this has been," she told him when they were heading back to the hotel.

That night she asked him to her room. Two themes marched through his mind as they undressed. One was his admiration for her beauty, her warmth and intelligence, her desirability. And the other was *zanjak, zanjak, zanjak.*

What to do? By dimmed light he came to her. He imagined himself saying, "Forgive me, Marbella, but I need to know. That terrible parasite—that monstrous disease—" And he could see her turning bleak and furious as he blurted his tactless questions, demanding icily whether he thought she were the sort of woman who might deliberately hide from him anything so ghastly and shoving him into the hall, slamming the door, screaming curses after him—

He faltered. She smiled. Her eyes were bright with desire and refusing her was absurd. He drew her into his arms.

They were inseparable, night and day, the rest of the week. He had no illusions: this was only a resort-planet romance, and when his time was up he would go back to Waldemar and that would be the end of it. But it was wondrous while it lasted. She was a fine companion, and she appeared to be altogether in love with him, sincerely and a little worrisomely so. He was already rehearsing the speech he was going to have to make after breaking the news to her that business responsibilities would not permit him to extend his Sempoangan holiday beyond the five days that remained.

Then one drowsy morning as they were lying in bed he felt a dismaying internal twitch, as if some tiny supple creature were trying to swim downsteam in his urethra.

He said nothing to her. But after breakfast he invented the need to put a call through to his firm on Waldemar and, in terror, got himself off to the hotel medical office, where a blandly unsympathetic doctor processed him through the diagnostat and told him he had *zanjak*. "You see those little red flecks in your urine? Just a couple of microns in diameter. They're symptomatic. And this blood sample—it's loaded with *zanjak* excreta."

Helmut shivered. "I can't have had it more than a couple of days. Perhaps because we've detected it so soon—"

"Sorry. It doesn't work that way."

"What do I do now?" he asked tonelessly.

The doctor was already tapping data into a terminal. "We put you on the master list, first. That slaps a hold on your passport. You know about the quarantine, don't you? If your home world is covered by the covenant, your government will pay the expenses of transferring your funds and a certain quantity of your possessions to Sempoanga. You can live in the hotel as long as you can afford to, of course. After that, you're entitled to a rent-free room at the Quarantine Center, which is on the southern continent in a very pleasant region where the fishing is said to be superb. You'll be asked to take part in the various test programs for cures, but otherwise you'll be left alone."

"I don't believe this," Helmut muttered.

"These harsh measures are absolutely necessary, of course. You must realize that. The parasite has passed through your genito-urinary tract and has taken up residence in your bloodstream, where it's busy filling you with threadlike reproductive bodies known as microfilariae. Whenever you have sexual relations with a woman—or with another man, for that matter, or with any mammalian organism at all—you'll inevitably transmit microfilariae. If the organism you infect is female, the microfilariae will travel in a few weeks to the ovaries, infiltrate unfertilized eggs and impose their own genetic material by a process we call pseudofertilization, causing the eggs to mature into hybrids, part *zanjak* and part host-species. What appears to be a normal pregnancy follows, though the term is only about twelve weeks in human hosts; offspring are born in litters, adapted quite cunningly to penetrate whatever ecosphere they find themselves in."

"All right. Don't tell me any more."

"No need to. You see the picture. These things could take over the universe if they ever got beyond Sempoanga."

"Then Sempoanga should be closed to interplanetary travel!"

"Ah, but this is a major resort area! Besides, the quarantine is one hundred percent effective. If only new tourists were not so careless or unethical as they seem to be, we would isolate all cases in a matter of weeks and after that—"

"I thought I was being careful!"

"Not careful enough, it seems."

"And you? Don't *you* worry about getting it?"

The doctor gave Helmut a scathing look. "When I was a small child, I learned quickly not to put my fingers into electrical sockets. I conduct my sexual activities with the same philosophy. Good morning, Mr. Schweid. I'll have your quarantine documents sent round to your room when they're ready."

Numbed, staggering, Helmut wandered in a lurching dazed way over the hotel's vast grounds, looking for Marbella. He felt unclean and outcast; he could not bear to look at any of the other guests who amiably greeted him as he went by; he yearned to thrust his fouled body into a vat of corrosive acid. Infected! Quarantined! Exiled, maybe forever, from his home! No. No. It went beyond all comprehension. That he, that precise and intelligent and meticulous man, with his insurance policies and his alarm systems and his annual medical checkups, should—should have—

He found her watching a game of body-tennis, caught her by the wrist from behind and whispered savagely, "I've got *zanjak!*"

She looked at him, startled. "Of course you do, love."

"You say it so casually? You let me believe you were clean!"

"Yes. Certainly. I knew you were already infected, even if you didn't. Since you apparently didn't know it yourself then, you'd never have gone to bed with me if I admitted I was carrying. And I wanted you so much, love. I'd have told any kind of harmless little lie then for the sake of—"

"Wait a minute. What do you mean, you knew I was already carrying?"

"That blonde bitch from Rigel, the night before you and I met—I saw the two of you together at dinner. I had my eye on you even then, you know. And I could tell that that unscrupulous little tramp would conceal from you that she was carrying. When I saw you go off to her room with her, I knew you'd be joining the club."

Icily he said, "I didn't sleep with her, Marbella."

"What? But I was sure—"

"You were, were you?" He laughed bitterly. "I walked her home and she told me she was a carrier and I kissed her goodnight and went away. You can't catch it from a kiss, can you? *Can you?*"

"No," she said in a very small voice.

"So you knowingly and shamelessly gave me a hideous incurable disease because you had decided I had been dumb enough to sleep with someone who was carrying it. I guess you were right about that, in a way."

She turned away, looking stricken. "Helmut, please—if you knew how sorry I am—"

"No sorrier than I am. Do you realize I'm quarantined here, and maybe for life?"

She shrugged. "Well, yes. So am I. There are worse places to spend one's life."

"I ought to kill you!"

She began to tremble. "I suppose I'd deserve it. Oh, Helmut—I was so completely fascinated by you—I didn't want to take the slightest risk of losing you. I should have waited until the infection I thought you got from *her* had showed itself. Then it wouldn't have mattered. But I couldn't wait—I tried, I couldn't—and I figured that we'd fall in love and by the time your *zanjak* showed it would be all right for me to admit that I had it, too."

He was silent a long moment. Then he said, "Maybe you figured that even if I *didn't* have it, you'd give it to me, by way of making absolutely sure I'd be stuck here on Sempoanga?"

"No. I swear it." There was shock and horror in her eyes. "You have to believe me, Helmut!"

"I could really kill you now," he said, and for an instant he thought he would. But instead he turned and fled, running in long loping, crazy strides, across the field of octopus palms and down a garden of electric orchids that flashed indignant lights at him and rang their bells, and through a swamp of warm sticky mud filled with little furry snakes, and up the side of Stinivong Chute, thinking he might throw himself over the edge. But halfway up he yielded to exhaustion and fell to the ground and lay there panting and gasping for what seemed like hours. When he returned to his room at dusk, there was a thick packet of documents beside his bed—his responsibilities and rights under the quarantine, how to transfer assets from his home world, pros and cons of applying for Sempoangan citizenship, and much more. He skimmed it quickly and tossed it aside before he was midway through. Thinking about such things was impossible now. He closed his eyes and pressed his face against his pillow, and suddenly scenes from Waldemar burned in his mind: the Great Glacier at Christmas, the ice-yacht races, the warm well-lit tunnels of his city, his snug dome-roofed home, his last night in it with Elissa, his trim little office with the rows of communicator panels—

He would never see any of that again, and it was all so stupid, so impossibly dumb, that he could not believe it.

He could not go to the dining room for dinner that evening. He ordered a meal from room service but left it untouched and nibbled a little of it the next morning after a night of loathsome dreams. That day he wandered at random, alone, getting used to what had happened to him. It was a magnificent day, the sky pink and soft, the flame-trees glowing, but it was all lost on him now. Even though this place might be paradise, he was condemned to dwell in it, and paradise on that basis was not very different from hell.

For two days he haunted the hotel grounds like his own ghost, speaking to no one. He didn't see Marbella again until the third evening after the *zanjak* had emerged in him. To break free of his depression he had gone to the cocktail lounge, and she was there, alone, apparently brooding. She brightened when he appeared, but he glared coldly at her and went past, to the bar. A newcomer was sitting there by herself, an attractive fragile-looking woman with large dark eyes and frosted auburn hair. Deliberately, maliciously, Helmut made a point of picking her up in front of Marbella. Her name was Sinuise; she came from a planet called Donegal; like so many others here, she was trying to forget a bad marriage. When they left the cocktail lounge together, Helmut could feel Marbella's eyes on him and it was like being skewered with hard radiation.

He and Sinuise dined and danced and drifted toward the evening's inevitable conclusion. In the casino he spotted Marbella again, watching them somberly from a distance. "Come," he said to the woman from Donegal. "Let's go for a walk." He slipped his arm over her shoulder. She was delicate and lovely and beyond doubt she was hungry for warmth and closeness, and he knew that he need only ask and she would go to his room with him. But as they strolled down the leafy paths he knew he could not do it. To carry his revenge on Marbella to the point of giving *zanjak* to an unsuspecting woman—no. No.

Under the rustling fronds of a limberwillow tree, he kissed her long and lovingly, and when he released her he said, "It's been a beautiful evening, Sinuise."

"Yes. For me also."

"Perhaps we'll go puff gliding tomorrow."

"I'd like that. But—tonight—I thought—"

"I can't. Not with you, I have *zanjak*, you know. And unless you've already got it also—"

Her face seemed to crumple. The great dark eyes swam with tears. He took her hand lightly, but a convulsive quiver of disappointment and anguish ran through her, and she pulled away and fled from him, sobbing.

"I'm sorry," he called after her. "More than you can imagine!"

Marbella was still in the casino, still alone. She looked astonished that he had returned. He shot her a venomous look and headed for the gravity-dice table, and in fifteen minutes managed to lose half the money he was carrying. He thought of lovely little Sinuise alone in her bed. He thought of Helmut Schweid, infested by bizarre alien organisms. He thought of Marbella, her energy, her passionate little cries, her quick wit and sly humor. Perhaps she was telling the truth, he thought bleakly. Perhaps she genuinely thought I had picked up a dose from the blonde from Rigel.

Besides, what choice do I have now?

Slowly, wearily, he made his way across the huge room. Marbella was playing five-chip cargo in a reckless way. He watched her lose her stake. Then he lightly touched her arm.

"You win," he said.

They stayed together at the hotel another eight days, and then, because his money was gone and he would not take any from her, they moved to the Quarantine Center. It was, he quickly discovered, just as beautiful as the hotel, with glorious natural features every bit as strange and wonderful. They shared a small cabin and spent their days swimming and fishing and their nights making love. Over the next ten weeks Marbella's breasts grew heavy and her belly began to swell; but when her time came she would not go to the Quarantine Center hospital. Instead she bore her Sempoangan young behind the cabin, a litter of sleek little creatures like tiny green otters, ten or fifteen of them that came sliding out of her without effort. Helmut dug a pit and shoveled them all in, and after she had rested for an hour or so they went down to the beach to watch the translucent waves lapping against the azure sand. He thought of the snows of Waldemar, and of his home there, his lovers, his friends, and it all seemed terribly long ago and more than a million light-years far away.

THE SIXTH PALACE

In 1964, after six or seven years away from the center of the science fiction scene, I was writing s-f again, thanks to the warm encouragement of Frederik Pohl, editor of *Galaxy Science Fiction* magazine. I wrote "The Sixth Palace" for him in February, 1964, and he published it in his February, 1965 issue.

For many years after I was unable to remember where I had found the quote from Hebrew mystical literature that was the spark for the story. I must have stumbled across the Ben Azai story in some secondary source, since I am not myself a student of arcane Jewish lore. Around 1975 I asked Avram Davidson, the most Orthodox of my Jewish friends, about it, but he, too, for all his extraordinary erudition, was unable to provide any information. And in time I came to assume I would never know. No knowledge remains lost forever, though, especially theological knowledge. One day late in 2014 there came an e-mail from Boruch Perl of Brooklyn, who has made a careful study of Jewish mystical lore. "The quote," he told me, "is from *Jewish Gnosticism: Merkabah Mystic and Talmudic Tradition*, by Gershom Scholem." It is drawn, he said, from "an extremely obscure book of Kabbalah (Jewish mysticism) and is based on an incident recorded in the Talmud . . . in which 'Ben Azai' gazed (at the Divine Presence) and was killed. . . . "

There's much more that Boruch Perl told me about Ben Azai and his adventures, but this is not the place to discuss it. What matters here is that I took that one line about Jewish Gnosticism and turned it into a science fiction story about two soldiers of fortune who travel to a small world orbiting the star Valzar, where a fabulous treasure is known to be guarded by a gigantic robot who will admit to the treasure vault only that person who can correctly answer a series of difficult questions. Anyone who fails to give the proper answers will be immediately annihilated. It's a classic fairy-tale plot, converted into science fiction by setting it on an alien world and using a robot instead of a dragon as the guardian of the treasure. As herewith.

Ben Azai was deemed worthy and stood at the gate of the sixth palace and saw the ethereal splendor of the pure marble plates. He opened his mouth and said twice, "Water! Water!" In the twinkling of an eye they decapitated him and threw eleven thousand iron bars at him. This shall be a sign for all generations that no one should err at the gate of the sixth palace.

—*Lesser Hekhaloth*

THERE WAS THE TREASURE, AND there was the guardian of the treasure. And there were the whitening bones of those who had tried in vain to make the treasure their own. Even the bones had taken on a kind of beauty, lying out there by the gate of the treasure vault, under the blazing arch of heavens. The treasure itself lent beauty to everything near it—even the scattered bones, even the grim guardian.

The home of the treasure was a small world that belonged to red Valzar. Hardly more than moon-sized, really, with no atmosphere to speak of, a silent, dead little world that spun through darkness a billion miles from its cooling primary. A wayfarer had stopped there once. Where from, where bound? No one knew. He had established a cache there, and there it lay, changeless and eternal, treasure beyond belief, presided over by the faceless metal man who waited with metal patience for his master's return.

There were those who would have the treasure. They came, and were challenged by the guardian, and died.

On another world of the Valzar system, men undiscouraged by the fate of their predecessors dreamed of the hoard, and schemed to possess it. Lipescu was one: a tower of a man, golden beard, fists like hammers, gullet of brass, back as broad as a tree of a thousand years. Bolzano was another: awl-shaped, bright of eye, fast of finger, twig thick, razor sharp. They had no wish to die.

Lipescu's voice was like the rumble of island galaxies in collision. He wrapped himself around a tankard of good black ale and said, "I go tomorrow, Bolzano."

"Is the computer ready?"

"Programmed with everything the beast could ask me," the big man boomed. "There won't be a slip."

"And if there is?" Bolzano asked, peering idly into the blue, oddly pale, strangely meek eyes of the giant. "And if the robot kills you?"

"I've dealt with robots before."

Bolzano laughed. "That plain is littered with bones, friend. Yours will join the rest. Great bulky bones, Lipescu. I can see them now."

"You're a cheerful one, friend."

"I'm realistic."

Lipescu shook his head heavily. "If you were realistic, you wouldn't be in this with me," he said slowly. "Only a dreamer would do such a thing as this." One meaty paw hovered in the air, pounced, caught Bolzano's forearm. The little man winced as bones ground together. Lipescu said, "You won't back out? If I die, you'll make the attempt?"

"Of course I will, you idiot."

"Will you? You're a coward, like all little men. You'll watch me die, and then you'll turn tail and head for another part of the universe as fast as you know how. Won't you?"

"I intend to profit by your mistakes," Bolzano said in a clear, testy voice. "Let go of my arm."

Lipescu released his grip. The little man sank back in his chair, rubbing his arm. He gulped ale. He grinned at his partner and raised his glass.

"To success," Bolzano said.

"Yes. To the treasure."

"And to long life afterward."

"For both of us," the big man boomed.

"Perhaps," said Bolzano. "Perhaps."

HE HAD HIS DOUBTS. THE big man was sly, Ferd Bolzano knew, and that was a good combination, not often found: slyness and size. Yet the risks were great. Bolzano wondered which he preferred—that Lipescu should gain the treasure on his attempt, thus assuring Bolzano of a share without risk, or that Lipescu should die, forcing Bolzano to venture his own life. Which was better, a third of the treasure without hazard, or the whole thing for the highest stake?

Bolzano was a good enough gambler to know the answer to that. Yet there was more than yellowness to the man; in his own way, he longed for the chance to risk his life on the airless treasure world.

Lipescu would go first. That was the agreement. Bolzano had stolen the computer, had turned it over to the big man, and Lipescu would make the initial attempt. If he gained the prize, his was the greater share. If he perished, it was Bolzano's moment next. An odd partnership, odd terms, but Lipescu would have it no other way, and Ferd Bolzano did not argue the point with his beefy compatriot. Lipescu would return with the treasure, or he would not return at all. There would be no middle way, they both were certain.

Bolzano spent an uneasy night. His apartment, in an airy shaft of a building overlooking glittering Lake His, was a comfortable place, and he had little longing to leave it. Lipescu, by preference, lived in the stinking slums beyond the southern shore of the lake, and when the two men parted for the night they went in opposite ways. Bolzano considered bringing a woman home for the night but did not. Instead, he sat moody and wakeful before the televector screen, watching the procession of worlds, peering at the green and gold and ochre planets as they sailed through the emptiness.

Toward dawn, he ran the tape of the treasure. Octave Merlin had made that tape, a hundred years before, as he orbited sixty miles above the surface of the airless little world. Now Merlin's bones bleached on the plain, but the tape had come home and bootlegged copies commanded a high price in hidden markets. His camera's sharp eye had seen much.

There was the gate; there was the guardian. Gleaming, ageless, splendid. The robot stood ten feet high, a square, blocky, black shape topped by the tiny anthropomorphic head dome, featureless and sleek. Behind him the gate, wide open but impassable all the same. And behind him, the treasure, culled from the craftsmanship of a thousand worlds, left here who knew why, untold years ago.

No more mere jewels. No dreary slabs of so-called precious metal. The wealth here was not intrinsic; no vandal would think of melting the treasure into dead ingots. Here were statuettes of spun iron that seemed to move and breathe. Plaques of purest lead, engraved with lathe-work that dazzled the mind and made the heart hesitate. Cunning intaglios in granite, from the workshops of a frosty world half a parsec from nowhere. A scatter of opals, burning with an inner light, fashioned into artful loops of brightness.

A helix of rainbow-colored wood. A series of interlocking strips of some beast's bone, bent and splayed so that the pattern blurred and perhaps abutted some other dimensional continuum. Cleverly carved shells, one within the other, descending to infinity. Burnished leaves of nameless trees. Polished pebbles from unknown beaches. A dizzying spew of wonders, covering some fifty square yards, sprawled out behind the gate in stunning profusion.

Rough men unschooled in the tenets of esthetics had given their lives to possess the treasure. It took no fancy knowledge to realize the wealth of it, to know that collectors strung from galaxy to galaxy would fight with bared fangs to claim their share. Gold bars did not a treasure make. But these things? Beyond duplication, almost beyond price?

Bolzano was wet with a fever of yearning before the tape had run its course. When it was over, he slumped in his chair, drained, depleted.

Dawn came. The silvery moons fell from the sky. The red sun splashed across the heavens. Bolzano allowed himself the luxury of an hour's sleep.

And then it was time to begin . . .

As a precautionary measure, they left the ship in a parking orbit three miles above the airless world. Past reports were unreliable, and there was no telling how far the robot guardian's power extended. If Lipescu were successful, Bolzano could descend and get him—and the treasure. If Lipescu failed, Bolzano would land and make his own attempt.

The big man looked even bigger, encased in his suit and in the outer casement of a dropshaft. Against his massive chest he wore the computer, an extra brain as lovingly crafted as any object in the treasure hoard. The guardian would ask him questions; the computer would help him answer. And Bolzano would listen. If Lipescu erred, possibly his partner could benefit by knowledge of the error and succeed.

"Can you hear me?" Lipescu asked.

"Perfectly. Go on, get going!"

"What's the hurry? Eager to see me die?"

"Are you that lacking in confidence?"' Bolzano asked. "Do you want me to go first?"

"Fool," Lipescu muttered. "Listen carefully. If I die, I don't want it to be in vain."

"What would it matter to you?"

The bulky figure wheeled around. Bolzano could not see his partner's face, but he knew Lipescu must be scowling. The giant rumbled, "Is life that valuable? Can't I take a risk?"

"For my benefit?"

"For mine," Lipescu said. "I'll be coming back."

"Go, then. The robot is waiting."

Lipescu walked to the lock. A moment later he was through and gliding downward, a one-man spaceship, jets flaring beneath his feet. Bolzano settled by the scanner to watch. A televector pickup homed in on Lipescu just as he made his landing, coming down in a blaze of fire. The treasure and its guardian lay about a mile away. Lipescu rid himself of the dropshaft, stepping with giant bounds toward the waiting guardian.

Bolzano watched.

Bolzano listened.

The televector pickup provided full fidelity. It was useful for Bolzano's purposes, and useful, too, for Lipescu's vanity, for the big man wanted his every moment taped for posterity. It was interesting to see Lipescu dwarfed by the guardian. The black faceless robot, squat and motionless, topped the big man by better than three feet.

Lipescu said, "Step aside."

The robot's reply came in surprisingly human tones, though void of any distinguishing accent. "What I guard is not to be plundered."

"I claim them by right," Lipescu said.

"So have many others. But their right did not exist. Nor does yours. I cannot step aside for you."

"Test me," Lipescu said. "See if I have the right or not!"

"Only my master may pass."

"Who is your master? I am your master!"

"My master is he who can command me. And no one can command me who shows ignorance before me."

"Test me, then," Lipescu demanded.

"Death is the penalty for failure."

"Test me."

"The treasure does not belong to you."

"Test me and step aside."

"Your bones will join the rest here."

"Test me," Lipescu said.

Watching from aloft, Bolzano went tense. His thin body drew together like that of a chilled spider. Anything might happen now. The robot might propound riddles, like the Sphinx confronting Oedipus.

It might demand the proofs of mathematical theorems. It might ask the translation of strange words. So they gathered, from their knowledge of what had befallen other men here. And, so it seemed, to give a wrong answer was to earn instant death.

He and Lipescu had ransacked the libraries of the world. They had packed all knowledge, so they hoped, into their computer. It had taken months, even with multi-stage programming. The tiny shining globe of metal on Lipescu's chest contained an infinity of answers to an infinity of questions.

Below, there was long silence as man and robot studied one another. Then the guardian said, "Define latitude."

"Do you mean geographical latitude?" Lipescu asked.

Bolzano congealed with fear. The idiot, asking for a clarification! He would die before he began!

The robot said, "Define latitude."

Lipescu's voice was calm. "The angular distance of a point on a planet's surface north or south of the equator, as measured from the center of the planet."

"Which is more consonant," the robot asked, "the minor third or the major sixth?"

There was a pause. Lipescu was no musician. But the computer would feed him the answer.

"The minor third," Lipescu said.

Without a pause, the robot fired another question. "Name the prime numbers between 5,237 and 7,641."

Bolzano smiled as Lipescu handled the question with ease. So far, so good. The robot had stuck to strictly factual questions, schoolbook stuff, posing no real problems to Lipescu. And after the initial hesitation and quibble over latitude, Lipescu had seemed to grow in confidence from moment to moment. Bolzano squinted at the scanner, looking beyond the robot, through the open gate, to the helter-skelter pile of treasures. He wondered which would fall to his lot when he and Lipescu divided them, two-thirds for Lipescu, the rest for him.

"Name the seven tragic poets of Elifora," the robot said.

"Domiphar, Halionis, Slegg, Hork-Sekan—"

"The fourteen signs of the zodiac as seen from Morneez," the robot demanded.

"The Teeth, the Serpents, the Leaves, the Waterfall, the Blot—"

"What is a pedicel?"

"The stalk of an individual flower of an inflorescence."

"How many years did the Siege of Lamina last?"

"Eight."

"What did the flower cry in the third canto of Somner's *Vehicles*?"

"'I ache, I sob, I whimper, I die,'" Lipescu boomed.

"Distinguish between the stamen and the pistil."

"The stamen is the pollen-producing organ of the flower; the pistil—"

And so it went. Question after question. The robot was not content with the legendary three questions of mythology; it asked a dozen, and then asked more. Lipescu answered perfectly, prompted by the murmuring of the peerless compendium of knowledge strapped to his chest. Bolzano kept careful count: the big man had dealt magnificently with seventeen questions When would the robot concede defeat? When would it end its grim quiz and step aside?

It asked an eighteenth question, pathetically easy. All it wanted was an exposition of the Pythagorean Theorem. Lipescu did not even need the computer for that. He answered, briefly, concisely, correctly. Bolzano was proud of his burly partner.

Then the robot struck Lipescu dead.

It happened in the flickering of an eyelid. Lipescu's voice had ceased, and he stood there, ready for the next question, but the next question did not come. Rather, a panel in the robot's vaulted belly slid open, and something bright and sinuous lashed out, uncoiling over the ten feet or so that separated guardian from challenger, and sliced Lipescu in half. The bright something slid back out of sight. Lipescu's trunk toppled to one side. His massive legs remained absurdly planted for a moment; then they crumpled, and a spacesuited leg kicked once, and all was still.

Stunned, Bolzano trembled in the loneliness of the cabin, and his lymph turned to water. What had gone wrong? Lipescu had given the proper answer to every question, and yet the robot had slain him. Why? Could the big man possibly have misphrased Pythagoras? No: Bolzano had listened. The answer had been flawless, as had the seventeen that preceded it. Seemingly the robot had lost patience with the game, then. The robot had cheated. Arbitrarily, maliciously, it had lashed out at Lipescu, punishing him for the correct answer.

Did robots cheat, Bolzano wondered? Could they act in malicious spite? No robot he knew was capable of such actions; but this robot was unlike all others.

For a long while, Bolzano remained huddled in the cabin. The temptation was strong to blast free of orbit and head home, treasureless but alive. Yet the treasure called to him. Some suicidal impulse drove him on. Siren-like, the robot drew him downward.

There had to be a way to make the robot yield, Bolzano thought, as he guided his small ship down the broad barren plain. Using the computer had been a good idea, whose only defect was that it hadn't worked. The records were uncertain, but it appeared that in the past men had died when they finally gave a wrong answer after a series of right ones. Lipescu had given no wrong answers. Yet he too had died. It was inconceivable that the robot understood some relationship of the squares on the hypotenuse and on the other two sides that was different from the relationship Lipescu had expressed.

Bolzano wondered what method would work.

He plodded leadenly across the plain toward the gate and its guardian. The germ of an idea formed in him as he walked doggedly on.

He was, he knew, condemned to death by his own greed. Only extreme agility of mind would save him from sharing Lipescu's fate. Ordinary intelligence would not work. Odyssean cleverness was the only salvation.

Bolzano approached the robot. Bones lay everywhere. Lipescu weltered in his own blood. Against that vast dead chest lay the computer, Bolzano knew. But he shrank from reaching for it. He would do without it. He looked away, unwilling to let the sight of Lipescu's severed body interfere with the coolness of his thoughts.

He collected his courage. The robot showed no interest in him.

"Give ground," Bolzano said. "I am here. I come for the treasure."

"Win your right to it."

"What must I do?"

"Demonstrate truth," the robot said. "Reveal inwardness. Display understanding."

"I am ready," said Bolzano.

The robot offered a question. "What is the excretory unit of the vertebrate kidney called?"

Bolzano contemplated. He had no idea. The computer could tell him, but the computer lay strapped to fallen Lipescu. No matter. The robot wanted truth, inwardness, understanding. Lipescu had offered information. Lipescu had perished.

"The frog in the pond," Bolzano said, "utters an azure cry."

There was silence. Bolzano watched the robot's front, waiting for the panel to slide open, the sinuous something to chop him in half.

The robot said, "During the War of Dogs on Vanderveer IX, the embattled colonists drew up thirty-eight dogmas of defiance. Quote the third, the ninth, the twenty-second, and the thirty-fifth."

Bolzano pondered. This was an alien robot, product of unknown hand. How did its maker's mind work? Did it respect knowledge? Did it treasure facts for their own sake? Or did it recognize that information is meaningless, insight a nonlogical process?

Lipescu had been logical. He lay in pieces.

"The mereness of pain," Bolzano responded, "is ineffable and refreshing."

The robot said, "The monastery of Kwaisen was besieged by the soldiers of Oda Nobunaga on the third of April, 1582. What words of wisdom did the abbot utter?"

Bolzano spoke quickly and buoyantly. "Eleven, forty-one, elephant, voluminous."

The last word slipped from his lips despite an effort to retrieve it. Elephants *were* voluminous, he thought. A fatal slip? The robot did not appear to notice.

Sonorously, ponderously, the great machine delivered the next question.

"What is the percentage of oxygen in the atmosphere of Muldonar VII?"

"False witness bears a swift sword," Bolzano replied.

The robot made an odd humming sound. Abruptly it rolled on massive treads, moving some six feet to its left. The gate of the treasure trove stood wide, beckoning.

"You may enter," the robot said.

Bolzano's heart leaped. He had won! He had gained the high prize!

Others had failed, most recently less than an hour before, and their bones glistened on the plain. They had tried to answer the robot, sometimes giving right answers, sometimes giving wrong ones, and they had died. Bolzano lived.

It was a miracle, he thought. Luck? Shrewdness? Some of each, he told himself. He had watched a man give eighteen right answers and die. So the accuracy of the responses did not matter to the robot. What did? Inwardness. Understanding. Truth.

There could be inwardness and understanding and truth in random answers, Bolzano realized. Where earnest striving had failed, mockery had succeeded. He had staked his life on nonsense, and the prize was his.

He staggered forward, into the treasure trove. Even in the light gravity, his feet were like leaden weights. Tension ebbed in him. He knelt among the treasures.

The tapes, the sharp-eyed televector scanners, had not begun to indicate the splendor of what lay here. Bolzano stared in awe and rapture at a tiny disk, no greater in diameter than a man's eye, on which myriad coiling lines writhed and twisted in patterns of rare beauty. He caught his breath, sobbing with the pain of perception as a gleaming marble spire, angled in mysterious swerves, came into view. Here, a bright beetle of some fragile waxy substance rested on a pedestal of yellow jade. There, a tangle of metallic cloth spurted dizzying patterns of luminescence. And over there—and beyond—and there—

The ransom of a universe, Bolzano thought.

It would take many trips to carry all this to his ship. Perhaps it would be better to bring the ship to the hoard, eh? He wondered, though, if he would lose his advantage if he stepped back through the gate. Was it possible that he would have to win entrance all over again? And would the robot accept his answers as willingly the second time?

It was something he would have to chance, Bolzano decided. His nimble mind worked out a plan. He would select a dozen, two dozen of the finest treasures, as much as he could comfortably carry, and take them back to the ship. Then he would lift the ship and set it down next to the gate. If the robot raised objections about his entering, Bolzano would simply depart, taking what he had already secured. There was no point in running undue risks. When he had sold this cargo, and felt pinched for money, he could always return and try to win admission once again. Certainly, no one else would steal the hoard if he abandoned it.

Selection, that was the key now.

Crouching, Bolzano picked through the treasure, choosing for portability and easy marketability. The marble spire? Too big. But the coiling disk, yes, certainly, and the beetle, of course, and this small statuette of dull hue, and the cameos showing scenes no human eye had ever beheld, and this, and this, and this—

His pulse raced. His heart thundered. He saw himself traveling from world to world, vending his wares. Collectors, museums, governments would vie with one another to have these prizes. He would let them bid each object up into the millions before he sold. And, of course, he would keep one or two for himself—or perhaps three or four—souvenirs of this great adventure.

And someday when wealth bored him he would return and face the challenge again. And he would dare the robot to question him, and he would reply with random absurdities, demonstrating his grasp of the fundamental insight that in knowledge there is only hollow merit, and the robot would admit him once more to the treasure trove.

Bolzano rose. He cradled his lovelies in his arms. Carefully, carefully, he thought. Turning, he made his way through the gate.

The robot had not moved. It had shown no interest as Bolzano plundered the hoard. The small man walked calmly past it.

The robot said, "Why have you taken those? What do you want with them?"

Bolzano smiled. Nonchalantly he replied, "I've taken them because they're beautiful. Because I want them. Is there a better reason?"

"No," the robot said, and the panel slid open in its ponderous black chest.

Too late, Bolzano realized that the test had not yet ended, that the robot's question had arisen out of no idle curiosity. And this time he had replied in earnest, speaking in rational terms.

Bolzano shrieked. He saw the brightness coming toward him.

Death followed instantly.

WHY?

I think this one might have pleased Horace Gold or Tony Boucher, two of the top science fiction editors of the time, if I had ever submitted it to them. But I was at the beginning of my career, not even a year out of college and faced with all sorts of new adult expenses like buying furniture and paying rent, and most of the time I was unwilling to take the risk of a speculative submission when I had an assured sale thing right at hand: like many of my stories at that time, this was written to order—for Robert Lowndes' modest little magazine *Science Fiction Stories*—to go with a cover painting the magazine already had on hand, and I got a safe, easy $85 for it in March, 1957, half of what *Galaxy* would have paid for it if I had taken the risk of sending it there on a speculative basis instead of embodying my story idea in a sure-thing commission for Lowndes. (I should also point out, since we are dealing in alternative realities here, that I might never have had the idea for this story in the first place without the inspiration that Ed Emshwiller's vivid cover painting provided.)

"Why?" ran in Lowndes' November, 1957 issue. I have no notion how much it cost me in the long run to do these sold-in-advance stories for the lower-paying magazines instead of taking my chances on everything with the top-paying ones first. But at least the rent got paid on time every month, a fact which, as you surely must have gathered by now, was a matter of no trivial concern to me back then.

AND WE LEFT CAPELLA XXII, after a six-month stay, and hopskipped across the galaxy to Dschubba, in the forehead of the Scorpion. And after the eight worlds of Dschubba had been seen and digested and recorded and classified, and after we had programmed all our material for transmission back to Earth, we moved on again, Brock and I.

We zeroed into warp and doublesqueaked into the star Pavo, which from Earth is seen to be the brightest star of the Peacock. And Pavo proved to be planetless, save for one ball of mud and methane a billion miles out; we chalked the mission off as unpromising, and moved on once again.

Brock was the coordinator; I, the fine-tooth man. He saw in patterns; I, in particulars. We had been teamed for eleven years. We had visited seventy-eight stars and one hundred sixty-three planets. The end was not quite in sight.

We hung in the greyness of warp, suspended neither in space nor in not-space, hovering in an interstice. Brock said, "I vote for Markab."

"Alpha Pegasi? No. I vote for Etamin."

But Gamma Draconis held little magic for him. He rubbed his angular hands through his tight-cropped hair and said, "The Wheel, then."

I nodded. "The Wheel."

The Wheel was our guide: not really a wheel so much as a map of the heavens in three dimensions, a lens of the galaxy, sprinkled brightly with stars. I pulled a switch; a beam of light lanced down from the ship's wall, needle-thin, playing against the Wheel. Brock seized the handle and imparted axial spin to the Wheel. Over and over for three, four, five rotations; then, stop. The light-beam stung Alphecca.

"Alphecca it will be," Brock said.

"Yes. Alphecca." I noted it in the log, and began setting up the coordinates on the drive. Brock was frowning uneasily.

"This failure to agree," he said. "This inability to decide on a matter so simple as our next destination—"

"Yes. Elucidate. Expound. Exegetize. What pattern do you see in that?"

Scowling he said, "Disagreement for the sake of disagreement is unhealthy. Conflict is valuable, but not for its own sake. It worries me."

"Perhaps we've been in space too long. Perhaps we should resign our commissions, leave the Exploratory Corps, return to Earth and settle there."

His face drained of blood. "No," he said. "No. No."

* * *

WE EMERGED FROM WARP WITHIN humming-distance of Alphecca, a bright star orbited by four worlds. Brock was playing calculus at the time; driblets of sweat glossed his face at each integration. I peered through the thick quartz of the observation panel and counted planets.

"Four worlds," I said. "One, two, three, and four."

I looked at him. His unfleshy face was tight with pain. After nearly a minute he said, "Pick one."

"Me?"

"Pick one!"

"Alphecca II."

"All right. We'll land there. I won't contest the point, Hammond. I *want* to land on Alphecca II." He grinned at me—a bright-eyed wild grin that I found unpleasant. But I saw what he was doing. He was easing a stress-pattern between us, eliminating a source of conflict before the chafing friction exploded. When two men live in a spaceship eleven years, such things are necessary.

Calmly and untensely I took a reading on Alphecca II. I sighted us in and actuated the computer. This was the way a landing was effected; this was the way Brock and I had effected one hundred sixty-three landings. The ion-drive exploded into life.

We dropped "downward." Alphecca II rose to meet us as our slim pale-green needle of a ship dived tail-first towards the world below.

The landing was routine. I sketched out a big 164 on my chart, and we donned spacesuits to make our preliminary explorations. Brock paused a moment at the airlock, smoothing the purple cloth of his suit, adjusting his air-intake, tightening his belt cincture. The corners of his mouth twitched nervously. Within the head-globe he looked frightened, and very tired.

I said, "You're not well. Maybe we should postpone our first look-see."

"Maybe we should go back to Earth, Hammond. And live in a beehive and breathe filthy grey soup." His voice was edged with bitter reproach. "Let's go outside," he said. He turned away, face shadowed morosely, and touched the stud that peeled back the airlock hatch.

I followed him into the lock and down the elevator. He was silent, stiff, reserved. I wished I had his talent for glimpsing patterns: this mood of his had probably been a long time building.

But I saw no cause for it. After eleven years, I thought, I should know him almost as well as I do myself. Or better. But no easy answers came, and I followed him out onto the exit stage and dropped gently down.

Landing One Six Four was entering the exploratory stage.

* * *

THE GROUND SPREAD OUT FAR to the horizon, a dull orange in color, rough in texture, pebbly, thick of consistency. We saw a few trees, bare-trunked, bluish. Green vines swarmed over the ground, twisted and gnarled.

Otherwise, nothing.

"Another uninhabited planet," I said. "That makes one hundred eight out of the hundred sixty-four."

"Don't be premature. You can't judge a world by a few acres. Land at a pole; extrapolate utter barrenness. It's not a valid pattern. Not enough evidence."

I cut him short. "Here's one time when I perceive a pattern. I perceive that this world's uninhabited. It's too damned quiet."

Chuckling, Brock said, "I incline to agree. But remember Adhara XI."

I remembered Adhara XI: the small, sandy world far from its primary, which seemed nothing but endless yellow sand dunes, rolling westward round and round the planet. We had joked about the desert-world, dry and parched, inhabited only by the restless dunes. But after the report was written, after our data were codified and flung through subspace towards Earth, we found the oasis on the eastern continent, the tiny garden of green things and sweet air that so sharply was unlike the rest of Adhara XI. I remembered sleek scaly creatures slithering through the crystal lake, and an indolent old worm sleeping beneath a heavy-fruited tree.

"Adhara XI is probably swarming with Earth tourists," I said. "Now that our amended report is public knowledge. I often think we should have concealed the oasis from Earth, and returned there ourselves when we grew tired of exploring the galaxy."

Brock's head snapped up sharply. He ripped a sprouting tip from a leathery vine and said, "*When* we grow tired? Hammond, aren't you tired already? Eleven years, a hundred sixty-four worlds?"

Now I saw the pattern taking fairly clear shape. I shook my head, throttling the conversation. "Let's get down the data, Brock. We can talk later."

We proceeded with the measurements of our particular sector of Alphecca II. We nailed down the dry vital statistics, bracketing them off so Earth could enter the neat figures in its giant catalogue of explored worlds.

GRAVITY—1.02 E.
ATMOSPHERIC CONSTITUTION—
ammonia/carbon dioxide
Type ab7, unbreathable
ESTIMATED PLANETARY DIAMETER—.87 E.
INTELLIGENT LIFE—*none*

We filled out the standard tests, took the standard soil samples. Exploration had become a smooth mechanical routine.

Our first tour lasted three hours. We wandered over the slowly rising hills, with the spaceship always at our backs, and Alphecca high behind us. The dry soil crunched unpleasantly beneath our heavy boots.

Conversation was at a minimum. Brock and I rarely spoke when it was not absolutely necessary—and when we did speak, it was to let a tight, tense remark escape confinement, not to communicate anything. We shared too many silent memories. Eleven years and one hundred sixty-four planets. All Brock had to do was say *"Fomalhaut,"* or I *"Theta Eridani,"* and a train of associations and memories was set off in whose depths we could browse silently for hours and hours.

Alphecca II did not promise to be as memorable as those worlds. There would be nothing here to match the fantastic moonrise of Fomalhaut VI, the five hundred mirror-bright moons in stately procession through the sky, each glinting in a different hue. That moonrise had overwhelmed us four years ago, and remained yet bright. Alphecca II, dead world that it was, or rather world not yet alive, would leave no marks on our memories.

But bitterness was rising in Brock. I saw the pattern forming; I saw the question bubbling up through the layers of his mind, ready to be asked.

And on the fourth day, he let it be asked. After four days on Alphecca II, four days of staring at the grotesque twisted green shapes of the angular sprawling vines, four days of watching the lethargic fission of the pond protozoa who seemed to be the world's only animal life, Brock suddenly looked up at me.

He asked the shattering question that should never be asked.

"Why?" he said.

* * *

Eleven years and a hundred sixty-four worlds earlier, the seeds of that unanswered question had been sown. I was fresh out of the

Academy, twenty-three, a tall, sharp-nosed boy with what some said was an irritatingly precise way of looking at things.

I should say that I bitterly resented being told I was coldly precise. People accused me of Teutonic heaviness. A girl I once had known said that to me, after a notably unsuccessful romance had come trailing to a halt. I recall turning to her, glaring at the light dusting of freckles across her nose, and telling her, "I have no Teutonic blood whatsoever. If you'll take the trouble to think of the probable Scandinavian derivation of my name—"

She slapped me.

Shortly after that, I met Brock—Brock, who at twenty-four was already the Brock I would know at thirty-five, harsh of face and voice, dark of complexion, with an expression of nervous wariness registering in his blue-black eyes always and ever. Brock never accused me of Teutonicism; he laughed when I cited some minor detail from memory, but the laugh was one of respect.

We were both Academy graduates; we both were restless. It showed in Brock's face, and I don't doubt it showed in mine. Earth was small and dirty and crowded, and each night the stars, those bright enough to glint through the haze and brightness of the cities, seemed to mock at us.

Brock and I gravitated naturally together. We shared a room in Appalachia North, we shared a library planchet, we shared reading tapes and music-discs and occasionally lovers. And eight weeks after my twenty-third birthday, seven weeks before Brock's twenty-fourth, we hailed a cab and invested our last four coins in a trip downtown to the Administration of External Exploration.

There, we spoke to a bland-faced, smiling man with one leg prosthetic—he boasted of it—and his left hand a waxy synthetic one. "I got that way on Sirius VI," he told us. "But I'm an exception. Most of the exploration teams keep going for years and years, and nothing ever happens to them. McKees and Haugmuth have been out twenty-three years now. That's the record. We hear from them, every few months or so. They keep on going, farther and farther out."

Brock nodded. "Good. Give us the forms."

He signed first. I added my name below, finishing with a flourish. I stacked the triplicate forms neatly together and shoved them back at the half-synthetic recruiter.

"Excellent. Excellent. Welcome to the Corps."

He shook our hands, giving the hairy-knuckled right hand to Brock, the waxy left to me. I gripped it tightly, wondering if he could feel my grip.

Three days later we were in space, bound outward. In all the time since the original idea had sprung up unvoiced between us, neither Brock nor myself had paused to ask the damnable question.

Why?

We had joined the Corps. We had renounced Earth. Motive, unstated. Or unknown. We let the matter lie dormant between us for eleven years, through a procession of strange and then less strange worlds.

Until Brock's agony broke forth to the surface. He destroyed eleven years of numb peace with one half-whispered syllable, there in the ship's lab our fourth morning on Alphecca II.

* * *

I LOOKED AT HIM FOR perhaps thirty seconds. Moistening my lips, I said, "What do you mean, Brock?"

"You know what I mean." The flat declarative tone was one of simple truth. "The one thing we haven't been asking ourselves all these years, because we knew we didn't have an answer for it and we *like* to have answers for things. Why are we here, on Alphecca II—with a hundred sixty-three visited worlds behind us?"

I shrugged. "You didn't have to start this, Brock." Outside the sun was climbing towards noon height, but I felt cold and dry, as if the ammonia atmosphere were seeping into the ship. It wasn't.

"No," he said. "I didn't have to start this. I could have let it fester for another eleven years. But it came popping out, and I want to settle it. We left Earth because we didn't like it there. Agreed?"

I nodded.

"But that's not *why* enough," he persisted. "Why do we explore? Why do we keep running from planet to planet, from one crazy airless ball to the next, out here where there are no people and no cities? Green crabs on Rigel V, sand-fish on Caph. Dammit, Hammond, what are we looking for?"

Very calmly I said, "Ourselves, maybe?"

His face crinkled scornfully. "Foggy-eyed and imprecise, and you know it. We're not looking for ourselves out here. We're trying to *lose* ourselves. Eh?"

"No!"

"Admit it!"

I stared through the quartz window at the stiff, almost wooden vines that covered the pebbly ground. They seemed to be moving faintly, to be stretching their rigid bodies in a contraction of some sort. In a dull, tired voice, Brock said, "We left Earth because we couldn't cope with it. It was too crowded and too dirty for sensitive shrinking souls like us. We had the choice of withdrawing into shells and huddling there for eighty or ninety years, or else pulling up and leaving for space. We left. There's no society out here, just each other."

"We've adjusted to each other," I pointed out.

"So? Does that mean we could fit into Earth society? Would you want to go back? Remember the team—McKees and Haugmuth, is it?—who spent thirty-three years in space and came back. They were catatonic eight minutes after landing, the report said."

"Let me give you a simpler *why*," I ventured. "Why did you start griping all of a sudden? Why couldn't you hold it in?"

"That's not a simpler *why*. It's part of the same one. I came to an answer, and I didn't like it. I got the answer that we were out here because we couldn't make the grade on Earth."

"No!"

He smiled apologetically. "No? All right, then. Give me another answer. I want an answer, Hammond. I need one, now."

I pointed to the synthesizer. "Why don't you have a drink instead?"

"That comes later," he said somberly. "After I've given up trying to find out."

The stippling of fine details was becoming a sharp-focus picture. Brock—self-reliant Brock, self-contained, self-sufficient—had come to the end of his self-sufficiency. He had looked too deeply beneath the surface.

"At the age of eight," I began, "I asked my father what was outside the universe. That is, defining the universe as That Which Contains Everything, could there possibly be something or someplace outside its bounds? He looked at me for a minute or two, then laughed and told me not to worry about it. But I did worry about it. I stayed up half the night worrying about it, and my head hurt by morning. I never found out what was outside the universe."

"The universe is infinite," said Brock moodily. "Recurving in on itself, topologically—"

"Maybe. But I worried over it. I worried over First Cause. I worried all through my adolescence. Then I stopped worrying."

He smiled acidly. "You became a vegetable. You rooted yourself in the mud of your own ignorance, and decided not to pull loose because it was too painful. Am I right, Hammond?"

"No. I joined the Exploratory Corps."

* * *

I DREAMED, THAT NIGHT, AS I swung in my hammock. It was a vivid and unpleasant dream, which stayed with me well into the following morning as a sort of misshapen reality that had attached itself to me in the night.

I had been a long time falling asleep. Brock had brooded most of the day, and a long hike over the bleak tundra had done little to improve his mood. Towards nightfall he dialed a few drinks, inserted a disc of Sibelius in his ear, and sat staring glumly at the darkening sky outside the ship. Alphecca II was moonless. The night was the black of space, but the atmosphere blurred the neighboring stars.

I remember drifting off into a semi-sleep: a half-somnolence in which I was aware of Brock's harsh breathing to my left, but yet in which I had no volition, no control over my limbs. And after that state came sleep, and with it dreams.

The dream must have grown from Brock's bitter remark of earlier: *You became a vegetable. You rooted yourself in the mud of your own ignorance.*

I accepted the statement literally. Suddenly I *was* a vegetable, possessed of all my former faculties, but rooted in the soil.

Rooted.

Straining for freedom, straining to break away, caught eternally by my legs, thinking, thinking . . .

Never to move, except for a certain thrashing of the upper limbs.

Rooted.

I writhed, longed to get as far as the rocky hill beyond, only as far as the next yard, the next inch. But I had lost all motility. It was as if my legs were grasped in a mighty trap, and, without pain, without torment, I was bound to the earth.

I woke, finally, damp with perspiration. In his hammock, Brock slept, seemingly peacefully. I considered waking him and telling him of the nightmare, but decided against it. I tried to return to sleep.

At length, I slept.

Dreamlessly.

The pre-set alarm throbbed at 0700; dawn had preceded us by nearly an hour.

Brock was up first; I sensed him moving about even as I stirred towards wakefulness. Still caught up in the strange unreal reality of my nightmare, I wondered on a conscious level if today would be like yesterday—if Brock, obsessed by his sudden thirst for an answer, would continue to brood and sulk.

I hoped not. It would mean the end of our team if Brock cracked up; after eleven years, I was not anxious for a new partner.

"Hammond? You up yet?"

His voice had lost the edgy quality of yesterday, but there was something new and subliminally frightening in it.

Yawning, I said, "Just about. Dial breakfast for me, will you?"

"I did already. But get out of the sack and come look at this."

I lurched from the hammock, shook my head to clear it, and started forward.

"Where are you?"

"Second level," he said. "At the window. Come take a look."

I climbed the spiral catwalk to the viewing-station; Brock stood with his back towards me, looking out. As I drew near I said, "I had the strangest dream last night—"

"The hell with that. Look."

At first I didn't notice anything strange. The bright-colored landscape looked unchanged, the pebbly orange soil, the dark blue trees, the tangle of green vines, the murk of the morning atmosphere. But then I saw I had been looking too far from home.

Writhing up the side of the window, just barely visible to the right, was a gnarled knobby green rope. Rope? No. It was one of the vines.

"They're all over the ship," Brock said. "I've checked all the ports. During the night the damned things must have come crawling up the side of the ship like so many snakes and wrapped themselves around us. I guess they figure we're here to stay, and they can use us as bracing-posts the way they do those trees."

I stared with mixed repugnance and fascination at the hard bark of the vine, at the tiny suckers that held it fast to the smooth skin of our ship.

"That's funny," I said. "It's sort of an attack by extraterrestrial monsters, isn't it?"

* * *

We suited up and went outside to have a look at the "attackers." At a distance of a hundred yards, the ship looked weirdly bemired. Its graceful lines were broken by the winding fingers of the vine, spiraling up its sleek sides from a thick parent stem on the ground. Other shoots of the vine sprawled near us, clutching futilely at us as we moved among them.

I was reminded of my dream. Somewhat hesitantly I told Brock about it.

Why?

He laughed. "Rooted, eh? You were dreaming *that* while those vines were busy wrapping themselves around the ship. Significant?"

"Perhaps." I eyed the tough vines speculatively. "Maybe we'd better move the ship. If much more of that stuff gets around it, we may not be able to blast off at all."

Brock knelt and flexed a shoot of vine. "The ship could be completely cocooned in this stuff and we'd still be able to take off," he said. "A space-drive wields a devil of a lot of thrust. We'll manage."

And *whick!*

A tapering finger of the vine arched suddenly and whipped around Brock's middle. *Whick! Whick!*

Like animated rope, like a bark-covered serpent, it curled about him. I drew back, staring. He seemed half amused, half perplexed.

"The thing's got pull, all right," he said. He was smiling lopsidedly, annoyed at having let so simple a thing as a vine interfere with his freedom of motion. But then he winced in obvious pain.

"—Tightening," he gasped.

The vine contracted muscularly; it skittered two or three feet towards the tree from which its parent stock sprang, and Brock was jerked suddenly off balance. As the corded arm of the vine yanked him backward he began to topple, poising for what seemed like seconds on his left foot, right jutting awkwardly in the air, arms clawing for balance.

Then he fell.

I was at his side in a moment, carefully avoiding the innocent looking vine-tips to right and left. I planted my foot on the trailing vine that held Brock. I levered downward and grabbed the tip where it bound his waist. I pulled; Brock pushed.

The vine yielded.

"It's giving," he grunted. "A little more."

"Maybe I'd better go back for the blaster," I said.

"No. No telling what this thing may do while you're gone. Cut me in two, maybe. Pull!"

I pulled. The vine struggled against our combined strength, writhed, twisted. But gradually we prevailed. It curled upward, loosened, went limp. Finally it drooped away, leaving Brock in liberty.

* * *

He got up slowly, rubbing his waist.

"Hurt?"

"Just the surprise," he said. "Tropistic reaction on the plant's part; I must have triggered some hormone chain to make it do that." He eyed the now quiescent vine with respect.

"It's not the first time we've been attacked," I said. "Alpheraz III—"

"Yes."

I hadn't even needed to mention it. Alpheraz III had been a hellish jungle planet; the image in his mind, as it was in mine, was undoubtedly that of a tawny beast the size of a goat held in the inexorable grip of some stocky-trunked plant, rising in the air, vanishing into a waiting mouth of the carnivorous tree—

—and moments later a second tendril dragging me aloft, and only a hasty blaster-shot by Brock keeping me from being a plant's dinner.

We returned to the ship, entering the hatch a few feet from one of the vines that now encrusted it. Brock unsuited; the vine had left a red, raw line about his waist.

"The plant tried," I said.

"To kill me?"

"No. To move on. To get going. To see what was behind the next hill."

He frowned and said, "What are you talking about?"

"I'm not so sure, yet. I'm not good at seeing patterns. But it's taking shape. I'm getting it now, Brock. I'm getting it all. I'm getting your answer!"

He massaged his stomach. "Go ahead," he said. "Think it out loud."

"I'm putting it together out of my dream and out of the things you said and out of the vines down there." I walked slowly about the cabin. "Those plants—they're stuck there, aren't they? They grow in a certain place and that's where they remain. Maybe they wiggle a little, and maybe they writhe, but that's the size of it."

"They can grow long."

"Sure. But not infinitely long. They can't grow long enough to reach another planet. They're rooted, Brock. Their condition is permanently fixed. Brock, suppose those plants had brains?"

"I don't think this has anything to do with—"

"It does," I said. "Just assume those plants were intelligent. They want to go. They're stuck. So one of them lashes out in fury at you. *Jealous* fury."

He nodded, seeing it clearly now. "Sure. We don't have roots. We can go places. We can visit a hundred sixty-four worlds and walk all over them."

"That's your answer, Brock. There's the *why* you were looking for." I took a deep breath. "You know why we go out to explore? Not because we're running away. Not because there's some inner compulsion driving us to coast from planet to planet. Uh-uh. It's because we *can* do it. That's all the why you need. We explore because it's possible for us to explore."

Some of the harshness faded from his face. "We're special," he said. "We can move. It's the privilege of humanity. The thing that makes us *us.*"

I didn't need to say any more. After eleven years, we don't need to vocalize every thought. But we had it, now: the special uniqueness that those clutching vines down there envied so much. Motility.

We left Alphecca II finally, and moved on. We did the other worlds of the system and headed outward, far out this time, as much of a hop as we could make. And we moved on from there to the next sun, and from there to the next, and onward.

We took a souvenir with us from Alphecca II though. When we blasted off, the vine that had wrapped itself round the ship gripped us so tightly that it wasn't shaken loose by the impact of blastoff. It remained hugging us as we thrust into space, dangling, roots and all. We finally got tired of looking at it, and Brock went out in a spacesuit to chop it away from the ship. He gave a push, imparted velocity to it, and the vine went drifting off sunward.

If had achieved its goal: it had left its home world. But it had died in the attempt. And that was the difference, we thought, all the difference in the universe, as we headed outward and outward, across the boundless gulfs to the next world we would visit.

THE PLEASURE OF THEIR COMPANY

Here's one from 1969, a time when it was starting to seem certain that the day of the science fiction magazine was ending. Just a handful of the magazines for which I had written in the early days of my career a decade and a half earlier still survived after the distribution cataclysm of 1958 and the general magazine attrition of the years immediately afterward, and those that were still with us were looking very unhealthy. The center of gravity of the science fiction-short-story field was now the steadily expanding group of original-fiction anthologies. Damon Knight had started his *Orbit* series in 1966, and my *New Dimensions* would follow a couple of years later, along with Terry Carr's *Universe*, Harry Harrison's *Nova*, Samuel R. Delany's *Quark*, and a whole host of one-shot collections. I did stories for just about all of them, *Quark* being the only exception that comes to mind.

One of the best of the new series was *Infinity*, published in paperback form by the same company that fifteen years earlier had brought out Larry Shaw's fine magazine *Infinity Science Fiction*. The editor this time was the long-time s-f reader and writer Bob Hoskins, who now was employed at the paperback company that had risen out of the ashes of the old Infinity and its companion magazines. He asked me to be a regular contributor, and as things turned out I could not have been more regular than I was: there were five issues of the new *Infinity* and I had stories in all five of them. This was the first, written in August of 1969 and published in *Infinity One* late in 1970—a journey for one, but he is not alone.

HE WAS THE ONLY MAN aboard the ship, one man inside a sleek shining cylinder heading away from Bradley's World at ten thousand miles a second, and yet he was far from alone. He had wife, father, daughter, son for company, and plenty of others, Ovid and Hemingway and Plato, and Shakespeare and Goethe, Attila the Hun and Alexander the Great, a stack of fancy cubes to go with the family ones. And his old friend Juan was along, too, the man who had shared his dream, his utopian fantasy, Juan who had been with him at the beginning and almost until the end. He had a dozen fellow voyagers in all. He wouldn't be lonely, though he had three years of solitary travel ahead of him before he reached his landfall, his place of exile.

It was the third hour of his voyage. He was growing calm, now, after the frenzy of his escape. Aboard ship he had showered, changed, rested. The sweat and grime of that wild dash through the safety tunnel were gone, now, though he wouldn't quickly shake from his mind the smell of that passageway, like rotting teeth, nor the memory of his terrifying fumbling with the security gate's copper arms as the junta's stormtroopers trotted toward him. But the gate had opened, and the ship had been there, and he had escaped, and he was safe. And he was safe.

I'll try some cubes, he thought.

The receptor slots in the control room held six cubes at once. He picked six at random, slipped them into place, actuated the evoker. Then he went into the ship's garden. There were screens and speakers all over the ship.

The air was moist and sweet in the garden. A plump, toga-clad man, clean-shaven, big-nosed, blossomed on one screen and said, "What a lovely garden! How I adore plants! You must have a gift for making things grow."

"Everything grows by itself. You're—"

"Publius Ovidius Naso."

"Thomas Voigtland. Former President of the Citizens' Council on Bradley's World. Now president-in-exile, I guess. A coup d'etat by the military."

"My sympathies. Tragic, tragic!"

"I was lucky to escape alive. I may never be able to return. They've probably got a price on my head."

"I know how terrible it is to be sundered from your homeland. Were you able to bring your wife?"

"I'm over here," Lydia said. "Tom? Tom, introduce me to Mr. Naso."

"I didn't have time to bring her," Voigtland said. "But at least I took a cube of her with me."

Lydia was three screens down from Ovid, just above a clump of glistening ferns. She looked glorious, her auburn hair a little too deep in tone but otherwise quite a convincing replica. He had cubed her two years before; her face showed none of the lines that the recent troubles had engraved on it. Voigtland said to her, "Not Mr. Naso, dear. Ovid. The poet Ovid."

"Of course. I'm sorry. How did you happen to choose him?"

"Because he's charming and civilized. And he understands what exile is like."

Ovid said softly, "Ten years by the Black Sea. Smelly barbarians my only companions. Yet one learns to adapt. My wife remained in Rome to manage my property and to intercede for me—"

"And mine remains on Bradley's World," said Voigtland. "Along with—along with—"

Lydia said, "What's this about exile, Tom? What happened?"

He began to explain about McAllister and the junta. He hadn't told her, back when he was having her cubed, why he wanted a cube of her. He had seen the coup coming. She hadn't.

As he spoke, a screen brightened between Ovid and Lydia and the seamed, leathery face of old Juan appeared. They had redrafted the constitution of Bradley's World together, twenty years earlier.

"It happened, then," Juan said instantly. "Well, we both knew it would. Did they kill very many?"

"I don't know. I got out fast once they started to—" He faltered. "It was a perfectly executed coup. You're still there. I suppose you're organizing the underground resistance by now. And I—And I—"

Needles of fire sprouted in his brain.

And I ran away, he said silently.

The other screens were alive now. On the fourth, someone with white robes, gentle eyes, dark curling hair. Voigtland guessed him to be Plato. On the fifth, Shakespeare, instantly recognizable, for the cube-makers had modeled him after the First Folio portrait: high forehead, long hair, pursed quizzical lips. On the sixth, a fierce, demonic-looking little man. Attila the Hun? They were all talking, activating themselves at random, introducing themselves to one another and to him. Their voices danced along the top of his skull. He could not follow their words. Restless, he moved among the plants, touching their leaves, inhaling the perfume of their flowers.

Out of the chaos came Lydia's voice.

"Where are you heading now, Tom?"

"Rigel XIX. I'll wait out the revolution there. It was my only option once hell broke loose. Get in the ship and—"

"It's so far," she said. "You're traveling alone?"

"I have you, don't I? And Mark and Lynx, and Juan, and Dad, and all these others."

"Cubes, that's all."

"Cubes will have to do," Voigtland said. Suddenly the fragrance of the garden seemed to be choking him. He went out, into the viewing salon next door, where the black splendor of space glistened through a wide port. Screens were mounted opposite the window. Juan and Attila seemed to be getting along marvelously well; Plato and Ovid were bickering; Shakespeare brooded silently; Lydia, looking worried, stared out of her screen at him. He studied the sweep of the stars.

"Which is our world?" Lydia asked.

"This," he said.

"So small. So far away."

"I've only been traveling a few hours. It'll get smaller."

* * *

He hadn't had time to take anyone with him. The members of his family had been scattered all over the planet when the alarm came, not one of them within five hours of home—Lydia and Lynx holidaying in the South Polar Sea, Mark archaeologizing on the Westerland Plateau. The integrator net told him it was a Contingency C situation: get off-planet within ninety minutes, or get ready to die. The forces of the junta had reached the capital and were on their way to pick him up. The escape ship had been ready, gathering dust in its buried vault. He hadn't been able to reach Juan. He hadn't been able to reach anybody. He used up sixty of his ninety minutes trying to get in touch with people, and then, with stunner shells already hissing overhead, he had gone into the ship and taken off. Alone.

But he had the cubes.

Cunning things. A whole personality encapsulated in a shimmering plastic box a couple of centimeters high. Over the past few years, as the likelihood of Contingency C had grown steadily greater, Voigtland had cubed everyone who was really close to him and stored the cubes aboard the escape ship, just in case.

It took an hour to get yourself cubed; and at the end of it, they had your soul in the box, your motion habits, your speech patterns, your way of thinking, your entire package of standard reactions. Plug your cube into a receptor slot and you came to life on the screen, smiling as you would smile, moving as you would move, sounding as you would sound, saying things you would say. Of course, the thing on the screen was unreal, a computer-actuated mockup, but it was programmed to respond to conversation, to absorb new data and change its outlook in the light of what it learned, to generate questions without the need of previous inputs; in short, to behave as a real person would.

The cube-makers also could supply a cube of anyone who had ever lived, or, for that matter, any character of fiction. Why not? It wasn't necessary to draw a cube's program from a living subject. How hard was it to tabulate and synthesize a collection of responses, typical phrases, and attitudes, feed them into a cube, and call what came out Plato or Shakespeare or Attila? Naturally a custom-made synthesized cube of some historical figure ran high, because of the man-hours of research and programming involved, and a cube of someone's own departed great-aunt was even more costly, since there wasn't much chance that it could be used as a manufacturer's prototype for further sales. But there was a wide array of standard-model historicals in the catalog when he was stocking his getaway ship; Voigtland had chosen eight of them.

Fellow voyagers. Companions on the long solitary journey into exile that he knew that he might someday have to take. Great thinkers. Heroes and villains. He flattered himself that he was worthy of their company. He had picked a mix of personality types, to keep him from losing his mind on his trip. There wasn't another habitable planet within a light-year of Bradley's World. If he ever had to flee, he would have to flee *far.*

He walked from the viewing salon to the sleeping cabin, and from there to the galley, and on into the control room. The voices of his companions followed him from room to room. He paid little attention to what they were saying, but they didn't seem to mind. They were talking to each other. Lydia and Shakespeare, Ovid and Plato, Juan and Attila, like old friends at a cosmic cocktail party.

"—not for its own sake, no but I'd say it's necessary to encourage mass killing and looting in order to keep your people from losing momentum, I guess, when—"

"—such a sad moment, when Prince Hal says he doesn't know Falstaff. I cry every time—"

"—when I said what I did about poets and musicians in an ideal Republic, it was not, I assure you, with the intent that *I* should have to live in such a Republic myself—"

"—the short sword, such as the Romans use, that's best, but—"

"—a throng of men and women in the brain, and one must let them find their freedom on the page—"

"—a slender young lad is fine, but yet I always had a leaning toward the ladies, you understand—"

"—massacre as a technique of political manipulation—"

"—Tom and I read your plays aloud to one another—"

"—good thick red wine, hardly watered—"

"—I loved Hamlet the dearest, my true son he was—"

"—the axe, ah, the axe!—"

Voigtland closed his throbbing eyes. He realized that it was soon in his voyage for company, too soon, too soon. Only the first day of his escape, it was. He had lost his world in an instant, in the twinkling of an eye. He needed time to come to terms with that, time and solitude, while he examined his soul. Later he could talk to his fellow voyagers. Later he could play with his cubed playmates.

He began pulling the cubes from the slots, Attila first, then Plato, Ovid, Shakespeare. One by one the screens went dark. Juan winked at him as he vanished, Lydia dabbed at her eyes. Voigtland pulled her cube too.

When they were all gone, he felt as if he had killed them.

* * *

For three days he roamed the ship in silence. There was nothing for him to do except read, think, watch, eat, sleep, and try to relax. The ship was self-programmed and entirely homeostatic; it ran without need of him, and indeed he had no notion of how to operate it. He knew how to program a takeoff, a landing, and a change of course, and the ship did all the rest. Sometimes he spent hours in front of his viewing port, watching Bradley's World disappear into the maze of the heavens. Sometimes he took his cubes out and arranged them in little stacks, four stacks of three, then three stacks of four, then six of two. But he did not play any of them. Goethe and Plato and Lydia and Lynx and Mark remained silent. They were his opiates against loneliness; very well, he would wait until the loneliness became intolerable.

He considered starting to write his memoirs. He decided to let them wait a while, too, until time had given him a clearer perspective on his downfall.

He thought a great deal about what might be taking place on Bradley's World just now. The jailings, the kangaroo trials, the purges. Lydia in prison? His son and daughter? Juan? Were those whom he had left behind cursing him for a coward, running off to Rigel this way in his plush little escape vessel? Did you desert your planet, Voigtland? Did you run out?

No. No. No. No.

Better to live in exile than to join the glorious company of martyrs. This way you can send inspiring messages to the underground, you can serve as a symbol of resistance, you can go back someday and guide the oppressed fatherland toward freedom, you can lead the counterrevolution and return to the capital with everybody cheering . . . Can a martyr do any of that?

So he had saved himself. So he had stayed alive to fight another day.

It sounded good. He was almost convinced.

He wanted desperately to know what was going on back there on Bradley's World, though.

The trouble with fleeing to another star system was that it wasn't the same thing as fleeing to a mountain-top hideout or some remote island on your own world. It would take so long to get to the other system, so long to make the triumphant return. His ship was a pleasure cruiser, not really meant for big interstellar hops. It wasn't capable of heavy acceleration, and its top velocity, which it reached only after a buildup of many weeks, was less than .50 lights. If he went all the way to the Rigel system and headed right back home, six years would have elapsed on Bradley's World between his departure and his return. What would happen in those six years?

What was happening there now?

His ship had a tachyon-beam ultrawave communicator. He could reach with it any world within a sphere ten light-years in radius, in a matter of minutes. If he chose, he could call clear across the galaxy, right to the limits of man's expansion, and get an answer in less than an hour.

He could call Bradley's World and find out how all those he loved had fared in the first hours of the dictatorship.

If he did, though, he'd paint a tachyon trail like a blazing line across the cosmos. And they could track him and come after him in their ramjet fighters at .75 lights, and there was about one chance in three that they could locate him with only a single point-source coordinate, and overtake him, and pick him up. He didn't want to risk it, not yet, not while he was still this close to home.

But what if the junta had been crushed at the outset? What if the coup had failed? What if he spent the next three years foolishly fleeing toward Rigel, when all was well at home, and a single call could tell him that?

He stared at the ultrawave set. He nearly turned it on.

A thousand times during those three days he reached toward it, hesitated, halted.

Don't. Don't. They'll detect you and come after you.

But what if I don't need to keep running?

It was Contingency C. The cause was lost.

That's what our integrator net said. But machines can be wrong. Suppose our side managed to stay on top? I want to talk to Juan. I want to talk to Mark. I want to talk to Lydia.

That's why you brought the cubes along. Keep away from the ultrawave.

On the fourth day, he picked out six cubes and put them in the receptor slots.

* * *

SCREENS GLOWED. HE SAW HIS father, his son, his oldest friend. He also saw Hemingway, Goethe, Alexander the Great.

"I have to know what's happening at home," Voigtland said. "I want to call them."

"I'll tell you." It was Juan who spoke, the man who was closer to him than any brother. The old revolutionary, the student of conspiracies. "The junta is rounding up everyone who might have dangerous ideas and locking them away. It's telling everybody else not to worry, stability is here at last. McAllister is in full control; calling himself provisional president or something similar."

"Maybe not. Maybe it's safe for me to turn and go back."

"What happened?" Voigtland's son asked. His cube hadn't been activated before. He knew nothing of events since he had been cubed, ten months earlier. "Were you overthrown?"

Juan started to explain about the coup to Mark. Voigtland turned to his father. At least the old man was safe from the rebellious colonels; he had died two years ago, in his eighties, just after making the cube. The cube was all that was left of him. "I'm glad this didn't happen in your time," Voigtland said. "Do you remember, when I was a boy, and you were President of the Council, how you told me about the uprisings on other colonies? And I said, No, Bradley's World is different, we all work together here."

The old man smiled. He looked pale and waxy, an echo of the man he had been. "No world is different, Tom. Political entities go through similar cycles everywhere, and part of the cycle involves an impatience with democracy. I'm sorry that the impatience had to strike while you were in charge, son."

"Homer tells us that men would rather have their fill of sleep, love, singing, and dancing than of war," Goethe offered, smooth-voiced, courtly, civilized. "But there will always be some who love war above all else. Who can say why the gods gave us Achilles?"

"I can," Hemingway growled. "You define man by looking at the opposites inside him. Love and hate. War and peace. Kissing and killing. That's where his borders are. What's wrong with that? Every man's a bundle of opposites. So is every society. And sometimes the killers get the upper hand on the kissers. Besides, how do you know the fellows who overthrew you were so wrong?"

"Let me speak of Achilles," said Alexander, tossing his ringlets, holding his hands high. "I know him better than any of you, for I carry his spirit within me. And I tell you that warriors are best fit to rule, so long as they have wisdom as well as strength, for they have given their lives as pledges in return for the power they hold. Achilles—"

Voigtland was not interested in Achilles. To Juan he said, "I have to call. It's four days, now. I can't just sit in this ship and remain cut off."

"If you call, they're likely to catch you."

"I know that. But what if the coup failed?" Voigtland was trembling. He moved closer to the ultrawave set.

Mark said, "Dad, if the coup failed, Juan will be sending a ship to intercept you. They won't let you just ride all the way to Rigel for nothing."

Yes, Voigtland thought, dazed with relief. Yes, yes, of course. How simple. Why hadn't I thought of that?

"You hear that?" Juan asked. "You won't call?"

"I won't call," Voigtland promised.

* * *

THE DAYS PASSED. HE PLAYED all twelve cubes, chatted with Mark and Lynx, Lydia, Juan. Idle chatter, talk of old holidays, friends, growing up. He loved the sight of his cool elegant daughter and his rugged long-limbed son, and wondered how he could have sired them, he who was short and thick-bodied, with blunt features and massive bones. He talked with his father about government, with Juan about revolution. He talked with Ovid about exile, and with Plato about the nature of injustice, and with Hemingway about the definition of courage. They helped him through some of the difficult moments. Each day had its difficult moments.

The nights were much worse.

He ran screaming and ablaze down the tunnels of his own soul. He saw faces looming like huge white lamps above him. Men in black uniforms and mirror-bright boots paraded in somber phalanxes over his fallen body. Citizens lined up to jeer him. ENEMY OF THE STATE. ENEMY OF THE STATE. ENEMY OF THE STATE. They brought Juan to him in his dreams. COWARD. COWARD. COWARD. Juan's lean bony body was ridged and gouged; he had been put through the tortures, the wires in the skull, the lights in the eyes, the truncheons in the ribs. I STAYED. YOU FLED. I STAYED. YOU FLED. I STAYED. YOU FLED. They showed him his own face in a mirror, a jackal's face, with long yellow teeth and little twitching eyes. ARE YOU PROUD OF YOURSELF? ARE YOU PLEASED? ARE YOU HAPPY TO BE ALIVE?

He asked the ship for help. The ship wrapped him in a cradle of silvery fibers and slid snouts against his skin that filled his veins with cold droplets of unknown drugs. He slipped into a deeper sleep, and underneath the sleep, burrowing up, came dragons and gorgons and serpents and basilisks, whispering mockery as he slept. TRAITOR. TRAITOR. TRAITOR. HOW CAN YOU HOPE TO SLEEP SOUNDLY, HAVING DONE WHAT YOU HAVE DONE?

"Look," he said to Lydia, "they would have killed me within the hour. There wasn't any possible way of finding you, Mark, Juan, anybody. What sense was there in waiting longer?"

"No sense at all, Tom. You did the smartest thing."

"But was it the *right* thing, Lydia?"

Lynx said, "Father, you had no choice. It was run or die."

He wandered through the ship, making an unending circuit. How soft the walls were, how beautifully upholstered! The lighting was gentle. Restful images flowed and coalesced and transformed themselves on the sloping ceilings. The little garden was a vale of beauty. He had music, fine food, books, cubes. What was it like in the sewers of the underground now?

"We didn't need more martyrs," he told Plato. "The junta was making enough martyrs as it was. We needed leaders. What good is a dead leader?"

"Very wise, my friend. You have made yourself a symbol of heroism, distant, idealized, untouchable, while your colleagues carry on the struggle in your name," Plato said silkily. "And yet you are able to return and serve your people in the future. The service a martyr gives is limited, finite, locked to a single point in time. Eh?"

"I have to disagree," said Ovid. "If a man wants to be a hero, he ought to hold his ground and take what comes. Of course, what sane man wants to be a hero? You did well, friend Voigtland! Give yourself over to feasting and love, and live longer and more happily."

"You're mocking me," he said to Ovid.

"I do not mock. I console. I amuse. I do not mock."

In the night came tinkling sounds, faint bells, crystalline laughter. Figures capered through his brain, demons, jesters, witches, ghouls. He tumbled down into mustiness and decay, into a realm of spiders, where empty husks hung on vast arching webs. THIS IS WHERE THE HEROES GO. Hags embraced him. WELCOME TO VALHALLA. Gnarled midgets offered him horns of mead, and the mead was bitter, leaving a coating of ash on his lips. ALL HAIL. ALL HAIL. ALL HAIL.

"Help me," he said hoarsely to the cubes. "What did I bring you along for, if not to help me?"

"We're trying to help," Hemingway said. "We agree that you did the sensible thing."

"You're saying it to make me happy, You aren't sincere."

"You bastard, call me a liar again and I'll step out of this screen and—"

"Maybe I can put it another way," Juan said craftily. "Tom, you had an *obligation* to save yourself. Saving yourself was the most valuable thing you could have done for the cause. Listen, for all you knew the rest of us had already been wiped out, right?"

"Yes. Yes."

"Then what would you accomplish by staying and being wiped out too? Outside of some phony heroics, what?" Juan shook his head. "A leader in exile is better than a leader in the grave. You can direct the resistance from Rigel, if the rest of us are gone. Do you see the dynamics of it, Tom?"

"I see. I see. You make it sound so reasonable, Juan."

Juan winked. "We always understood each other."

He activated the cube of his father. "What do you say? Should I have stayed or gone?"

"Maybe stay, maybe go. How can I speak for you? Certainly taking the ship was more practical. Staying would have been more dramatic. Tom, Tom, how can I speak for you?"

"Mark?"

"I would have stayed and fought right to the end. Teeth, nails, everything. But that's me. I think maybe you did the right thing, Dad. The way Juan explains it. The right thing for *you*, that is."

Voigtland frowned. "Stop talking in circles. Just tell me this: do you despise me for going?"

"You know I don't," Mark said.

* * *

THE CUBES CONSOLED HIM. HE began to sleep more soundly, after a while. He stopped fretting about the morality of his flight. He remembered how to relax.

He talked military tactics with Attila, and was surprised to find a complex human being behind the one-dimensional ferocity. He tried to discuss the nature of tragedy with Shakespeare, but Shakespeare seemed more interested in talking about taverns, politics, and the problems of a playwright's finances. He spoke to Goethe about the second part of Faust, asking if Goethe really felt that the highest kind of redemption came through governing well, and Goethe said, yes, yes, of course. And when Voigtland wearied of matching wits with his cubed great ones, he set them going against one another, Attila and Alexander, Shakespeare and Goethe, Hemingway and Plato, and sat back, listening to such talk as mortal man had never heard. And there were humbler sessions with Juan and his family. He blessed the cubes; he blessed their makers.

"You seem much happier these days," Lydia said.

"All that nasty guilt washed away," said Lynx.

"It was just a matter of looking at the logic of the situation," Juan observed.

Mark said, "And cutting out all the masochism, the self-flagellation."

"Wait a second," said Voigtland. "Let's not hit below the belt, young man."

"But it *was* masochism, Dad. Weren't you wallowing in your guilt? Admit it."

"I suppose I—"

"And looking to us to pull you out," Lynx said. "Which we did."

" Yes. You did."

"And it's all clear to you now, eh?" Juan asked. "Maybe you *thought* you were afraid, thought you were running out, but you were actually performing a service to the republic. Eh?"

Voigtland grinned. "Doing the right thing for the wrong reason."

"Exactly. Exactly."

"The important thing is the contribution you still can make to Bradley's World," his father's voice said. "You're still young. There's time to rebuild what we used to have there."

"Yes. Certainly."

"Instead of dying a futile but heroic death," said Juan.

"On the other hand," Lynx said, "what did Eliot write? *'The last temptation is the greatest treason: To do the right deed for the wrong reason.'*"

Voigtland frowned. "Are you trying to say—"

"And it *is* true," Mark cut in, "that you were planning your escape far in advance. I mean, making the cubes and all, picking out the famous men you wanted to take—"

"As though you had decided that at the first sign of trouble you were going to skip out," said Lynx.

"They've got a point," his father said. "Rational self-protection is one thing, but an excessive concern for your mode of safety in case of emergency is another."

"I don't say you should have stayed and died," Lydia said. "I never would say that. But all the same—"

"Hold on!" Voigtland said. The cubes were turning against him suddenly. "What kind of talk is this?"

Juan said, "And strictly as a pragmatic point, if the people were to find out how far in advance you engineered your way out, and how comfortable you are as you head for exile—"

"You're supposed to help me," Voigtland shouted. "Why are you starting this? What are you trying to do?"

"You know we all love you," said Lydia.

"We hate to see you not thinking clearly, Father," Lynx said.

"Weren't you planning to run out all along?" said Mark.

"Wait! Stop! Wait!"

"Strictly as a matter of—"

Voigtland rushed into the control room and pulled the Juan-cube from the slot.

"We're trying to explain to you, dear—"

He pulled the Lydia-cube, the Mark-cube, the Lynx-cube, the father-cube.

The ship was silent.

He crouched, gasping, sweat-soaked, face rigid, eyes clenched tight shut, waiting for the shouting in his skull to die away.

* * *

AN HOUR LATER, WHEN HE was calm again, he began setting up his ultrawave call, tapping out the frequency that the underground would probably be using, if any underground existed. The tachyon beam sprang across the void, an all but instantaneous carrier wave, and he heard cracklings, and then a guarded voice saying, "Four Nine Eight Three, we read your signal, do you read me? This is Four Nine Eight Three, come in, come in, who are you?"

"Voigtland," he said. "President Voigtland, calling Juan. Can you get Juan on the line?"

"Give me your numbers, and—"

"What numbers? This is *Voigtland.* I'm I don't know how many billion miles out in space, and I want to talk to Juan. Get me Juan. *Get me Juan.*"

"You wait," the voice said.

Voigtland waited, while the ultrawave spewed energy wantonly into the void. He heard clickings, scrapings, clatterings. "You still there?" the voice said, after a while. "We're patching him in. But be quick. He's busy."

"Well? Who is it?" Juan's voice, beyond doubt.

"Tom here. Tom Voigtland, Juan!"

"It's really you?" Coldly. From a billion parsecs away, from some other universe. "Enjoying your trip, Tom?"

"I had to call. To find out—to find out—how it was going, how everybody is. How Mark—Lydia—you—"

"Mark's dead. Killed the second week, trying to blow up McAllister in a parade."

"Oh. Oh."

"Lydia and Lynx are in prison somewhere. Most of the others are dead. Maybe ten of us left, and they'll get us soon, too. Of course, there's you."

"Yes."

"You bastard," Juan said quietly. "You rotten bastard. All of us getting rounded up and shot, and you get into your ship and fly away!"

"They would have killed me too, Juan. They were coming after me. I only just made it."

"You should have stayed," Juan said.

"No. No. That isn't what you just said to me! You told me I did the right thing, that I'd serve as a symbol of resistance, inspiring everybody from my place of exile, a living symbol of the overthrown government—"

"I said this?"

"You, yes," Voigtland told him. "Your cube, anyway."

"Go to hell," said Juan. "You lunatic bastard."

"Your cube—we discussed it, you explained—"

"Are you crazy, Tom? Listen, those cubes are programmed to tell you whatever you want to hear. Don't you know that? You want to feel like a hero for running away, they tell you you're a hero. It's that simple. How can you sit there and quote what my cube said to you, and make me believe that *I* said it?"

"But I—you—"

"Have a nice flight, Tom. Give my love to everybody, wherever you're going."

"I couldn't just stay there to be killed. What good would it have been? Help me, Juan! What shall I do now? Help me!"

"I don't give a damn what you do," Juan said. "Ask your cubes for help. So long, Tom."

"Juan—"

"So long, you bastard."

Contact broke.

* * *

Voigtland sat quietly for a while, pressing his knuckles together. *Listen, those cubes are programmed to tell you whatever you want to hear. Don't you know that? You want to feel like a hero for running away, they tell you you're a hero.* And if you want to feel like a villain? They tell you that too. They meet all needs. They aren't people. They're cubes.

He put Goethe in the slot. "Tell me about martyrdom," he said.

Goethe said, "It has its tempting side. One may be covered with sins, scaly and rough-skinned with them, and in a single fiery moment of self-immolation one wins redemption and absolution, and one's name is forever cherished."

He put Juan in the slot. "Tell me about the symbolic impact of getting killed in the line of duty."

"It can transform a mediocre public official into a magnificent historical figure," Juan said.

He put Mark in the slot. "Which is a better father to have: a live coward or a dead hero?"

"Go down fighting, Dad."

He put Hemingway in the slot. "What would you do if someone called you a rotten bastard?"

"I'd stop to think if he was right or wrong. If he was wrong, I'd give him to the sharks. If he was right, well, maybe the sharks would get fed anyway."

He put Lydia in the slot. Lynx. His father. Alexander. Attila. Shakespeare. Plato. Ovid. Lit in their various ways they were all quite eloquent. They spoke of bravery, self-sacrifice, nobility, redemption.

He picked up the Mark-cube. "You're dead," he said. "Just like your grandfather. There isn't any Mark anymore. What comes out of this cube isn't Mark. It's me, speaking with Mark's voice, talking through Mark's mind. You're just a dummy."

He put the Mark-cube in the ship's converter input, and it tumbled down the slideway to become reaction mass. He put the Lydia-cube in next. Lynx. His father. Alexander. Attila. Shakespeare. Plato. Ovid. Goethe.

He picked up the Juan-cube. He put it in a slot again. "Tell me the truth," he yelled. "What'll happen to me if I go back to Bradley's World?"

"You'll make your way safely to the underground and take charge, Tom. You'll help us throw McAllister out: We can win with you, Tom."

"Crap," Voigtland said. "I'll tell you what'll really happen. I'll be intercepted before I go into my landing orbit. I'll be taken down and put on trial. And then I'll be shot. Right? Right? Tell me the truth, for once. Tell me I'll be shot!"

"You misunderstand the dynamics of the situation, Tom. The impact of your return will be so great that—"

He took the Juan-cube from the slot and put it into the chute that went to the converter.

"Hello?" Voigtland said. "Anyone here?"

The ship was silent.

"I'll miss all that scintillating conversation," he said. "I miss you already. Yes. Yes. But I'm glad you're gone."

He countermanded the ship's navigational instructions and tapped out the program headed RETURN TO POINT OF DEPARTURE. His hands were shaking, just a little, but the message went through. The instruments showed him the change of course as the ship began to turn around. As it began to take him home.

Alone.

THEBES OF THE HUNDRED GATES

I had always wanted to visit Egypt and see the Pyramids and the other monuments of the Pharaohs, even as a small boy, and when I began writing books on archaeological subjects (*Lost Cities and Vanished Civilizations*, *Empires in the Dust*, and many others, starting in 1961) that desire grew even stronger. But not until 1990, after having traveled far and wide throughout the world, did I finally do anything about going there.

Our plan was to make the trip in conjunction with Brian and Margaret Aldiss, who had been there before and who had offered much good advice on how to cope with the mysteries of that ancient land. At the last moment the Aldisses had to cancel, I forget why; but, thanks to Brian's useful suggestion, we had engaged the services of an excellent tour company, Kuoni Tours, which put together an Egyptian adventure for us which, for the most part, took us from place to place in a private car with a guide, and so we saw everything we wanted to see without having to sign up for the sort of group tour that I have always tried to avoid.

We landed in Cairo, found ourselves almost immediately staring up at the Great Pyramid of Khufu—far more massive than I had ever imagined, and I hadn't imagined that the Great Pyramid was a tiny thing—and the Sphinx nearby. After a couple of days wandering in chaotic Cairo we embarked on a dazzling ten-day journey by car and plane that took us south as far as Aswan and the awesome cliffside statues of Rameses II, and then came back to Luxor, Sakkara, Memphis, and nearly all the other memorable sights along the way before we returned to Cairo and a return visit to the Pyramids. (We stayed, our final night, at the Mena Hotel, with the Pyramids virtually within reach just outside our window.) Egypt was everything I had expected it to be and then some, and I spent the next few months steeping myself in archaeological texts and translations of the sacred scriptures of the Pharaonic era.

There was at that time a vigorous small-press publishing company based in Seattle, Pulphouse Press, that was doing a series of books of stand-alone novellas under the direction of Kristine Kathryn Rusch. My regular trade publisher in that period was Bantam Books, then under the command of the brilliant and ambitious Lou Aronica. Lou just then had the idea of publishing a series of stand-alone novellas also, and had no objections to co-publishing with Pulphouse, and, since the novella is my favorite length for fiction (cf. "Sailing to Byzantium," "The Secret Sharer," "Hawksbill Station," "Born with the Dead," and five or six more of mine) I leaped at the opportunity to write an Egyptian novella for them. The opening lines of "Thebes of the Hundred Gates," which I wrote in January, 1991, very precisely capture the emotions I felt myself at the outset of my own Egyptian trip:

> The sensory impact pressed in on him from all sides at once in the first dazzling moment of his arrival: a fierce bombardment of smells, sights, sounds, everything alien, everything much too intense, animated by a strange inner life.

Exactly so. I wrote the 30,000-word story with furious intensity, working at a pace I hadn't been able to sustain for years, and finished in about a month. Pulphouse published it in November, 1991 in several limited-edition formats, and Bantam followed with a paperback edition in July, 1992.

Heaven is opened, the company of gods shines forth!
Amon-Re, Lord of Karnak, is exalted upon the great seat!
The Great Nine are exalted upon their seats!
Thy beauties are thine, O Amon-Re, Lord of Karnak!

—The Liturgy of Amon

Flame which came forth backwards, I have not stolen the god's-offerings.
O Bone-breaker who came forth from Heracleopolis, I have not told lies.
O Eater of entrails who came forth from the House of Thirty, I have not committed perjury.
O You of the darkness who came forth from the darkness, I have not been quarrelsome.
O Nefertum who came forth from Memphis, I have done no wrong, I have seen no evil.

—The Negative Confession

ONE

THE SENSORY IMPACT PRESSED IN on him from all sides at once in the first dazzling moment of his arrival: a fierce bombardment of smells, sights, sounds, everything alien, everything much too intense, animated by a strange inner life. Luminous visions assailed him. He wandered for some indeterminate span of astounded time in shimmering dream-forests. Even the air had texture, contradictory and confusing, a softness and a roughness, a heaviness and a giddy lightness. Egypt coursed through him like an uncheckable river, sparking and fizzing, stunning him with its immensity, with its stupefying aliveness.

He was inhaling magic, and he was choking on it. Breathing was a struggle—he was so stunned that he had to remind himself how it was done—but the real problem was the disorientation. There was too much information and he was having trouble processing it. It was like sticking not just your fingertip but your whole head into the light-socket. He was a dozen different sizes and he was experiencing every moment of his life, including moments he hadn't yet lived, in a single simultaneous flash.

He had prepared for this moment for months—for nearly all his life, you might almost say—and yet nothing could really prepare anyone for *this,* not really. He had made three training jumps, two hundred years, then four hundred, then six hundred, and he thought he knew what to expect, that sickening sense of breathlessness, of dizziness, of having crashed into the side of a mountain at full tilt; but everyone had warned him that even the impact of a six-C jump was nothing at all compared with the zap of a really big one, and everyone had been right. This one was thirty-five C's, and it was a killer. *Just hold on and try to catch your breath,* that's what the old hands had told him, Charlie Farhad who had made the Babylon jump and Nick Efthimiou who had seen the dancers leaping over bulls at the court of King Minos and Amiel Gordon who had attended a royal bar mitzvah at the temple of Solomon when the paint was still fresh. *It's a parachute jump without the parachute,* Efthimiou had said. *The trick is to roll with the punch and not try to offer any resistance. If you live through the first five minutes you'll be okay.* You built up a charge of temporal potential as you went, and the farther back in time you went, the stiffer the charge, in more ways than one.

Gradually the world stopped spinning wildly around him. Gradually the dizziness ebbed.

The actual extent of what he could see was quite limited. They did their best to drop you off someplace where your arrival wouldn't be noticed. He was in an unpaved alleyway maybe six feet wide, flanked by high walls of dirty whitewashed mud-brick that blocked his view to either side. The last bright traces of the golden aura of the jump field were still visible as a series of concentric rings with him at its center, a glittering spiderweb of light, but they were dwindling fast. Two donkeys stood just in front of him, chewing on straw, studying him with no great curiosity. A dozen yards or so behind him was some sort of rubble-heap, filling the alley almost completely. His sandal-clad left foot was inches from a row of warm green turds that one of the donkeys must have laid down not very long before. To his right flowed a thin runnel of brownish water so foul that it seemed to him he could make out the movements of giant microorganisms in it, huge amoebas and paramecia, grim predatory rotifers swimming angrily against the tide. Of the city that lay beyond the nasty, scruffy little slot where he had materialized, nothing was visible except a single tall, skinny palm tree, rising like an arrow against the blank blue sky above the alley wall. He could have been anywhere in any of a hundred Asian or African or Latin American countries. But when he glanced a second time at the wall to his left he caught sight of a scrawled graffito, a scribbled line of faded words hastily applied; and the script was the vaguely Arabic-looking squiggles and dots and boxes of Eighteenth Dynasty hieratic and his well-trained mind instantly provided a translation: *May the serpent Amakhu devourer of spirits swallow the soul of Ipuky the wine-merchant, may he fall into the Lake of Fire, may he be trapped in the Room of Monsters, may he die for a million years, may his* ka *perish eternally, may his tomb be full of scorpions, for he is a cheat and a teller of falsehoods.* In that moment the totality of the world which he had just entered, the inescapable bizarre reality of it, came sweeping in on him in tidal surges of sensation, Thoth and Amon, Isis and Osiris, temples and tombs, obelisks and pyramids, hawk-faced gods, black earth, beetles that talked, snakes with legs, baboon-gods, vulture-gods, winking sphinxes, incense fumes drifting upward, the smell of sweet beer, sacks of barley and beans, half-mummified bodies lying in tubs of natron, birds with the heads of women, women with the heads of birds, processions of masked priests moving through forests of fat-bellied stone columns, water-wheels turning slowly at the river's edge, oxen and jackals, cattle and dogs, alabaster vessels and breastplates of gold, plump Pharaoh on his throne sweating beneath the weight of his two-toned crown, and above all else the sun, the sun, the sun, the inescapable implacable sun, reaching down with insinuating fingers to caress everything that lived or did not live in this land of the living and the dead. The whole of it was coming through to him in one great shot. His head was expanding like a balloon. He was drowning in data.

He wanted to cry. He was so dazed, so weakened by the impact of his leap through time, so overwhelmed. There was so much he needed to defend himself against, and he had so few resources with which to do it. He was frightened. He was eight years old again, suddenly promoted to a higher grade in school because of his quick mind and his restless spirit, and abruptly confronted with the mysteries of subjects that for once were too difficult for him instead of too easy—long division, geography—and a classroom full of unfamiliar new classmates, older than he was, dumber, bigger, hostile.

His cheeks blazed with the shame of it. Failure wasn't a permissible mode.

Maybe it was time to start moving out of this alleyway, he decided. The worst of the somatics seemed to be past, now, pulse more or less normal, vision unblurred—*if you live through the first five minutes you'll be okay*—and he felt steady enough on his feet. Warily he made his way around the two donkeys. There was barely enough clearance between the beasts and the wall. One of the donkeys rubbed his shoulder with its bristly nose. He was bare to the waist, wearing a white linen kilt, sandals of red leather, a woven skullcap to protect his head. He didn't for a moment think he looked convincingly Egyptian, but he didn't have to; here in the great age of the New Empire the place was full of foreigners—Hittites, Cretans, Assyrians, Babylonians, maybe even a Chinaman or two or some sleek little Dravidian voyager from far-off India—*tell them you're a Hebrew*, Amiel had advised, *tell them you're Moses' great-grandfather and they'd better not fuck around with you or you'll hit them with the twelve plagues a hundred years ahead of schedule*. All he had to do was find some short-term way of fitting in, keep himself fed somehow until he had completed his mission, sign on for work of any sort where he could simulate a skill—a scribe, a butler, a maker of pots, a fashioner of bricks. Anything. He only had to cope for thirty days.

The alley took a sharp bend twenty feet beyond the donkeys. He paused there for a long careful look, fixing the details in his mind: the graffito, the rubble-heap, a bare place where the whitewash had worn through, the angle of the bend, the height and declination of the palm tree. He was going to have to find his way back here, of course, on the thirtieth day. They would be trawling through time for him, and that was like fishing with a bent pin: he had to give them all the help he could. For a moment his heart sank. Probably there were fifty thousand alleys just like this one in Thebes. But he was supposed to be an intelligent life-form, he reminded himself. He'd make note of the landmarks; he'd file away all the specifics. His life depended on it.

Now at last he was at the end of the alley.

He peered out into the street and had his first glimpse of Thebes of the Hundred Gates.

The city hit him in the face with a blast of sensation so heavy that he felt almost as shaken as he had in the first instant of the time-jump. Everything was noise, bustle, heat, dust. The smell of dung and rotting fruit was so ripe he had to fight to keep from gagging. There were people everywhere, huge throngs of them, moving with startling purposefulness, jostling past him, bumping him, pushing him aside as though he were invisible to them as he stood slack-jawed in the midst of all this frenzy; this could be New York's Fifth Avenue on a spring afternoon, except that many of them were naked or nearly so in the astonishing furnace-like heat, and huge herds of goats and sheep and oxen and asses and weird long-horned hump-backed cattle were moving serenely among them. Pigs snorted and snuffled at his feet. He had emerged into a sort of plaza, with tangled clusters of little mud-walled shops and taverns and, very likely, brothels, all around him. The river was on his right just a few dozen steps away, very low but flowing fast, a swift green monster cluttered with hundreds of ships with curving prows and towering masts, and right in front of him, no more than a hundred yards distant, was a vast walled structure which, from the double row of giant papyrus-bud stone columns and the hint of intricate antechambers beyond, he supposed was the building that in modern times was known as Luxor Temple. At least it was in the proper north-south alignment along the Nile. But what he saw now was very different from the temple he had explored just two weeks ago—two weeks? Thirty-five hundred years!—on his orientation trip to contemporary Egypt. The Avenue of the Sphinxes was missing, and so were the obelisks and the colossi that stood before the great flaring wings of the north pylon. The pylon didn't seem to be there either. Of course. The Luxor Temple sphinxes were Thirtieth Dynasty work, still a dozen centuries in the future. The obelisks and the colossi were the doing of Rameses II, whose reign lay five or six kingships from now, and so too was the north pylon itself. In their place was an unfamiliar covered colonnade that looked almost dainty by Egyptian architectural standards, and two small square shrines of pink granite, with a low, slender pylon of a clearly archaic style behind them, bedecked with bright fluttering pennants. He felt a small scholarly thrill at the sight of them: these were Twelfth Dynasty structures, perhaps, ancient even in this era, which Rameses' inexorable builders would eventually sweep away to make room for their own more grandiose contributions. But what was more bewildering than the differences in floor plan was the contrast between this temple and the bare, brown, skeletal ruin that he had seen in latter-day Luxor. The white limestone blocks of the facades and columns were almost unbearably brilliant under the sun's unblinking gaze. And they were covered everywhere by gaudy reliefs painted in mercilessly bright colors, red, yellow, blue, green. From every cornice and joist glittered inlays of precious metal: silver, gold, rare alloys. The temple pulsed with reflected sunlight. It was like a second sun itself, radiating shattering jolts of energy into the frantic plaza.

Too much, he thought, beginning to sway. Too much. He was overloading. His head throbbed. His stomach lurched. He was having trouble focusing his eyes. He felt chills even in the midst of all this heat. Because of it, most likely. He imagined that he was turning green with nausea.

"You are ill? Yes, I can see that you are ill, very ill." A sudden deep voice, virile and harsh. A hand closing tight around his wrist. A man's face thrust practically up against his, thin lips, hawk nose, shaven scalp. Dark brooding eyes bright with concern. "You look very bad. You will be an Osiris soon, I think."

"I—I—"

"To die like a pig in the street—that is not good, not good at all, my friend."

It was astonishing that anyone had spoken to him and even more astonishing—despite all his training—that he could understand. Of course they had filled his brain with Egypt, pumped him to the brim, language, art, history, customs, everything. And he had learned a good deal on his own before that. But still he was surprised to find that he had comprehended the other man's words so easily. His tutors hadn't guessed quite right on the pronunciation, but they had been close enough. The vowels were wrong, everything shifted into the back of the throat, "e" turning into "i," "o" turning into "u," but he was able quickly enough to adjust for that. His benefactor was holding him upright with that vise-like grip; otherwise he would fall. He tried to think of something to say, but no words would come. His fluency failed him when it was his moment to speak. He couldn't frame a single sentence. *You will be an Osiris soon.* Was he dying, then? How strange, putting it that way. He must be starting to look like Osiris already, the dead god, green-faced, mummified.

The stranger was drawing him out of the sun, into the sparse shade of a five-branched palm at the edge of the plaza.

"I am very ill, yes—" he managed finally. "The heat—my head—"

"Yes. Yes. It is so sad. But look, my friend, the god is coming now."

He thought at first that some apparition was descending, that Horus or Thoth had come to carry him off to the Land of the Dead. But no, no, that wasn't what the stranger meant at all. A stupefying roar had gone up from the crowd, a bursting swell of incredible noise. The man pointed. He managed to follow the outstretched arm. His vision was blurring again, but he could make out a commotion near the front of the temple, brawny men wearing nothing but strips of blue and gold cloth advancing, wielding whips, people falling back, and then a chariot appearing from somewhere, everything gilded, blindingly bright, falcons on the yoke-pole, a great solar disk above them, winged goddesses on the sides, horned creatures behind; and out of the temple and into the chariot, then, there came a slow portly figure, ornately robed in the stifling heat—the blue crown on his head, the *khepresh*, and the two scepters in his hands, the crook and the flail, and the stiff little false beard strapped to his chin—

The king, it was—it must be—the Pharaoh, getting into the chariot—he has been at some ceremony in the temple, and now he will return to his palace across the river—

Drums and trumpets, and the sound of high-pitched things something like oboes. An immense roar. "Horus!" the crowd was crying now. Ten thousand voices at once, a single throat. "Horus! Neb-Maat-Re! Life! Health! Strength!"

Neb-Maat-Re. The Pharaoh Amenhotep III, that was what that meant. His coronation name. It was the king himself, yes. Standing there, smiling, acknowledging the crowd, before his very eyes.

"Lord of the Two Lands!" they were shouting. "Son of Re! Living image of Amon! Mighty one! Benefactor of Egypt! Life! Health! Strength!"

Too much, too much, too much. He was totally overwhelmed by it all. He was thirty-five centuries out of his proper time, a displacement that he had been confident he would be able to comprehend until the moment he found himself actually experiencing it. Now his entire body convulsed in a tremor born of fatigue and confusion and panic. He tottered and desperately grasped the palm tree's rough scaly trunk. The last of his little strength was fleeing under the impact of all this staggering unthinkable reality. Thebes as a living city—Amenhotep III himself, wearing the blue crown—the masked priests, hawk-faced, ibis-faced, dog-faced—the dark mysterious figure of a woman coming out now, surely the queen, taking her place beside the Pharaoh—the chariot beginning to move—

"Life! Health! Strength!"

For the king, maybe. Not for him. How had he ever managed to pass the psychological tests for this mission? He was flunking now. He had been able to fake his way successfully among tougher people all his life, but the truth was coming out at last. His legs were turning to water. His eyes were rolling in his head. They had sent the wrong man for the job: he saw that clearly now. Indeed it was the only thing he could see clearly. He was too complicated, too—*delicate.* They should have sent some stolid unimaginative jock, some prosaic astronaut type, invulnerable to emotion, to the hot dark unreasoning side of life, poetry-free, magic-free, someone who would not become overwhelmed like this by the sight of a fat middle-aged man in a silly costume getting into a Hollywood chariot.

Was it that? Or simply the heat, and the lingering shock of the thirty-five-C jump itself?

"Ah, my friend, my friend," the dark-eyed stranger was saying. "I fear you are becoming an Osiris this very minute. It is so sad for you. I will do what I can to help you. I will use my skills. But you must pray, my dear friend. Ask the king to spare your life. Ask the Lady Isis. Ask the mercy of Thoth the Healer, my friend, or you will die as surely as—"

It was the last thing he heard as he pitched forward and crumpled to the ground at the palm tree's base.

TWO

THE STRANGER RESTED QUIETLY ON a bed in the House of Life in the Precinct of Mut that lay just to the south of Ipet-sut, the great temple of Amon, in the baffling jumble of holy buildings that future ages would call Karnak. The pavilion he was in was open to the sky, a simple colonnade; its slim pillars, rising like stems to the swollen lotus-buds at the top, were painted a soothing pink and blue and white. The stranger's eyes were closed and peaceful and his breath was coming slowly and easily, but there was the gleam of fever on his face and his lips were drawn back in an odd grimace, an ugly lopsided smile. Now and again a powerful shudder rippled through his body.

"He will die very soon, I think," the physician said. His name was Hapu-seneb and he was the one who had been with the stranger when he collapsed outside the Temple of the Southern Harem of Amon.

"No," said the priestess. "I think he will live. I am quite sure that he will live."

The physician made a soft smothered sound of scorn.

But the priestess paid no heed to that. She moved closer to the bed, which stood high off the floor of the room and sloped noticeably from head to foot. The stranger lay naked on a mattress of cord matting, tightly stretched and covered with cushions, and his head rested on a curving block of wood. He was slender and light-boned, almost feminine in his delicacy, though his lean body was muscular and covered with a thick mat of dark curling hair.

Her hand lightly touched his forehead.

"Very warm," she said.

"A demon is in him," said Hapu-seneb. "There is little hope. He will be an Osiris soon. I think the crocodile of the West has him, or perhaps the rerek-snake is at his heart."

Now it was the priestess' turn to utter a little skeptical snort.

She was a priestess in the service of Isis, although this was the Precinct of Mut and the entire temple complex was dedicated to Amon; but there was nothing unusual about that. Things overlapped; boundaries were fluid; one god turned easily into another. Isis must be served, even in Amon's temple. The priestess was tall for a woman, and her skin was very pale. She wore a light linen shift that was no more substantial than a mist: her breasts showed through, and the dark triangle at her loins. A heavy black wig of natural hair, intricately interwoven in hundreds of tight plaits, covered her shaven scalp.

The stranger was muttering now in his sleep, making harsh congested sounds, a babble of alien words.

"He speaks demon-language," Hapu-seneb said.

"Shh! I'm trying to hear!"

"You understand the language of demons, do you?"

"Shh!"

She put her ear close by his mouth. Little spurts and freshets of words came from him: babble, delirium, then a pause, then more feverish muttering. Her eyes widened a little as she listened. Her forehead grew furrowed; she tucked her lower lip in, and nibbled it lightly.

"What is he saying, then?" asked Hapu-seneb.

"Words in a foreign language."

"But you understand them. After all, you're foreign yourself. Is he a countryman of yours?"

"Please," said the priestess, growing irritated. "What good are these questions?"

"No good at all," the physician said. "Well, I will do what I can to save him, I suppose. Your countryman. If that is what he is." He had brought his equipment with him, his wooden chest of medicines, his pouch of amulets. He gave some thought to selecting an amulet, picking one finally that showed the figure of Amon with four rams' heads, trampling on a crocodile while eight gods adored him in the background. He whispered a spell over it and fastened it to a knotted cord, which he tied to the stranger's kilt. He placed the amulet over the stranger's heart and made magical passes, and said in a deep, impressive tone, "I am this Osiris here in the West. Osiris knows his day, and if he does not exist in it, then I will not exist in it. I am Re who is with the gods and I will not perish; stand up, Horus, that I may number you among the gods."

The priestess watched, smiling a little.

The physician said, "There are other spells I can use." He closed his eyes a moment and breathed deeply. "Behind me, crocodile, son of Set!" he intoned. "Float not with thy tail. Seize not with thy two arms. Open not thy mouth. May the water become a sheet of fire before thee! The charm of thirty-seven gods is in thine eye. Thou art bound to the four bronze pillars of the south, in front of the barge of Re. Stop, crocodile, son of Set! Protect this man, Amon, husband of thy mother!"

"That must be a good spell," said the priestess. "See, he's stirring a little. And I think his forehead grows cool."

"It is one of the most effective spells, yes. But medicines are important too." The physician began to rummage through the wooden chest, drawing forth little jars, some containing crushed insects, some containing live ones, some holding the powdered dung of powerful animals.

The priestess laid her hand lightly on Hapu-seneb's arm.

"No," she said. "No medicines."

"He needs—"

"What he needs is to rest. I think you should go now."

"But the powder of the scorpion—"

"Another time, Hapu-seneb."

"Lady, I am the physician, not you."

"Yes," she said gently. "And a very fine physician you are. And your spells have been very fine also. But I feel Isis in my veins, and the goddess tells me that what will heal this man is sleep, nothing other than sleep."

"Without medicine he will die, lady. And then Isis will have her Osiris."

"Go, Hapu-seneb."

"The oil of serpent, at least—"

"Go."

The physician scowled and began to say something; but then he converted his anger deftly into a shrug and started to pack up his medical equipment. The priestess was a favorite of the young Prince Amenhotep; everyone knew that. It was perhaps not a good idea to disagree with her too strongly. And if she thought she knew what sort of care this stranger needed better than he did, well—

When Hapu-Seneb was gone, the priestess threw some grains of incense on the brazier in the corner of the pavilion and stood for a time staring out into the deepening darkness, breathing deeply and trying to calm herself, for she was not at all calm just now, however she may have seemed to the physician. In the distance she heard chanting. A darkening blue was descending from the sky and changing the river's color. The first stars were appearing overhead. A few fireflies flickered past the tops of the columns. From far away came the mournful sound of the night-trumpet, floating across the water from the royal palace on the west bank.

Well then, she thought.

She considered what had to be done now.

She clapped her hands twice, and two slave-girls came running. To the older and more intelligent one she said, "Go to the House of Stars which is behind the shrine of Men-Kheper-Re, Eyaseyab, and tell

Senmut-Ptah the astronomer to come to me right away. He will tell you that he has important work to do. Say to him that I know that, and want him to come all the same, that it's absolutely essential, an emergency." The priestess sent the other slave off to fetch cloths steeped in cool water, so that she could bathe the stranger's forehead.

The stranger was still unconscious, but he had stopped babbling now. His face was no longer so rigidly set and the sheen of fever was nearly gone. Perhaps he was simply asleep. The priestess stood above him, frowning.

She leaned close to him and said, "Can you hear me?"

He shifted about a bit, but his eyes remained closed.

"I am Isis," she said softly. "You are Osiris. You are my Osiris. You are the lost Osiris who was cut asunder and restored to life in my care."

He said something now, indistinctly, muttering in his own language again.

"I am Isis," she said a second time.

She rested her hand on his shoulder and let it travel down his body, pausing over his heart to feel the steady beating, then lower, and lower still. His loins were cool and soft, but she felt a quickening in them as her fingers lingered. The priestess smiled. Turning away, she picked up the cool cloth that the young slave-girl had brought, and lightly mopped his forehead with it. His eyes fluttered open. Had the cool cloth awakened him, she wondered? Or had it been the touch of her hand at the base of his belly a moment before?

He was staring at her.

"How do you feel?" she asked.

"A little better." He spoke very softly, so that she had to strain to hear him.

He glanced down at his nakedness. She saw the movement of his eyes and draped a strip of cloth that she had not yet moistened across his middle.

"Where am I?"

"The House of Life in the Precinct of Mut. The physician Hapuseneb found you in the street outside the southern temple and brought you here. I am Nefret. Isis is the one I serve."

"Am I dying, Nefret?"

"I don't think so."

"The man who found me said I was. He told me I was about to become Osiris. That means I'm dying, doesn't it?"

"It can mean that. It can mean other things. Hapu-seneb is a very fine physician, but he's not always right. You aren't dying. I think the heat was too much for you, that's all. That and perhaps the strain of your voyage." She studied him thoughtfully. "You came a long way?"

He hesitated before replying. "You can tell, can you?"

"A child could tell. Where are you from?"

Another little pause. A moistening of the lips. "It's a place called America."

"That must be very far away."

"Very."

"Farther than Syria? Farther than Crete?"

"Farther, yes. Much farther."

"And your name?" the priestess asked.

"Edward Davis."

"Ed-ward Da-vis."

"You pronounce it very well."

"Edward Davis," she said again, less awkwardly. "Is that better?"

"You did it well enough the first time."

"What language do they speak in the place called America?" she asked.

"English."

"Not American?"

"Not American, no. English."

"You were speaking in your English while you were asleep, I think."

He looked at her. "Was I?"

"I suppose," she said. "How would I know? I heard foreign words, that's all I can tell you. But you speak our language very well, for someone who comes from so far away."

"Thank you."

"Very well indeed. You arrived just today, did you?"

"Yes."

"By the ship that sailed in from Crete?"

"Yes," he said. "No. No, not that one. It was a different ship, the one that came from—" He paused again. "It was the ship from Canada."

"Canada. Is that near America?"

"Very near, yes."

"And ships from Canada come here often?"

"Not really. Not very often."

"Ah," she said. "But one came today."

"Or yesterday. Everything's so confused for me—since I became sick—"

"I understand," the priestess said. She swabbed his forehead with the cool cloth again. "Are you hungry?"

"No, not at all." Then he frowned. Messages seemed to be traveling around inside his body. "Well, a little."

"We have some cold roast goose, and some bread. And a little beer. Can you handle that?"

"I could try," he said.

"We'll bring you some, then."

The slave-girl who had gone to fetch the astronomer had returned. She was standing just outside the perimeter of the pavilion, waiting. The priestess glanced at her.

"The priest Senmut-Ptah is here, Lady. Shall I bring him to you?"

"No. No, I'll go to him. This is Edward-Davis. He was ill, but I think he's recovering. He'd like to have some food, and something to drink."

"Yes, Lady."

The priestess turned to the stranger again. He was sitting up on the bed now, looking off toward the west, toward the river. Night had fully arrived by this time and the torches had been lit along the west bank promenade, and in the hills where the kings' tombs were. He appeared to be caught up in some enchantment.

"The city is very beautiful at night, yes," she said.

"I can hardly believe I'm really here."

"There's no city like it in all the land. How fortunate you are to see it at its greatest."

"Yes," he said. "I know."

His eyes were shining. He turned to stare at her, and she knew that he was staring at her body through her filmy gown, backlit by the torches behind her. She felt exposed and curiously vulnerable, and found herself wishing she was wearing something less revealing. It was a long time since she had last cared about that.

The priestess wondered how old he was. Twenty-five, perhaps? Perhaps even less. Younger than she by a good many years, that much was certain.

She said, "This is Eyaseyab. She'll bring you food. If you want anything else, just ask her."

"Are you going?"

"There's someone I have to speak with," the priestess said.

"And then you'll come back?"

"Later."

"Not too much later, I hope."

"Eat. Rest. That's what's important now. Eyaseyab will take care of you." She smiled and turned away. She could feel his eyes on her as she left the pavilion.

THREE

SENMUT-PTAH WAS WAITING FOR HER outside, by the great sphinx that bore the inscription of Tuthmosis III. He was wearing a kilt of scarlet cloth into which golden ibises had been woven, and a tall priestly crown with three long feathers set in it. His shoulders and chest were bare. He was a long-limbed, bony man, very broad through the shoulders, and his features were sharp and powerful, giving him a falcon-face, a Horus-hawk face. Just now he looked angry and impatient.

"You know you've made me miss the rising of the Bull's Thigh," he said at once, when she appeared. "The North Star will be past the meridian by the time I—"

"Shh," she said. "The North Star won't go anywhere unusual tonight, and the Bull's Thigh will look just the same tomorrow. Walk with me. We have to talk."

"What about?"

"Walk," she said. "We can't talk here. Let's go down toward the Sacred Lake."

"I don't understand why we can't—"

"*Because we can't,*" she said in a fierce whisper. "Come on. Walk with me. The astronomer and the priestess of Isis, out for a little stroll by starlight."

"I have important observations that absolutely have to be made this evening, and—"

"Yes, I know," she said.

She loathed the all-enveloping obsessive concern with his astronomical duties that had taken possession of him in recent years. He was like a machine, now. Or like an insect of some sort, clicking along busily in his preprogrammed routines. Day and night preoccupied with his viewing apertures and his transits, his reflecting bowls, his azimuths and meridians and ascensions, his sundials and his water-clocks. Once, when the two of them were new here and first struggling with the terrible challenge of building lives for themselves in Egypt, he had been aflame with wonder and eager curiosity and a kind of burning dauntlessness, but that was all gone now. Nothing seemed to matter to him any longer except his observations of the stars. Somewhere along the way a vast leaden indifference had come to engulf all the rest of him. Why was it so important to him, that absurd compilation of astronomical data, probably inaccurate and in any case useless? And where had he misplaced the warmth and passion that had carried the two of them through all the difficulties they had had to face in this strange land in earlier days?

He glared at her now as though he would send her to the Lake of Fire with a single flash of his eyes, if he could. By the chilly light of the stars his eyes seemed cruel and cold to her, and his face, sculpted to harshness by the years, had some of the nightmare look of the gods whose images were engraved on every wall of every temple. She had once thought he was handsome, even romantic, but time had made his face and body gaunt just as it had turned his soul to stone. He was as ugly as Thoth now, she thought. And as horrid as Set.

But he was the closest thing to an ally that she had in this eternally strange land, unless she counted the prince; and the prince was dangerously unstable, and an Egyptian besides. However much the man who stood before her had changed since he and she had first come to Thebes, he was nevertheless someone of her own kind. She needed him. She couldn't let herself ever forget that.

She slipped her arm into his and tugged him along, through the colonnade that surrounded the Precinct of Mut, down the new avenue that Pharaoh had built, lined by a double row of cobras, and across the field toward the Sacred Lake. When they had gone far enough from the House of Life so that there was no chance the breeze might carry her voice upward to the sick man in the pavilion she said, speaking suddenly in English, "Someone from downtime showed up in Thebes today, Roger. From Home Era."

The shift to English was like the throwing of a switch. It was years since she had spoken it, and the effect was immediate and emphatic for her. She felt her former identity, so long suppressed, come leaping forth now from its entombment. Her heart pounded; her breasts rose and fell quickly.

The man who called himself Senmut-Ptah seemed shaken as though by an earthquake. He made a choking sound and pulled himself free of her. Then his icy self-control reasserted itself.

"You can't be serious. And why are you speaking English?"

"Because Egyptian doesn't have the words I need in order to tell you what I have to tell you. And because I wouldn't want anyone who might overhear us to understand."

"I hate speaking it."

"I know you do. Speak it anyway."

"All right. English, then."

"And I *am* serious."

"Someone else from downtime is here? Really?"

"Yes. Really."

The corner of his mouth made a little quirking motion. He was trying to comprehend her news and obviously having a difficult time of it. She had finally broken through that indifference of his. But it had taken something like this to do it.

"His name's Edward Davis. He's very young, very innocent in a charming way. He was staggering around outside Luxor Temple this afternoon right about the time the king was leaving, and he passed out with heatstroke and a bad case of temporal shock practically at Hapu-seneb's feet. Hapu-seneb brought him to me. I've got him in the House of Life this very minute. Eyaseyab's trying to get a little food into him."

The astronomer stared. His nostrils flickered tensely. She could see him fighting to maintain his poise.

Sullenly he said, "This is all a fantasy. You're making it up."

"I wish. He's real."

"Is he? Is he?"

"I could take you to him right now. You can say hello to him in English and hear what he says."

"No. No, I don't want to do that."

"What are you afraid of?"

"I'm not afraid of anything. But if you've got someone from Home Era up there in your temple, the last thing I would want to do is go to him and give him a big happy handshake. The absolutely last thing."

"Will you believe me without seeing him, then?"

"If I have to."

"You have to, yes. Why would I want to invent something like this?"

His lips worked, but for a moment no sound came out.

"Yes, why would you?" he said, finally. And then, after another pause: "When is he from?"

"I don't know, but it's got to be a year pretty close to ours. He told me right flat out that he's from America—what should he care, he must figure the word's just a meaningless noise to me?—and that he came in today or yesterday on a ship from Canada. He started to say he sailed in from Crete, but maybe it occurred to him that I could check up on that. Or maybe he just enjoys telling whoppers. Did you know an Edward Davis when you were in the Service?"

"I don't remember any."

"Neither do I."

"He must be later than we are."

"I suppose. But not much. I'm sure of that."

The astronomer shrugged. "He could come from five hundred years after our time, for all we can tell. Isn't that so?"

"He could. But I don't think he does."

"Intuition?"

"He just doesn't seem to. *Edward Davis.* Is that your idea of a Twenty-Seventh Century name?"

"How would I know what a Twenty-Seventh Century name would sound like?" he asked, his voice rising angrily. By the glimmering light of the torches set in the sconces ringing the Sacred Lake she saw agitation returning to his face. Ordinarily he was as expressionless as a granite statue. She had broken through, all right.

He began to pace rapidly along the perimeter of the lake. She was hard pressed to keep up with him.

Then he turned and looked back at her.

Hoarsely he said, "What do you think he wants here, Elaine?"

"What do you think he wants? What else would he be doing here but to study Eighteenth Dynasty Egypt? He speaks the language so well that he must be trained in Egyptology. So he's come on the usual kind of preliminary exploration mission, the sort of thing we were going to do in Rome. Did you really believe that nobody was ever going to come here? Did you, Roger?"

"I wanted to believe that."

She laughed. "It had to happen sooner or later."

"They've got five thousand years of Egyptian history to play with. They could have gone to Memphis to watch the pyramids being built. Or to Alexandria to see Antony screwing Cleopatra. Or to the court of Rameses II."

"They've probably been to all those places," the priestess said. "But they'd want to come here too. Thebes is a fabulous city. And it's absolutely at its peak right now. It's an obvious destination."

The man who called himself Senmut-Ptah nodded glumly. He was silent for a time. He walked even faster. He held his shoulders hunched in an odd way and now and then one of them rose abruptly as though he was being swept by a tic.

At length he said, in a new and oddly flat, unresonant tone, a dead man's voice, "Well, so someone came at long last. And fell right into your lap on his very first day."

"Was dumped."

"Whatever. There he is, up there in your temple, not more than five hundred feet away from us. He could have landed anywhere in Thebes and used up his whole time here without ever laying eyes on either of us or having the slightest notion that we're here, and instead somehow he finds his way to you in a single day. How neat that is."

"He doesn't know anything about me, Roger."

"Are you sure of that?"

"Positive."

"You didn't tell him you aren't Egyptian, did you?"

"I didn't tell him anything."

"Do you think he could have guessed?"

"He doesn't have a clue. He's still groggy from the jump and he thinks I'm a priestess of Isis."

"You are a priestess of Isis," the astronomer said.

"Of course I am. But that's all he knows about me."

"Right. You didn't say a thing. You wouldn't have." He came to a halt and stood rigidly with his back toward her, staring off toward the Precinct of Amon. There was another long silence. Then he said, his voice still flat and dead, "Okay. So we've got a young man from Home Era on our hands, and you know what he is, but he doesn't know what you are. Well. Well, well, well. All right: what are we going to do about him, Elaine?"

"Is there any question about that? I have to get rid of him."

"Get rid? How? What do you mean?"

"Get him out of the temple, is what I mean. Move him along, send him on his way. See to it that he uses up his time in Thebes without finding out anything about us."

He gave her a long peculiar look. She had no idea what was going on in his mind. He seemed to be cracking apart. He frightened her, reacting to the coming of the visitor as he was, in all these different contradictory ways.

He moistened his lips and said, "So you don't want to speak to him at all?"

"Speak to him about what?"

The look on his face grew even more strange. She couldn't remember a time when he had ever seemed so disturbed, not even in the first chaotic days after their arrival. "Anything. The news from Home Era. What's going on in the world. The Service, our friends. He may know some of them. We haven't heard a thing in fifteen years. Aren't you even curious?"

"Of course I am. But the risks—"

"Yes," he said.

"We've talked about this so many times. What we would do if somebody from down there showed up."

"Yes."

"And now that someone actually has—"

"That changes everything, having someone from down there actually arrive here."

"It doesn't change a thing," she said coolly. "You only think it does. I'm amazed, Roger. You said only a couple of minutes ago that revealing yourself to him was the last thing you'd want to do. You aren't seriously suggesting now that we do it, are you?"

He contemplated that.

"Are you?" she asked.

"No," he said. "Not seriously. And you don't want to either."

"Of course I don't. I just want to be left alone to live my life."

"Well, so do I."

"Then we can't let him know anything, can we?"

"No."

"But you're tempted, all of a sudden. I can see that you are. I didn't expect this of you, Roger."

He looked past her, into the night, as though she were not there at all. He seemed once again to be rebuilding some of his old glacial indifference. But she knew now that it was only a pose. He was more confused than she had ever imagined.

"Maybe I am tempted, just a little," he said grudgingly. "Is that so surprising, that the idea should cross my mind? But of course I don't mean it."

"Of course not."

"Of course."

"Good. I'll take care of this, then. I just wanted you to know what was happening. You can go back to your observatory, now. Maybe there's still time to find the North Star tonight. Or whatever it is that you do."

She realized that somewhere during the conversation she had gone back to speaking Egyptian, and so had he. She wasn't sure when that had been.

FOUR

In the morning the slave-girl Eyaseyab came into the pavilion where he was lying on the sloping bed and said, "You are awake? You are better? You are strong today?"

He blinked at her. It must be well along in the morning. The sky was like a blue shield above him and the air was already warming toward the midday scorch. He realized that he was awake and that he felt reasonably strong. During the night the worst effects of the shock of his arrival in Eighteenth Dynasty Egypt seemed to have left him. His throat was dry and his stomach felt hollow, but he was probably strong enough to stand.

He swung his legs over the side of the bed and cautiously got up. The flimsy cloth that was covering him fell away, leaving him naked. That was a little strange; but Eyaseyab was just about naked too, as naked as any of the girls in the tomb paintings in the Valley of the Kings, just a little beaded belt around her hips and a tiny loincloth covering the pubic area. Little anklets of blue beads jingled as she moved. She was sixteen or seventeen, he supposed, though it was hard to tell, and she seemed cheerful and healthy and reasonably clean. Her eyes were dark and glossy and so was her hair, and her skin was a pleasing olive color with a hint of red in it and a golden underhue.

She had brought a basin of water and a flask of perfumed oil. Carefully she washed him, in a way that was the nearest thing to being intimate, but wasn't. He suspected that it could be, if he asked. He had never been washed by a woman like this, at least not since he was a child, and it was enticing and unnerving both at once. When she was done washing him she anointed him with the warm, fragrant oil, rubbing it into his chest and back and thighs. That too was new to him, and very strange. She is a slave, he told himself. She's accustomed to doing this. Now and again she giggled. Once her eyes came up to meet his, and he saw provocation in them; but it seemed unthinkable for him to reach for her now, in this open place, in this *temple*. To draw her to him, to *use* her. She is a slave, he told himself again. She expects to be used. Which makes it all the more impossible.

She handed him his white kilt and watched without embarrassment as he clambered into it.

"I have brought food," she said. "You will eat and then we will go."

"Go where?"

"To the place where you will live."

"On the temple grounds?"

"In town," she said. "You will not stay here. The priestess Nefret has said I am to take you to a lodging in the town."

That was upsetting. He had been hoping to stay here, to be taken into the service of the temple in some fashion. He wanted to speak with that serene, mysterious, aloof priestess again; in this profoundly unfamiliar place she had already begun to seem like an island of security and succor. He had felt a strange kind of rapport with her, some curious sort of kinship, and he would gladly have remained in her domain a little longer. But finding some safe nest to hide in, he knew, would not be a useful way of achieving the goals of his mission here.

Eyaseyab went out and returned shortly with a tray of food for him: a bowl of broth, a piece of grilled fish, some flat bread and a few sweet cakes and a little stone pot of dates. It seemed much too much food. Last night he had only been able to nibble at the meat and beer the girl had brought him. But to his surprise his appetite was enormous today; he emptied the broth bowl in gulps, gobbled the dates, went on to the fish and bread and cakes without hesitating. Vaguely he wondered what sort of microbes he might be ingesting. But of course he had been loaded to the brim with antigens before leaving downtime: one whole division of the Service did nothing but immunological research, and travelers setting out for the past went forth well protected, not just against the great obsolete plagues of yesteryear but against the subtlest of intestinal bugs. He probably had been at greater medical risk during his orientation visit to modern Cairo and Luxor than he was here.

"You want more to eat?" she asked him.

"I don't think I should."

"You should eat, if you're hungry. Here at the temple there's plenty of food."

He understood what she was telling him. All well and good; but he couldn't pack away a month's worth of eating at a single sitting.

"Come, then," she said. "I will take you to your lodging-place."

They left the temple precinct by a side gate. A dusty unpaved path took them quickly to the river promenade, just a short walk away. The temples were much closer to the Nile than they would be thirty-five centuries later. Millennia of sedimentation had changed the river's course to a startling extent. In this era the Nile flowed where, in modern-day Luxor, there was a broad stretch of land covering several blocks, running from the riverfront promenade to the taxi plaza that served the Karnak ruins, the ticket-booth area, the approach to the avenue of sphinxes at the temple's first pylon.

She walked swiftly, keeping half a dozen paces in front of him, never looking back. He watched with amusement the rhythmic movements of her buttocks. She was heading south, into the bewildering maze that was the city proper.

He could see now why he had been so dazed yesterday. Not only had he had to cope with the shock of temporal displacement far beyond anything he had ever experienced on his training jumps, but the city itself was immense and immediately overpowering. Thebes of the Pharaohs was far bigger than the modern Luxor that occupied its site, and it hit you with all its force the moment you set foot in it. Luxor, its splendid ruins aside, was no more than a small provincial town: a few tourist hotels, a one-room museum, a little airport, a railway station, and some shops. Thebes was a metropolis. What was the line from the *Iliad*? "The world's great empress on the Egyptian plain, that spreads her conquests o'er a thousand states." Yes.

The general shape of the place was familiar. Like everything else in Egypt it was strung out along the north-south line of the Nile. The two ends of the city were anchored by the great temples he knew as Luxor and Karnak: Luxor at the southern end, where he had made his appearance yesterday, and the vast complex of Karnak, where he had spent the night, a mile or so to the north. As he faced south now, the river was on his right, cluttered with bright-sailed vessels of every size and design, and beyond it, across the way to the west, were the jagged tawny mountains of the Valley of the Kings, where the great ones of the land had their tombs, with a long row of grand imperial palaces stretching before them in the river plain, Pharaoh's golden house and the dwellings of his family. When he looked the other way he could see, sharp against the cloudless desert sky, the three lofty hills that marked the eastern boundary, and the massive hundred-gated walls that had still been standing in Homer's time.

What was so overwhelming about Thebes was not so much its temples and palaces and all its other sectors of monumental grandeur—though they were impressive enough—as it was the feverish multifariousness of the sprawling streets that occupied the spaces between them. They spread out as far as he could see, a zone of habitation limited only by the river on the one side and the inexorable barrenness of the desert on the other. City planning was an unknown concept here. Incomprehensibly twisting lanes of swarming tenements stood cheek by jowl beside the villas of the rich. Here was a street of filthy little ramshackle shops, squat shanties of mud brick, and just beyond rose a huge wall that concealed cool gardened courtyards, blue pools, and sparkling fountains, quiet hallways bedecked with colored frescoes; and just on the far side of that nobleman's grand estate were the tangled alleys of the poor again. The air was so hot that it seemed to be aflame, and a shimmering haze of dust-motes danced constantly in it, however pure the sky might be in the distance. Insects buzzed unceasingly, flies and locusts and beetles making angry, ominous sounds as they whizzed past, and animals browsed casually in the streets as though they owned them. The smoke of a hundred thousand cooking-fires rose high; the smell of meat grilling on spits and fish frying in oil was everywhere. And a steady pounding of traffic was moving in all directions at once through the narrow, congested streets, the nobles in their chariots or litters, ox-carts carrying produce to the markets, nearly naked slaves jogging along beneath huge mounds of neatly wrapped bundles, donkeys staggering under untidier loads half the size of pyramids, children underfoot, vendors of pots and utensils hauling their wagons, everybody yelling, laughing, bickering, singing, hailing friends with loud whoops. He had been in big exotic cities before—Hong Kong, Honolulu, maddening gigantic Cairo itself—but even they, with all their smoke-belching trucks and autos and motorbikes, were no match for the wondrous chaos of Thebes. This was a disorder beyond anything he had ever experienced: indeed, beyond anything he had ever imagined.

They were near the southern temple now. He recognized the plaza where he had collapsed the day before. But abruptly Eyaseyab turned toward the river and led him down a flight of stone steps into a waterfront quarter that had not been visible from above, where squalid taverns and little smoky food-kiosks huddled in a cluster beside a long stone wharf.

A flat barge crowded with people was waiting at the wharf, and a burly man who seemed obviously to be an overseer was waving his arms and crying out something unintelligible in thick, guttural tones.

"It's going to leave," Eyaseyab said. "Quick, let's get on board."

"Where are we going?"

"To the other side."

He stared at her blankly. "You said I'd be lodging in town."

"It is also the town over there. You will be lodging near the place where you will work. The priestess has arranged everything. You are a very lucky man, Edward-Davis."

"I don't understand. What sort of work?"

"With the embalmers," the girl said. "You will be an apprentice in the House of Purification, in the City of the Dead." She tugged at his wrist. "Come quickly! If we miss the ferry, there won't be another one going across for an hour."

Too astonished to protest, he stumbled on board after her. Almost at once, the overseer bellowed a command and slaves along quayside tugged on the ropes that tied the barge down, pulling them free of the bollards that held them. A huge man wielding an enormous pole pushed the vessel loose and it drifted out into the channel of the Nile. The great red and yellow sails scooped up such breeze as was there for the scooping. The lunatic bustle of Thebes receded swiftly behind them. He stared back at it in dismay.

An embalmer, in the City of the Dead?

A lodging-place on the wrong side of the river?

Some of yesterday's confusion and panic began to surface in him again. He looked toward the distant western shore. His assignment here was difficult enough as it was; but how was he supposed to carry it out while living over there in the mortuary village? Presumably the two people he had come here to find were living in Thebes proper, if they were here at all. He had expected to circulate in the city, to ask questions and generally sniff about in search of unusual strangers, to pursue whatever clues to their whereabouts he might discover. But the priestess, in her great kindness, had essentially exiled him from the place where he had to be. Now he would have to steal time from his work—whatever that was going to be!—and get himself somehow back to the main part of Thebes every day, or as often as he could arrange it, if he was going to carry out his little Sherlock Holmes operation. It was a complication he hadn't anticipated.

In the crush of passengers aboard the greatly overcrowded ferry, the slave-girl was jammed right up against him. He found himself enjoying the contact. But he wondered how often one of these boats foundered and sank. He thought of the crocodiles that still inhabited the Nile in this era.

She laughed and said, "It is too many people, yes?"

"Yes. Many too many."

"It's always this busy this time. Better to go early, but you were sleeping."

"Do the ferries run all day?"

"All day, yes, and less often in the night. Everyone uses them. You are still feeling all right, Edward-Davis?"

"Yes," he said. He let his hands rest on her bare shoulders. "Fine." For a moment he found himself wondering what he was going to use to pay the ferry fare; and then he remembered that this entire empire managed somehow to function without any sort of cash. All transactions involving goods or services were done by barter, and by a system of exchange that used weights and spirals of copper as units of currency, but only in the abstract: workers were paid in measures of grain or flasks of oil that could be traded for other necessities, and more complex sales and purchases were handled by bookkeeping entries, not by the exchange of actual metal. The ferries, most likely, were free of charge, provided by the government by way of offering some return on the labor-taxes that everyone paid.

The ferry wallowed westward across the green sluggish river. The east bank was no more now than a shadowy line on the horizon, with the lofty walls and columns of the two temple compounds the only discernible individual features. On the rapidly approaching western shore he could see now another many-streeted tangle of low mud-brick buildings, though not nearly as congested as the very much larger one across the way, and a towering row of dusty-leaved palm trees just behind the town as a sort of line of demarcation cutting it off from the emptiness beyond. Further in the distance was the sandy bosom of the western desert, rising gradually toward the bleak bare hills on the horizon.

At the quay-side Eyaseyab spoke briefly with a man in a soiled, ragged kilt, apparently to ask directions. They seemed to know each other; they grinned warmly, exchanged a quick handclasp, traded a quip or two. Davis felt an odd, unexpected pang of jealousy as he watched them. The man turned and pointed toward the left: Davis saw as he swung around that his face was terribly scarred and he had only one eye.

“My brother,” Eyaseyab said, coming back toward him. “He belongs to the ferry-master. We go this way.”

“Was he injured in battle?”

She looked baffled a moment. “His face? Oh, no, he is no soldier. He ran away once, when he was a boy, and slept in the desert one night, and there was an animal. He says a lion, but a jackal, I think. Come, please.”

They plunged into the City of the Dead, Eyaseyab once more going first and leaving him to trudge along behind, keeping his eyes trained on the tapering glossy wedge of her bare back. On every side the industry of death was operating at full throttle. Here was a street of coffin-makers, and here were artisans assembling funerary furniture in open-fronted arcades, and in another street sculptors were at work polishing memorial statues. A showroom displayed gilded mummy-cases in a startling range of sizes, some no bigger than a cat might need, others enormous and ornate. Silent priests with shaven heads moved solemnly through the busy, crowded streets like wraiths. Now and again Davis caught a whiff of some acrid fumes: embalming fluids, he supposed.

The district where the workers lived was only a short distance behind the main commercial area, but the layout of the village was so confusing that Eyaseyab had to ask directions twice more before she delivered him to his new lodging-place. It was a cave-like warren of dark little mud-walled rooms lopsidedly arranged in a U-shaped curve around a sandy courtyard. Misery Motel, Davis thought. A florid, beefy man named Pewero presided over it. The place was almost comically dismal, filthy and dank and reeking of urine, but even so it had its own proud little garden, one dusty acacia tree and one weary and practically leafless sycamore.

“You will take your meals here,” Eyaseyab explained. “They are supplied by the House of Purification. There will be beer if you want it, but no wine. Check your room for scorpions before you go to sleep. On this side of the river they are very common.”

“I’ll remember that,” Davis said.

She stood waiting for a moment at the door to his little cubicle as though expecting something from him. But of course he had nothing to offer her.

Was that what she wanted, though? A gift? Perhaps that look of expectation meant something else.

"Stay with me this afternoon," he said impulsively.

She smiled almost demurely. "The priestess expects me back. There is much work to do."

"Tonight, then? Can you come back?"

"I can do that, yes," she said. There wasn't much likelihood of it in her tone. She touched his cheek pleasantly. "Edward-Davis. What an odd name that is, Edward-Davis. Does everyone in your country have such odd names?"

"Even worse," he said.

She nodded. Perhaps that was the limit of her curiosity.

He watched her from his doorway as she went down the dusty path. Her slender back, her bare plump buttocks, suddenly seemed almost infinitely appealing to him. But she turned the corner and was gone. I will never see her again, he thought; and he felt himself plummeting without warning into an abyss of loneliness and something approaching terror as he looked back into the dark little hole of a room that was his new home in this strange land.

You wanted this, he told himself.

You volunteered for this. Going back to find a couple of Service people who hadn't come back from a mission was only the pretext, the excuse. What you wanted was to experience the real Egypt. Well, kid, here's the real Egypt, and welcome to it!

He wondered what he was supposed to do next. Report for work? Where? To whom?

Pewero said, "In the morning. Go with them, when they leave."

"Who?"

But Pewero had already lost interest in him.

He made his way back through the confusion that was the village, staring about him in wonder at the frantic intensity of it all. He had known, of course, that to an Egyptian death was the most important part of life, the beginning of one's true existence, one's long residence in eternity: but still it was astonishing to see these hordes of men hard at work, turning out a seemingly endless stream of coffins, scrolls, grave-goods, carvings. It was like a gigantic factory. Death was big business in this country. A dozen guilds were at work here. Only the embalmers were not to be seen, though he suspected their workshops would not be far away; but doubtless they kept to one side, in some quieter quarter, out of respect for the corpses over whom they toiled. The dead here were an active and ever-present part of the population, after all. Their sensibilities had to be considered.

He wandered down toward the river and stood by the quay for a while, looking for crocodiles. There didn't seem to be any here, only long ugly fish. Unexpectedly he felt calmness settle over him. He was growing accustomed to the heat; he barely heard the noise of the town. The river, even though at low ebb, was strikingly beautiful, a great smooth green ribbon coming out of the inconceivably remote south and vanishing serenely into the unimaginable north, an elemental force cutting through the desert like the will of God. But it stank of decay; he was astounded, standing by it, to see what was unmistakably a dead body go floating by, perhaps a hundred yards out from the bank. No mummifying for that one, no tomb, no eternal life. A beggar, he supposed, an outcast, the merest debris of society: yet what thoughts had gone through his mind at the last moment, knowing as he did that for him death was the end of everything and not the grand beginning?

A trick of the sunlight turned the muddy banks to gold. The corpse drifted past and the river was beautiful again. When Davis returned to the lodging-house, four men were squatting outside, roasting strips of fish over a charcoal fire. They offered him one, asking him no questions, and gave him a little mug of warm rancid beer. He was one of them, the new apprentice. Perhaps they noticed that his features were those of a foreigner and his accent was an odd one, perhaps not. They were incurious, and why not? Their lives were heading nowhere. They understood that he was as unimportant as they were. Important men did not become apprentices in the House of Purification. The priestess Nefret, meaning to do well by the stranger, had buried him in the obscurity of the most menial of labor over here.

It was going to be a long thirty days, he thought. Here in the real Egypt.

To his utter amazement Eyaseyab appeared in his doorway not long after dark as he sat somberly staring at nothing in particular.

"Edward-Davis," she said, grinning.

"You? But—"

"I said I would be back."

So at least there would be some consolations.

FIVE

THE REAL EGYPT GOT EVEN realer, much too real, in the days immediately following.

On the first morning he followed the other men of his little mud tenement when they set out for work soon after sunrise. Silently they marched single file through the rapidly awakening City of the Dead, past the residential district and out a short way into the fringe of the desert. The line of demarcation was unmistakable: no transitional zone, but rather two utterly different worlds butting up against each other, fertile humus and green vegetation and the coolness of the river air on one side, and, on the other, arid sand and rock and the blast-furnace heat of the realm of the dead, striking with the force of a punch even this early in the day. The dawn breeze brought him the briny smell of the embalmers' chemicals, far more pungent than it had been the night before. They must be approaching the House of Purification, he realized.

And then he saw it, not any kind of house at all but a raggle-taggle pseudo-village, scores of flimsy little booths made of sheets of cloth tacked together in frameworks of wooden struts. It was spread out like a Gypsy encampment over a strip of the desert plain that was probably a thousand yards long and fifty yards or so deep. As he watched, workmen began disassembling a booth not far from him, revealing the workshop within: soiled and wadded cloths, mounds of damp sawdust, rows of phials and flasks and unpainted pottery jars, racks of fearsome-looking tools, a scattering of discarded bandages, and, in the center of the room, a ponderous rectangular table made of four huge wooden butcher's-blocks. The workmen were carefully packing everything up, sweeping the sawdust into large jars, stuffing the cloths in on top, gathering all the tools and chemicals together and putting them in elegant wooden satchels. He thought he understood. The job was finished here; the dead man had gone to his grave; now the booth where his body had lain for the seventy days of his mummification was being dismantled and every scrap, every bit of cloth, every stray hair, was being taken away lest it fall into the hands of some enemy of his who might use it against him in an enchantment. All these booths were temporary things. Each had been constructed for a specific occupant, and it was taken down when he had been safely seen into the next world.

He looked about in wonder. The great work of preparing the dead for the glorious afterlife was proceeding with awesome alacrity on all sides.

He had studied the process, naturally. He had studied every aspect of Egyptian life while preparing for this mission: they had poured it into him, hypnogogic training day and night, a torrent of facts, an electronic encyclopedia engraved on his mind. He knew how they drew the brain out through the nostrils with an iron hook and squirted chemicals in to dissolve whatever remained. How they made an incision in the left flank through which to remove the entrails for their separate interment in stone jars. The cleansing and scouring of the body, the washing of it in palm-wine; the packing of the interior cavity with myrrh and cassia and other aromatics; the many days of curing in a tub of dry natron to purge the body of all putrefying matter, the thirsty salts devouring every drop of the body's moisture, leaving it as hard as wood. The coating of the skin with a carapace of resinous paste. And then the bandaging, the body enveloped in its protective layers of cloth, the hundreds of yards of fine linen so carefully wrapped, each finger and toe individually, thimbles covering the nails to keep them in place, the pouring of unguents, the reciting of prayers and the uttering of magic formulas—

But still, to see it all happening right in front of him—to *smell* it happening—

Someone whacked him on the back.

"Move along, you! Get to work!"

He stumbled and nearly fell.

"Yes—sir—"

Work? Where was he supposed to work? What did they want him to do?

He drifted as though in a dream toward a nearby booth. Its linen door was folded back, half open, and he could see figures moving about within. A naked body lay face down on the great wooden table. Above it stood two figures out of some terrifying dream, men in golden kilts whose heads were concealed by dark Anubis masks—the dog-faced god, the black god of death, tapered narrow ears rising high, dainty pointed muzzles projecting half a foot. These must be the embalmers themselves, members of the secret hereditary guild. A priest stood to one side, droning prayers. There were three other men in the booth, maskless and dressed only in loincloths, handing tools back and forth in response to brief harsh commands. Would an apprentice be useful here? He took a deep breath and went in.

"More oil," one of the men in loincloths said to him at once, brusquely thrusting a huge sweet-smelling red jar into his arms.

He nodded and backed out of the booth, and looked about in perplexity. An overseer glowered at him. He avoided making eye contact and turned away, trudging up the path as though he knew where he was going. But he hesitated to ask. At any moment, he thought, he would be recognized as an outsider, an impious interloper with no business here. Overseers would take him by the scruff of the neck and carry him to the river—toss him in to provide the crocodiles with breakfast—

Toward him came a boy of thirteen or fourteen, tottering under an immense roll of bandages. The boy, at least, didn't seem to pose a threat. Davis took up a position in the middle of the path, deliberately blocking it. The boy shot him an angry glance and gestured furiously with his head, wordlessly telling him to move aside.

Davis said, "I need to get some more oil."

"Then get more oil," the boy said. "You're standing in my way."

"I'm new. I don't know where to go."

"Fool," the boy said in disgust. Then he softened a little. "Cedar oil, is it?"

"Yes," said Davis, hoping he was right.

"Over there." The boy nodded toward the side. "Now get out of the path."

He saw a dispensing station of some sort where an old withered man, as parched as a mummy himself, was dispensing a dark fluid from a clay jar nearly as tall as he was. A line of workmen stood before it. Davis waited his turn and presented the jar, and the old man ladled the new supply in, splashing it about so liberally that Davis' arms and chest were covered with it.

"You took your time about it," grunted one of the men in the booth, relieving him of the jar.

"Sorry."

"Start loading those pipes, will you?"

They were tubes—syringes of a sort—stacked on the floor of the booth. It took a moment for Davis to figure out how they worked; but then he got the knack of it and began filling them with oil and handing them up to the other men, who passed them along to the Anubis-headed embalmers. Who deftly unloaded them into the corpse on the table through the anus.

What was taking place here, he realized, was a bargain-rate mummification. No incisions had been made in this man, no internal organs withdrawn. They were simply pumping him full of a powerful solvent that would leach away the bowels. Then they would sew him up and cover him with natron to dry him out while the oil inside did its work; and when the prescribed number of days had elapsed, they would cut the stitches and let the oil out and send the new Osiris to his final resting- place. There was a cheaper kind of mummification yet, Davis knew, in which they dispensed even with the cedar oil, and simply treated the corpse with natron until it was properly dry. He wondered whether those who were given such skimpy treatment could hope to live forever in the afterlife also, and ride through the heavens with the gods on the boat of the sun. No doubt they did. He began to see why these Egyptians were all so exuberant. So long as they could give their bodies some sort of preparation for the life to come, they were guaranteed virtual immortality, not only the kings but even the humble merchants, the boatmen, the peasants. No reason to be bitter about one's lot in life: better times were coming, and they would endure forever.

His first day in the necropolis seemed to endure forever also. He drifted from booth to booth, filling in wherever he seemed to be needed, doing whatever they seemed to want him to do. The day was a fever-dream of intestines and stinks, of salts and oils, of dead bodies lying like meat on wooden blocks. It astonished him that death had undone so many this day in Thebes. But then he reminded himself that this wasn't only one day's crop; the mummification process lasted a couple of months and there were bodies here in all stages of preparation, ranging from those who had just undergone their preliminary cleaning to those who had attained the requisite level of desiccation and were ready to be carried to their resting places in the hills. Several times during the day new deads arrived at the necropolis, borne on litters with their friends and members of their family grieving by their sides and parties of professional mourners, women with bare breasts and disheveled hair, sobbing along behind. Davis helped to construct the embalmers' booth for one of these new arrivals; it was the most pleasing thing he had done all day, swift, neat, clean work. In late afternoon just as the sky was beginning to redden behind the jagged hills he witnessed the other end of the process, the departure of a funeral cortege toward the actual place of burial. It must have been someone of note who had died, for the procession was extensive: first servants carrying intricately carved alabaster jars that very likely contained foodstuffs and perfumed oils for the use of the dead man in the next world, and then men bearing heavy, ornately decorated wooden chests that must hold his fine clothing, his prized possessions, all the treasure that he was taking with him to the afterlife; and after them came the four jars of polished stone containing the deceased's embalmed viscera, carried upon a sled. A priest was alongside, chanting. The mummy itself was next, handsomely encased and resting on a couch beneath a canopy, all mounted upon another sled, this one gilded, with ebony runners. Four more priests accompanied it: and then the family and friends, not grieving now, but looking calm and rather proud of the fine show of which they were a part. In the rear once again were the professional mourners, a dozen of them wailing desperately and beating their breasts, each of them every bit as distraught as though it was her own husband or father who had been taken from her that very morning.

The procession passed through the embalmers' village and out the far side, heading toward the looming cliffs just to the west. It was grand enough, Davis thought, for a vizier, a judge, a high priest, at the very least. A prince, perhaps.

"Who's being carried there, do you know?" Davis asked the man by his side.

"Mahu, I think. Overseer of the royal granaries, he was."

"A rich man?"

"Rich? Mahu? No, not really. Too honest, Mahu was."

Davis stared at the retreating cortege. How splendid it looked against the light of the setting sun! And this was only a bureaucrat's funeral. He wondered what a nobleman's must be like, or a king's.

He had seen some of the royal tombs during his orientation visit to Luxor, those haunting surreal catacombs endlessly decorated with the bewildering profuse mysteries of the Book of Gates and the Book of the Night and the Book of the Underworld, and he had seen the smaller but jollier tombs of nobles and high officials as well. Had Mahu's tomb survived to come before the eyes of modern-day archeologists and tourists? He had no idea. Perhaps it had, but no one cared. Mahu had been an honest man; his tomb must not have compared with those of the great lords.

The great ones, Davis already knew, did not undergo their mummifications amidst the vulgar hubbub of the embalmers' village. For them the booths were set up closer to the tomb sites, well away from the stares of the curious; and they were guarded day and night until they were at last safely packed away underground amidst all their worldly wealth. Which had made no difference in the long run, for all the tombs had been plundered eventually, all but insignificant Tut-ankh-Amen's, and even his had been broken into a couple of times, though the thieves had left most of the treasure behind. But the mummies themselves, some of them, had survived. In the Cairo Museum Davis had looked upon the actual face of Rameses the Great, stern and fierce, ninety years old and still outraged by the idea of dying: he was one who had meant to stay on the throne forever, to have his afterlife and his first life at the same time. *My name is Ozymandias, King of Kings. Look on my works, ye mighty, and despair!* And—shivering now—he realized that he had seen Amenhotep III's mummy in the museum also, the mortal remains of the plump sleek-cheeked man whom he had watched, only two days before, as he came forth from Luxor Temple, a living god, happy and well, becrowned and bejeweled, who had clambered into his royal chariot and driven off while his adoring subjects cheered—*Life! Health! Strength!*

Davis trembled. He had been with the Service for five years; and it seemed to him that it was only in this moment that the full power of the meaning of being able to travel in time came home to him. The awesome privilege, the utter magnificence of having the gates of the past rolled back for him. For him!

I must not have much of an imagination, he thought.

"You! Standing and watching!"

A whip came out of somewhere and coiled around his bare shoulders like a fiery cobra.

He turned. An overseer was laughing at him.

"Work to do. Who do you think you are?"

Work, yes. Soiled rags to collect. Blood-stained rags, left-over salts, broken pots. He entered one booth where a fat man lay on his back, staring through empty sockets at the darkening sky. A vivid line of stitches crossed his belly, holding in the packing of myrrh and cassia. The fat man's jaw sagged in the stupefaction of death. All those fine dinners: what did they matter now? *Look on my works, ye mighty!* On a table in the adjoining booth was a woman, a girl, perhaps fifteen or twenty years old, small-breasted and slender. She had just arrived;

the craftsmen of the necropolis had not yet begun their work on her. The elaborate wig of dense midnight-blue hair that she had worn in life sat beside her on the table. Her shaven skull was like porcelain. Her fingernails and toenails were dyed dark red with henna and there was blue-green eye-paint around her sightless eyes. A gold bracelet encircled her lovely arm: maybe she had worn it since a child and it could no longer be removed. Her nakedness was heartbreaking. He felt an impulse to cover it. But he moved on, only remotely aware now of the odor of death and of the chemicals of the embalmers. It was dark now. The Anubis-masked embalmers had gone home. His body ached everywhere from his day's work, and he knew the pain was just beginning. He was stained with oils and assorted aromatics. His shoulders burned from the sting of the overseer's whip. The real Egypt, all right. Seen from the underside. Could he leave now, or would he be whipped again? No, no, all the workers were leaving. Night-guards were coming on duty; one of them glanced at him and made a jerking motion with his head, telling him to get out, go back to his village, call it a day.

He had grilled fish for dinner again, and rancid beer.

Later he sat up, staring at the impossibly brilliant stars in the astonishingly clear sky, and wondered whether Eyaseyab would come to him again. But why should she? What was he to her? A comet in the night, a random visitor to whom she had granted a moment of kindness. After a time he went inside his foul little cubicle and lay down on the straw that was his bed.

I must get back across the river, he told himself. I need to find—

And sleep came up in the midst of the thought and took him like a bandit who had thrown a heavy hood over his head.

SIX

Four days went by very much like the first one, in a dreamlike haze of hard work and overmastering strangeness.

He knew he needed to get out of this place, that he had to go back across the river and set about the search for the two missing members of the Service whose trajectories had gone astray and who—so the calculations indicated—were somewhere hereabouts. And, while he was at it, take in as much as he could of mighty Thebes. He had no business settling down like this in the necropolis. He had been sent here in part to rescue the vanished Roger Lehman and Elaine Sandburg, and in part as a scholar of sorts who had been trained to observe and report on one of the most glorious of all ancient cities; and although it might be useful for him to be learning the things that he was concerning the village of the embalmers, it was definitely time to move along. He owed that much to Sandburg, to Lehman, to the Service. Yet a curious trance-like lassitude held him. He sensed that the exhaustion of the day of his arrival had never really lifted from him. He had *seemed* to recover, he had gone past that frightening stage of dizziness and fainting, he could even cope with the hellish heat, he was able to put in a full working day at manual labor, some of it quite nasty; but in truth he realized that he had drawn back into this awful place as a kind of refuge and he was unable to muster the energy to get out and get on with his real work.

On the fourth night Eyaseyab unexpectedly returned. He had given up all hope of her.

When she appeared, trudging into the compound wearing little more than a shawl over her shoulders, the other men looked enviously at him, with a certain puzzlement and awe in their expressions. A slave-girl of the temple, a young and pretty one at that, coming to see him! Why, the stranger must not be as stupid as he seems. Or else he has some other merit that must not be readily apparent.

He wondered about it himself. And decided that he must seem elegant and exotic to her, courtly, even, a man with manners far beyond those of the class to which he obviously belonged. He was a luxury for her.

As she lay beside him that night she said, "You like it here? You are doing well?"

"Very well."

"You work hard, you will rise in the House. Perhaps your children will be embalmers, even."

He brought his hand up her side and cupped her breast.

"Children? What children?"

"Of course you will have children."

What was she talking about? The children that she would bear for him?

"Even if I did," he said, "how could they become embalmers? Isn't the guild hereditary?"

"You could marry an embalmer's daughter," she told him. "They would have you. You are very handsome. You are very intelligent. An embalmer's daughter would do well to be married to a man like you. You could choose the best of the daughters of the House of Purification. And then your wife's father would bring your children into the guild. How fine that would be for you and all your descendants!"

"Yes," he said dispiritedly.

The conversation was drifting into strange places. He imagined himself sitting at his dining-room table at the head of his clan, with his sons around him, each one wearing his little Anubis mask, gravely discussing the fine points of embalming with his father-in-law. How fine that would be, yes.

He was struck by the realization that Eyaseyab seemed to expect him to remain in the House of Purification for the rest of his life. A wonderful career opportunity, evidently. And of course she had automatically ruled herself out as a potential mate for him. She was a slave; he was a free man, and handsome and intelligent besides. Not for the likes of her. Perhaps slaves weren't allowed to marry. He was a divertissement for her, a novelty item who would pass swiftly through her life—like a comet, yes, the image was a good one—and disappear.

To distract himself he stroked the plump pleasant spheroid of her breast. But it had lost all erotic charge for him. It was flesh, only flesh. He had a sudden horrifying vision of good-hearted Eyaseyab lying face-up on a wooden table in one of the booths of the House of Purification. But no, no, they wouldn't send a slave's body there. What did they do with them, throw them into the Nile?

Abruptly he said, "In the morning I want to go across the river. I have to see the priestess Nefret again."

"Oh, no. That would be impossible."

"You can get me into the temple."

"The priestess sees no one from the outside."

"Nevertheless," he said. "Do it for me. Tell her it's urgent, tell her that Edward-Davis has important business with her." He hovered over her in the darkness. His thumb lightly caressed her nipple, which began to grow rigid again. In a low voice he said, "Tell her that Edward-Davis is in truth an ambassador from a foreign land, and needs to speak with her about highly significant matters."

She began to laugh. She wriggled and slipped her knee between his thighs and began to slide it back and forth.

"I'm serious," he said.

"Yes. Of course you are. Now stop talking and put it in me the way you do so well."

"Eyaseyab—"

"Like this."

"I want you—to talk—to the priestess—"

"Shh."

"Eyaseyab."

"Yes. Yes. Good. Oh, you are Amon! You are Min! Oh, yes! Yes, Edward-Davis! Oh—don't stop—"

Was he supposed to include this in his report? he wondered.

The Service had no vow of chastity. But some things were none of their business.

"You are Amon! You are Min!"

She was slippery with sweat in the heat of the night. He said no more to her about going across the river to see the priestess, and eventually they slept.

But when he heard her up and moving about the room a few hours later, getting her things together, he reached out, hooked his finger into her anklet in the darkness, and whispered, "Wait for me. I'm coming with you."

"You mustn't!" She sounded frightened.

"I need to see the priestess."

She seemed baffled by his insistent need to do what could not be done. But in the end she yielded: she was a slave, after all, accustomed to obeying. As they crossed the Nile on the early-morning ferry she still appeared tense and apprehensive, but he stroked her soft shoulders and she grew calm. The river at sunrise was glorious, a streak of polished turquoise running between the two lion-colored strips of land. Two little elongated puffs of cloud were drifting above the western hills and the early light turned them to pennants of flame. He saw white ibises clustering in the sycamore trees along the shore.

They entered the temple grounds through the side gate by which they had left, nearly a week before. A burly pockmarked guard scowled at him as he passed through, but he kept his head up and moved as though he belonged there. On the steps of the House of Life Eyaseyab paused and said, "You wait here. I will see what can be managed."

"No, don't leave me here. Take me inside with—"

Too late. She was gone. He prowled outside the building, uneasily looking around. But no one seemed to care that he was there. He studied a pair of elegant stone cobras, one wearing the red crown of Lower Egypt, the other wearing the white crown of the southern kingdom. He dug about in the sandy soil with the tip of his big toe and unearthed a superb scarab of blue faience that any museum would have been proud to own. He touched his hand wonderingly to the flawlessly executed and brightly painted bas-relief that was carved along the wall: Pharaoh before the gods, Isis to his left, Osiris to the right, Thoth and Horus in the background, the ibis-head and the hawk.

Egypt. Egypt. Egypt.

He had dreamed all his life of coming here. And here he was. Well ahead of normal Service schedule for such a major mission, and all because of Elaine Sandburg and Roger Lehman.

"I'm not so sure I want to find out what they've turned into," Charlie Farhad had told him, explaining why he had refused to take on the assignment. "The past's a weird place. It can make you pretty weird yourself, if you stay in it long enough."

"They've only been there a year and a half."

"Not necessarily," Farhad had said. "Think about it."

Sandburg and Lehman had been heading for the Rome of Tiberius, a ninety-day reconnaissance. But they had missed their return rendezvous and an analysis of the field spectrum indicated some serious anomalies—i.e., an overshoot. How much of an overshoot had taken almost a year to calculate. A lot of algorithmic massage produced the conclusion that instead of landing in 32 A.D. they had plopped down at least thirteen centuries earlier and a goodly distance to the east: Eighteenth Dynasty Egypt, the calculations indicated. "Poor Roger," Charlie Farhad said. "He was so damned proud of his Latin, too. Won't do him a fucking bit of good now, will it?" The algorithm was a murky one; the calculation was only probabilistic. Sandburg and Lehman might have landed right on top of the Nile or they could have turned up in some merciless corner of the Arabian desert. The high-probability line said Thebes. The most likely year was 1390 B.C., but the time range was plus or minus ten years. Not a hope in hell of finding them again, right? Nevertheless an attempt to rescue them had to be made, but none of the veteran time-jockeys wanted to touch it. That was their privilege. They hinted darkly about serious risk and the considerable unlikelihood of success. And in any case they had their own projects to worry about.

Davis heard what they had to say, but in the end he had volunteered anyway. Fools rush in, et cetera. He hadn't known Sandburg and Lehman at all: the Service was a big operation, and he was pretty far down in junior staff. So he wasn't doing it out of friendship. He took the job on partly because he was in love with the idea of experiencing Egypt in the prime of its greatness, partly because he was young enough still to see something romantic as well as useful to his career about being a hero, and partly because his own real-time life had taken some nasty turns lately—a collapsed romance, a bitter unexpected parting—and he was willing enough to go ricocheting off thirty-five centuries regardless of the risks. And so he had. And here he was.

Eyaseyab appeared at the head of the stairs and beckoned to him. "The prince is with her. But he will be leaving soon."

"The prince?"

"Pharaoh's son, yes. The young Amenhotep." A mischievous look came into the slave-girl's eyes. "He is Nefret's brother."

Davis was bewildered by that for a moment. Then he recognized the idiom. This was an incestuous land: Eyaseyab meant that the priestess and the prince were lovers. A tingle of awe traveled quickly along his spine. She was talking about the fourth Amenhotep, the future Pharaoh Akhnaten, he who would in another few years attempt to overthrow the old gods of Egypt and install a new cult of solar worship that had only a single deity. Akhnaten? Could it be? Up there now, just a hundred feet away, at this moment caressing the priestess Nefret? Davis shook his head in wonder. This was like standing in the plaza and watching Pharaoh himself come out of the temple. He had expected to lurk around the periphery of history here, not to be thrust right into the heart of it. That he was seeing these people in the flesh was remarkable, but not entirely pleasing. It cheapened things, in a way, to be running into actual major historical figures; it made it all seem too much like a movie. But at least it was a well-done movie. The producers hadn't spared any expense.

"Is that him?" Davis asked.

Of course it was. The tingle returned, redoubled. A figure had appeared on the portico of the House of Life. He gaped at it: a very peculiar figure indeed, a slender young man in a loose pleated linen robe with wide sleeves trimmed with blue bows. The upper half of his body seemed frail, but from the waist down he was fleshy, thick-thighed, soft-bellied. A long jutting jaw, a narrow head, full lips: an odd-looking mysterious face. He was instantly recognizable. Only a few weeks before Davis had peered wonder-struck at the four giant statues of him in the Amarna gallery at the far end of the ground floor at the Cairo Museum. Now here was the man himself.

Here and gone. He smiled at Davis in an eerie otherworldly way as if to say, *Yes, you know who I am and I know who you are,* and went quickly down the back steps of the temple's podium. A litter must have been waiting for him there. Davis watched as he was borne away.

"Now," he said to Eyaseyab, forcing himself to snap from his trance. "Did you tell the priestess I'm here?"

"Yes. She says no. She says she will not see you."

"Go back inside. Ask her again."

"She seemed angry that you are here. She seemed very annoyed. *Very* annoyed."

"Tell her that it's a matter of life and death."

"It will do no good."

"Tell her. Tell her that I'm here and it's extremely important that I get to see her. Lives are at stake, the lives of good, innocent people. Remind her who I am."

"She knows who you are."

"Remind her. Edward-Davis, the man from America."

"A-meri-ca."

"America, yes."

She trotted up the stairs again. Some moments passed, and then a few more. And then Eyaseyab returned, eyes wide with amazement, face ruddy and bright with surprise and chagrin.

"Nefret will see you!"

"I knew she would."

"You must be very important!"

"Yes," he said. "I am."

The priestess was waiting for him in an antechamber. As before, she was wearing a filmy gown, casually revealing in what he was coming to regard as the usual Egyptian way; but she was more splendidly bedecked this time, lips painted a glowing yellow-red, cheeks touched with the same color, the rims of her eyes dark with kohl, the eyelids deep green. A muskiness of perfume clung to her. An intricate golden chain lay on her breast; pendant beads of carnelian and amethyst and lapis-lazuli dangled from it. The presence of her royal lover seemed still to be about her, like an aura. She seemed imperious, magnificent, splendid. For someone her age—she had to be past forty—she was remarkably beautiful, in a chilly, regal way.

And unusual-looking. There was something exotic about her that he hadn't noticed the other time, when he was too too dazzled by the whole sweep of Egypt and in any event too sick to focus closely on anything. He realized now that she probably was not an Egyptian. Her skin was much too white, her eyes had an un-Egyptian touch of violet in them. Perhaps she was Hittite, or Syrian, or a native of one of the mysterious lands beyond the Mediterranean. Or Helen of Troy's great-great-grandmother.

She seemed strangely tense: a coiled spring. Her eyes gleamed with expressions of—what? Uneasiness? Uncertainty? Powerful curiosity? Even a tinge of sexual attraction, maybe. But she appeared to be holding herself under tight control.

She said, "The stranger returns, the man from America. You look healthier now. Hard work must agree with you."

"Yes," he said. "I suppose it does."

"Eyaseyab says you are an ambassador."

"In a manner of speaking."

"Ambassadors should present themselves at court, not at the temple of the goddess."

"I suppose so. But I can't do that." His eyes met hers. "I don't have any credentials that would get me access to the court. In all of Thebes you're the only person of any importance that I have access to. I've come to you today to ask for your help. To beg you for it."

"Help? What kind of help?"

He moistened his lips.

"Two people from my country are living somewhere in Thebes. I've come to Egypt to find them."

"Two people from America, you say."

"Yes."

"Living in Thebes."

"Yes."

"Friends of yours?"

"Not exactly. But I need to find them."

"You need to."

"Yes."

She nodded. Her eyes drifted away from his. She seemed to be staring past his left cheekbone.

"Who are these people? Why are they here?"

"Well—"

"And why is finding them so important to you?" she asked.

"It's—a long story."

"Tell me. I want to know everything."

He had nothing to lose. But where to begin? He hesitated a moment. Then the words began to flow freely. He poured it all out. My country, he told her, is so far away that you could never comprehend it. There is a Service—a kind of priesthood, think of it as a priesthood—that sends emissaries to distant lands. A little while ago they sent two to a place called Rome, a man and a woman—Rome is very distant, almost as far as my own country—but they went astray in their journey, they traveled much too far, they wandered even as far as the land of the Nile and have not been heard from since—

He listened to himself speaking for what seemed to be an hour. It must all have been the wildest nonsense to her. He watched her watching him with what might have been irritation or incredulity or even shock on her face, but which was probably just bewilderment. At last he ran down and fell silent. Her face had tightened: it was like a mask now.

But to his amazement the mask suddenly cracked. He saw unexpected tears welling in her eyes, flowing, darkening her cheeks with tracks of liquefied kohl.

She was trembling. Holding her arms crossed over her breasts, pacing the stone floor in agitation.

What had he said, what had he done?

She turned and stared straight at him from the far side of the room. Even at that distance he could see restless movements in her cheeks, her lips, her throat. She was trying to say something but would not allow it to emerge.

At last she got it out: "What are the names of the two people you're looking for."

"They won't mean anything to you."

"Tell me."

"They're American names. They wouldn't be using them here, if they were here."

"Tell me their names," she said.

He shrugged. "One is called Elaine Sandburg. The other is Roger Lehman."

There was a long moment of silence. She moistened her lips, a quick tense serpent-flicker of her tongue. Her throat moved wordlessly once again. She paced furiously. Some powerful emotion seemed to be racking her: but what? What? Why would a couple of strange names have such an effect on her? He waited, wondering what was going on.

"I have to be crazy for telling you this," she said finally, in a low, husky voice he could scarcely identify as hers. He was stunned to realize that she was speaking in English. "But I can't go on lying to you any longer. You've already found one of the people you're looking for. I'm Elaine Sandburg."

"You?"

"Yes. Yes."

It was the last thing he had expected to hear. Vortices whirled about him. He felt numb with shock, almost dazed.

"But that isn't possible," he said inanely. "She's only thirty-two." His face flamed. "And you're at least—"

His voice trailed off in embarrassment.

She said, "I've been here almost fifteen years."

She had to be telling the truth. There was no other possibility. She spoke English; she knew Elaine Sandburg's name. Who else could she be if not the woman he had come here to find? But it was a struggle for him to believe it. She had had him completely fooled; she seemed completely a woman of her time. He had memorized photos of Elaine Sandburg from every angle; but he would never have recognized this woman as Sandburg, not in a thousand years, not in a million. Her face had changed: considerably sharpened by time, lengthened by her journey into middle age. The tight brown curls of the photographs must have been shaved off long ago, replaced by the traditional black Egyptian wig of an upper-class woman. Her eyebrows had been plucked. And then there was the strange jewelry, the transparent robes. Her lips and cheeks painted in this alien way. Everything about her masked her identity: she had transformed herself fully into an Egyptian. But she was the one. No doubt of it, no doubt at all. This priestess, this devotee of Isis, was Elaine Sandburg. Who had given him cuddly Eyaseyab to play with. And had told Eyaseyab to take him across the river to the City of the Dead and lose him over there.

Sudden searing anger went roaring through him.

"You were simply playing with me, that other time. Pretending you had no idea where I was from. Asking me where America was, whether it was farther from here than Syria."

"Yes. I was playing with you, I suppose. Do you blame me?"

"You knew I was from Home Era. You could have told me who you were."

"If I had wanted to, yes."

He was mystified by that. "Why hide it? You saw right away that I was Service. Why'd you hold back from identifying yourself? And why ship me over to the other side of the river and stash me among the embalmers, for God's sake?"

"I had my reasons."

"But I came here to help you!"

"Did you?" she asked.

SEVEN

LEHMAN SAID, "WHERE IS HE now?"

"In one of the temple storerooms. Under guard."

"I still can't understand why you told him. After chewing me out the way you did last week when I was the one talking about doing it. You made a complete hundred-eighty-degree reversal in a single week. Why? Why?"

Sandburg glowered at him. She was furious—with herself, with Lehman, with the hapless boy that the Service had sent. But mainly she was furious with herself. And yet, even in her fury, she realized that she was beginning to forgive herself.

"Originally we thought he was simply here on an independent research mission, remember? But when he told me that in fact he had come here looking for us—that he had come to rescue us—"

"Even so. Especially so. You recall what you said last week? You just want to be left alone to live your life. Your life in Eighteenth Dynasty Egypt. And therefore we can't let him know a thing, you said. But then you did, anyway."

"It was an impulse that I couldn't overcome," she said. "Have you ever had an impulse like that, Roger? Have you?"

"Don't call me Roger. Not here. My name is Senmut-Ptah. And speak Egyptian."

"Stop being such an asshole, will you?"

"I'm being an Egyptian. That's what we are now: Egyptians."

They were in his astronomical chamber, a small domed outbuilding behind the oldest shrine of the main Karnak temple. Cool bright sprinklings of starlight penetrated the openings in the roof and sketched patterns on the brick floor. Across the blue-black vault of the ceiling the fantastically attenuated naked figure of the goddess Nut, the deity of the sky, stretched from one side of the room to the other, great spidery arms and legs yards and yards long spanning the starry cosmos, with the Earth-god Shu supporting her arched nude form from below and complacently smiling figures of ram-headed Khnum standing beside him. Dense rows of hieroglyphs filled every adjacent inch of free space, offering intense assertions of arcane cosmological truths.

Sandburg said, "I was being just as Egyptian as I could be. But there he was solemnly telling me all about the Service, really sweating at it, trying to explain to a priestess of Isis where America was and where Rome was and how two people from this Service of his had overshot their mark and disappeared somewhere in the depths of time—no, wait, he didn't try to tell me it was time-travel, he just used geographical analogies—and suddenly I couldn't hold it in any longer. I couldn't just go on standing there in front of him pretending to be a fucking ancient priestess of Isis, looking lofty and esoteric and mystical, when this kid, this *kid* who had come three and a half thousand years to find us, who I had sent over to the City of the Dead to work as a pickler of mummy-guts because we wanted to get him out of our hair, was begging for my help so that he could find you and me. Our rescuer, and I was treating him like shit. Playing games with his head, making him reel off yard after yard of completely needless explanation. I couldn't keep the pretense up another minute. So I blurted out the truth, just like that."

"An impulse."

"An impulse, yes. A simple irrational impulse. You've never had one of those, have you? No—no, of course not. Who am I asking? Roger Lehman, the human computer. Of course you haven't."

"That isn't true and you damned well know it. You like to think of me as some sort of android, some kind of mechanical man, but in fact I'm every bit as human as you are, and maybe a little more so." In his agitation he snatched up one of his astronomical instruments, a little gleaming armillary disk from whose center a hippopotamus image yawned, and ran his long tapering fingers around its edges. "Remember, I was the one who originally wanted to have a little talk with him, to find out, at least, what might be going on down the line. You said you shouldn't do it, and you were right. And then you did it. An impulse. Christ, an *impulse*! Well, I have impulses too, whatever you may think. But even so I still have enough sense not to jump out of a third-floor window simply because I happen to be on the third floor. And enough sense not to say the one thing I shouldn't be saying to the one person I shouldn't be saying it to."

"If I seriously thought that it could have done any harm—"

"You don't think it can?"

"He's here alone. I've got him in custody. He can't make us do anything we don't want to do. We've got complete control of the situation. Really we do."

"I suppose," Lehman said grudgingly. He wandered around the room, fingering his charts and instruments. He rubbed his hands over the bits of gold and lapis-lazuli embedded in the wall. He picked up three long tight rolls of sacred papyri that he used in his divinations and set them fussily down again in slightly different places. "How do you think they were able to trace us?" he asked.

"How would I know? Something with their computers, I guess. Calculating probable trajectories. Maybe they took a guess. Or a bunch of guesses. You know they sweat a lot whenever any mission goes astray. So they sweated the computers until they came up with a hypothetical location where we might have landed. And sent this kid to check it out."

"And what happens now?"

"We go to talk to him. You and me both."

"Why?"

"Because I think we owe it to him. There's no sense pretending any longer, is there? He's here, and he knows I'm here, and he's probably guessed that you're here too. He's Service, Roger. We can't simply leave him in the dark, now. We've got to make him understand the way this has to be handled."

"I don't agree. I think the best thing for us is just to keep away from him. I wish you hadn't said anything to him in the first place."

"It's too late for that. I have. Anyway, he's probably got news from people we knew in Home Era. Carrying messages, even."

"That's exactly what worries me."

"Don't you want to hear anything about—"

Lehman gave her a wild-eyed stare. "Elaine, those people are thirty-five centuries in the future. I want to keep them there." He sounded almost desperate about it.

"Last week you were hot to hear the gossip," she said.

"That was last week. I've had a week to think about things. I don't want to stir all that old stuff up again. Let it stay where it is. And let us stay where *we* are. I'm not going to go near him."

His lower lip was quivering. He seemed actually afraid, she thought. Where had granite-faced Senmut-Ptah gone?

She said, "We can't simply stonewall him. We *can't.* We owe him at least the opportunity to talk to us."

"Why? We don't owe him anything."

"For Christ's sake, Roger. He's a human being. He came here with the intention of helping us."

"I'm aware of that. But—"

"No buts. Come on with me. Right now. You'll be sorry if you don't. I can guarantee that."

"You're a terrible woman."

"Yes. I know that—Listen, do you remember how it was for us when we first landed here? Helpless, bewildered, hopelessly lost in time, dressed like a couple of Romans fifteen centuries out of place, unable to read or write Egyptian, not speaking a word of the language, not the first inkling of it, hardly knowing anything about this civilization except what we learned in high school? Wondering how the hell we were going to survive? You remember how frightening that was?"

"We survived, though. We did more than survive."

"Because we were good. We were adaptable, we were versatile, we were clever. Even so, we went through two years of hell before we started to make things happen for us. You remember? I certainly do. Life as a temple whore? You didn't have to do that, at least, but you had your bad times too, plenty of them."

"So? What does that have to do with—"

"This kid is here now, up against some of the same things we were. And the only two people in the world that he has anything in common with choose to turn their backs on him. I hate that."

"What are you, in love with him?"

"I feel sorry for him."

"We didn't ask him to come here."

"It was lousy of me just to dump him out on the streets to shift for himself in the City of the Dead. It's going to be lousy of us to tell him that he's wasted his time coming here, that we don't want to be rescued, thank you very much but no deal. How would you feel if you came charging in to be somebody's savior and got told something like that?" She shook her head firmly. "We have to go to see him."

"You're suddenly so soft-hearted. You surprise me."

"Do I?" she said. "And here I was thinking you were the soft-hearted one. Secretly, behind the grim facade."

"How discerning you are. But I still don't want to see him."

"Why not?"

"I just don't."

She moved closer to him.

"We have to. That's all there is to it."

"Well—"

"Do you think he's a magician? A hypnotist? He's just a kid, and we've got him locked safely away besides. He can't make you do anything you don't want to do. Come with me."

"No."

"Come on, Roger."

"Well—"

"Come. Now."

She led him, still grumbling, out of the building, past the temple of Amenhotep II and the pylons of Tuthmosis I and Tuthmosis III, down the avenue of ram-headed sphinxes and into the Precinct of Mut. The storeroom where she had parked Davis for safe-keeping was partly below-ground, a cool, clammy-walled crypt not very different from a dungeon. When they entered it, Davis was sitting huddled on the straw-covered floor next to a shattered statue in pink granite of some forgotten king that had been tossed into the room for storage two or three or five hundred years earlier. The Egyptians never threw anything away.

He looked up and glared balefully at her.

"This is Roger Lehman," she said. "Roger, I want you to meet Edward Davis."

"It's about fucking time," Davis said.

Lehman extended his hand in a tentative, uncertain way. Davis ignored it.

"You look a whole lot older than I expected," Davis said. "I would never have recognized you. Especially in that cockeyed costume."

"Thank you."

"You expect me to be polite?" Davis asked bitterly. "Why? What the hell kind of fucking reception did you people give me? You think it was fun, falling across three and a half thousand years? Have you forgotten what that feels like? And then what happens to me when I get here? First she ships me across the river to be an embalmer's apprentice. After which she throws me in this hole in the ground when I come back over. What am I, your enemy? Don't you two stupid monkeys realize that I'm here to goddamn *rescue* you?"

"There's a lot you don't understand," Sandburg said.

"Damn right there is. I'd like you to tell me—"

"Wait," Lehman said. Sandburg shot him an irritated look and started to speak, but he held up his hand to silence her. To Davis he said, "Talk to us about this rescue plan of yours, first. What's the arrangement?"

"I'm on a thirty-day mission. We don't need the full thirty, now that I've found you so fast, but we've got to wait it out anyway, right? On the thirtieth day they'll drop the jump field into an alleyway just north of Luxor Temple. It's the one I landed in, with a graffito on the wall pronouncing a curse on some wine-merchant who screwed one of his customers. The field arrives at noon sharp, but of course we're there waiting for it a couple of hours before that. The rainbow lights up, the three of us step inside, away we go. Back home in a flash. You don't know how hard they've been working, trying to locate you two."

"They couldn't have been in much of a hurry," Lehman said. "Did Elaine tell you we've been here fifteen years?"

"In the Home Era time-line you've only been missing for a year and a half. And they've been running calculations non-stop most of that time. I'm sorry we couldn't match up the displacement factors any better, but you've got to understand it was really just a stab in the dark sending me to the year they did. We had a twenty-year probability window to deal with."

"I'm sure they did their best," Sandburg said. "And you too. We appreciate your coming here."

"Then why did you send me to—"

She held up her hand. "You don't understand the situation, Edward."

"Damned right I don't."

"There are certain factors that we have to explain. You see, we don't actually—"

"Wait a second, Elaine," Lehman said sharply.

"Roger, I—"

"Wait a second."

It was his priest-voice again, his stony Senmut-Ptah voice. Sandburg peered at him in astonishment. His face was flushed, his eyes were strangely glossy.

He said, "Before you tell him anything, we need to have a discussion, Elaine. You and I."

She looked at him blankly. "What's to discuss?"

"Come outside and I'll tell you."

"What the hell is this all about?"

"Outside," Lehman said. "I have to insist."

She gave him a glance of cool appraisal. But he was unreadable.

"Whatever you say, O Senmut-Ptah."

EIGHT

THEY STOOD IN THE DARKNESS of the garden of the Precinct of Mut. Torches flickered in the distance. Somewhere, far away, the priests of Amon were chanting the evening prayer. From another direction came a more raucous sound: sailors singing down by the riverfront.

Lehman's long, gaunt figure towered above her. Lines of strain were evident in his face. It had taken on the same strange expression that had come over him the week before, the night when she had first told him of the arrival of a member of the Service in Thebes.

"Well?" she said, perhaps a little too harshly.

"Let me think how to put this, Elaine."

"Put what?"

He made a despairing gesture. "Wait, will you? Let me think."

"Think, then."

She paced in a fretful circle around him. A dim figure appeared on the pylon of a distant temple and unhurriedly began to take in the pennants for the night. Some dark-winged nocturnal bird fluttered by just overhead, stirring faint currents in the warm air.

Lehman said finally, speaking as though every word were very expensive, "What I need to tell you, Elaine, is that I'm half inclined to go back with him. More than half."

"You son of a bitch!"

He looked abashed, uncomfortable. "Now do you see why I told you I didn't want to see him? You yourself pointed out last week that there were risks in talking to him, that it could stir up troublesome old memories. Well, it has." Lehman touched his hand to his forehead. "If you only knew how I've been churning inside since he got here. Every day it's gotten a little worse. We should have simply kept clear of him, the way we had always planned to do if anyone came. But no. No. Bad enough that he stumbled right into you first thing. You still had the option of keeping your mouth shut. No, you had to spill everything, didn't you? And now—now—" He scowled at her. "I was wavering even then, last week."

"I know you were. I saw it. We talked about it."

"I was able to put the idea away then. But now—"

"Just seeing him, that was enough to make you want to go back down the line? Why, Roger? Why?"

Lehman was silent again for a time. He scuffed at the ground with his sandaled foot. A young priest appeared from somewhere, staggering under the jeweled and gilded image of a cobra taller than he was, and came stumbling toward Lehman as though wanting to ask him some question about it. Lehman waved the boy away with a curt, furious gesture.

Then in a remote voice he said, "Because I'm starting to think that maybe we should. We've done all right for ourselves here, sure, but how long can our luck hold out? For one thing, consider the health angle. I don't mean the exotic diseases they have here: I assume our immunizations will continue to hold out. I'm just talking about the normal aging process. We have to keep in mind that this is a primitive country in many ways, especially where it comes to medicine, and we're starting to get older. It won't be easy for us here when the medical problems begin—the big ones, the little ones, the medium ones. You want someone to help you get through your menopause with powdered scarab and a tincture of goose turds and a prayer to Thoth?"

"I'm doing all right so far."

"And if you develop a lump in one of your breasts?"

"They have surgeons here. It isn't all goose turds and powdered beetles. Why this sudden burst of hypochondria, Roger?"

"I'm just being realistic."

"Well, so am I. I don't know what you're worrying about. This is a clean, healthy place, if you happen to belong to the privileged classes, and we do. We've kept ourselves in good condition the whole time we've been here and we're in terrific shape right now with no sign of problems ahead and we're going to have really beautiful mummies. What other reasons do you have for going home?"

"I don't know. Homesickness? Curiosity about what's been happening back there? Maybe I've just had enough of Egypt, that's all."

"I'm sorry to hear that. I haven't."

"So you want to stay?"

"Of course I do. That hasn't changed. This is where I want to be, Roger. This is the time and the place that I prefer. I have a good life in a tremendously fascinating period of history and I'm waited on hand and foot and I don't have to put up with any of the shit of the modern world. I like it here. I thought you did too."

"I did," he said. "I do. For so many reasons. But—"

"But now you want to go home."

"Maybe."

"Then go," she said disgustedly. "If that's what you think you want."

"Without you?"

"Yes."

He looked startled. "Do you mean that, Elaine?"

"If they ask where I am, just don't say anything. Tell them you simply don't know what happened to me when we overshot Rome. You came out of the jump field and discovered that you weren't in Rome at all, that you were stranded on your own in Thebes, and there you stayed, shifting for yourself, until this Davis came and got you."

"I can't do that. You know what their debriefings are like. Anyway, *he'd* tell them."

"Even if I asked him not to?"

"Why would he want to lie for you, Elaine?"

"Maybe he would, if I asked him very nicely. Or maybe he wouldn't. But in any case, you've just said that you'd tell them where I am."

"I'd have to. Whether or not I wanted to."

"Then I don't want you going back, Roger." Her tone was cold and quiet.

"But—"

"I don't. I won't let you do it."

"Won't *let* me?" he repeated.

"That's right. Not if you'd give me away. And I see now that that's exactly what you'd do. So I'm not going to let you leave here."

"How could you stop me?"

She reached out. Her hand rested lightly on his bony wrist. She rubbed her fingertips back and forth over his skin.

Softly she said, "Maybe I'm putting it too strongly. You know I couldn't stop you if you were really determined to go. But I don't *want* you to go. Please. Please, Roger? What I want is for you to stay here with me. I don't want to be left by myself here."

"Then come with me."

"No. No, I won't do that." She leaned close to him. "Don't go, Roger."

He stared at her, mesmerized.

"We can be wonderful together," she said, smiling up at him. "We *were.* We can be again. I'll see to that, I promise you. It'll be the way it was for us in the beginning."

He looked skeptical. "Will it, now?"

"I promise. But stay. There's nothing for you back there. You're homesick? For what? You want to rejoin the Service? Hop when they tell you to? Let them ship you around to a lot of strange places? The glory of the Time Service! What glory? It's just a job, and a damned hard one. You don't want that any more, do you, Roger? Or maybe they'd give you a desk job. And a nice little one-room apartment with a view of the Potomac, and in ten years you can have your pension and move to Arizona and sit on your porch and watch the cactus grow until you get old. No, listen to me: You want to stay here. This is the right place for us. You've said it a million times. You have a life here, a damned good one. Your estate, your slaves, your chariot, your observatory, your—all of it. You don't want to go back there and be Roger Lehman again. There's nothing for you in that. You very much prefer being Senmut-Ptah. Don't you? Don't you, Roger? Tell me the truth."

Now he was plainly wavering again, back the other way.

"Well—"

"I know it's a temptation, wanting to see your own time again. Don't you think I've felt it too, now and then? But it's not worth it. Giving up all this."

"Well—"

"Think about it."

He looked into the distance. The faint warm breeze brought the sound of a harp, some temple slave playing to amuse the elder priests in the Amon temple.

"Think."

"Yes."

She watched him. She saw the knots come and go in his craggy face. He was adding up the columns in that precise mathematical way of his, tallying the profits and the losses.

"Well?" she said.

"All right," he told her. He sounded almost relieved. "Forget what I've been saying. We stay in Egypt. Both of us."

"You're sure of that?"

"Yes. Yes."

"Good," she said. She grinned at him and winked. "And now we ought to go back in there and finish talking to him."

He nodded. "Yes. We do."

"Do we understand each other completely now, Roger?"

"Yes. Yes."

She gave him a long cool look. "Let's go back inside, then, and get it over with."

"Not there," Lehman said. "Not in that miserable musty storeroom. It's too depressing down in a hole like that. Let's take him over to my chambers in the observatory, at least. It'll be a little more civilized, talking to him over there."

"If you want to."

"I think we should," Lehman said.

NINE

THIS PART OF THE KARNAK complex that they had brought him to was new to him, a round two-story domed building behind the main temple. Since Roger Lehman's priestly specialty was supposed to be astronomy, the building was surely his observatory, Davis thought. So far as he could recall there had been no trace of any such structure in the modern-day Karnak ruins that he had visited on the orientation trip. Perhaps it had been demolished during the tremendous religious upheavals that were due to hit Egypt after Amenhotep III died.

"How about a little wine?" Lehman asked, with unconvincing geniality. "This is good stuff, from the royal vineyards in the Delta. The very best."

"You must have good connections at the court," Davis said.

"The very best," said Lehman.

From a cupboard in the wall he drew forth three alabaster drinking-cups embellished elaborately with hieroglyphics and a tall graceful terracotta amphora with two small handles and a pointed base. A clay stopper plugged its narrow mouth. As he broke it he said, "Elaine? Wine?"

"Please."

Davis took a sip, and then a deeper draught. The wine was sweet and thick, with a raisiny underflavor. Not bad, really. And the cup he was drinking out of was a little masterpiece, museum quality. The room itself, Lehman's private priestly chamber, was splendidly furnished, the walls magnificently covered with dark, vividly realistic murals of gods and demons and stars. It had a look of quiet luxury. Sandburg and Lehman had done all right for themselves in Egypt, especially considering that they had started with absolutely nothing only fifteen years ago, worse off than slaves, having no identities, not even knowing how to speak the language. Lehman seemed to have made himself into an important figure in the scientific establishment, such as it was. And she a high priestess and the mistress of the heir to the throne, no less. Both of them obviously wealthy, powerful, well connected. He had felt sorry for them a year ago when he first had heard the story of their being lost in time, far from the Imperial Rome that had been their intended destination, marooned in some alien hostile place where they were doubtlessly eking out miserable, difficult lives. He couldn't have been more wrong about that. They had proved to be paragons of adaptability. But of course they were Service personnel, trained to handle themselves satisfactorily under all sorts of unfamiliar and bewildering conditions.

Lehman turned to the cupboard again. This time he took from it a lovely little game-board, ebony inlaid with golden hieroglyphic inscriptions. Thirty gleaming squares of ivory veneer were set into it, arranged in three rows of ten, each square separated from its neighbors by ebony strips. From a box at its base he withdrew a pair of odd curving dice and a handful of pawn-shaped gaming-pieces made of some polished blue stone.

"You know what this is?" he asked.

"A *senet*-board?" Davis said at once.

"They really gave you a good briefing."

"The works. But I've always been interested in Egypt. I made special studies on my own."

"You don't know how to play, though, do you?"

"*Senet?* No. The rules are lost."

"Not here they aren't. Everyone plays it. Soldiers, slaves, construction workers, whores. The king plays it very well. So does the royal astronomer."

From a corner of the room Sandburg said, "Roger, why don't you get down to business?"

"Please, Elaine," Lehman said.

Calmly he arranged the pieces on the game-board.

"It even figures in the Book of the Dead, you know. Spell 17: the dead man plays *senet* with an invisible adversary, and has to win the game in order to continue his passage safely through the Netherworld."

"I know," said Davis. "But I'm not dead, and this isn't the Netherworld. Ms. Sandburg is right. If there's business for us to get down to, let's get down to it."

"Let me show you the rules of the game first, at least. We arrange the pieces like this. And then—a roll of the dice to determine who the challenger is and who's the defender—"

"Roger," Sandburg said.

"There. You challenge. I defend. Now, we start at this end of the board—"

"Roger."

Lehman smiled. "Well then. *Senet* afterward, perhaps."

He poured more wine into Davis' cup and his own and leaned forward across the table, bringing his face uncomfortably close. Davis saw what fifteen years of the Egyptian sun had done to Lehman's skin: he was as dry as a mummy, his skin drumhead-tight over his bones.

He said, "About this rescue proposal of yours, Davis. It was very kind of you to take the leap all the way back here for the sake of locating us. And marvelous luck that you found us at all. But I have to tell you: it's no go."

"What?"

"We're staying here, Elaine and I."

Staying?

Davis stared. Yes, yes, of course. It all fit together now, their odd fidgety elusiveness; her failure to disclose herself to him the first day, when she had heard him babbling deliriously in English; her sidetracking of him to the City of the Dead; her clapping him in that dungeon-like storeroom once she finally had blurted out the truth about herself. They were renegades. They were deserters. So dumb of him to have failed to see it.

He could hear Charlie Farhad's words echoing in his mind.

The past's a weird place. It can make you pretty weird yourself if you stay in it long enough.

Farhad hadn't been willing to go looking for them.

I'm not so sure I want to find out what they've turned into, Farhad had said.

Yes.

"You like it here that much?" Davis asked, after a bit.

"We've settled in," Elaine Sandburg said from across the room. "We have our niches here."

"We're Egyptians now," said Lehman. "Very highly placed court figures leading very pleasant lives."

"So I see. But still, to turn your back forever on your own era, your own world—"

"We've been here a long time," Lehman said. "To you we've only been missing a year or so. But we've lived a third of our lives here. Egypt's a real place to us. It's fantastic, it's bizarre, it's full of magic and mumbo-jumbo that doesn't make the slightest bit of sense to modern-day people. But it's beginning to make sense to us."

"Osiris? Thoth? Gods with the heads of birds and beetles and goats? They make sense to you?"

"In a larger sense. A metaphorical sense. You want more wine, Davis?"

"Yes. I think I do."

He drank more deeply this time.

"So this place is real to you and Home Era isn't?" he asked.

Lehman smiled. "I won't deny that Elaine and I feel a certain pull toward Home Era. Certainly I do. I suppose I still have family there, friends, people who remember me, who would be happy to see me again. I have to admit that when you first showed up I felt a powerful temptation to go back there with you when the jump field comes to get you. What is it, a thirty-day mission, you said?"

"Thirty, yes."

"But the moment of temptation passed. I worked my way through it. We're not going to go. The decision is final."

"That's a hell of a thing. Desertion, in fact. Completely against all the rules."

"It is, isn't it? But it's what we want. We're sorry about the rules. We didn't ask to come here, or expect it or want it. But somehow we did, and we made our own way upward. *Clawed* our way. You think working in the mummy factory is bad? You ought to know some of the things Elaine and I had to do. But we put new lives together for ourselves, against all the odds. Damned fine new lives, as a matter of fact. And now we want to keep them."

"The Time Service is a damned fine life too."

"Screw the Time Service," Lehman said. He wasn't smiling now. "What did the Service ever do for us except dump us fifteen hundred years from where we were hoping to go?" His long skeletal fingers toyed with the pieces on the *senet*-board. He fondled them a moment; then, in a single swift motion, he swept them brusquely off the board and into their box. "That's it," he said. "That's what we had to tell you. Your kind offer is refused with thanks. No deal. No rescue. That's the whole story. Please don't try to hassle us about it."

Davis looked at them in disbelief.

"I wouldn't dream of it," he said. "Stay here, if that's what your choice is. I can't force you to do anything you aren't willing to do."

"Thank you."

Davis helped himself to a little more of Lehman's wine.

They were both watching him in a strange way. There was something more, he realized.

"Well, what happens next?" he asked. "Now do you take me back to that beautiful little room under Ms. Sandburg's temple so I can get a little sleep? Or am I supposed to catch the night ferry over to the City of the Dead, so that I can learn a little more about how to make mummies before my time in Egypt runs out?"

"Don't you understand?" Sandburg said.

"Understand what?"

"Your time in Egypt isn't going to run out. You're staying here too, for keeps. We can't possibly let you go back. You mean to say you haven't figured that out?"

TEN

At least this time they had given him a room that was above ground-level, instead of returning him to the cheerless subterranean hole they had stashed him in before. He actually had a window of sorts—a rectangular slot, about fifteen feet high up in the wall, which admitted a long shaft of dusty light for five or six hours every day. He could hear the occasional twitterings of birds outside and now and then the distant chanting of priests. And, since the Egyptians evidently hated to leave so much as a square inch of any stone surface uncovered by incredible artistic masterpieces, there were superbly done bas-reliefs of gods on the walls of his cell to give him something to look at: good old ibis-headed Thoth aloofly accepting an offering of fruit and loaves of bread from some worshipful king, and the crocodile-faced god Sobek on the opposite wall holding a pleasant conversation with winged Isis while Osiris in his mummy-wrappings looked on benignly. Three times a day someone opened a little window in the door and passed a tray of food through for him. It wasn't bad food. They gave him a mug of beer or wine at least once every day. There could be worse places to be imprisoned.

This was the fourteenth day of the thirty. He was still keeping meticulous count.

Through the niche in the wall came the sound of singing voices, high-pitched, eerily meeting in harmonies that made his ears ache:

O my Sister, says Isis to Nepthys
Here is our brother
Let us raise up his head
Let us join his sundered bones
Let us restore his limbs to his body
O Sister, come, let us make an end to all his sorrow.

He had no idea where he was, because they had brought him here in the middle of the night, but he assumed that he must be in one of the innumerable outbuildings of the Karnak Temple complex. What Sandburg and Lehman intended, he assumed, was to keep him bottled up in here until the thirtieth day had passed and the jump field had come and gone in the alleyway near Luxor Temple. After that they would be safe, since he'd have no way of getting back to Home Era and letting the authorities know where and in what year the two missing renegades were hiding out. So they could afford to let him go free, then: stranded in time just like them, forever cut off from any chance of making his return journey, one more unsolved and probably unsolvable mystery of the Time Service.

Thinking about that made his temples pound and his chest ache. Trapped? Stranded here forever?

Over and over again he tried to understand where he had made his critical mistake. Maybe it had been to reveal the nature of his mission to the supposed priestess Nefret before he knew that she was Sandburg and Sandburg was dangerous. But she had already known the nature of his mission, because he evidently had been muttering in English during that time of delirium. So she was always a step ahead of him, or maybe two or three.

If he had been able to recognize Nefret as being Elaine Sandburg, either the first time when she was taking care of him, or a week later when he had walked back into her grasp, so that he could have been on his guard against—

No, that wouldn't have made any difference either. He hadn't had any reason to expect treachery from her. He had come here to rescue her, after all; why would she greet him with anything other than gratitude?

That was his mistake, he saw. Failing to anticipate that Sandburg and Lehman were deserters who didn't want to be rescued. Why hadn't anyone warned him of that? They had simply sent him off to Thebes and let him blithely walk right into the clutches of two people who had every reason to prevent him from returning to Home Era with news of their whereabouts and their whenabouts.

He heard a sound outside the door. Someone scrabbling around out there, fooling with the bolt.

He felt a foolish surge of hope.

"Eyaseyab? Is that you?"

Yesterday, when his evening food-tray had arrived, he had been waiting by the window in the door. "Tell the slave-girl Eyaseyab I'm here," he had said through the tiny opening. "Tell her her friend Edward-Davis needs help." A desperate grasping at straws, sure. But what else was there? He had to escape from this room. He didn't want to spend the rest of his life in ancient Egypt. Egypt was remarkable, yes, Egypt was astounding, he'd never deny that; but as a member of the Service he had the whole range of human history open to him, and prehistory too, for that matter, and to have that snatched away from him by these two, to be sentenced to a lifetime in the land of the Pharaohs—

The bolt slid back.

"Eyaseyab?"

He imagined her bribing his guards with jewels stolen from Nefret's bedchamber, with amphoras of royal wine, promises of wild nights of love, anything—anything, so long as she was able to let him out of here. And then she and that one-eyed brother of hers, maybe, would help him make his way across the river to the City of the Dead, where he could probably hide out safely in that maze of tiny streets until the thirtieth day. Then he could slip aboard the ferry again, entering Thebes proper, finding his alleyway with the graffito and the palm tree, waiting for the shimmering rainbow of the jump field to appear. And he'd get himself clear of this place. To hell with Sandburg and Lehman: let them stay if that was what they wanted to do. He'd report what had happened—he was under no obligation to cover for them; if anything quite the contrary—and then it was up to the Service. They could send someone else to bring them back. The defection would be expunged; the unauthorized intrusion into the domain of the past would be undone.

If only. If.

Now the door was opening. The dim smoky light of a little oil lamp came sputtering through from the hallway, just enough illumination to allow him to see that the veiled figure of a woman was entering his room.

Not Eyaseyab, no. Too tall, too slender.

It was Sandburg. "You?" he said, astonished. "What the hell are you doing—"

"Shh. And don't get any funny ideas. The guards are right outside and they'll be in here in two seconds if they hear anything they don't like."

She set her lamp down on the floor and came toward him. Close enough to grab, he thought. She didn't seem to be carrying a weapon. He could twist one of her arms up behind her back and put his hand on her throat and tell her that unless she issued an order to have him released and gave him a safe-conduct out of this building he would strangle her.

"Don't," she said. "Whatever you're thinking, don't even toy with the idea. You wouldn't stand a chance of finding your way out of here no matter what you did. And you'd be throwing away the only chance you have to salvage things for yourself."

"Where do I have any chance of salvaging anything?"

"It's all up to you," she said. "I've come here to try to help you work things out."

She came closer to him and pulled aside her veil. In the flickering glow of the lamplight her violet-flecked eyes had an amethyst sheen. Her face looked younger than it did by day. She seemed unexpectedly beautiful. That sudden revelation of beauty jarred him, and he was startled by his own reaction.

He said, "There's only one way you could help me. I want you to let me out of here."

"I know you do. I can't do that."

"Why not?"

"Don't try to sound naive. If we release you, you'll go back to Home Era and tell them exactly where and when we are. And the next time they'll send out a whole crew to get us and bring us back."

He thought for a moment.

"I could tell them I never located any trace of you," he said.

"You would do that?"

"If that was the price of my being allowed to go home, yes. Why not? You think I want to be stuck here forever?"

"How could we trust you?" she asked. "I know: you'd give us your word of honor, right? You'll swear a solemn oath at the high altar of Amon, maybe? Oh, Davis, Davis, how silly do you think we are? You'll simply go back where you came from and let us live out our lives in peace? Sure you will. Five minutes after you're back there you'll be spilling the whole thing out to them."

"No."

"You will. Or they'll pry it out of you. Come on, boy: don't try to weasel around like this. You aren't fooling me for a second and you're simply making yourself look sneaky. Listen, Davis, there's no sense either of us pretending anything. You're screwed and that's all there is to it. There's no way we're going to let you go home, regardless of anything you might promise us."

Her voice was low, steady, unyielding. He felt her words sinking in. He could hear the hundred gates of Thebes closing on him with a great metallic clangor.

"Then why have you come here?" he asked, staring into those troublesome amethyst eyes.

She waited a beat or two.

"I had to. To let you know how much I hate having to do this to you. How sorry I am that it's necessary."

"I bet you are."

"No. I want you to believe me. You're a completely innocent victim, and what we're doing is incredibly shitty. I want to make it clear to you that that's how I feel. Roger feels that way too, for that matter."

"Well," he said. "I'm really tremendously sorry that you're forced to suffer such terrible pangs of guilt on my behalf."

"You don't understand a thing, do you?"

"Probably not."

"Do you have family back there down the line?"

"A mother. In Indiana."

"No wife? Children?"

"No. I was engaged, but it fell apart. You feel any better now?"

"And how old are you?"

"27."

"I figured you to be a little younger than that."

"I'm very tricky that way," Davis said.

"So you joined the Service to see the marvels of the past. This your first mission?"

"Yes. And apparently my last, right?"

"It looks that way, doesn't it?"

"It doesn't have to be," he said. "You still could let me go and take your chances that I'll cover up for you, or that the Service will have lost interest in you. Or you could opt to go back with me. Why the hell do you want to stay in Egypt so much, anyway?"

"We want to, that's all. We're accustomed to it. We've been here fifteen years. This is our life now."

"The hell it is."

"No. You're wrong. We've come up from nowhere and we're part of the inside establishment now. Roger's considered practically a miracle man, the way he's revolutionized Egyptian astronomy. And I've got my temple responsibilities, which I take a lot more seriously than you could ever imagine. It's a fantastically compelling religion." Her voice changed, taking on an odd quavering intensity. "I have to tell you—there are moments when I can feel the wings of Isis beating—when I'm the Goddess—the Bride, the Mother, the Healer." She hesitated a moment, as though she was taken aback by her own sudden rhapsodic tone. When she spoke again it was in a more normal voice. "Also I have high connections at the court, very powerful friends who make my life extremely rewarding in various material ways."

"I know about those connections. I saw one of your very powerful friends leaving your temple just as I was arriving. He's crazy, isn't he, your prince? And you sound pretty crazy too, I have to tell you. Jesus! Two lunatics take me prisoner and I have to spend the rest of my life marooned in Eighteenth Dynasty Egypt for their convenience. A hell of a thing. Don't you see what you're doing to me? Don't you *see*?"

"Of course we do," she said. "I've already told you so."

Tears were glistening on her cheeks, suddenly. Making deep tracks in the elaborate makeup. He had seen her weep like that once before.

"You're a good actress, too."

"No. No."

She reached for him. He jerked his hand away angrily; but she held him tight, and then she was up against him, and, to his amazement, her lips were seeking his. His whole body stiffened. The alien perfume of her filled his nostrils, overwhelming him with mysterious scents. And then, as her fingertips drew a light trail down the skin of his back, he shivered and trembled, and all resistance went from him.

They tumbled down together onto the pile of furs that served him as a bed.

"Osiris—" she crooned. "You are Osiris—"

She was muttering deep in her throat, Egyptian words, words he hadn't been taught at Service headquarters but whose meaning he could guess. There was something frightening about her intensity, something so grotesque about this stream of erotic babble that he couldn't bear to listen to it, and to shut it off he pressed his mouth over hers. Her tongue came at him like a spear. Her pelvis arched; her legs wrapped themselves around him. He closed his eyes and lost himself in her.

Afterward he sat with his back against the wall, looking at her, stunned.

She grinned at him.

"I've wanted to do that since the day you came here, do you know that? Ever since I first saw you stretched out on that bed in the House of Life."

His heart was still thundering. He could scarcely breathe. The air in the room, hot and close and dense, sizzled with her strange aromas.

"And now you have," he said, when he could speak again. "All right. Now you have." A new idea was blossoming in his mind. "We were pretty good together, weren't we?"

"Yes. I'll say we were."

"Well, it doesn't have to stop there. We can go back together, you and I. Lehman can do whatever he damned pleases. But we could become a team. The Service would send us anywhere, and—"

"Stop it. Don't talk nonsense."

"We could. We *could*."

"I'm almost old enough to be your mother."

"It didn't seem that way just now."

"It would in broad daylight. But regardless. I choose to stay in Egypt. And therefore you have to stay too."

Her words came at him like a volley of punches.

He had almost hoped, for a moment, that he had won her over. But what folly that was! Change her mind with a single roll in the furs? Expect her to walk away from her plush life at Pharaoh's court for the sake of a little heavy breathing? What a child you are, he told himself.

He heard the hundred gates clanging shut again.

"Now you listen to me," she said. She crouched opposite him, on the far side of the little lamp, under the bas-relief of Sobek and Isis. She was still naked and her body had an oiled gleam in the near darkness. She still looked beautiful to him, too. Although now, in the aftermath of passion, he was able to see more clearly the signs of aging on her. "You said a little while ago that you think Roger and I are crazy for wanting to stay here. You want to save us from ourselves. Well, you're wrong about that. We're staying here because it's where we want to be. And you'll feel the same way yourself, after you've been here for a little while longer."

"I don't—"

"*Listen* to me," she said. "Here are your options. There's an embassy leaving next month for Assyria. It's an ugly crossing, passing through a pretty desolate stretch of wasteland that someday will be called the Sinai Peninsula. We can arrange to have you become a slave attached to the ambassador's party, with the understanding that at some disagreeable place in the middle of the Sinai you'll be left behind to fend for yourself. That's your first choice. If you opt for it, it's extremely unlikely that you'll ever find your way back to Thebes. In which case you're not going to be here to greet any possible rescuers that the Service may decide to send out to find you."

"Let me hear some other options."

"Option Two. You stay in Thebes. I use my influence to have you appointed a captain in the army—it's safe, there's no significant military activity going on these days—or a priest of Amon or anything else that might strike your fancy. We get you a nice villa in a good part of town. You can have Eyaseyab as your personal slave, if you like, and a dozen more pretty much like her. A certain priestess of Isis might pay visits to your villa also, possibly. That would be up to you. You'll have a very pleasant and comfortable existence, with every luxury you can imagine. And when the Service sends a mission out to rescue you—and they will, I'm sure they will—we'll help you deal with the problem of staying out of their clutches. You'll *want* to stay out of their clutches, believe me, because by the time they come for you you'll be an Egyptian just like us. And once you've had a chance to discover what life is like as a member of the privileged classes in the capital city of Eighteenth Dynasty Egypt, you won't want to go back to Home Era any more than we do. Believe me."

"Are there any further choices?"

"That's it. Go with the ambassador's party to Assyria and end up chewing sand, or stay here and live like a prince. Either way, of course, we keep you secluded in this room for another couple of weeks, until the time of the jump field's return is safely past." She stood up and began to don her filmy robe. Smiling, she said, "You don't have to tell me which one you choose right now. Think it over. I wouldn't want you to be too hasty about your decision. You can let me know when we come to let you out."

She kissed him lightly on the lips and went quickly out of the room.

"No—wait—come back!"

He heard the bolt slamming home.

ELEVEN

THE DAYS WENT BY, SLOWLY at first, then with bewildering swiftness, then with an excruciating unwillingness to end. He took care to keep count of them, as he had been trained to do, but he knew there was no hope. Sandburg's last lighthearted words tolled in his brain again and again and again, like the sound of somber leaden bells. He lived in a frozen abyss of despair.

The chanting priestly voices from outside went on and on, all day long, and by now the strange clashing harmonies seemed not at all strange to him:

I am Nepthys.
Here comes Horus at your call, O Osiris.
He will take you upon his arms.
You will be safe in his embrace.

As the time passed he could feel his former existence running out of him as if through a funnel. All his memories were slipping away, every shred of identity: mother, father, school days, girls, books, sports, college, Service, everything. Leaving nothing but an empty shell, gossamer-thin.

He had danced his way through life, *sneaked* his way through, dealt somehow with all the uncertainties and the perils and the cruelties. Held his own. More than held his own. He had done very well for himself, in fact. And then had taken one risk too many; and now the game was up. He had run up against a pair of players who were willing to cast him aside without hesitation and with nothing more than the pretense of remorse.

He had only one day left, now. Tomorrow the jump field would return and wait for him to enter it, and after a little while, whether he had entered it or not, it would take off again for his own era.

I am Nepthys.
How beautiful you are that rise this day!
Like Horus of the Underworld
Rising this day, emerging from the great flood.
You are purified with those four jars
With which the gods have washed themselves.

He stared at the wall. Gradually the weirdly serene faces of the monstrous gods that were carved into it began to emerge out of the darkness. The first light of morning was coming through the slot high overhead. The last day: his final chance. But there was no hope. The door was bolted and would stay that way. The day would come and go and the jump field would leave without him and that would be that.

He stood empty and tottering, waiting for the breeze that would blow him to dust.

But he was surprised to discover that he seemed to be filling again. A new Edward Davis was rushing in. An Egyptian Edward Davis.

Already he felt Thebes spinning its web around him, as it had around *them.* A new life, rich and strange. The daily company of Horus and Thoth, Isis and Osiris, Sobek and Khnum. Fine robes; lovely women; fountains and gardens. A life spent playing *senet* and sipping sherbet in his villa and attending elegant parties of the sort portrayed on all the tombs of the nobility across the river in the Valley of the Kings. And eventually to have his own fine tomb over there, where his own splendiferous mummy would be put to rest.

No. No. He was amazed at himself. What kind of insane fantasy was this? How could he even be thinking such stuff? Angrily he thrust it from his mind.

Which left him empty again, marooned, defenseless.

He trembled.

He felt once more the devastating inrush of fear, mingled with savage resentment. They had trapped him. They had stolen his life from him.

But had they really? Was the situation actually that bad?

> *Horus has cleansed you.*
> *Thoth has glorified you.*
> *The masters of the Great White Crown have abolished the troubles of your flesh.*
> *Now you can stand on your own legs, entirely restored.*
> *You will open the way for the gods.*
> *For them you will act as the Opener of the Way.*

They had him. He might as well give in. What choice did he have, really? When they finally let him out of here, he would allow Sandburg and Lehman to help him. And they would, if only out of guilt. He would take full advantage of what had happened to him. Build a new life for himself. He could go a long way here.

He knew the history of the years that lay ahead, after all. The whole thing was there, neatly filed in the electronic memory that the Service had poured into his brain. The upheavals that would come after the death of Amenhotep III and the succession of crazy Prince Amenhotep to the throne, the idealistic religious revolution and the bitter counter-revolution that would follow it, the short and turbulent reigns of Tut-ankh-Amen and the others who would follow him—he knew it all, every twist and turn of events. And could benefit from his special knowledge. He would rise high in the kingdom. Higher than Lehman had, higher than Sandburg. A grand vizier, say. A viceroy. The power behind the throne. The powerful men had lovely titles here. *The Eyes and Ears of the King. The Fan-Bearer at Pharaoh's Right Hand.* Edward C. Davis of Muncie, Indiana, Fan-Bearer at Pharaoh's Right Hand. Why not? Why not? He laughed. It was almost a giggle. You are getting a little hysterical, Mr. Fan-Bearer, he told himself.

But then came a bewildering thought. What if he achieved all that—and then a rescue team arrived from Home Era to bring him back? A year from now, say. Five years. They couldn't pinpoint the delivery time all that precisely. They'd know what year they had sent him to, but they couldn't be absolutely certain he'd reached it, and there was likely to be a little overshoot on the part of the rescue mission, too. Five years, say. Ten. Enough for him to get really comfortably established.

The Service will send a mission out to rescue you, Sandburg had said. *They will, I'm sure they will.*

Who? Charlie Farhad? Nick Efthimiou?

Yes. Somebody like that. A couple of the tough, capable operators who always knew how to manage things the right way. That's who he'd have to deal with. But how soon? And was he going to welcome them, when they came?

We'll help you to stay out of their clutches, she had promised. *Because by the time they come for you you'll be an Egyptian just like us.*

He wondered. He didn't know.

Priests were beginning to sound the morning chants at the temple, now. The unearthly music of Amon and Horus and Anubis came floating through the little slot-like window in the wall. A shaft of bright sunlight poured into his room and lit up the carvings. He stared at the calm figures of the gods: winged Isis, full of love, and mummified Osiris and bird-headed Thoth and smiling crocodile-faced Sobek, high above. They stared back at him.

And then he heard the bolt sliding back. Voices outside: Sandburg's voice, Lehman's.

He couldn't believe it. Here on the last day, they had relented after all! The guilt, the shame, had been too much for them, finally. They were giving him back his life. Tears of gratitude burst from him suddenly. They would want him to cover up for them, of course, when he got back down the line. And he would. He would. Just let me out of here, he thought, and I'll tell any lie you want me to.

"Hello, there," Sandburg said cheerily. She was wearing some sort of elaborate priestess-rig, white linen done up in curl upon stiff curl and a shimmering diadem in her black ringlets. "Ready for some fresh air?"

"So you've decided not to keep me here?" he said.

"What?"

"This is the day the jump field is coming back, isn't it? And you're letting me out."

She blinked and peered at him as though he had spoken in some unknown language.

"What? What?"

"I've been keeping count. This is the day."

"Oh, no," she said, with an odd little laugh. "The field came yesterday. We found your alleyway, and we were there to see it. Oh, I'm so sorry, Edward. Your count must be off by a day."

He was bewildered. "My count—off a day—"

"No doubt of it."

He couldn't believe it. He had ticked off the dawn of each new day so carefully, updating in his mind. The tally couldn't be off. Couldn't.

But it was. Why else would they be here? He saw Lehman standing behind her, now, looking fidgety and guilty. There were others there also. Eyaseyab, for one. A little party to celebrate his release. In the solitude of his cell he had lost track of the days somehow. He must have.

Sandburg took him by the hand. Numbly he let her lead him out into the hall.

"These are your slaves," she said. "I'm giving Eyaseyab to you."

"Thank you." What else did you say, when they gave you a slave?

And a charioteer, and a cook, and some others.

Davis nodded. "Thank you very much," he said stonily.

She leaned close to him. "Are you ever going to forgive us?" she asked in a soft, earnest tone. "You know we really had no choice. I wish you had never come looking for us. But once you did, we had to do what we did. If you could only believe how sorry I am, Edward—"

"Yes. Yes. Of course you are."

He stepped past her, and into the hall, and on beyond, around a row of huge columns and into the open air. It was a hot, dry day, like all the other days. The sun was immense. It took up half the sky. I am an Egyptian now, he thought. I will never see my own era again. Fine. Fine. Whatever will be, will be. He took a deep breath. The air was like fire. It had a burning smell. Somewhere down at the far end of the colonnade, priests in splendid brocaded robes were carrying out some sort of rite, an incomprehensible passing back and forth of alabaster vessels, golden crowns, images of vultures and cobras. One priest wore the hawk-mask, one the crocodile-mask, one the ibis-mask. They no longer looked strange to him. They could have stepped right out of the reliefs on the wall of his cell.

Eyaseyab came up beside him and took his arm. She nestled close.

"You will not miss your old home," she said. "I will see to that."

So she knew the story too.

"You're very kind," he said.

"Believe me," Eyaseyab said. "You will be happy here."

"Yes," he said. "Yes. Perhaps I will."

* * *

THE MASKED PRIESTS WERE CASTING handfuls of some aromatic oil on a little fire in front of a small shrine. Flames rose from it, green and turquoise and crimson ones. Then one of them turned toward him and held out a tapering white vessel of the oil as if inviting him to throw some on too.

How different from Indiana all this is, Davis thought. And then he smiled. Indiana was 3500 years away. No: farther even than that. There was no Indiana. There never had been. Indiana was something out of a dream that had ended. This was a different dream now.

"It is the Nekhabet fire," Eyaseyab said. "He wants you to make an offering. Go on. Do it, Edward-Davis. Do it!"

He looked back toward Sandburg and Lehman. They were nodding and pointing. They wanted him to do it too.

He had no idea what the Nekhabet fire was. But he shrugged and walked toward the shrine, and the priest handed him the vessel of oil. Hesitating only a moment, Davis upended it over the fire, and watched a sudden burst of colors come blazing up at him, for a moment as bright as the colors of the jump-field vortex itself. Then they died away and the fire was as it had been.

"What was that all about?" he asked Sandburg.

"The new citizen asks the protection of Isis," she said. "And it is granted. Isis watches over you, now and forever. Come, now. We'll take you to your new home."